The Smuggler Code

(The Rob Blackstock series – Book 3)

By Bill Yeates

****

The Smuggler's Code

Millionaire Rob Blackstock and his wife Susan, plan to take a break from the chaos of the first few months of their marriage and get away on their yacht, sailing around the British coastline. But their plans must change when Susan inherits a remote estate in Scotland, from a relative she knew nothing of.

Together they learn about the Clan Morgan of Sutherland, but digging into history proves to be dangerous, where the codes of past generations are still being practiced. They both barely escape death when they visit the estate and discover the secrets it holds. Smugglers and pirates still exist in these remote lands but their modern day trade is far more dangerous than barrels of brandy and bales of silk.

Hindered by the local Clan, Rob and Sue work to stop the unlawful trading that is going on and to discover who the mastermind is that is running the operation and bring them to justice.

To my son Benjamin Stewart

Chapter 1

"This looks like a gangland execution to me gov. The girl has has obviously been strangled. She appears to have put up quite a struggle. We found blood and skin under her nails. Someone is certainly going to have some nasty scratches on his or her face for a week or two. Her clothes and general appearance lead us to believe her to be from Eastern Europe, most likely Russia. The bag found near her contained several pieces of correspondence all in Russian, including a recent letter from someone that we think is probably her sister."

****

Millionaire Rob Blackstock and his wife of four months, Sue, sat talking about the shock of Rob's father Eric's late wedding gift while they waited for Rob's daughter Luci and her two Russian girl friends to change out of their stage clothes. They needed to be in clothes more suitable for walking the mile home from the 'Dog and Gun' to Blackstock Horse racing stables, which Eric had just signed over to Rob and Sue. It was almost 1:00 in the morning of New Year's day.

With a quick goodbye to the landlord they set out to walk home. There were still several people in the pub car park, mostly the worse for drink. Justin, Rob's son, showed the way with his torch and they quickly left the revellers behind. As they reached the crest of the hill they heard a vehicle coming up the hill behind them. Fearing they might be hit they stepped up onto the verge as the car raced by. Rob shouted after it. "Slow down you idiot. Are you okay Sue?" he turned to look behind.

"SUE…….."

Rob woke suddenly. This was more than just a dream, it was the memory of a real event of some six months earlier. When returning from a New Year's Eve party, an attempt was made to run down Susan Blackstock, Rob's wife of just a few months. It was possibly the forth attempt on her life by someone not yet identified.

5

It was originally thought that the person stalking Sue, was the wife of an army general who had committed suicide after being arrested for drug dealing by Sue when she was a military police captain. Although she was the prime suspect, there was some doubt because of her strong alibi at the time of this latest attempt. The incident had left both Rob and Sue shaken but no one had suffered serious injury. In fact once they had all regained their senses the whole incident caused them great amusement at Sue's expense. Where she had tried to step up onto the verge there was no verge. The grass had grown over a gully cut through the verge to take away excess water when it rained. So when in the dark Sue stepped up onto the verge there was nothing under her foot and she simply collapsed in a heap on the ground. Apart from a severely bruised pride, she was unharmed and was soon laughing about it with the others. They later discovered that the driver of the car was a friend who had been in the pub most of the evening and was well over the limit for driving.

Rob had this dream more often than he cared to remember. He never got as far as discovering that Sue had simply fallen in a hole, but always stopped with him turning and being unable to see her.

He looked across the bed to reassure himself that she was there safe and well, then looked beyond her to the bedside table and the clock with its red glowing number. 4:15. Too early to get up and maybe too late to be able to get any more sleep. He looked back at Sue and thought how lucky he was to have found her and to have her as his wife. They had only met nine months ago when Sue had helped him when his children were in serious danger from some criminal types. He thought how well she had got on with his two children, Justin almost fifteen and away at boarding school and Luci seventeen and doing 'A' levels at school in York.

He remembered the first time she met his parents, Eric and Rose, and how well they got on right from that time. He had brought her up to the racehorse stables near York. They were then owned by his dad, but given over to Sue and himself as a wedding present and which Sue now managed.

It was a good time for the Blackstock family and Rob lay back and smiled at his good fortune. He was a rich man from his own efforts back when he was an accountant working in the financial side of the American movie business. Then after his first wife and their eldest son had been killed in a car crash, he had changed career and taken ownership of the family business of training horses and riders to be used in movies. More recently he had started academies in both Britain and America to train stunt artists for film and TV.

Looking back at Sue sleeping peacefully next to him, she looked so much like his first wife Jayne. They would be about the same age, they had the same long auburn hair and skin colouring and similar classic high cheekbones but that was where the similarities ended. They were totally different in almost everything else. Jayne had been a homebuilder who had given up a promising acting career when she married Rob and she became a full time mum. Whereas Sue was an action girl and a leader. She had been a Captain in the Military Police and had been a task force leader in a security company when she met Rob and now for the last six months she had been a racehorse stable manager and trainer with a rapidly growing record of success. He would always love Jayne, but he had lost her eight years ago and now he had Sue and he was deeply in love with her.

The sun was up and beginning to shine through a gap in the curtains. It was the 1st of June. A new month and hopefully a warm dry month following an extremely wet May, so different to the blistering hot weather of last year. 2018 had broken so many records, hours of sunshine and soaring temperatures it would be remembered for many years to come. But 2019 was more likely to be remembered as one of the wettest years.

Justin had been home from school all week for half term. He had not done well in a couple of subjects so had spent the week revising for his end of term exams and rarely left his room. He had a difficult act to follow; Luci having scored all A's in her GCSE's last year. She on the other hand had spent most of her week with her boyfriend Peter, either at his house or hers. She was studying for her end of year exams and he was revising hard for his A levels, the first papers beginning the first week of the new half term. He needed good results, he wanted to be a vet and the University of Edinburgh had offered him a place on a five year course but he needed a minimum of two A's and a B to be accepted. Luci had been together with Peter for more than eight months now and Rob still couldn't believe that his daughter's first love is the nephew of his own first

7

love and was living in the same house as she had lived in. He just hoped that Luci and Peter weren't having sex in the bike sheds like he and Tracy had done twenty five years ago. Tracy had come back into his life less than a year ago when by chance they were asked to join an MI-6 task force set up to prevent a major incident in London. He last saw her on New Year's eve, she had moved to live permanently in London and taken a full time position in MI-6. He had sent her a message a couple of days ago via Peter to invite her to the annual Blackstock barbecue tonight but he doubted whether she would be able to make it.

The annual Blackstock barbecue has been held on the Saturday after May Bank Holiday since Rob's Grandfather was alive. It is a thank you to all the employees at the stables and their families plus a few invited friends. It starts at noon with traditional fun activities like skittles, horseshoe tossing, blindfold branding, lasso tossing and, as a special attraction this year, Rob had hired a bucking bronco machine. Food comes out late afternoon then the party really gets going with a barn dance. With a bar open all day things will be really swinging by the time the dance starts and it has been known for the event to run into the early hours of Sunday. Music this year was coming from a local country band made up of a father on keyboard, his two sons on guitars, the father's brother on fiddle and the mother calling the dances. Both of the sons worked as stable lads at the yard and the family was well known by everyone.

Blackstock Catering will be managing all the food at this years event. Rob had explained the requirements to Ana and Eva, the catering managers and was confident enough in them to leave everything in their hands. Rob had bought the two Russian girls out of the London sex trade as a thank you to them for looking after Luci when she was having a rough time. He subsequently appointed Ana and Eva as managers of a company set up specifically to provide food and refreshment for his teams on location, making movies and TV programmes. They had built a sound business plan and run a trial for three months which was so successful that Rob financed two new vehicles and allowed them to recruit two staff to help operate them.

To add to the entertainment Ana, Eva and Luci would be singing two sets, one mid afternoon and another mid evening. They were regular performers at the Dog and Gun down in the village and were occasionally joined by Luci. The two Russians were graduates of Moscow University, they had been brought into Britain by the Russian mafia and provided with false papers. They were forced to become erotic dancers to earn money to pay back the Russian mafia. They had found Luci lost and alone wandering the London streets and had helped her get reunited with Rob who rewarded them by paying off their debt and giving them a job. When they first moved to Yorkshire Rob allowed them to live in a two room flat above the stables, but now they were renting a small house in the village on the same street as the 'Dog and Gun'.

With so much going on in his head, there was no way he was going to get any more sleep. The clock now read 6:55. He gently slipped out from under the duvet so as not to disturb Sue. He pulled on a pair of shorts and a tee shirt then quietly left the bedroom and went to the kitchen to make some coffee. He didn't notice the housekeepers coat on the hook behind the kitchen door and nearly jumped out of his skin when a voice behind him said. "You sit down Mr. Robert I'll make you a coffee. Will Miss Susan want one?"

"Christ, Madge you almost gave me a heart attack creeping up behind me like that!"

"Sorry, sir," she apologised. "There's a lot to get ready today so I'm in early to get started. Does Miss Susan have sugar?"

Sue was awake when Rob re-entered the bedroom with a tray carrying two cups of black coffee. "Good morning lover if one of those is mine I'm just about ready for it."

"Tell me, again, darling how many winners did you have yesterday at Kempton Park?"

"Three."

"And how much prize money did you win?"

"Just a few pounds short of £16,000 in trainer's prize money from the seven races. Not bad for a day at the races eh?"

"I make that eighteen winners in twenty weeks since you got your licence and you've done it with the same horses that dad had, with nowhere near the same success rate."

"Ah well. It must be the woman's touch or beginner's luck," she answered. "Now come over here and give me my good morning kiss."

Rob sat on the edge of the bed next to her and bent over so that their lips just barely touched. Sue reacted throwing her arms around him and pulling him down into her and their tongues danced together. "I do like these," he said as he played with the gold stud that pierced her nipple. "I just can't believe that a woman of forty would have it done!"

"After ten years of restricted life in the army, I guess it was just the rebel in me coming out," she replied. "But I glad you like them and if you keep playing with them like that our coffee will get cold. Not that I want you to stop but we do have a lot to do today."

Guests started to arrive before 12:00 but everything was ready and the party was very quickly underway. Cars were parked in every possible spot and between eighty and a hundred people aged from pre-school children to a pensioner in a wheelchair were having fun. After such a wet May, June was starting with a warm sunny summers day, perfect for the event which went incredibly well. The food was totally different from previous years with offerings of Asian food, pasta, pizzas and salads as well as the traditional burgers and hot dogs.

"Your girls certainly know how to cater for the masses," Eric said to Rob as they stood together at the bar looking out across the crowd.

"Yes, it's going down very well isn't it," Rob replied. "Something for everyone and they've been very clever in going direct to the suppliers to get the food and agreed that any unopened foods can be returned and refunded."

"And Rose tells me that they have arranged that any leftovers will be collected first thing tomorrow to go to the homeless shelter in York. What a great idea. Such a waste otherwise," Eric added.

"What about this amazing bar they've set up. All supplied by the brewery," Rob explained. "They came in on Thursday and set up the counter and the optics plus the real ales, so that they had chance to settle out then brought the rest this morning. They have also had a hundred wine glasses and a hundred beer glasses printed with our company logo on one side and the brewer logo on the other. Guests will be able to take them home as souvenirs, plus it's their staff serving and they are staying until 11:00 tonight."

"It must be costing a fortune, but is certainly going down well with everyone," Eric continued.

"It's not costing a penny dad," Rob answered. "It was an idea the girl's passed by me a couple of months ago and we approached the brewery for sponsorship for the stables. They jumped at the opportunity to be linked with us, especially as Sue is being so successful at the moment. The bar is just part of the package we've agreed. In return the brewery name will appear on our horse boxes. It's certainly an incredible bar. The chap pulling pints at the bar now is the brewery manager. Come on over and I'll introduce you."

"Dad, look who Peter has brought with him," Luci called from the other end of the bar. Rob looks across and smiled at the woman standing next to his daughter and her boyfriend.

"Tracy! What a pleasant surprise so good to see you. You're looking well," Sue said as she came up to the bar at that moment to get herself a drink. "What can I get you to drink? If you're here to take my husband away again I'm going to have to shoot you." They both laughed and gave one another a welcoming hug.

"Hi gorgeous," Rob said as he came up behind Sue and put his arms around her waist and his head on her shoulder. "What brings our favourite police officer up to these remote parts."

"Hello you two, nice to see you both again. I'll have a red wine please, Sue," she replied. "Well I'm up here to celebrate really. My divorce came through last week. I'm Tracy Mills again now and as it is half term I've spent the week with my two kids. I don't see them too often these days now that I'm London based. I'm staying with my brother over at the big house and when Peter said about this do, I thought I'd gatecrash."

"Well, you're very welcome Tracy," Sue said as she handed her a large glass of red wine and linked arms with her. "Let's go and find somewhere to sit and catch up on things."

11

Numbers slowly reduced as afternoon became evening. Most of the families with young children had gone home to put the little ones to bed but at the same time there had been several late comers. The girls were beginning their second spell on the makeshift stage performing to a very responsive audience of seventy plus.

Rose found Rob at the barbecue talking to a young lad who was cooking burgers. 'What's wrong mum? You look worried."

"Darling, there are two police officers at the house asking to speak to Oxsana Kolanski."

"That's our Ana," Rob replied. "Did they say why they wanted to see her?"

"Just that it was a personal matter."

"Don't worry, I'll go and speak to them."

"Officers, I'm Rob Blackstock, Miss Kolanski works for me, can you tell me what this is about?"

"We'd rather speak directly to Miss Kolanski sir. Is she about?" answered the older officer, with a very heavy Scottish accent.

"I'm afraid she's on stage performing at the moment. Can this wait for twenty minutes or so? Perhaps you can come through and have a drink."

The officers looked at one another and the younger one nodded then the older officer replied. "We're on duty sir, but a soft drink would be welcome. We've just driven down from Glasgow and its been a rather warm drive."

"Ana, there are two policemen here that want to have a word with you. They are over at the bar. You go into the big house and I'll go and fetch them and bring them into the lounge. Eva why don't you go with her."

"Miss Kolanski. We are with the Glasgow Central force. This letter was found a few days ago at a crime scene in Glasgow," the older officer said as he handed Ana a folded piece of paper. "As you see it is written in Russian. We've had it interpreted and it appears to have been sent by you to a relative."

12

"Yes officer. It's a letter I sent to my sister Yasmin. I sent her some money. She's just finished university and want's to come and visit me. Has something happened to her?"

"I regret to inform you that this letter was found on the body of a young lady of approximately twenty two years, found dead in Glasgow's dockland district."

Ana's eyes watered and she gripped Eva's hand very firmly. "Can you describe your sister for us?" the officer asked.

"She's a lot shorter than me, about five feet two. She has blond hair like me and we look very similar. She was twenty two last December."

"I'm very sorry. Do you recognise this?" PC Taylor passed across a small clutch bag.

"Yes. I sent it to Yasmin for her birthday." Tears were now rolling down Ana's cheeks.

"From what you have said the victim could be your sister. We will need you to come back to Glasgow with us to make a formal identification of the body."

"Officer, Ana is clearly very upset," Rob interrupted. "Is it okay if I drive her up to Glasgow tomorrow morning?"

"That will be fine sir, Taylor and I will be driving back this evening. Please ask for Inspector Howard when you get there. Thank you for your time." The two officers left, Rob went back to the party and Eva stayed with Ana in the lounge.

'Where have you been for the last half hour Rob?" Sue asked.

"Ana has had some very bad news. A couple of coppers from Glasgow have just been talking with her. The body of a young woman has been found and they believe it to be Ana's sister. I'm taking her up to Glasgow for the formal identification tomorrow morning."

"Poor Ana, is she alright?" Sue enquired.

"She's in tears, as you'd expect," Rob answered. "Eva is with her and mum is making up a bed for them. They'll stay here tonight."

"This has all gone very well today," Sue said. "Is it like this every year, or is this something special?"

"This year has been exceptional, mainly thanks to those two girls I think. They have put in a huge amount of work and it's all paid off. They were talking the other day about applying for British citizenship and I'm going to offer to be their sponsor. I didn't get much opposition when I applied to get them official British work permits so I'll see if I can oil a few wheels for them. Now, let's see this party through to the end. Have you seen the kids?"

Chapter 2

"Are you sure none of this can be traced back to any of us? It should never have gone this far. It will only draw attention to our business and could mean we need to suspend operations for a few weeks. There are many ways she could have been silenced without killing her and leaving her to be found so easily. It would have been so simple to take her out in one of the boats and simply tip her overboard and let her drown. The body would probably never turn up. But what you've done has given the police a murder to investigate."

****

Ryman, Rob's driver, pulled Rob's car up to the front door of the house. Rob climbed into the front passenger seat, Ana climbed in the back and Eva, coming along to support her closest friend, sat next to Ana. Sue and Luci stood on the front doorstep wished them a safe journey and waved them off as they drove down the driveway.

Ryman was not just Rob's driver. He had been with the family since October. Originally hired as Rob's body guard when Rob went to South America, Ryman had saved Rob's life at least twice. He was ex-army but had bought himself out to look after his two small children, after his wife had been murdered by a drug addict.

The journey of close on two hundred and fifty miles should have taken them four hours but as it was Sunday traffic was light. After only three and a half hours they were parking the car in Dundasvale Car Park, next to the Police Scotland office on Stewart Street. It was raining quite heavily so Rob and the girls ran from the car park, across the road and up the stone steps into the police station. Ana was again in tears as Rob asked for Inspector Howard and was told to take a seat. Just minutes later a tall plain clothes officer came through a side door to where they were sitting.

"Miss Kolanski?" Ana could only nod in response then stood.

"I've been expecting you. Please come this way. Your friends are welcome to come as well," he said holding the door open for them to pass through.

They followed him along a long corridor and into a small room containing just two simple chairs. There was a window in the wall opposite the door with curtains drawn shut on the other side and next to the window was a closed door.

"I'm afraid I have to ask you for some proof of identification before we proceed." Ana took her passport from her handbag and opened it at the picture page. The inspector nodded then walked across the room to the window.

"Are you ready miss?" Ana nodded and the inspector pressed a button and the curtains slowly began to roll back to reveal a woman's body draped with a sheet with just the head and shoulders showing.

Three pairs of eyes were watching Ana for her reaction. She actually started to smile. "It's not her. It's not Yasmin," she said.

"Are you sure, miss?"

"I'm absolutely certain," Ana responded immediately. "She does look like my sister and could easily pass for her, but Yasmin has a large birthmark on the front of her left shoulder shaped like Australia. As kids we always called her Ozzy. She hated it."

"Thank you miss. Sorry we had to ask you to come all this way." The inspector said. "Can you think of why this young lady would have had your sister's handbag?"

"I can't explain that at all inspector," She replied. "Can I take the bag home with me?"

"I'm sorry, miss but it is evidence in an ongoing murder enquiry. I will make sure you get it back as soon as possible. Now can I see you all out?"

The mood, when walking back to the car, was totally different, even the rain had stopped. Rob had planned for a pub lunch before they left Glasgow, but it was still too early, so they decided to pick something up at the services on the motorway.

As soon as they were clear of the car park and he could get a good signal Rob rang Sue.

"Hi darling, how did it go?"

"It wasn't Yasmin. We're on our way home."

"That's great news. I bet Ana is pleased."

16

"Yep, all smiles again and jabbering away with Eva in Russian in the back here." Rob looked over his shoulder at the two girls and smiled. Ana looked up at that moment and smiled back at him. Then suddenly her expression change.

"Where is Yasmin's phone? It wasn't in her bag. Her passport wasn't there either," She said.

"Maybe the murderer took them both," Eva suggested.

"Then why leave all that money behind. It looked like at least £500. My guess is that they weren't in the bag when she was a murdered," Rob concluded.

"Maybe Yasmin still has them," Eva said. "Why don't you ring her phone?"

"I'll try a message first and see if I get a response," Ana said.

She scrolled her contact list and selected Yasmin's number. *'Hi Ozzy,'* was all she typed, then she pressed send. Within a couple of minutes she had a response. "It's her, she's used the name she used to call me when we were kids. She says, *'Oxy ring me'*. Something must be wrong," she said as she pressed the call button. After a few seconds she began talking in Russian obviously in conversation with someone.

"Ana is talking to her sister on the phone right now. I'll call you again darling," Rob said as he ended his call to Sue.

"What's she saying Eva?" Rob asked.

"It sounds like Yasmin has been attacked. Something about a letter and her coming to England."

Finally Ana ended the call. "She's in big trouble, Rob. I sent her some money last month and suggested she come to Britain to visit. She wrote back giving all the details of what flight she had booked, but she sent it to our old London address and it hasn't been forwarded yet."

"That Post Office forwarding system is far from perfect. I've known it take weeks for mail to get to me," Rob interrupted.

"She sent that letter on 2nd May. Her flight was booked for 20th with a taxi arranged to take her to the airport. Apparently the taxi arrived early. The driver said the car was a hire car, while his car was being repaired which explained why it wasn't marked as a taxi.

On the way to the airport the driver stopped and climbed in the back with her making suggestive comments. Thinking he was about to rape her she kicked out striking him on the head. While he was dazed she got out of the car and ran for her life."

"That's terrible," Rob said. "Did she call your parents?"

"Our father died in an accident at his workplace a few weeks before Yasmin was born. We were raised by our mother, but she died of cancer two years ago. We've got an uncle, but he lives a long way away," Ana continued. "In her haste to get away she had left behind her handbag and her luggage. She only had her phone and her purse containing her credit cards and a small amount of money. Anyway she went into a coffee shop to get her self sorted. She was sitting with a coffee when a pleasant young man stopped by her table and asked if she was okay. She said she was crying at the time. She said he was very nice and they got talking. She told him about the taxi and he said he was on leave from a ship currently in port at St Petersburg and would be sailing for London in six days. He told her that if she could get to St. Petersburg, he would smuggle her on board and get her to London where he knew a man who could get her papers. She jumped at the opportunity and caught a train to St. Petersburg five days ago."

"So where is she now?" Rob asked.

"She's on a ship anchored at sea somewhere. When she got to St. Petersburg, she was met by the nice young man but now he wasn't so nice and had two other men with him. She was taken onto a ship in the harbour and put in a room with six other girls and that's where she still is."

"You say she's got no idea where she is?" Rob enquired.

"She says she can see land. A beach with a jetty but no buildings."

"That sounds like it is some remote landing stage that could be anywhere," Rob said.

"Not anywhere boss," Ryman commented. "She must be in range of a mobile phone aerial. So not too remote either."

"Unless the ship has a satellite link," Rob said. "Did she give you any names of her abductors at all?"

"That's the thing I find most horrific in all this," Ana said. "The man that she first met was Ivan Gorkov."

"Mikhail Gorkov's brother," Eva spoke up. "We know Ivan don't we Ana?"

"Yes, he was the one who promised us a great new life in Britain and sold us passports and new identities. It wasn't until months later that found out that we had been given the identity of other girls tricked in the same way," Ana explained.

"Do you think that's how that girl in Glasgow ended up with Yasmin's things?" Rob asked.

"Yes I do. It's the only possible answer, don't you think?" Ana answered.

"All this doesn't help your sister but we should tell Inspector Howard. It might help his enquiry. I'll ring him first thing tomorrow. If Ivan Gorkov is anything like his brother, there are one or two people in London who would be interested in knowing what he is up to."

They stopped at the motorway services for a coffee and a bite to eat. Before moving off again, Rob rang Sue again and updated her with the news of Ana's sister and then asked her how the clearing up after the party was going.

"We've almost finished," Sue told him. "The brewery rang to say they had a problem with their van and they can't collect the counter and the beer barrels until tomorrow afternoon. Rose, Madge and I sorted out the unopened food in the cool house, ready to go back to the suppliers tomorrow and the people from the homeless shelter have to collect the food left that can't be returned. They were well organised with containers and they went away very happy with a car boot full of food. Six of the lads plus Sally and Lizzy stayed on and have worked hard to get everywhere looking business like again. So I said they could light up the barbecue and have some of the sausages and burgers left over and whatever beer was left in the barrels. They've had quite a party out there for the last hour or so but it's beginning to rain now so they've started to clear away."

"You've done very well and Eva says thank you for organising it all for them. We should be home around 4:00, it's been quite a trip."

The girls wanted to be dropped off at the 'Dog and Gun'. Ana said she needed a good drink and they agreed that sharing a bottle of wine with a meal would be the best way to finish the day. Although Ryman now lived in the village with his two children and his retired parents, he still had to go back to the stables with Rob to collect his own car, which he had left at the stables that morning.

Sue greeted Rob, as he entered the house through the back door which opened into the spacious kitchen

"Hello darling, you're not as late as you said you might be." She walked across the kitchen and gave him a kiss. "Why don't you go and have a shower then come back down for a drink and relax before dinner."

"That's a very good idea," Rob replied. "Dinner smells good, what have we got?"

"Marge has prepared a traditional Sunday roast and Rose is just finishing it off for us. It's beef."

Rob returned to the kitchen a few minutes later. "I've just poured Eric and Rose a sherry, can I get you a drink, darling?" Sue said.

"What is that you've got?" he asked.

"Gin and tonic," came her reply.

"Yes, I think I could manage one of those, please."

"Coming right up." Sue responded as she left the room to go to the lounge to get Rob's drink.

"Rob," Sue called from the lounge, you had a message on your phone while you were upstairs, from someone called Vic or Nick. Who or what is the 'Lovely Jayne'?" She walked back into the kitchen with his phone and his watch and set both down on the table in front of her husband. Rob turned the phone on and listened to the message *'Ric here, the 'Lovely Jayne' laid back and waiting for you'*.

'It's actually Ric, Ric Mahoney in Dublin. The Poolbeg Yacht and Boat Club to be more accurate. The 'Lovely Jayne' is a

20

seventeen meter four berth motor yacht. I asked Ric to get her out of mothballs and ready for sea. I thought it was about time we had a honeymoon."

"She's a boat. You've never mentioned you had a boat." Sue said.

"'Lovely Jayne' is a bit more that just a boat," Rob huffed. "She's a fibreglass hull, luxury motor cruiser, with twin seven hundred horsepower engines, two cabins, a day room and fitted with navigation equipment that can take us anywhere in the world. I bought her in 2010. Jayne and I only used her three or four times before Jayne was killed. Since then she's been laid up in Dublin and Ric has been looking after her."

"Sounds nice. Where are you going to take me and when, I've got a busy summer of race meetings. There aren't many free days."

"I thought a trip round Britain. But before we plan too much we need to get used to handling her and maybe get her in a yard closer to us here. Dublin was okay when I lived in Birmingham, it was just a quick flight from Birmingham to Dublin. Perhaps we can find something at the Hull Marina. We'll need a couple of days to get her round there, when have you got a two day window."

Sue checked a big wall chart they had mounted on the wall by the back door, it showed all events. "Next Sunday through to next Friday are free." She said. "This Thursday is free but I've got two runners at York on Friday and seeing a new prospective owner on Saturday. So is next Sunday okay or is it too soon?"

"No, I'm sure I can get everything organised by then." Rob agreed. "Sunday it is then, I'll make a few calls first thing tomorrow. I've also got to ring Inspector Howard in Glasgow to tell him about Ana's conversation with her sister and I thought it might be worth giving James Bull at MI-5 a ring and tell him about Ivan Gorkov."

Chapter 3

"How did that girl get hold of a phone? Was it hers or did one of the other girls give it to her? I hope that there is nothing on it that can be used to link her to us. Why the hell didn't you destroy it. There might even be pictures of the boats or the beach, worse still there could be pictures of us on that fucking thing."

****

"We should be able to find Yasmin by tracking her phone," Justin said. The whole family were sitting around the dining table eating Sunday roast and Rob had talked to them about his trip to Glasgow and what Ana had discovered from Yasmin.

"Do you know how to do that?" Rob asked.

"Of course he does, I don't know why we hadn't thought of doing that before," Luci said. "You just need the app loaded on your phone and you can pinpoint any iPhone or iPad you want to. What I don't understand is how Yasmin has been able to keep hold of her phone, while she is being held captive and able to charge the battery as well. It's been over a week."

"She probably has it turned off so that it doesn't ring and be heard by her captors," Justin suggested. "The battery would last two to three weeks if it had been fully charged to start with."

"If that's the case, how did she get the message from Ana?" Luci argued.

"Perhaps she had just turned it on to try and get some help." Justin replied.

"That's a blooming big coincidence. Turning it on just as the moment Ana rang it," Luci claimed.

"It fits what we know," Justin said. "If she left her phone on and allowed it to ring her captive would be certain to discover it. Plus she would have needed to recharge it at least twice in the time. I doubt she or any of the other girls had a charger with them when they were taken."

"If she has her phone turned off all the time will your app be able to locate it?" Rob asked.

"Possibly not, but if we keep trying we could get lucky if she switches it on again," Justin said.

"Well, we'll try tomorrow. We'll be leaving here at about 9:00 to get you back to school, so you can try your app while we're travelling. That will give you four hours to try and make contact," Rob said. "You never did explain why term restarts on Tuesday and not tomorrow."

"It's a teacher training day dad," Justin said, "they are going to be learning about the new GCSE grading system."

"I don't see why they need to keep changing these things. When I was at school we had two levels General GCE and Secondary CSE, both with grades one to nine, one being the best. Then they were merged together to be GCSE when Rob was at school, with grades A-G. Now if I understand it right, they are going back to grades one to nine again but this time nine is the best. How are we employers expected to compare what level qualification their job applicants have achieved?" Eric complained.

"Forget it dad," Rob said. "It what politicians do best. Interfere with something that works fine, rather than tackle one of the more pressing needs like fixing the NHS."

Rob and Justin left for Edinburgh just after 8:00 the next morning. Justin was keen to start tracking Yasmin's phone, but sat frustrated with only an intermittent poor service to his phone until they reached the A1 and headed north. With a constant 4G signal now available, he launched the app but the target wasn't located. He continued launching it every five minutes for almost an hour and a half. Then finally he was successful.

"I've got it, dad!" He announced. "I'll send the grid reference to google and find out where it is on the map."

He pressed a few buttons. "The phone at least is at Harthill services off the M90 between Edinburgh and Glasgow."

"Well done, son. Leave it ten to fifteen minutes then try again to see if she's moving and the direction she's going." Forty five minutes later the app was still returning the same location.

"She's still hasn't moved. I've entered everything into google and it's saying the services are just thirty minutes from my school. So can we go there now?"

"I'm not sure what we might find, so I don't think so."

"But dad, she has had her phone switched on now for over an hour, so she must be somewhere she feels safe and not in danger of being found with a phone. There can't possibly be any risk."

"Well, I guess you're right and if we do find Yasmin you could help me to convince her to come with us and I'll take her back to Ana."

As they got closer, the map displayed by the app slowly moved to a larger scale and as they pulled into the services it was showing that the signal was being generated from somewhere behind the main building. Rob parked the car and they both walked to the source of the signal which they eventually discovered was coming from a large wheelie bin. Lifting the lid they saw that the bin was full of black bin bags crammed full of rubbish from the various outlets around the site. "Looks like the phone has been just dumped," Rob said.

"Maybe Yasmin's captors found her with it and took it off her and threw it away," Justin suggested.

"You're most probably right," Rob agreed, "let's see if we can find it. It may give us a clue as to what's been going on. Give me a hand and we'll tip it over and then if you ring the number we can identify which bag to look in."

The two of them struggled to upturn the bin. It was much heavier than they expected it to be but eventually it fell over on its side and they stood looking down at twenty or more black bags of rubbish and the body of a woman in her early twenties.

Rob and Justin both stepped back as the shock of what they had uncovered hit them.

"Is she dead?" the boy asked.

"She certainly looks dead but I will check," Rob replied. He bent over the body and placed two fingers on the neck of the young woman. There was no pulse. "She's dead alright and quite cold, so must have been dumped here some time ago.

"Do you think it's Yasmin?" Justin asked.

"I'm pretty sure it isn't. Ana said that Yasmin was blonde and facially similar to her. This poor girl is a red head and looks nothing like Ana."

"So how come she's got Yasmin's phone?" Justin queried.

"We don't know that she has," Rob replied. "Give it a ring and see if we can hear it."

Justin selected the number from his contacts and moments after he had pressed the dial button they heard a phone vibrating on the concrete floor under one of the black bags next to the body. Rob carefully lifted the bag to reveal the phone lying face up and turned on. Justin knelt to take a closer look.

"The person last using this was having a messenger conversation with someone in a foreign language that could be Russian, certainly some of the letters are strange. It looks like there are three messages on the screen. The first sent from this phone, then a reply and the final one from here, which has never been sent."

"Can you take a picture and send it to Ana to see if she can translate it." Rob asked.

Justin got as close as he could to get a good clear image which he sent on to Ana with a message.

"Right we need to report this," Rob said "You stay here and don't let anyone near. I'll go and find a security person."

He returned a couple of minutes later with two uniformed security staff, a young man who looked as though he was hired for his brawn rather than his brains and a woman of about Rob's age who appeared to know what to do. She assessed the situation with a very quick scan of the area then spoke into her radio. "Sixty one to control."

"Yes Jane, what can I do for you?" came the response.

"Stan, can you call the police and report a suspicious death found amongst the bins in the west compound?"

"Will do."

She turned to her colleague. "William, go out to the car park and as soon as the police arrive bring them through to here. Don't run, we don't want to alert the public." He nodded his acknowledgement and left. She turned to Rob. "Is this how you found things?"

"No miss. We tipped the bin over to find the mobile phone stolen from our friend. My son had tracked the phone to here. We didn't see the young lady until she fell out."

At that moment the phone on the floor beeped and displayed the message '*BATTERY LOW*'.

"Is that the phone?" she asked.

"Yes."

"Is that you're friend?"

"No. We don't know who that is."

A voice from the radio interrupted them. "Control to sixty one. Come in Jane."

"What's happening Stan?"

"The police say there will be a car here within five minutes. They are only a couple of miles away."

"Thanks Stan."

They must have been a lot closer than a couple of miles because Rob could already hear the two tone sound of a police car approaching.

"They're coming from Glasgow so will be in the East car park. I'll have to go and direct them. You and your son stay here please, sir the police are sure to want to speak to you."

Justin's phone rang. It was a reply message from Ana. "Ana has sent a translation." He announced. "First message, '*Help me please father*' the response was, '*Petra where are you?*' and the final part which didn't get sent was. '*In England I think. In a wagon six other girls travelling all night*'. Ana says can we send her a photo because she knows a girl called Petra, a friend of Yasmin's."

"Do it," Rob said.

Two police officer followed the security woman into the compound.

"I'm P.C. McNab this is P.C. Charlton, we are from Glasgow central and you are, sir?"

"Hello constable my name is Robert Blackstock from York and this is my son Justin."

"And what exactly brought you here into this compound."

"Well, my son attends a boarding school in Edinburgh and I was driving him back to school today."

"So why are you here miles away from your destination, in the wrong direction?"

"Because a friend had her phone stolen and asked us to try and find it. My son tracked it to here and we tipped over the bin looking for it."

"Have you touched anything sir?"

"I touched the girl's neck to check for a pulse, that's all."

The other constable who had been writing in his notebook said. "We had better report this in Ray, D.I. Howard will need to know and we need the forensic team here to go over the area. I'll contact the station and get things rolling. Can you tape off the area?"

It was a full thirty minutes before the forensic officers arrived and a further ten before the detective inspector arrived. In that time Ana had sent them the name of the young woman who lay in the compound.

"Mr. Blackstock, I didn't expect to see you here today. My officer says that it was you who discovered the body," the inspector said.

"As I told the constable earlier. I was driving my son Justin back to his school in Edinburgh. As you know Miss Ana Kolanski had spoken to her sister yesterday afternoon and Justin had the idea that we could locate Yasmin by tracking her phone. So as we were driving along this morning Justin was using his phone to try and locate it. When he discovered it was just a few miles from his school, we decided to come and check it out and hopefully take Yasmin to her sister."

"So is this Yasmin Kolanski?"

"No, but we sent a picture to Ana Kolanski and she is positive that this is a friend of Yasmin's named Petra Litvinova."

"She is certain about that?"

"She is and there is a message on the phone just there that mentions the name Petra."

The Inspector bent down and carefully picked up the phone in his gloved hand. "The phone is not on," he said.

"It was on when we first saw it but the battery died about half an hour ago. Justin show the inspector the photo of the messages."

"Do you know what these say? I assume they are in Russian."

Justin showed the inspector the message he had received from Ana.

The inspector turned to the forensic officer who was kneeling next to the body. The officer looked up at the inspector and said, "Provisionally I would say the cause of death was a broken neck, there are marks on her neck consistent with a thin rope or cord in an attempt to strangle her but I'm certain the neck is broken."

"And time of death?"

"Going by the body temperature and the warm weather we have today I would place her death as being sometime between 6:00 and 10:00 this morning."

Rob interrupted. "The last message on the phone was timed at 08:13 so we know she was still alive then."

"Only if it was her sending the messages," the inspector replied. "We'll see what the experts come up with when they examine the phone. Thank you Mr. Blackstock, you and your son may leave now. We have your contact details if we need to speak to you again. Good bye."

The inspector turned his back on Rob, as if not wanting to hear anything else from Rob or Justin.

As they walked back to the car, Rob rang Sue and told her about everything that had happened.

"You sound tired, darling," Sue said. "Once you've got Justin back to school why not book yourself into a hotel, have a nice meal and get an early night. You've had a very busy few days, the drive home will be so much easier after a good night's sleep."

"That sounds a good idea," he replied, "I think I might just do that.

After leaving the car park they had to continue driving west until the next motorway exit, where they crossed the motorway and headed back to Edinburgh. It was almost 6:00 when he eventually dropped Justin off at his school. Sue was right, there was no way he would be safe driving back to Yorkshire now. So after leaving the Edinburgh suburbs and getting on to the route home, he pulled into the first decent looking hotel that he came to.

He felt a lot better after a shower and decided he'd have a drink at the bar before going to the restaurant. He perched on a stool at the bar, ordered a double Glenlivet and sat looking down into his glass, thinking over the events of the last couple of days

"Rob Blackstock, what a pleasant surprise!" He instantly recognised the voice and turned to greet the smiling face that had called his name and was walking up behind him.

"Tracy Mills. What are you doing in Scotland?"

She lent in and kissed his cheek before answering. "I'm here on business. What's your excuse? Is Sue with you?"

"Justin is at school in Edinburgh, I've just driven him back after half term. Can I get you a drink? Are you on your own?"

"It's just me tonight, I'm being joined by somebody local tomorrow morning. What are you drinking?" she asked looking into his glass.

"Malt."

"Oh no, I couldn't drink anything as strong as that, I haven't eaten anything since breakfast. I'll have a glass of Prosecco, please." The barman nodded an acknowledgment and Tracy edged backwards onto the bar stool next to Rob.

"Don't tell me you drove back to London yesterday, then all the way up here today?" Rob said.

Tracy smiled at the barman as he placed her drink on the bar in front of her. "No, yesterday I was in Newcastle collecting some evidence for the case I'm working."

"Big case is it?" Rob asked.

Tracy looked around to check no one could overhear them, then quietly said, "I'm following up on a lead which we hope will lead to a new drug importer and distribution network. We think the drugs are coming in on very small boats onto a beach somewhere on the Scottish coast, then passed through Glasgow and Edinburgh for distribution to all the major cities in England."

"Pretty big then," Rob commented.

"And very important," Tracy continued. "These drugs are targeted at a specific market. They have been found on children as young as eight years old. We've got a list of over a hundred and fifty schools across the country that have reported a problem and new cases are being reported every day."

"You say a Scottish beach. There are hundreds of places that could be."

"You are right, Rob. For centuries smugglers have brought in their goods through Scotland and avoided the customs officers. Spirits, silk and tobacco brought in and whisky taken out. They operate a code of working together recognising there is enough profit for everyone, so they help one another and keep the locals happy enough not to give them away."

"I don't envy you trying to find that beach," Rob said.

"It's not just one beach Rob. They use several. We are aware of a dozen or so."

"You said earlier that you were going to be joined by someone local, does he have knowledge of all these beaches?"

"It's a she, D.S. Mary Howard, from Glasgow Central. She's been working this case for years. Only recently has it grown rapidly and that's why we've got involved."

"Is she any relation to D.I. Howard?" Rob asked.

"He's her husband. Why do you ask?"

Rob gave Tracy a summary of the events of the passed forty eight hours and the off hand manner the Inspector had with him at the scene of the second body that day.

"Well good luck to you, is all I can say. Now I'm in need of some food. Will you join me?" Rob asked.

"That would be nice, thank you," she said smiling back at Rob.

30

Over their meal Rob told Tracy what he knew about Yasmin and everything about the two bodies eventually saying that they needed to talk about something less depressing. Rob asked Tracy how her children were doing since her divorce. She told him that there was very little difference because before the divorce she didn't see much of them because of work.

"Is there anyone special in your life at the moment?" Rob asked.

"No, I live the life of a nun these days," she answered.

"I did have Hilda Luggard spend a couple of nights with me, back in March, when she came to London for a specialist plastic surgeon to look her over. It was nice to see her again and we did have some good times, if you know what I mean. But I have to say I do on the whole prefer men and I haven't had sex with a man for more than a year."

"I can't help you there, I'm afraid," Rob said.

"I wasn't suggesting anything," she said. "I've seen what you and Sue have got and wouldn't want to interfere."

Rob changed the subject to avoid further embarrassment. "I saw building work going on up at your old house. Is your brother expanding his business?"

"He's got some big plans and he's hoping that when my little brother Tim leaves the army next month, he will join him to help run the place."

"I didn't know Tim was in the army. Is he off fighting somewhere?"

"No, for the last six years he's been with horse guards doing ceremonial duties. He's qualified as a vet, now so would be a big asset."

After finishing their meal, they returned to the bar for another drink and continued chatting until Rob felt he really needed to get some sleep.

Chapter 4

*"The post-mortem reports on those two girls are back, sir.
Death by strangulation in both cases, sir. The second young lady
had dental treatment consistent with a style commonly seen in
Eastern Europe, but other than that no clue as to where they came
from and as expected fingerprint matching drew a blank. It seems
likely that both girls were sex workers. The M.E. found multiple
samples of semen in the vagina and anus of both. It would appear
that they both had sex with at least seven men shortly before they
died and tissue damage suggests it was not consensual in either
case. We've got a DNA match with one of the samples to known
Russian Mafia thug Ivan Gorkov. Blood and skin found under the
nails of the first girl has been matched to his sister-in-law Yeta
Gorkov."*

****

It was gone 8:00 when Rob woke and it took him a moment or
two to work out that it was Tuesday morning. He wouldn't get home
now until early afternoon and there would be a pile of paper work
waiting on his desk. That did nothing to encourage him to rush
home. He showered, dressed and went down for breakfast. The
restaurant was almost empty, he was possibly the last to come down.
He only wanted a coffee and a Danish.

He had no luggage to go back to his room for, so when he left
the restaurant he went straight to reception and settled his bill, then
went out into the sunshine bathing, the car park and making his car
glow as if lit from inside. He opened the drivers door, turned and sat
sideways in the driver's seat and dangled his feet outside. He pulled
his phone from his pocket and dialled Sue. When she saw who was
calling she answered it quickly. "Good morning darling, do you feel
better this morning? Are you on your way home?"

"I'm actually still in the hotel car park. It's a long time since I slept as well as I did last night, but I had some weird dreams."

"Anything to do with the murdered girls?"

"No, it wasn't the horror kind, just very strange. I was at a fairground with a rifle at the duck shooting stall but they were not ducks, they were pirates or smugglers and they weren't going across from side to side but coming straight towards me and the faster I shot them, the faster they came. Any idea what it means?"

"I don't think it means anything. It was just a weird dream."

"Don't be so dismissive, dreams always mean something. You wait and see."

"I'm glad you had a good sleep, I guess you'll be back here early afternoon. I should be back at around 4:30, I've got two runners at Thirsk this afternoon, one in the 1:00 and one in the 2:45, both should be placed." Sue said.

"I expect nothing less than two winners. Good luck darling, see you later." He ended the call, climbed into the car and slowly left the car park.

He eased into the motorway traffic and headed south. He was listening to Ken Bruce and pop master, he only got one question right from the first set and two in the second set, that was normal for him because he had really only taken an interest in music recently, by listening to Radio 2 on his regular journeys between York and London. All his answers were about guns and shooting, which worried him. First there was his dream about shooting pirates then all his answers referred to guns, was his subconscious trying to tell him something.

He was coming up on junction fifty and the road sign was reading '*A61 Thirsk*'. before he realised what he was doing he had slowed down and moved from the fast lane onto the slip-road to leave the motorway. Sue was just seven miles away and he felt he needed to see her.

Thirsk race course is actually on the A61 just a couple of miles before the town, so it only took Rob about ten minutes to get there. The Jockey Club sticker on his windscreen allowed him to drive past the queue of cars waiting to be checked into the public car park and he quickly found a space in the Premier Enclosure car park for owners and trainers. It was just a short walk from there to the parade ring. A quick glance at his watch told him it was 12:40. Sue had said the first race was at 1:00 so he should find her in the parade ring, waiting for the horses to come out to be shown to the public.

He couldn't see her at first, then she stepped out from behind a horse. She was being careful how she walked so that the heels of her ankle boots didn't sink into the ground. The last week had been dry and warm but after twenty six days of rain before that, the ground was still very soft. Rob stood for a moment just watching her. She was immaculately dressed as always, in a black leather skirt and a black leather waistcoat over a flower pattern blouse. She wasn't wearing a hat, as many of the ladies were, but just a simple spray of flower buds above her left ear and a pair of large lense sun glasses pushed up onto her head, holding her long auburn hair back off her lightly made up face. This was a busy few minutes for her, as she did a final check over the horse and gave the jockey his last minute instructions, so Rob held back and didn't break her routine.

The horse was 'Moscow Magic' and the jockey was a favourite of Sue's, Willy Jobe. He'd won several races for Sue and with this horse he could well have another. Rob saw that the bookies behind him thought so too and the odds slipped from eight to one down to five to one almost as soon as 'Moscow Magic' entered the ring. Rob checked his wallet and walked over to the first bookie in a long line all offering similar odds.

"£50 to win on number two 'Moscow Magic' please, Sid." Rob said.

"Mr. Blackstock, we don't see you here very often these days. Your wife is learning the trade very quickly. She's a natural. Here you go then sir." The bookie said as he handed Rob a betting slip and turned to the next customer. The odds slipped again, now down to nine to two. Rob checked his slip to confirm he had five to one.

Sue was now talking with Willy, they laughed and Willy walked over to the mounting steps and climbed into the saddle, to be led out onto the course. The winner of the best turned out horse was 'Moscow Magic' which was no surprise to any one. Right from her first day, Sue had given instructions on how she wanted her horses turned out and the care she expected to be taken in preparing for any race. Her horse won best turned out with boring regularity and the girls were rewarded with a steady income from prize money. Things were now out of Sue's hands. As the crowd move off to take their seats in the stands Rob moved towards the ring and Sue caught sight of him. She smiled and walked to greet him planting a kiss on his lips before he could say a word.

"Wow that was worth a three hour drive for!" he said.

"What are you doing here? I wasn't expecting to see you until later this afternoon."

"Well, I was just passing and thought I'd pop in to see how you were doing."

"As you can see I'm doing OK. I think we've got a good chance with this one."

"I hope so, I've just put £50 to win on him."

"Lizzy is happy as well. She's just picked up the prize money for best turned out. We'd better go and find a seat, they'll be off soon."

First time past the grandstand '*Moscow Magic*' was third from last but moving easily.

The next time they came into view '*Moscow Magic*' had a clear lead. All he needed to do was stay the pace. To great applause Willy stood in the stirrups and wave to the cheering crowd as he cantered the horse passed the post, winning by ten lengths.

Rob collected his winnings and met Sue at the winner's enclosure, she had just been presented with the trainer's trophy and prize money.

"I can afford to buy you a drink now," Rob said as he took her hand and walked her to the Woolpack bar.

"I must keep an eye on the time. The biggest race of the day the Sir Lenard's Trophy is at 2:45. '*Chanced Romance*' is my runner, he was very poor last time out and the time before that he was a bad third in a three horse race. So he is not fancied, but I think he just didn't like his jockey. Willy Jobe will get a lot more out of him and I quite fancy him for a place at least. It's a big field, more than twenty runners and he likes it best when he's in a crowd."

"You've really taken to this role haven't you? You love every minute," Rob said.

"Let's talk later. I've got work to do. If you are staying a while longer I'll go home with you. I just need to let the others know I won't be going with them, so they can leave just as soon as they are all packed up. Now I really must focus on the next race," She kissed his cheek and headed back towards the parade ring.

Rob felt in his pocket for his winnings. £250, not life changing but a lot more than he had left home with. He thought to himself about what Sue had said about *'Chanced Romance'* being ridden by Willy Jobe. Again he looked down at the money in his hand and said to himself *'Easy come, easy go.'*

He knew Sid wouldn't take a large bet and he expected the other small bookies would not either so he went straight to the Ladbrook's marquee and placed his bet. £250 to Win on number sixteen *'Chanced Romance'* at twelve to one. He wouldn't usually bet recklessly like that but if he lost he would only have lost his winnings.

The last horses were being led from the parade ring out onto the course when Rob got to Sue. He came up behind her placed his hands on her upper arms then lent over her shoulder and said quietly, "Relax darling, you've done everything you can. Willy looks up for it, I'm sure he'll get the best out of that beast."

"He's really good isn't he? I just wish he was available to ride all our horses," Sue said.

"A guy like him will be wanting at least a dozen rides a week. On a good week Blackstock stables can only put out ten rides and only half of those would be flat races," Rob continued.

"They should all be down at the start by now. I told Willy to hold back until the last minute. That horse loves to be in a crowd, when he gets out in front on his own he tends to slow and let the others catch up," Sue announced

"They're under starter's orders." A voice announced over the speakers. "And they're off and running at first time of asking."

The early leaders set a steady pace, this was not a sprint it was a for mile three furlongs endurance event, more than twice around the track. As they came off the bend and onto the run in for the third and final time *'Chanced Romance'* was on the outside of the leading bunch of seven horses and Willy was moving him wide. "That's right Willy, just a little wider, timing is everything." Sue thought out loud. They were just entering the final 2 furlongs "Sue called out "Now Willy, now!" Willy stopped holding his mount wide and gave him his head with freedom to run. The excelleration was noticable and his muscles rippled under the strain as *'Chanced Romance'* raced to get back into the group. Such was his momentum that he rushed up to join the others and got his head out in front, as they dived over the finish line.

Both Sue and Rob punched the air to celebrate victory even though the result was being held waiting for the photo. Technology confirmmed another Blackstock winner by a short head. "He did it Rob, he bloody well did it!" Sue almost screamed. They made their way through the crowd to the winners enclosure to greet the smiling victor.

"How much did you win Rob?" Sue asked as they sat in the queue of vehicles leaving the course at the end of the day.

"£3,000," Rob answered.

"And with two winners I'm bringing home more than twice that in prize money." Sue added. "I do love this life Rob. I just wish I had more Class One horses, then I could compete against the top trainers in the classics'"

They eventually got out of the car park and on to the A61. Rob remembered then why he didn't go to Thirsk as often as he went to other courses. It was the traffic when it was time to leave. Apart from a couple of minor roads, the A61 was really the only way out and you either went west for the A1 or as Rob did, go east for York, the coast or the North Yorkshire Moors. Unfortunately going east meant going through the town of Thirsk in order to get onto the A19 south for York and with the volume of traffic coming off the course at the same time it meant they were bumper to tail and stop start for the first three miles which gave them time to talk.

"I spoke with Willy Jobe before he left," Sue said. "We talked about him taking more rides from Blackstock's."

"Oh yes, and what did he say?" Rob interrupted.

"He's keen to do more. He really likes the way we operate and our attention to detail but he has to go where the work is. He only had two rides today. If he could have got more rides elsewhere then we wouldn't have seen him here. He also said that the owners make a difference. The richer ones give the jockeys a little bonus when they win."

"You haven't got any of those have you? Aren't most of yours syndicate owned?"

"They are, but with my recent successes, I have had one or two interesting enquiries. The problem is I'm full and can't take any more on."

"I don't think you can take on any more, it would be too much. As it is you are out at a race meeting three times most weeks. Then there's the paperwork, managing the yard, staff issues and the money side of things as well. I know you want more but like the yard you've reached capacity."

"Ryman is picking up some of the office work load. He's doing all the customer billing and I've got him starting on running the payroll. He has also looked after the yard, fitted in well, all the lads like him."

"Ryman is not the answer, love," Rob argued. "He's very good at most things but he knows nothing about horses. What you need is someone who can seamlessly step into your shoes, either at the racecourse or at the stables."

"Of course you are right. Ryman is not the right person, but I'm glad we've got him. Madge is glad we've got him too. He's teaching her his style of cooking in return she's teaching him about baking. I believe he is producing a Black Forest Gateaux for dinner this evening," she announced.

"Is the Queen coming or something. What's the occasion?"

"Not the Queen but someone equally important, at least to Luci, Peter is coming to diner this evening. It's his eighteenth birthday tomorrow and Luci wants to start the celebration this evening."

Rob pulled a face, but said nothing for the rest of the journey.

Chapter 5

"Sir Bernard, I saw Rob Blackstock when I was in Edinburgh, we happened to be staying at the same hotel. He told me that he believed Mikhail Gorkov's younger brother Ivor, has taken over Mikhail's role and is shipping in fresh girls from Russia. Scottish police want to speak to Ivor and Mikhail's widow Yeta in connection with the murder of two women in the Glasgow area"

****

The sun shine falling across his face from a gap in the curtains woke Rob. He rolled over intending to cuddle up behind Sue, only to discover she wasn't there. Looking across to their bathroom, it was clear that she wasn't in there either. Wondering where she was, he quickly scrambled out of bed pulled on shorts and a t-shirt then went down to the kitchen, where he found Sue sitting at the table writing something in a notebook with several pages torn out and spread in front of her.

"Perfect timing darling," Sue said, "grab yourself a coffee, then come here and let me show you what I've been doing."

Sue was wearing one of his shirts, she had not done any of the buttons up down the front so Rob could see she was still naked beneath.

"I think you should do a couple of buttons up. Mum will be down soon to make dad's breakfast."

"You have no idea what time it is, have you?" she replied. "It's almost 10:30. Rose and Eric left to go into York half an hour ago. Now come here and listen."

Rob poured a coffee and went and sat next to his wife.

"I was awake in the night thinking about what we were talking about yesterday afternoon," she began, "I've decided that I'm going to expand the stables. In fact I'm going to double the capacity."

"But......."

"No Rob, let me finish. We own the land either side of the stable block so we can extend in either or both directions. I know it will take months to build, but I'm planning on three months to get plans drawn up and get building permission, three months building and ready to open at New Year. I'll need help running the place, so I'll start looking now, get someone trained so that they can take on much of my workload when building work starts, so that I can oversee the building and line up some new clients. I may then take on another assistant and leave myself in a sort of overseeing role. I've only got £84,000 in the bank, so I need to get the bank on my side with a loan or a mortgage. I'll need more staff. I'll need to speak with the vet because we'll need more of his time and I think Rose may have solved some of the paperwork overload problem."

"Don't tell me mum is joining the firm as office girl."

"No silly, She has put me in touch with the most wonderful person you're likely to meet. Tricia Lamb, she's our age and a fully qualified accountant. Until five years ago she worked for a biggish firm of accountants in York but didn't agree with some of their practices, so left and started up her own company. Her husband gave up his job and is training as an accountant. Rose says that all her clients love her because of the personal service they get. I've looked at her website and she can provide full accounts and auditing, bookkeeping and payroll services. So I rang her and she's coming to see me this afternoon."

"You have had a busy morning," he said.

"I've still got an awful lot of work to do, but it's coming and I'm getting very excited."

As they continued talking there was a knock on the back door. Sue pulled the two shirt fronts together as Rob went to answer the door. Ryman was stood on the step.

"This gent came into the yard looking for Miss Susan," he said and stepped aside so that Rob could see a tall man, who looked to be in his sixties, wearing an expensive looking suit, carrying a document case under his arm.

"This is Mr. Robert Blackstock, Miss Susan's husband." Ryman said to the stranger.

"Good morning sir." The tall gent said holding out his hand."My name is William Blake. I represent Howell, Blake and McPhee solicitors of Inverness, I have a letter for Miss Susan Kowinski, which I have been instructed to deliver personally and await a reply."

Rob was struggling to follow the heavy Scottish accent but Sue had overheard and said. "Let him come in Rob, so we can see what this is all about." The gent looked a little embarrassed by Sue's choice of clothes but she had at least had time to do up three or four buttons down the front. "I am Susan Blackstock maiden name Kowinski. What can I do for you?" she said.

"I'm sorry, miss but do you have any proof of identity?" he responded.

"Will a driving licence do?" she asked. "Rob pass me my hand bag please. It's on the dresser."

"Thank you miss, that's perfect," Blake said and he opened his document case and pulled out a letter and handed it to her.

She admired the quality of the paper as she tore it open and carefully read the single sheet she found inside.

"It says an uncle of mine has died and I have been identified as his only living relative and am to inherit his property in Scotland. I am to provide this gentleman with my contact details, phone number, email address and that sort of stuff and give him three dates when I can possibly be in Inverness to meet with the solicitors and discuss what we want to do."

"Darling, can you look on the chart and see when I could be free?" Sue asked. I guess we'll need three days, a day to get up to Inverness, day two to meet with the solicitor, then the third day to get home."

Rob walked over to a large wall chart stuck on the kitchen wall, next to the back door and ran his finger along the row of dates for June then on into July.

"The first gap is July 5th. You've got several two day breaks but that is the first three day one," Rob reported. "The next is July 14th then July 19th."

"So that suggests the three dates for a meeting would be 6th, 15th and 20th of July," Sue said and she wrote the dates down on a blank page in her note book and added her business email address, her mobile number and office landline. When she'd finished she carefully tore the page out of the book and handed it to the gentleman patiently waiting.

"Is that okay? Is there anything else you need from me?"

"I do need to see your marriage licence," he replied, "and I understand that this is your second marriage so I'll need to see papers relating to the termination of your first marriage."

"My first husband was a soldier killed in action. Will his death certificate suffice?"

"I'm sorry I didn't know that. Yes, his death certificate will be good."

Sue told Rob where to find her papers and he went upstairs to their room to get them. He was quickly back and William Blake looked the documents over, wrote something in his notebook and used his phone to take pictures of all the papers.

"Well that is all I need. Thank you both. I look forward to seeing you in Inverness. I would imagine the 5th July will be the date, as it is a month away. I'll say good day to you Mrs. Blackstock, Mr. Blackstock."

"Hang on, I'll see you out," Rob said and opened the door followed him out and walked him to the taxi sitting on the drive. Rob recognised the taxi as an airport taxi from Leeds-Bradford airport. He'd used them in the past and recognised the logo in the taxi's door. Obviously the estate on this uncle of Sue's was wealthy enough to fund this solicitor flying down from Inverness, just for a ten minute visit.

When Rob got back to the kitchen Sue had poured herself another coffee. "Do you want another," She asked holding up her mug.

"Something stronger wouldn't go amiss," he replied. "But a coffee will do for now. Tell me more about this uncle of yours."

"It's complete news to me," she replied. "My mother never spoke about having a brother and my fathers parents were Jews who had left Russia when they were only thirteen to avoid Nazi persecution. Tony did some family tree stuff when we were first married and he did find a record of a christening of a boy named George, with my grandparents listed in the parish records as his parents, but Tony found no other record of him. Mother was born in London, 5th September 1940. Both her parents were killed when the flats they lived in were totally destroyed in one of the first raids in the Battle of Britain. Records showed that several people known to have been in the building were never found. We assumed George had been killed as well. Records from that period are very sketchy, so much was lost in the bombing. Apparently my mother was found in the rubble the next day. Less than a month old, she was labelled a miracle baby. A lady doctor saw her through the next few days and when she was well enough she was shipped to Edinburgh to be brought up by the doctor's family, people that I called my grand parents when I was young.

When she left school mum trained as a secretary and landed a job with the Civil Service, eventually ending up working in a government department in London. There she met my father six years her junior. They were married in 1978 and had two children. Mother told me all this as soon as I was old enough to understand. I was eight years old when they died. They were on Pan Am flight 103 which crashed at Locherbie on 21st December 1988. They had been going to New York for Christmas to celebrate their tenth wedding anniversary. My adopted grandparents in Edinburgh had both died by this time, so my brother and I went to live with our father's parents who were in their early sixties. If you remember you met my granddad the day we first met. The rest of my life you already know."

"So this uncle you're inheriting from is most probably your mum's brother George, who your mother thought had been killed with her parents," Rob surmised.

"It's the only answer I can think of," she replied, "but what am I going to do with an old crofter's cottage in a remote part of mainland Scotland?"

"You could always rent it out as a holiday home," Rob suggested.

"If it's that remote it won't have electricity, running water or wi-fi. Who would want to stay in a place like that?"

"I think it may be a bit better than some tumbled down ruin. His estate must be worth a sum large enough to pay for that solicitor to fly down here from Inverness."

"Maybe it is. We won't know until next month, so I'm not going to think about it until then." She turned and set her empty mug down next to the sink and went upstairs leaving Rob to look over her plans to expand the stables.

". . . . . Thanks Tracy I'll give him a call right now. Good luck up there. 'Bye." Rob was ending a phone call when Sue returned to the kitchen. She gave Rob a quizzical look. Rob responded by saying. "While I was in Edinburgh Monday night I bumped into Tracy Mills. That was her I was just talking to on the phone. She's in Scotland, about to start a big drugs case. She just happened to be staying in the same hotel and we had dinner together. While we were talking her younger brother came up in the conversation. I think he may be the solution to two of your issues with your plan to expand."

"Explain."

Rob continued, "He's a lieutenant in the army getting a medical discharge. For the last few years he's been with the horse guards, that is until a horse kicked him and smashed his leg up and he needed plates and screws to fix it. He's on sick leave up here with his older brother, young Peter's dad, over at the Mill's house. The brother wants him to help run the livery business but Tim's not keen. He's an officer so must have something about him. As a horse guard, he is used to order and discipline which would suit you and more importantly he's qualified as a vet, specialising in horses. Apparently he's had a couple of papers published about the treatment of muscle damage in horses' legs."

"Sound too good to be true. He could be exactly what I'm looking for as an assistant," she smiled. "I'll forgive you for not telling me that you spent the night with another woman."

"I thought we could give him a call this morning, get him down here to meet him, have a chat then take it from there. I thought who ever you take on could stay in the flat above the stables. Ana and Eva made a good job of fitting it out in the months they lived there. It's now a very nice little set up and could be thrown in as part of the deal."

"Tim so good of you to come down, come into the office and meet my wife, she runs this place and it's her that really wants to talk to you." They shook hands and Tim followed Rob into the office. "Sue, this is Tim Mills. Tim, this is my wife Sue."

"I thought the name rang a bell and now I see the face. We've met before Lieutenant Mills. You were a witness for me at Colour Sergeant Bigger's Court Marshal in Colchester about five years ago," Sue said.

Tim's whole body stiffened. He grew to his full six foot three and his heels came smartly together. He only just managed to stop himself saluting.

"Captain Williams, it's a long time ago, I had just finished veterinarian college and been promoted to Lieutenant, so it must have been July 2013. You're looking well, Yorkshire air must suit you."

"Almost as much as being out of the army," she joked. "Rob says you know one another."

"Twenty five years ago I'd say yes. At one time he went out with my sister and we all went to the same high school. Of course, I was two years behind Rob, but my mates and I always looked up to him as a role model."

"I don't know what Rob told you on the phone earlier, but we've reached a point here at the stable where we need to grow to continue being successful. The plan is to double the capacity of the yard by extending the stable block at both ends," Sue explained. "I'm looking for someone to take on my current role so that I can be free to oversee the expansion plan and bring in some new customers."

"Can I stop you there?" Tim interrupted. "If you are offering me a job then the answer is yes please. I'm very interested, although I'm not sure whether I have the right experience to do it. I know about horses, but know nothing about racing. Since I've been staying with my brother, I've heard our Peter and your Luci continually going on about this and that happening here and how there is a real buzz generating and how many winners you are getting. To be honest walking in as I just have, there is definitely a positive atmosphere and I'd very much like to be part of it."

"The racing side of things is not difficult, but very demanding," Sue said.

"I'm not afraid of hard work or putting the hours in," Tim responded.

"Well, how about a six week trial and at the end of it we can decide what to do longer term. Once we are a bigger outfit, I can see a need to make use of your vetinarian training rather than increase our use of the local vet."

"When would you want me to start?" Tim asked.

"Hang on, we haven't discussed pay etcetera yet and I understand you are still in the army until the end of the month."

"That's right. I technically can't start a job until after I'm discharged. If I do then it would impact my army pension. But that doesn't stop me being trained and I can be free to start that right now. We can sort out the pay some other time."

"Today is actually a very good day to start. The vet will be in this afternoon for his weekly visit. He's here every Wednesday to do a general health check on the horses. Then at 4:30 I've got an accountant coming to see me to discuss what she can do to lighten the work load in the office. It would be useful if you sit in."

"All sounds good to me," Tim said.

"Fantastic. I'll sort out some paperwork this evening to clarify the role and we'll discuss it tomorrow. Officially you'll start on July 1st, but I'll find some way of paying you for the three weeks before then. Part of the package will be accomodation, there is small flat above the stables that goes with the job."

"This gets better and better," Tim said. "What time will the vet get here?"

Chapter 6

"The odd bit of smuggling of booze and tobacco I can turn a blind eye to, but you've escalated to significant volumes of drugs. Are these Eastern European girls that are being found strangled, anything to do with you? I've had two girls turn up dead on my patch this week. I'm an inspector, people watch me very carefully, waiting to trip me up. There is only so much I can do to direct the investigation away from you. My wife is now working with an MI-6 agent looking at the drug trafficing, it's only a matter of time before they make the link to these girls."

****

Trisha Lamb left, having signed up Blackstock Racing, as her latest client. The meeting had gone on for almost two hours and Sue was buzzing with enthusiasm when she walked into the kitchen. Rose had held back dinner so that they could all sit down together. There were only four of them because Luci had gone out almost as soon as she had come home from school. She'd rushed up to her bedroom and reappeared minutes later in a much shorter skirt and a boob tube. "Peter's folks are taking him out for a birthday meal and have invited me to go too," she had announced and left.

Rob and Eric were in the lounge discussing the forthcoming Rugby World Cup in Japan and agreeing that Wales having won the Six Nations Grand Slam, must be in with a good chance of winning the cup.

Now that Sue was in, Rose called Rob and Eric through for their meal.

"How did it go with Mrs. Lamb?" Rob asked Sue.

"Great. You were right Rose, she is a very nice lady," Sue said, "and knows what she's talking about. She only had a quick look at the books and said we are paying too much tax. She can get that sorted and claim a substantial refund. She said she can do all the company accounts, our bookkeeping and our payroll. She can even advise on the expansion work and assist in getting money from the bank. All that and she will only charge the same as we currently pay Grindle's and they only do the annual accounts and get them audited."

"If she's any good, I should be asking her to do work for the stunt academy. I hate the thought that I might be paying too much tax," Rob said.

"You can sound her out on Friday, if you come to York. I've invited Trisha to go as my guest, just to give her an insight into the horse racing business. She claims she's never been nor ever laid on a bet even on The National."

"I'll check my diary but I think I can free up the afternoon. What have you got running?"

"'Lord Jim' in the 1:30, it's his first time out so I'm not sure what to expect but he has shown good pace out on the gallops. Then 'Lucky Jean' in the 3:45, hopelessly outclassed last time out but I've convinced the owner to step down a class and she should be good for a place."

"'Lucky Jean', that's one of that pompass ass Ross Jenkin's horses isn't it. Always thinks his horses are better than they are and we don't know how to train winners."

"He does come on a bit strong sometimes, but since I met him face to face a few weeks ago, we have a better understanding of each other. He still hasn't had a winner. But last week at Redcar he came very close, beaten into second place by a short head in heavy going."

"Are you still free for two or three days from Sunday to go over to Dublin and take the boat round to Hull. I've booked a birth at the marina and the weather forecast is excellent for the Irish Sea, the Channel and the North Sea right through from Friday until Wednesday."

"Yes, I've got a runner on Thursday, but nothing until then," Sue replied.

"Good girl, I'll sort out some transport to get us to Dublin. If we can get onto the boat by lunch time we should make Falmouth before dark, then have plenty of time on Monday to get round up to Hull. Don't forget to pack your sun cream, even if we don't see the sun you can still get very burnt being exposed on the open deck and don't forget some light shoes with rubber soles, trainers will do."

The alarm on Rob's watch woke them both at 6:00 Sunday morning. "Come on sleepy head, we've got to get moving. We've only got half an hour to get ready." Rob said as he pulled the duvet from Sue's naked body. "Your face and shoulders are turning a lovely brown from standing around all these racecourses, you'll be able to top it up over the next couple of days. You go and get in the shower while I have a shave. Leave it running and I'll hop in as soon as you've finished."

"I'll only be a minute. Have we got time for a coffee?" Sue asked.

"Not really but we can take a couple of those insulated travel mugs with us and drink it as we go."

They were both dressed by 6:15 and heading down stairs. There was plenty of activity outside as the horses were being readied to be exercise. Rose was pouring a coffee and Eric was sitting at the table sipping his obviously hot coffee.

"Are you sure you are okay looking after things here, while we're away Eric?" Sue asked her father-in-law.

"Think nothing of it lass. I'm happy to be able to help out now and again. It was race days that were beginning to be too tiring. The day to day yard job I can easily cope with and I've got Tim to call on if I need any lifting doing. Tell me Robert, why are you going to Dublin by helicopter and not using the regular Leeds/Bradford plane. It would be considerably cheaper."

"If we went on the scheduled flight, we wouldn't land until 2:15 so it would be around 5:30 before we would be ready to cast off. We wouldn't get very far before we'd have to stop somewhere for the night, so it would be a struggle to reach Hull. The helicopter will get us there in less than four hours. We can be casting off before mid-day, so will easily make it round to Falmouth by nightfall."

"Even so, it must be hellishly expensive," Eric suggested.

"If I was going alone I couldn't justify it. But the helicopter is like a taxi, you pay for the journey not the number of passengers, so for the two of us it's only costs a little more than the scheduled flight."

Sue came rushing into the kitchen and interrupted Rob and Eric. "Rob the helicopter has just landed in the paddock."

"Right girl, grab your things. Let's not keep the pilot waiting."

The pilot was out of the aircraft to greet them. After a brief safety talk they climbed aboard and were quickly airborne.

Flying low, they had an amazing view of the English countryside, then they followed the North Wales coast and low across Anglesey, out over the Irish Sea towards Dublin. They landed at Dublin Airport and took a short taxi ride to Poolbeck Yacht Club. The club house was a brick built 2 story building with a car park on three sides and what appeared to be a boat yard behind. Rob entered through the door, under the sign reading reception.

"Good day sir, can I help you?" a smiling red haired receptionist asked.

"Yes please. I'm here to see Ric Mahoney," Rob said.

"Just a moment please, sir. Would you and the lady like to take a seat?" She pointed to a short row of easy chairs. As Sue and Rob sat down to wait, the receptionist used the P.A. system to ask Ric to come to reception.

"Good morning Mr. Blackstock, miss. Lovely Jayne is all fuelled up and ready to go, the provisions you requested are all stowed and have been charged to your account. If you'd like to follow me I'll take you down to her, I expect you're keen to get away. It's been a long time. Do you want me to go over anything with you before you leave?"

"Yes please Ric. As you say it's been a long time, so you'd better treat me as a novice and my wife here is a real beginner."

"Well here she is, sir. I hope you find her in the state you'd expect. She is a very fine craft and doesn't show any sign of her age."

"Wow Rob, I'm impressed," Sue said.

"She is a good looker isn't she?" Rob responded.

Ric stepped down from the jetty onto the aft deck and held out his hand to help Sue down. "Careful miss it's quite a big step down," he said.

Rob threw their bags down onto the deck and stepped down to join the others. Ric took them into the cockpit and talked them through the array of controls and explained how to use the navigation system.

"You really should study the manual and get to know this equipment before you need to seriously use it to get anywhere. Same with the radio. If you ever get into a situation where your life depends on these systems, you won't want to be reading a manual to find out how to use them."

"Sound advice Ric," Sue said. "I'll see he gets familiar with all the controls, I'll also study it all as well."

They all moved into the day cabin and Ric showed them how to use the galley stove and other equipment. "I think that's just about everything, most things in here are basic and simple to use, you shouldn't have any trouble but if you do you can always call me."

"Thanks Ric for all your work over the last few years. It's very much appreciated," Rob said and pressed an envelope into Ric's hand.

"I know you're eager to get away so I'll leave you to it," Ric said as he turned to leave. "Good day miss, happy sailing. Take care now, sir. Go steady until you get the hang of her again."

"I will and thank you again for everything. Bye." Rob said.

"What did you just give him?" Sue asked.

"A good bonus, he's earned it. The boat looks better than she did when I bought her and I know the job doesn't pay well."

"You're such a nice guy, Mr. Blackstock. I do love you." She walked across the day room and kissed him. "Now are we almost ready to get moving. I just want to get out of these jeans, that sun is really getting hot."

She reappeared a couple of minutes later in shorts and a tee shirt knotted at the side. "That's better I was getting way too hot. What do you want me to do?"

"I'm ready to get moving. I'll start the engines, then if you can get up onto the jetty and untie the lines, front one first, then jump back onboard."

"Will do captain," Sue said and saluted.

Rob slowly manoeuvred his way out of the yacht club moorings, conscious that dozens of pairs of eyes were watching his every move. Space was very tight but he made his way out into the main harbour and on into the open waters of the Irish Sea.

"I thought we'd follow the coast down to Rosslare then follow the compass due south until we see Lands End on our port side. We'll keep the Cornish coast on our port and should make Falmouth late afternoon. Tomorrow, we just need to continue with the mainland on our port side, all the way to Hull."

"All sounds sensible to me. Do I get a turn at being captain sometime soon?"

"Sorry love, of course you can have a go, just keep her this distance from the shore." Rob stepped to one side and let Sue take the wheel. "Once you feel comfortable increase the speed a little by pulling those two leavers back just a fraction."

"This was a good idea Rob, I'm really enjoying today."

"I've been thinking Sue, we've got to go up to Inverness sometime in July, why don't we go in this and take a few extra days, perhaps even a week and have that round Britain trip I spoke about a few days ago, a late honeymoon."

"That is a great idea Rob, you're a true romantic at heart. I'll need to check the race days. Do you think Eric could cope running the stables?"

"I'm sure he'll do fine, he'll have Tim to assist him, he'll have been with you a month by then,

" Rob said.

"I still need to check the dates. Now if you take over here again I'll see what I can rustle up for lunch."

They arrived in Falmouth a little after 4:00 and tied up temporarily while Rob went to find the harbour master to pay for a berth for the night. Sue told Rob she had never been to Falmouth before and Rob admitted that he hadn't either. So they decide to get a map from the Harbour Master's office and explore together, eventually finding a cosy pub for their evening meal. It was a timber framed building, decorated to make the most of it's history, with pictures and images of smugglers and pirates plus artifacts from a period in history when more than half the townsfolk were involved in the illegal import export business. The menu was basic pub grub. Sue claimed a table in a quiet corner and Rob ordered two scampies and two real ales from a local brewery.

Although it was almost 8:00 it was still warm and they were happy that the window beside them was open. Sue was back in her jeans and the tee shirt had been replaced by one of Rob's shirts with the front tails tied in a loose knot. The sleeves were rolled back above her elbows and she'd left the top four buttons undone showing plenty of cleavage. As they sat waiting for their food they studied the various historical items mounted on the walls.

"It must have been big business in this area in the day," Rob said.

"Other than tin mining, I don't know that Cornwall is known for anything else," Sue added.

"Some of these labels refer to Roman times and there's a news paper clipping on the wall above your head dated 1948. It's about a gang caught smuggling three tons of butter which was still on ration after the war."

"And the business still goes on, but these days it's mostly drugs," Sue said.

"Drugs must certainly be the biggest problem, but don't forget the human trafficing. Just think about Ana and Eva, they were smuggled in illegally."

"Do you think that's what has happened to poor Yasmin?" Sue queried.

"I'm certain of it. Those two dead girls are connected to it in someway as well, I expect," Rob replied.

"Two scampies?" came a call from behind Rob.

Sue raised a hand and their food was delivered by a young blond girl with long legs topped by a denim skirt three inches shorter than her waitress apron and a tight top.

"Put your eyeballs back in Blackstock, look at these if you want to look at any." Sue said and pulled her shirt aside to give him a glimps of her pierced nipples. Then looked around to be certain no one else could see.

"You do know how to get a man's attention," Rob said. They smiled at one another across the table and began their meal.

"Well that was very ordinary," Sue said as she pushed her empty plate into the middle of the table.

"What do you expect for £7.99?" Rob said. "What do you want to do now? It's still early. We could have another drink or look around the town a bit more, or go back to the boat and open a bottle."

"We had an early start this morning so it would be wise to go back to the boat. I'm in need of a good eight hours sleep," Sue claimed.

"Could you manage with just six hours?" Rob said with a broad grin on his face.

"You're not suggesting something improper are you, sir?" Sue smiled back at him and they left the pub and walked back to the boat arm in arm.

Rose had invited Tim to join her and Eric for dinner. She had told him 7:00 and at 6:45 he knocked on the back door in clean jeans and tee shirt, his hair still looked damp from his shower. Rose answered the door and he came in walking with a slight limp.

"Please take a seat. I've cooked lasagne, I hope that's okay for you? Does your leg give you trouble at all Tim?" Rose asked.

"Not normally, just occasionally it lets me know it's held together with bits of metal and today I've been stood a lot which I haven't really done since it happened. I'm sure it will get used to more standing as the muscles strengthen."

"Do you miss the army, Tim?" Rose asked.

"I thought I would, but it's horses I love, just being around them makes me happy. I was so pleased when Sue offered me this job. I only hope I can fit in and be what she wants me to be."

Eric had walked into the kitchen and caught the end of the conversation. "You're doing great lad, from what I've seen of you today you'll fit in very well. You seem to get on well with the lads and they respect you. Lizzy and Sally of course, melt at the sight of you, but that's no big deal. They'd do the same at any man under forty."

"Thank you Eric, keep your lewd thoughts to yourself," Rose said as she placed a plate of lasagne in front of Tim and another in front of Eric.

"Do you have to do much training for the horse guards, Tim?" Rose asked.

"Quite a bit actually Mrs. Blackstock." He answered. "Firstly you have to do the twelve week basic military training that everybody has to do. Because the modern cavalry is all about tanks, we have to train as a driver or gunner down at Bovington in Dorset for six weeks. Then you get assigned to either The Life Guards or The Blues and Royals. Only the few selected for mounted duty go to Windsor to complete a sixteen week Riding School course. There you get given your own horse which you must feed and look after. A final four weeks is spent riding in ceremonial uniform before your passing out parade, then you join your regiment at Hyde Park barracks."

"That must be best part of a year?" Rose said.

"It's about nine months and is hard work, but the end result is something we are all proud to be part of."

"Can I interest you in strawberries and cream?" she asked.

"Yes please," he replied. "Can you tell me about the two ladies that had the flat I'm in."

"Ana and Eva are two very nice young Russian women. We've all become very fond of them. Why do you ask?" Eric questioned.

"Well I found a few items of clothing in the flat that I think I should let them have back, but it might be a little embarrassing," Tim answered.

"You mean you've found some of their knickers." Eric said. "I can assure you they won't be embarrassed, but you might be."

The evening on the south coast was still very warm, so Sue and Rob sat out on the deck with a glass of whisky, enjoying the sun going down in a blaze of red and gold, reflected perfectly in the calm dark sea. Sue had removed her jeans and untied the shirt to try and cool down a little.

"The forecast is for a real scorcher tomorrow," Rob said, "we'll be glad we're out at sea to pick up any breeze that there might be."

"I plan to make the most of it and top up my tan and let you play with your toy," Sue said. "I think I'll just ring home to check that Eric is okay. You can pour me another whisky while I'm on the phone."

She was smiling broadly when she ended the call.

"What's funny?" Rob asked.

"Tim's found some of Ana and Eva's knickers in the flat and is concerned that giving them back might embarrass them," Sue explained.

"He doesn't know those two. From what Luci has told me they are beyond embarrassing. He hasn't met them has he?" Rob said.

"Not yet," Sue replied. "Did Luci ever show you the video Ana gave her a copy of?"

"No."

"Would you like to. I think I've still got a copy on my phone." She tapped the screen of her phone several times and Rob heard some dance music begin. She handed him the phone and sat back with her drink and watched his expression. The video lasted about six minutes.

"Gee whiz. They don't hold back do they and they're not camera shy. I can see why they were so popular and got paid well," he said and handed the phone back to Sue before downing the contents of his glass.

"Luci was almost forced into something like that," Sue suggested. "And Yasmin could well be going the same way. Is there anything we can do?"

"I can't see what. We'll just have to hope Inspector Howard can track them down soon," Rob said.

"I'm ready for bed but I need a shower first," Sue said.

"I'll come and show you how it works," Rob said and followed.

Chapter 7

"You've brought in some very good looking girls this time Ivor, I'm sure our customers will be very pleased. But you told me you were bringing seven and there are only 5 here. Where are the other two? The one who gave me these scratches on my arm doesn't appear to be here nor the redhead."

****

The rocking motion of the boat as other craft passed by was enough to wake Sue. She could tell that the sun was already beating down on them because of the warm glow seeping around the edges of the blind at the window. She could smell coffee, so Rob must already be up. She found the shirt she had been wearing the previous evening, slipped it on to her shoulders and pulled the two fronts over one another then opened the door into the day room.

"Well, good morning gorgeous. Did you smell the coffee?" Rob said. He was sitting on the bench seat behind the table with the navigation system manual open in front of him. "I was just doing my homework."

Sue sat on the other bench seat on the opposite side of the cabin with her feet drawn up onto the seat in front of her and her knees against her chest. "I'll just have a coffee then I'll get some breakfast organised," she said.

"It's already over twenty degrees outside and there's practically no breeze at all. The forecast says that some parts of the south coast will see record temperatures this afternoon," Rob told her.

"I was thinking if we have a good breakfast here in the sheltered waters of the harbour, then a sandwich at lunch time will see us through. You said we should be home early evening so we'll have dinner when we get home," Sue suggested.

"Good plan. I'll get the breakfast underway while you get some clothes on. We can't have you frightening the seagulls can we?"

Sue went back into the bedroom and returned wearing her bikini under the shirt. Whilst they ate their breakfast, Rob suggested Sue take charge of their leaving the harbour and getting back out to sea. She readily agreed. By 9:00 breakfast had been cleared away, dishes washed, dried and stowed away.

Sue was bare footed and felt the heat of the deck uncomfortably on the soles of her feet. Fortunately the cockpit floor was covered by a rubber mat and shaded by the canopy above her head which made it all much more comfortable. She keyed in the six digit security code and pressed the button to start the twin engines. Rob was up on the jetty, as soon as the engines roared into life she heard him shout, "Bow line away." Immediately Sue felt the bow swing away from the jetty, forced by the fast flowing tide. Seconds later Rob shouted. "Stern line away," followed by a loud thud, as he jumped from the jetty down onto the deck. She pulled on the throttle leavers to give enough power to control the boat in the fast moving water. Carefully she moved them out into mid stream, increased their speed gently and headed for the open water.

Monday was a bigger challenge for Tim. His leg was objecting to the exertions of the previous day and the pain had kept him awake for long periods during the night. Pain killers were having very little effect, but somehow he had to get through it. Eric had set him the challenge of getting the yard including all the stables cleaned by lunchtime. He knew the stable lads hated the job, so the real challenge was to get them all motivated to do it.

It was 8:15, the morning exercises were just about all finished and the lads were mostly indoors getting their breakfast. Tim was perched on a shooting stick trying to keep the weight of his leg and for the next ten minutes he sat watching the various comings and goings. Then he called out to one of the older lads. "Billy, can you please get all the lads together out here in front of me now?" Looking confused, Billy rushed off to collect everybody.

When everyone was assembled Tim stood and stretched to his full height which was far above any of those in front of him.

"Gentlemen, today is clean up day," he said, causing a murmur to ripple around the group. He raised a hand to silence them then continued. "I know it's a chore we all hate, but I'm going to set you a challenge. I want you to split into two teams and take half the stables each and get them cleaned out. It's a straight race between two teams but they have to be done thoroughly. Mr. Eric will be out at 11:45 to check everything out. For every fault he finds that team will be awarded one point, the team with the most points will win the job of cleaning the yard as well. The other team will meet me in the 'Dog and Gun' at 7:00 this evening when I will buy all of them a pint. In the event that both teams score equal points then the first team will have one point deducted."

Everyone seemed to be enthusiastic about the challenge and they quickly divided into two teams and went about their challenge.

Eric had been stood close enough to hear what Tim had been saying, but was out of sight from the lads.

"That's a novel way of motivating them to do work they hate doing," he said as he walked towards Tim.

"It may be £20 or so well spent, if it works." Tim said.

"I'm sure it will. Well done."

Sue took the 'Lovely Jayne' straight out from the harbour until she judged them to be a mile off shore, then she turned east.

"Darling, can you put some sun cream on my shoulders please?" Sue asked and slowly eased off her shirt and casually tossed it onto one of the seats at the back of the cockpit.

"Sure, if you'll do the same for me."

Rob went down into the day cabin and came back with Sue's sun cream. He poured a little into his hand and began spreading it across her back and shoulders. As he did so she reached behind her back and pulled the cord of her bikini top then did the same with the cord at her neck allowing the top to drop to the floor. "Don't get any of that on my bikini, it will stain the fabric."

"That's your back all done. Do you want me to do the front?" He suggested.

"No thanks, I'm quite capable of that," she replied. "Now get that shirt off and take over at the wheel, while I do you."

They swapped places and Sue spread sun cream across his back, his shoulders, down his arms and across his chest. The surplus on her hands she rubbed into her own chest coating her breasts and her rapidly growing nipples. When Rob looked round she was spreading cream on her legs starting at her feet and ankles and moving upwards. Something moved and caught his eye. He looked down to see the Sue's bikini bottom on the floor at his feet. When he turned to look at her she was carefully applying sun cream around her groin and then stood to rub more across her backside.

"I'm all ready for some serious tanning. Am I alright lay on a towel on the cabin roof."

"Sure, no problem," he said then continued. "You continue to surprise me Sue. First the pierced nipples and now this."

"Well, you made a comment about Ana and Eva when you watched their video last night, so when I had my shower before bed, I got my razor out. There wasn't much light in the bedroom so you wouldn't have noticed." She smiled at the reaction she was seeing. "Call me in after a hour will you and I'll make us a coffee."

Ryman was at Hull marina for 5:30, as Rob had requested when he rang Ryman two hours earlier. Rob secured the boat then stopped off at the Marinas office to inform them of his arrival, they both then walked out to find Ryman. "Did you have a good trip, miss?" he asked as he put their bags into the boot.

"Very good thank you Ryman, except my shoulders are a bit sore, slight case of too much sun. I'll be fine in a couple of days."

"Have you got an Alovera plant, miss?"

"I don't think so. Why?"

"The juice squeezed from the leaves of an Alovera plant will heal your burns instantly. I've got a couple of spare plants at home. I'll detour to my house before I take you home and you can have one of my plants."

"Honestly Ryman, don't go to any trouble, I'll be fine."

"No trouble at all miss, it's more or less on our route."

They stopped long enough for Ryman to run into his house and return to the car carrying a strange looking spiky plant.

Luci heard the car pull onto the gravel drive and opened the front door to greet them.

"Welcome home you two. You just caught me before I left."

"Don't tell me you're going to see Peter," Rob said and gave his daughter a kiss on the forehead.

"Not tonight, dad. He's got a big day tomorrow, it's his last two A-level papers so he's busy cramming. I'm off to an Ann Summers party at the girls' place. Peter's mum is going too and she's giving me a lift. She's really nice you should meet her sometime. And isn't Peter's Uncle Tim a dish, for an older man that is. You'll need to watch Sue and him working closely together."

Another car pulled onto the drive. "There's my lift. I must go. See you later," she called over her shoulder as she ran down the drive.

"Okay Ryman, what do I do with this plant you've given me?"

"Simply break a piece off, squeeze out the syrupy juice from inside and spread that onto the burn. It truly is a wonderful plant, great for burns and can ease aching muscles. My parents swear by it."

"Thank you, I'll give it a go later."

"Hi dad, how's your day been?" Sue asked Eric who was sitting in the lounge reading his paper."

"It's been interesting shall I say."

"What do you mean? What's happened?"

"Nothing's happened it just that Tim has some interesting ways of getting things done. He got the lads cleaning the stables and the yard this morning with surprising results, I don't think I've ever seen the place so clean and everyone so keen to do the work."

"What do you think of Tim?"

"I think you got a good one there. He learns very quickly. The lads respect him and I've never seen anyone quite like him with the horses, it's like they talk the same language and think alike too. He is quite a remarkable chap."

"You had a letter arrive this morning dear," Rose told Sue. "I put it on the mantle piece in the lounge."

"Thanks Rose. Post for me normally costs me money. It's either a bill, a holiday brochure or a sales leaflet. I'll get it later. What's for dinner? The sea air has made me hungry."

"It's not a bill. At least it doesn't look like a bill. It's a very high quality envelope. It's postmarked Inverness."

"That will be from those solicitors dealing with your uncle's estate." Rob said, "probably confirming the date for your meeting."

"I'll open it and we'll see." She disappeared through the door into the lounge and returned with a torn envelop and what looked like a cheque in one hand and several sheets of paper in the other. She was reading from the first page as she walked back into the kitchen and sat at the table.

"It is from the solicitor. They want to meet me on 19th July at 10:30. They have sent a map of how to find them, a three day pass for free parking on 18th, 19th and 20th July in a car park near their offices and a list of four and five star hotels within half a mile of their office. They have also sent an advance on the estate to cover my expences." She looked at the cheque in her hand. "Christ, it's for £1,000!"

"I did say the estate must be worth quite a bit to fund that solicitor flying down here, just for that ten minute meeting with you," Rob said. "You must have £50,000 or more coming. You never know you may even have enough to fund your extension plans."

"Do you think so? That would be nice."

"Did you say the 19th, that's six weeks away, Tim should be more or less capable of running the whole operation by then and you could oversee and help out if he has a problem, couldn't you dad?"

Eric gave his son a blank look.

"I want to take Sue away for a couple of weeks. We haven't had a honeymoon, so we're thinking about taking the boat around Britain, stopping off anywhere that takes our fancy, but making sure we're in Inverness to meet these solicitors."

"That will be fine. We haven't got any plans for going away have we Rose? Like you say Tim should be up to speed by then anyway."

"Tim will get his first taste of race days this week. We've got three long hauls, with one runner at Fakenham on Thursday, two at Hereford on Friday then three at Chepstow on Saturday," Sue announced.

"If that doesn't put him off nothing will," Rob said.

"I've only got tomorrow and Wednesday to prepare him for what to expect. Thankfully, I've only got one runner on Thursday, so it won't be too hectic and I'll be able to spend time with him.

Yasmin had learnt a lot about the other four girls she was locked up with. Annika and Galina, like her were from the suburbs of Moscow, whilst Irina and Katina were from St Petersburg. There had been two other girls with them when they were first taken and put into a shipping container. One of the girls looked a little like her sister, Oxsana, suffered badly from claustrophobia and as soon as the container doors were closed on them she had started to scream so loudly that their captors came and took her away. The other girl no longer with them was Petra, a friend of Yasmin's. They had met at Moscow University both studying Hotel Management. Petra had been tricked into this in a similar way to Yasmin. She was a more outward going girl than Yasmin and most men were attracted by her flame red hair. Petra had been taken away seven days ago and hadn't been seen since.

They were obviously on a boat, the rolling motion told them that but after four days the rolling stopped, Yasmin believed that the boat had arrived at it's destination. It was at that time that Petra was taken away never to return. Since then each of the girls had been repeatedly raped and were punished if they complained. The food they were given was sufficient to keep them alive but had very little nourishment and even less flavour. Life couldn't be much worse.

They remained on board the ship for two days, after Petra had been taken. At least Yasmin's best guess was two days but being held in a shipping container they had no means of measuring the passing of time. They had all had their phones, watches and jewellery taken away from them, except Yasmin, whose phone hadn't been found when she had been searched. She had turned it off days ago in order to preserve the battery power for as long as she could. She made a point of turning it on when she was alone or the others were asleep, just to see if she had a signal and could call for help. The day Petra disappeared, Yasmin was leaning over a bucket throwing up, when their guards came to take the girls away one at a time. Yasmin assumed they were being used for sex again. The guards left her alone wanting nothing to do with her in the state she was in. As soon as she was alone, she turned the phone on and saw she had a full signal. Instantly dozens of emails flooded in plus one message. She decided to read the message first. It said just two words. '*Hi Ozzy.*' Only Oxsana called her Ozzy, she replied to the message '*Oxy, ring me.*' Within seconds the phone rang. She answered in a whisper and continued a conversation with her sister for several minutes. She ended the call quickly when she heard someone opening the door. A voice outside was complaining about being pushed, then Petra came tumbling in and the door shut quickly behind her.

"Is that a phone you've got hidden?" Petra asked.

"Not so loud," Yasmin whispered. "I don't want anyone to know, I'm trying to get us some help."

"I've got an alternative," Petra said. "I've been sent back in here to get my stuff together. The guard just told me I've passed some sort of test and I'm being taken somewhere else. Let me take the phone it will be easier to call for help away from this place."

"Take it if you think there might be a chance," Yasmin agreed. "The battery is down to 10% anyway. It will only last about one more day at best."

"Thanks, girl. Good luck, I'll look out for you at the next place wherever that might be."

Chapter 8

"There's a rumour going around the village that Mad George's solicitors have finally traced the niece that he left everything to in his will and they'll be handing over this place to her in a few weeks. We've had it good these last couple of years since the old bugger died. Let's hope she's as accommodating as he was. We still need that place for storing our stuff and keeping the girls safe until we can ship them on and that jetty out into the deep water is perfect for our boats."

****

Having seen the way the clean up went and how the teams actually stuck to the task, Tim agreed with everyone, that a draw was an acceptable result and if the yard was cleaned to the same standard he would buy everyone a drink. Morale was certainly at a high and everyone was talking about the new boss and his crazy ways.

Sue had always insisted that Monday afternoon would be the time to complete any outstanding paperwork and all bookkeeping had to be up to date. No matter how long it took the office and yard would not close until everything was complete. Only staff on race duty were exempt and there was rarely any racing on a Monday. However as soon as all paperwork was finished, everyone could finish for the day and still be paid up until 5:30. This incentive generally meant that everyone kept on top of the paperwork every day, just leaving anything outstanding from the weekend for Mondays. So at 4:30 Tim checked with Eric that there was nothing more to do and allowed everyone to finish and go home.

Eric told Tim that he had heard from Sue and she and Rob would not be back until 7:00, so she would review things with him first thing in the morning.

"I must say I like the way you work Tim and I've enjoyed working with you these last two days. I look forward to the next time," Eric said.

"Thank you Eric. I just hope I can meet Sue's high standards, I really like it here," Tim said.

Eric wished him good luck with his evening with the lads down at the 'Dog and Gun'. Then as he crossed the yard heading to back to his flat above the stables to shower and get ready to go out, Tim bumped into Lizzy and Sally who were locking up the tack room.

"Did you two get the message about this evening?" he asked.

"We did, Mr. Mills and we're off now to get all dressed up for you," Lizzy replied and smiled.

"Mr. Mills was my father, my name is Tim. I'll see you later then."

He had time after his shower, so turned on his TV to hear the 6:00 news bulletin. Brexit was the main subject as it always seemed to be these days. He had little interest whether Britain remained or left the EU, he just wished somebody would actually do something.

At 6:30 he set out to walk down to the village and the 'Dog and Gun'. As he passed the last cottage before the pub, two very attractive young ladies came out of the cottage door, pulled it so that it locked behind them and walked ahead of him to the pub. They were talking to one another and when they got to the door to the pub, they went straight in. The blonde held the door open for Tim to follow them in.

"Spasibo, vy ochen' dobry," he said.

"You speak perfect Russian," the blonde sounded surprised.

"I studied Russian at university," Tim said. "You must be Ana and your friend is Eva, am I right?"

Ana looked puzzled. "Do we know you?"

"Sorry, I should have introduced myself. I'm Tim, Tim Mills. I've just started working at Blackstock Stables."

"Pleased to meet you Tim, I expect we'll be seeing a lot of one another, but I'm sorry we can't talk now we have a table booked for 6:30 and we're already twenty minutes late, Sid wont be happy."

Tim looked around the pub and counted just five other customers.

"It's Monday, we're always quiet on Mondays," a voice from behind him said.

He spun round to see a smile quickly spread across the barmaid's face. "Jenny Buck," he said. "Last I heard you were singing on cruise ships."

"Until last month I was," she replied. "But after twenty years at sea I felt in need of a change. What about you? Are you still in the army?"

"I am technically, but I'm being invalided out at the end of the month. I'm hopefully going to be working at Blackstock Stables as an assistant manager."

"Tim, I can't talk now there's a crowd in the car park that are looking like they are coming in. Perhaps we can talk later when we're quiet again."

"That's my staff from the stables, I've invited them for a drink. Can you set up a tab and let everyone have whatever drink they ask for? No doubles and no fancy cocktails though."

"Good morning Tim." He was studying the diary in the office at 6:30 when Sue walked in. "As you can see we've got a busy end to this week."

"That's what I was looking at and to be honest with you Sue, it's the part of this job that I have least confidence in. The stables are not too dissimilar to those at Hyde Park barracks. But race day is not like anything I've ever done."

"I think you'll be surprised how much it is similar to parade day, making sure the horses are turned out as smartly as possible and a plan is understood and followed," Sue explained.

"I hope you don't mind if I reserve judgement on that," Tim said.

"By the end of Saturday you will have experienced every part of the job I'm looking to fill. From what I saw of you last week and what Eric has told me about the last two days, you've fitted in very quickly and are showing great promise," Sue said. "For today and tomorrow I want you to run the stables as manager. I'll be in here if you need advice or help. I'll be working on the expansion and getting some drawings ready for the planning meeting on 11th July."

"Good luck in doing that, it took my brother John three months to get his plans passed for his extension up at the livery stables."

"So I hear, that's why I want plans in so quickly. I need to have this completed by New Year."

"John used a retired civil architect. He did an extremely good job and because he is retired he was free to start almost immediately. Because he did John's work so recently and your job will be very similar construction, he should aware of what the planning committee are looking for, what they will agree to and what they will reject."

"Excellent, can you get me his details?"

"I'll send John a text right now, then I'd better get started on the day's workload."

Tim left the office and rode a quad bike down to the gallops to watch the horses being exercised. He stood with the head lad, Terry Martin. It was 7:00 a.m. and already warm again. Terry was following Sue's plans for general training of her horses for the seven days before a race. Day one was endurance, the horses would be galloped at seventy five percent of race speed for the full distance they would be racing. Day two, gentle exercise which meant a good gallop down the measured mile. Day three, full speed over the measured mile. Days four and five, a repeat of days two and three. Day six to be another gentle exercise day. Day seven race day, early morning walk only. Terry had been in racing for more than twenty years and he had never come across a trainer who had an exercise plan anything like this, but she was having a lot of success, so perhaps it was a successful regime.

To help Tim, Terry was identifying the horses as they reached the start of the mile gallop. Several horses that were not scheduled to race came by first. The plan for them was to run the measured mile, turn and run back to the start, giving the observers a chance to spot any potential movement problems. The horses ran the miles in pairs or in threes.

"These are two of this week's racers." Terry said. "On the far side is 'Cannibal's Child', racing at Fakenham on Thursday and near to us is 'Rail Car', one of the favourites at Chepstow on Saturday." As they raced past Tim it was obvious that 'Rail Car' was a higher class animal, 'Canibal's Child' was struggling to keep up well before the end.

"This next pair are both running at Chepstow, 'Brown Sugar' on the far side and the grey is 'Whimpole'."

"Stop them quickly Terry! 'Whimpole's' got a loose shoe, left hind leg," Tim called out.

Terry waved a red flag at the two riders who immediately pulled up their mounts. Tim approached the nervous grey and ran his hand gently down the horses flank then lifted the foot.

How could you see that from where we were?" Terry said as he looked at the shoe, with two nails with their heads broken off.

"I'm actually a qualified vet specialising in horses," Tim replied. "My special interest is in leg muscle. I could see that although she was running okay, she wasn't happy landing on that foot."

"Thank heavens you spotted it. I've seen too many horses in my time do all sorts of damage losing a shoe at full gallop. She's probably going to start favourite at Chepstow on Saturday, the boss wouldn't be happy if she got injured now," Terry said.

"Down you jump Ginger, walk her back to the yard and we'll get the farrier to sort her later," Terry said to the lad on Whimpole's back.

"Mary, is it me or are the people in these parts a bit reluctant to talk to us?" Tracy said as the Detective Sergeant drove them North towards the village of Durness.

"You've noticed that have you?" she responded. "I was stationed up here at Dornoch when I first joined the force. You quickly learn to spot areas that are involved in smuggling and there are dozens of villages up here where it is happening. In those villages anyone involved will say nothing to incriminate themselves and the ones not involved say nothing, because they are frightened of repercussions."

"Gosh it's like Cornwall two hundred years ago," Tracy remarked.

"With one significant difference," Mary explained. "Two hundred years ago there were over one hundred Revenue Officers and local army units to seek out the smugglers and stop the trade in Cornwall. I am just one of twelve police officers trying to police a coast line of a similar distance and so remote that the population is only five per square mile."

"I'm surprised you ever make any arrests," Tracy said.

"We do have a few successes, but that is largely down to a handful of major land owners, keen to clean up their patch and work with us to achieve it. They have installed hidden cameras at likely landing sites triggered with motion sensors. We've been able to identify individuals from the pictures, and then watch them closely, gather evidence against them and eventually get a conviction. It's still very labour intensive and a lengthy process."

"This chap you're taking me to see today, how is he different?" Tracy enquired.

"He's got a different approach. He is actually patrolling a large section of the coastline using a drone. This enables us to track smugglers' movements. We've been lucky once or twice and managed to get officers to the scene before the smugglers dispersed," Mary explained.

She continue, "he's the one who thinks he's located a new band operating in the area he patrols. He says that they appear to be well organised and whatever they are bringing in it's not the normal goods. Our thinking is that this could be the gang bringing in the drugs that are getting through to so many schools."

"The chances are that these are just the ones doing the importing. It's unlikely that the head of this gang is up here it's more likely he is closer to the sales end in London or Manchester," Tracy summarised. "We need to track these people, follow them in the hope that they lead us to the higher ranks."

They were now driving along the A838, passing the shallow sea inlet of the Kyle of Durness. They were heading for the isolated village of Durness, to meet the man who had sent pictures to Mary over the last six months. The pictures showed known smugglers and a boat lying just off shore then coming in to be unloaded.

"This man, James Blackburn, can he be trusted?" Tracy asked

"He's never given any concerns in the twelve months he's been working with us. But I can't be certain. He could be selling out the opposition to protect his own smuggling business," Mary speculated.

"I always thought the smuggler code was to protect one another against the authorities, honour amongst thieves, and all that." Tracy said.

"So we listen to everything he has to say but still gather our own evidence," Mary concluded. "I wouldn't trust any member of the Clan Morgan.

Chapter 9

"I've sent that dumb female cop all the fake video and pictures we took. Your boys did a fine job of pretending to be smuggling drugs, the guns were a good touch. She has definitely swallowed the story, she came to see me today. Brought some bitch from London with her who has been assigned to work with the cops in Glasgow. We've got nothing to worry about, they've got no idea at all."

****

Over the next few weeks Tim slowly took increased responsibility both in the yard and on race days. Sue had complete confidence in his abilities and he was now regularly managing race day unsupervised. In early July the Blackstock Stables had winners on two courses on the same day, with Tim winning at Wolverhampton and Sue winning at Red Car.

As Sue returned to the stables, Tim was just leaving his flat. They had talked on the phone after their races, so Sue was aware of his win.

"Congratulations on your first solo winner. Just look at you, all dressed up, are you off to celebrate?" Sue asked Tim.

"No, he's got a date," Eric's voice came from behind her.

"Oh, anyone I know?" Sue asked.

"I'm meeting Jenny Buck for a drink," Tim said.

"She's Sid's daughter from the 'Dog and Gun.'" Eric added.

"It's not a date as such." Tim said. "We were in the same class all through high school. We are meeting to catch up."

"Come on Tim you fancy her don't you?" Eric teased

"We're just having a drink together and talking," Tim insisted.

"Eric, Tim, while I have you here together can we get together tomorrow morning. Rob and I are off on our honeymoon on Friday and I want to make sure we're all clear as to what's happening here while I'm away. How about 10:00 in the office?"

Both men nodded their agreement and Tim walked on.

"That architect fellow, Willoby, called in this afternoon, brought some drawings for you to look over and some forms that need to be filled in for the planning meeting on Thursday. He said he'll come back tomorrow morning to collect them and take them directly to the planning offices well before the noon deadline for submissions. They're in the living room."

When Sue reached the lounge Rob had the plans open across the coffee table. "These are really very good, honey. He's got it just how you described it to me. Come and look, he's even done a sketch of what it will look like."

"Oh Rob, this is really happening isn't it? Tell me I'm not dreaming," Sue said.

"You're not dreaming," he reassured her. "There's some papers in the envelope that you need to deal with."

Sue smiled when she looked at the papers. "What a lovely little man that Brett Willoby is, he's filled in all the forms so all I've got to do is add my signature."

"Are you still going to be able to get away on Friday?" Rob asked.

"Of course I am," Sue replied. We agreed we both wanted to see Newcastle and the only way to do it this trip, was to get up there for Friday night to allow Saturday for exploring. Then Sunday we move on to Edinburgh and have Monday to explore and Tuesday we move on to Aberdeen. On Wednesday we move on to Inverness giving us Thursday to explore. On Friday we meet the solicitor."

"What a good memory you've got," he commented.

"Not really it's all in my diary," she said and tapped her phone that was hooked onto the waistband of her skirt. "I was only reading through the diary on our way home earlier."

"There was I thinking you were so looking forward to it that you remembered all our plans," Rob smiled.

"I am looking forward to it. We've both been so busy these last few weeks we've hardly had time for each other. A few days on the boat will be nice," Sue said.

"The days at sea won't be easy. Each step is roughly one hundred and fifty miles. Depending on weather conditions, that could take anything from eight to ten hours and whoever is at the helm will need to stay alert watching for anything in the water. I've checked the latest reports and if we stay three to four miles off shore, we should have no problems," Rob assured her.

"We'll be glad of our time ashore then."

"The long range weather forecast says we're in for a few wet days but no sign of any strong winds or rough seas for the next couple of weeks. It's about normal for the time of year, as soon as the schools break up it starts to rain," Rob jested.

"Talking of school holidays, Luci says that Peter is going with you tomorrow when you drive up to Edinburgh, to pick up Justin," Sue said.

"Yes, Luci asked me if he could. He's interested in how we train horses for some of the stunts, getting them to do things that they don't do naturally. I can't say I'm looking forward to four hours alone in the car with him. We'll have nothing to talk about after the first twenty minutes, but I couldn't say no could I?"

"I'm sure you'll be fine," Sue reassured him. "It's an ideal time for you to get to know him, he's a very nice young man and he and Luci make a lovely couple."

"I still think she's too young to be in a serious relationship," he said.

"You're just worried they'll do something silly and get her pregnant," Sue commented.

"What responsible father wouldn't worry about his daughter."

"You needn't worry about that. She is still a virgin. She told me when we were talking quietly together the other week that she had planned to have sex with him on his birthday, but when it came to it she felt she wasn't ready. Apparently Ana and Eva are talking to her on a regular basis and you know what she thinks of them."

"Luci being kidnapped last year was a terrible thing to have happened, but it brought those two young ladies into our lives and they've done so much for this family, I can't begin to thank them."

"They don't see it like you do. They strongly believe that they owe you their lives. This time last year they were in a world of corruption, sex and drugs and were unable to escape. But you came along as their knight in shining armour and bought their freedom," Sue kissed him.

"Maybe, but I'd like to do more. I wish I could help Ana find her sister, she must be so worried about her."

"There's nothing you can do Rob. You're just going to have to let that Scottish police inspector do his job and pray she's still alive when he finds her."

Rob set off early, stopping to pick up Peter. Sue was also up and dressed early and was on her second coffee looking over her plans for the extension which were spread over the kitchen table, when Rose and Eric walked in.

"Is this your new stable block, dear?" Rose said. "Do you mind if I have a look?"

"Not at all. Here this is an impression of what it will look like when it's finished." Sue pulled out the drawing that the architect had done.

"What are they?" Rose said pointing to windows in the roof.

"Flats," Sue replied. "Once we are up and running we'll need a lot more staff. We struggle now to get enough in from the local villages so we need to look further afield and that will mean providing accommodation."

"This is going to take an awful lot of organising and managing, will you be able to take on that workload?"

"That's why we took on Tim and shipped all the financial bits out to Lamb Accounting Services. Once the extension is operational I'll be getting another assistant manager in, then that person, Tim and I will share the workload."

"How many horses will there be room for, dear?" Rose queried.

"Seventy, because we are also going to modernise the loose boxes in the current block to add accommodation for a further 10 horses"

"That will take you way up into the big league. You'll be competing against the likes of Paul Nicholls," Eric commented.

"Hardly. He runs two stables with well over one hundred horses. He also has covered all weather gallops. But this is the first step."

"Doesn't this increase bring a risk that if one horse gets sick you could lose them all. Your insurance will go sky high," Eric said.

"We've thought of that. There will be three isolation stables with the latest technology to prevent any sickness transferring to other horses. These will also be used to quarantine any horse travelling abroad, plus with Tim we have a vet permanently on site. I've already sounded out our insurers and they've given me some idea of what the premium will be."

"So when does building work start?"Eric asked.

"I hope we can get started in September. I'm told that builders are always busy in July and August working on school contracts. We're only submitting plans for the first time this Thursday. I don't expect them to be passed first time, so optimistically we will have permission to build by mid August. I've got a couple of builders coming in at the end of the month to look over the site, check access and look the plans over to give me a provisional estimate and projected completion date. The next step after that will be to raise the money."

"Then I suppose you've got to find someone to fill all these empty boxes," Eric said.

"I've already got three clients lined up bringing in fifteen horses and I'm meeting Prince Hassan Saleh Al Shammari from the Emerates in London on the 31st. He's considering placing six horses in the UK early next year, so there is interest already."

"It would be very good for business if you can land a client of that status and can get a winner for him," Eric enthused.

"Well, I hope everything goes well for you dear. You've worked hard and you deserve some success," Rose said.

Ivan Gorkov stood on the jetty looking out five hundred metres to his ship stationary in deeper water. The moonlight was so bright that Ivan could just make out small images moving about the deck. He cursed the moon for being this bright, as he could easily see his crew drag five girls out of a shipping container on the deck and force them to descend a ladder into a small boat. Apart from the jetty and the overgrown dirt track leading from the road down to it, there were no sign of habitation. Kinlochbervie was only half a mile from the jetty, there were half a dozen crofter properties and a Kirk clustered together there in a hollow but with no view of what was happing on the jetty.

Yeta Gorkov stood next to her brother-in-law as the small boat approached the jetty.

"Why did you choose to off load here this time and not at Balnakiel. Not being able to bring your ship to the jetty there is a big risk that we will be noticed," She asked.

"We have to unload today. If the ship doesn't arrive in Liverpool tomorrow questions will be difficult. We can claim engine issues for a slight delay, but any longer will be suspicious. We're not using Balnakiel this time because we have heard that new owners are expected anytime and we don't want them watching us and setting alarms ringing," he explained.

"What was the reason for getting those other two girls off in Aberdee?."

"Our customer in Glasgow wanted his order delivered early. The two girls were causing me problems, so it was easy to decide which two. It's unfortunate that we had to terminate both of them. I've had a difficult conversation with him earlier and he'll take one of the remaining girls and take his second from the next batch."

"So you're only delivering four girls to London this trip. They wanted twelve and we agreed to deliver that number. I hope you're planning another delivery soon," Yeta said.

"There won't be any trouble, they're not really interested in the girls that's just their entertainment. It's the drugs they're interested in and there's almost two million pounds profit in this consignment."

It was beginning to rain as the boat tied up at the end of the jetty and it was pouring heavily as the girls were bundled into the back of a transit. One of Ivan's men took the boat back to the ship and the other two climbed into the front seats.

It took the driver several attempts to get the engine started. When it eventually started it only ran for a few second before stopping. Ivan, who had been in the passenger seat of Yeta's sports car, went across to the van to see why they hadn't moved off.

"We've got a problem, boss. We seem to be starved of fuel and she won't run smoothly."

"Can you fix it?"

"Sure boss, but not out here in this." The driver replied and looked up at the rain coming down heavier than ever.

"Can you get it running at all?"

"Possibly, but I don't think we'll be able to get very far. It really needs the carburettor stripped down and cleaned, which I can't do out in this rain."

"We're about twenty miles from Balnakiel Castle. Do you think you can get that far?"

"We can try, boss."

"You'll be able to get the van under cover there. We'll follow you. Get moving!"

"Something wrong?" Yeta asked when Ivan was back in her car.

"Engine trouble," he replied. "It's fixable but we need to get it under cover to work on. So like it or not we're heading for Balnakiel and will pray the new owner doesn't show up."

"Sorry I'm a little late guys, but I had a call from my architect that I had to deal with," Sue said as she entered the office.

"Did your plans get passed?" Eric enquired.

"Not quite," She answered.

"What do you mean not quite?"

"There is an issue about the insulation and fireproofing specified to go in the floors between the loose boxes and the flats," Sue explained. "Brett has specified a very new product which the planners say is not tested to British Standards. Brett's going to appeal on the basis that just because it hasn't yet got the British kite mark, doesn't mean it can't be used. He's saying it has a Swedish kite mark which is a far higher standard. He was calling to get my okay to appeal and of course the money."

"I'm sure half of these planning refusals are done simply to screw more money out of you," Eric moaned.

"That may well be the case." Sue stated. "I've asked you both to come in this morning just to clarify the situation while I'm away. Tim, Eric and I have discussed your training quite often in the past few weeks and we both believe you to be well capable of running the stables, but perhaps lack confidence in dealing with the customers."

Tim took a deep breath.

"That's okay, don't worry it will come," Sue continued. "So what I propose is for Eric to run the office, you Tim, to manage the horses with Eric going with you to race meetings to handle the owners. There are just two runners at York this Saturday and two at Doncaster next Thursday. Is that okay with the two of you?"

They both nodded.

"Good. Now if you will excuse me I have the accountant coming in at 11:00 for our quarterly review." As she was dismissing Tim and Eric the office phone rang.

"Sue?"

"Yes."

"Sue, this is Trisha Lamb. I'm terribly sorry but I'm going to be late for our meeting. My daughter is off school with bad period pain. Mother is coming over to sit with her. That means I won't get to you until about 11:30. Will that be okay?

"That's fine Trisha. I'll probably be somewhere out in the yard, so when you arrive can you call at the house and either my mother-in-law or the housekeeper will come and find me."

"Thanks Sue, I'll do that. See you later."

With half an hour extra to kill, Sue went out into the yard. She stood for a moment watching two of the lads washing the mud away. One with a slow running hosepipe, the other with a wide stiff broom. They were two of the younger lads, probably only a year out of school. They were larking about all the time they were working and Sue thought it was probably that attitude that had got them into trouble and Tim had given them this job for them to work off their excess energy. Normally it would not be done until after lunch when all horses and quad bikes were back from the muddy exercise fields.

'I wish I had an all weather training field like Paul Nicholls,' she thought to herself.

As she crossed to the side of the yard the lads had already swept, she looked into one of the loose boxes.

A voice behind her said, "They will be so much better when they've been modernised." It was Tim. "The stables at Hyde Park are the same. Poor lighting and bad air flow are the main problems, plus they are difficult to clean."

"I know," Sue said. "Twenty years ago I worked in a yard very similar to this and I remember the effort that went into cleaning the loose boxes. You're right, modernisation is definitely over due."

"I guess it will be the last phase of the building work, so we've got to live with these as they are for another twelve months."

"I'm sorry Tim, but that's what it has to be."

Looking back up the yard Sue saw Rose and Trisha heading towards her.

"Trisha, you needn't have come down here, Rose could have come and got me," she smiled a thank you to Rose who turned and went back to the house.

"No, I insisted. You've shown me the racing end of the business and I'm interested in seeing more. Perhaps you can also tell me about your plans."

Sue took Trish to look into one of the loose boxes then to the end of the row and with a lot of arm waving explained about the extension. They then went back to the house for Sue to show Trisha the plans and the artists impression of how it will all look.

"Those flats above the stables, are you just letting people live in them for free or will it be part of their pay deal?"

"I thought as part of their pay deal. Why?"

"Because there could well be National Insurance and Tax issues. I would suggest you rent them to your staff. The rent could be deducted from their pay but it will keep the tax man happier."

"We had better change the arrangement we have with Tim then, because we put him on a low wage supplemented by accommodation."

"You should do so really, it's better for everyone. If he ever wants a loan the higher wage will increase the amount he can borrow."

"I hadn't thought of that."

"Any idea how much all this building work is going to cost and how you are going to fund it?" Trisha asked.

"I've got no idea at all but Rob thinks it will be somewhere between eight hundred thousand and one million pounds.

"At least I would have thought. I know there is not that much money in the company accounts so where do you think it will come from?

"I was hoping the bank would give me a mortgage or something."

"I don't think it will be that easy. I'll make some enquiries for you. Now we had better go over these quarterly accounts," Trisha said.

"Are you in a rush to get away this afternoon?" Sue asked.

"Not particularly, why?"

"Because I had breakfast at 6:15 this morning and I'm starving." Sue said. "I thought we might slip down into the village and take a working lunch. It's a nice day and we haven't had many of those this year."

"That's a very tempting idea, I was sorting out Charlotte this morning and only managed a coffee for my breakfast."

"Oh how is she? I meant to ask when you arrived."

"She's suffering poor thing. This is her first heavy period and she's learning what we women have to go through. Is it far to the village?"

"Only a mile or so. We'll take my car."

Rob was pleasantly surprised with how well he got on with Peter. They talked about several topics as they travelled up the motorway. Peter even managed a score of twenty seven points in one of the Pop Master rounds on the radio, which impressed Rob. They didn't really talk much about the stuntman business and Rob thought that it had been an excuse Luci had used to get her dad to take him along. Rob was very surprised at Peter's knowledge of horses and even more surprised when he talked about cross breeding racehorses and why Arab horse lines were so important to the sport.

"Did you learn all this stuff about horses from your uncle Tim?" Rob asked.

"No, I've read a lot about the subject. It's of special interest to me and something I think I would like to specialise in when I'm qualified."

"That's a long way off, you might find something else of greater interest by then."

"Unlikely," he said. "Luci told me that when you took Justin back after half term you found a dead body. She said something about it being in a wheelie bin."

"That's right, murdered."

"I've never seen a dead person."

"It's not something I'd rush to see. Now can we talk about something a little more pleasant?" Rob said.

"Well man you've had three hours, have you sorted out that engine yet?" Ivan asked.

"I have found the problem boss but can't fix it. It's a broken spring clip that needs replacing."

"Can't it be repaired?"

"No boss. It's a significant piece," he said. "Any garage that services vehicles should have a stock of them they only cost a few pence but are critical for keeping the fuel flow continuous."

"Shit. Where do we need to go to get one?"

"I doubt that the villages around here have a garage. The closest is probably Thurso."

"That's more than seventy miles away. At least two hours each way on these roads, but I suppose it's what we'll have to do." He went to give Yeta the bad news.

"We're going to be stuck here for most of the day at least."

"But we don't have any food."

"I'm well aware of that and I was going to see if the local crofters are willing to sell me some," he said. "I need you to take Charles to Thurso for the part we need. Yan can watch over the girls."

"Won't the crofters give us away?"

"It's possible but very unlikely, most of them are smugglers anyway and they stick to the smugglers' code. They don't want the cops snooping around and discovering their own business. We don't have any other option. Those girls haven't had food for more than two days. We can't wait for you to pick up provisions and bring something back. I'll go and see James Blackburn he runs a sizeable operation out of Durness, he'll not give us away."

"Well, there's no point me sitting here, I'd better get on the road. If you can squeeze in the car we can drop you off in Durness then you'll only have to walk one way." Yeta stood and went to get her car.

Tracy and Mary were discussing their meeting the previous afternoon as they left the B&B in Durness where they had spent the night.

"There's a lot that doesn't ring true in what he was saying," Mary said.

"You noticed it as well did you? Some of his lies were not consistent and in one of his videos the smuggler kept on looking directly at the camera. If they knew the drone was filming them, why didn't they try and do something about it?" Tracy added.

"That's strange," Mary said.

"What?"

"That sports car coming out of the Balnakiel road back there. It's not the sort of car anyone up here would own and there were three people in it," Mary explained. "It might be worth taking a short detour."

"I agree. It does sound suspicious."

Mary quickly reversed back to the junction and turned into the side road.

"It's only five minutes down to Balnakiel. There's not much there, just a handful of crofters' cottages and a castle."

"If there is something going on there then it should be obvious," Tracy commented.

The road ended at the castle. Tracy and Mary got out of the car and walked slowly through the gate in the perimeter fence. Tracy pointed out tyre tracks through the mud in the gateway.

"Two vehicles I would say. One set from a medium size vehicle, perhaps a panel van going one way in or out and another much smaller vehicle possibly that sports car we saw going both in and out." Tracy announced after a closer look. Mary walked on ahead while Tracy was checking the tyre marks again, before following about twenty yards behind.

As she walked passed an out building with the doors open Mary pointed into the building but didn't stop. As Tracy came to the open door she saw that Mary had pointed out a transit van with its bonnet raised, she went in to check it. There was just enough space for Tracy to squeeze between the vehicle and the door frame, but once through she had more room and walked to the front of the van. The vehicle was obviously being repaired, bits she recognised but couldn't name, lay on a piece of sacking on the floor.

From beyond the open door Tracy heard what was unmistakably two rapid pistol shots, she instinctively ducked down behind the van. As soon as she realised the shots hadn't been fired at her, she worked her way slowly back to the doorway and squeezed herself back through the narrow space. She could see Mary lay on her back, she had been shot in the stomach, had her hand over the wound and blood was oozing between her fingers. Tracy drew her MI-6 issue Gloch 17 from her belt holster, ready to return fire. She peered carefully around the open door but could see no one. The shooter could have been behind any one of thirty windows or even on the roof.

Mary was obviously losing a lot of blood and needed help quickly. Tracy checked her phone. *'NO SIGNAL'.*

"Mary we've got to get out of here quickly," Tracy called. "Do you think you can walk?"

"I'll need help but I think so," Mary answered.

Cautiously, Tracy moved out into the open space between the doorway and Mary, continuously scanning the building ahead of her. She reached Mary and helped her stand. Mary was hurting badly but together they made it back to their car and Tracy helped Mary into the passenger seat and pulled the seat belt around her. Then she went to her overnight bag in the boot and pulled out a tee-shirt.

"Hold this over it to slow the bleeding," she said as she handed Mary the shirt.

"Where's the nearest hospital."

"Thurso, seventy two miles, back through Durness."

"Well, you just hold on and watch me do, my Lewis Hamilton impression." Tracy quickly strapped herself into the drivers seat and turned the key in the ignition.

Forty five minutes later Ivan Gorkov returned to the castle. It was raining again so he didn't notice the extra tyre marks outside the gate or the blood stain on the driveway.

"We had a visitor boss. Two women, they were checking out the van. I fired a couple of warning shots and they quickly went away." Yan confessed.

"You idiot! They were probably the new owners looking around. Why didn't you just sit tight until they went away again. Now they'll report being shot at and we'll have the authorities down on us before the day is out. You'd better hope that Charles can get the part he needs and gets the van moving quickly so that we can get away before anyone comes calling."

"Sorry boss."

"You will be sorry if we don't get away from here before mid afternoon. Now make yourself useful and get this food to the girls."

Chapter 10

"DS Howard was bleeding out Sir. I made the decision not to report in because in my opinion DS Howard needed every second I could give her and if I stopped to report, precious minutes would have been lost and she would have been dead before we reached hospital. As it was the journey was painfully slow. Fortunately there was no other traffic and I was able to keep up a reasonable speed, even so she was unconscious when we got to the hospital. They are operating on her now, but she is critical."

6:30 Friday morning and the yard was awake and horses being readied for exercise. Ryman had already loaded a box of provisions, a cool box of perishable food and two small suitcases into the boot and Justin was sitting in the front passenger seat. He was tagging along just to see the boat. He had only been four or five when Rob had mothballed her and he wanted to look her over. Rob and Sue climbed into the back and they were off. Two hours later Rob was at the helm carefully passing out of the harbour and into the mainstream of the Humber heading towards the North Sea.

"Well this is it Rob, we've managed to get away," Sue said excitedly.

"I hope dad doesn't overdo things and lets Tim do most of the work. I thought he was looking a bit grey this morning. What did you think?" Rob asked.

"I'm sure he's alright. Probably just had a bad night and is a bit tired. I certainly didn't get much sleep, I couldn't get the extension plans out of my head."

"The extension will work out fine, you'll see."

"The cost is my biggest worry. Where am I going to get that sort of money from and if I do get a loan or a mortgage, how will I be able to afford the repayments?"

"You need to find yourself a rich husband. Oh, you already have," Rob smiled down at her.

"I can't take money from you, Rob. You've already signed your half of the business over to me. No, this is my problem and I have to find the solution."

"I wasn't thinking of giving you the money, but getting Blackstock Stunts to invest in Blackstock Racing for a share of the profits. We could talk it through with Trisha when we get back."

"How far off shore did you say we needed to be?" Sue asked.

"Well, if you check the charts you'll see a number of hazards marked and the course I've plotted to avoid them. I loaded all the data onto my laptop and downloaded into the navigation system when we got onboard. In theory the boat can get us there without anyone at the helm, but I'm not comfortable letting a computer drive."

"Isn't technology great? It can do so much these days."

"Except stop the rain. It's started again. I don't think you'll be getting your bikini on this trip."

A police helicopter touched down at Glasgow airport and three armed police officers disembarked. They were picked up by a police car and taken back to the station for debriefing with Superintendent McNab present.

The senior officer on the armed unit gave his report reading from a small notebook.

"We received the call from dispatch at 14:08 and myself and two officers we're immediately transported to Glasgow airport. The helicopter set down on grass approximately half a mile from Balnakiel Castle at 16:37. We made our way to the target arriving at the gate at 16:53. It was evident from the tracks in the mud in the gateway, that several vehicles had passed through during the last twenty four hours. On the driveway we saw a blood stain, approximately twenty centimetres in diameter. We conducted a full search of all buildings, but we found the property to be entirely deserted. There were signs that someone had been there very recently, a set of vehicle number plates was found in one of the out buildings. We returned to our aircraft at 18:03."

"Thank you gentlemen, that is all."

The three armed officers left the room and the superintendent turned to the sergeant. "Dean what's the latest news on D.S. Howard?"

"The latest I heard, sir was that the operation to remove the bullet was a success but the doctors give her less than a fifty fifty chance of pulling through. It's thanks to that MI-6 agent that she's alive even now."

"Has D.I. Howard gone to be with his wife?"

"Yes sir, left about two hours ago. He's being flown to Wick airport then by car to Thurso hospital."

"This is big Dean, I mean really big. If MI-6 is involved we're looking at international criminals. I'm expected to give agent Mills whatever she needs to identify these drug traffickers and bring them down. The head of MI-6 wants me to update him daily on our progress so we'd better start making some bloody progress. Have we had any sightings of the van that agent Mills said was being repaired or the sports car she said had passed them?"

"The armed officers found a set of number plates in an outbuilding that correspond to the registration agent Mills gave, it proved to be false. These people know what they are doing. They will change the plates regularly, so we'll stand very little chance of finding them and that sports car may have stood out in the highlands but as it moves south it simply blends in with the masses. With just the vague description that agent Mills was able to give us, we can't really do much."

"So you're telling me we've made no progress nor are we likely to."

"What if we kept the castle under around the clock surveillance, sir?"

"A surveillance team wouldn't be able to do anything other than observe, unless the team was big enough to take on the smugglers. We know that this time there were at least three, next time there may be more, plus we have no guarantee they will use the same venue. But it's irrelevant anyway because I don't have the manpower or the budget. What the hell am I going to say to Sir Bernard Howe?"

"I can never remember which was built first, the Tyne Bridge or the Sydney Harbour Bridge." Sue said. She and Rob were sitting in the day cabin and Sue could see the famous Newcastle icon through the window above Rob's head.

"I know the answer to that one," Rob gloated. "They were both built in the 1920's. Sydney Harbour Bridge was started in 1923 and completed in 1932. The Tyne Bridge was started in 1925 and completed in 1928."

"I'm impressed with the crap your brain holds. We're a long way from the coast. I didn't realise Newcastle was so far inland," Sue said.

"About eight miles I think. We passed two or three other marinas further down stream but I chose the City Marina because it's only a stones throw from the city centre, for sight seeing tomorrow."

"Is there anything particular you wanted to do tomorrow?"

"If this rain eases off I was thinking we could get a taxi out to the Beamish open air museum. It's said to be one of the best in Europe."

"I'd be happy just to walk over the Millenium Bridge. I think it's so very unusual."

"Maybe we can keep an eye open for somewhere to eat in the evening. See if we can do better than that pub in Falmouth."

"What if it is still raining?"

"Then we do other stuff," Rob said and laughed. "As for this evening I'm too tired to go out. In truth the combination of sea air and concentrating for eight hours has knackered me. What have we got we can rustle up a meal from?"

Tracy sat at Mary's bedside on the intensive care ward. Mary's operation lasted almost two hours, her doctors were happy that there had been no complications and they had removed all the bullet fragments but she had not regained consciousness and that was a concern to everyone. She had reported the shooting to Mary's department and to her own supervisor at MI-6. Her thoughts took her back to Balnakiel Castle. What had they stumbled across? It was obviously a big operation to warrant them carrying guns. Could this be the gang she had been sent up here to find?

90

The monitor connected up to Mary showed the same numbers as it had the last time a nurse checked her. The doctor had asked the nurse for fifteen minute obs and Tracy could see that the last eight columns on the chart contained the same numbers. That's no change in over two hours she thought to herself. She'd only known Mary since Tuesday but she liked her, she seemed to be a good honest cop, she deserved better than to die like this."

Tom Howard arrived at his wife's bedside at 21:45 and a little after midnight, Tracy left him alone with her. Mary had told her that their marriage was going through a rough period. She said that she felt he was keeping something secret from her and perhaps he was having an affair. But DI Howard appeared very upset and concerned about his wife's condition. Either he was a very good actor or he was genuinely worried.

When Tracy returned next morning Mary was still unconscious and Tom Howard was sitting in the easy chair with his phone in his hand.

"Do you know if there's a public phone anywhere? I've got no signal on this," he said showing Tracy his mobile.

"You can use mine, I've got a full signal," Tracy offered.

"No, it's alright. I can use a public phone."

"I think I saw one in the day room, down the corridor, second turn on the left," she explained.

"Do you mind staying with Mary while I make a quick call? There is someone I must talk to."

"Take as long as you need, I'm going nowhere until she wakes," Tracy replied.

Tom Howard scrolled the contact list on his phone and typed the number he wanted into the public phone's keypad. He stood listening to the digits click through, then the phone ringing. It rang endlessly and Tom was about to hang up when it was answered.

"Hello, James Blackburn."

"James, it's Tom Howard. Those bloody Russians have shot Mary."

"Hang on a minute Tom, calm down and tell me what you mean."

"Mary and a colleague were in your area following a line of enquiry."

"I know, they came to see me yesterday. I've been laying a false trail for them over the last couple of weeks, to allow this new team to settle in."

"You've got us involved with some really dangerous people James. The woman with Mary is an MI-6 agent, she is working with Interpol to break a new drug ring that is getting drugs into schools all over Western Europe. Also I've had two Russian girls found dead on my patch last week. Now Mary being shot makes me think it's all down to the same team. Your Russian team."

"I know nothing about any girls being murdered or drugs getting into schools. As far as I'm concerned this is purely a drugs import deal and nothing else."

"Well this is all getting too hot for me to hide. I'm already spending endless hours hiding anything that could lead anyone to your operation. I'm sure Mary is beginning to suspect something."

"Yes, and you're paid well for what you do."

"Not enough to cover up murder. I'll warn you now James, if Mary dies I will come clean to MI-6, tell them everything I know about this new gang. To hell with the consequences, I'll have nothing more to lose."

"Only your head you damn fool. You said yourself how ruthless these Russians are."

"I don't care anymore, James." Tom hung up the phone and went back to his wife's bedside.

"That was a very interesting place," Rob said.

"Shame the rain came in this afternoon, I could have spent the whole day there. All those people dressed in period costumes bringing everything to life. It makes history far more interesting having people demonstrating how life used to be one hundred years ago. Today we can't imagine life without electricity."

"And those old vehicles, weren't they so basic? We've come a long way in the last century," Rob proclaimed.

"I'm glad we did the Millennium Bridge as well even though we got soaked to the skin, it is such a unique structure." Sue added.

"At least we tested the shower out," Rob said. "It didn't look big enough for two."

"I'm just going to give Tim a quick ring before I get ready to go out. He had two runners at York today and I'm wondering how he got on."

Whilst Sue was on the phone talking to Tim, Rob programmed the navigation system for the next leg of their journey ending at Port Edgar Marina in Edinburgh. *'Another iconic bridge,'* he thought to himself.

"Tim's very pleased with himself. One winner and one 3rd place."

"You see, they don't need you holding their hands all the time."

Tracy left Mary's bedside late Sunday afternoon. It had been forty eight hours since Mary's operation and she still hadn't woken. The tone of the doctors were sounding less confident each time they came to see her. Apart from twenty minutes at lunchtime she had been with Mary the whole day, fortunately she had a couple of books downloaded onto her phone which helped pass the time, but Tom Howard had spent long periods pacing up and down in deep thought.

Tracy had to get some proper sleep. Sir Bernard Howe would be expecting to hear her plan first thing tomorrow. But first she must find a hotel room somewhere.

The Forth estuary was far wider than Sue had imagined. She could see both the rail and the road bridges in the distance. They appeared to grow as each minute passed and the boat moved up stream. Rob had reserved space at the Port Edgar Marina, close to the bridges. He pulled the boat into the marina and tied her up, while he registered their arrival in the office and was allocated a berth.

"This is a pretty little spot. I do like Edinburgh, I've been here a few times but never been down here by the river nor been to the castle," Sue said.

"It would be nicer if the sun were shining, rather than this persistent drizzle," Rob moaned. "You've been here several times but never been up to the castle. I thought everyone went up there on their first visit."

"No, but I'm looking forward to seeing it tomorrow, rain or no rain," Sue said.

"Are you happy to stay in this evening? The weather is not very favourable for looking around for somewhere to eat."

"If you're doing the cooking I'm happy. How about a G and T while you plan the menu?" Sue suggested.

Despite her lack of sleep Tracy woke early Monday morning. The fact that she was expected to have a plan ready by 9:00, when Sir Bernard would be ringing her was nagging at her but she could only think of Mary, wondering if she was awake. By 8:30 she was back at the hospital pleased to see Mary awake and talking with Tom.

"Mary, I'm so happy to see you awake. You've had us so worried these past three days. How are you?"

"Alive, thanks to you Tracy. The doctor says I was just minutes from death when you got me here. You saved my life, thank you," Mary said.

"You won't thank me when you see your car. Not just your blood all over the passenger seat, but the suspension is probably ruined by the speed I drove on that track you call a road, up here. At one place I took a corner too wide and ripped a wing mirror off on an outcrop of rocks. The good news is your brakes are good, but I think most of the tread on your tyres I left on the road," Tracy said and Mary managed brief smile.

"The doctor is now concerned about her liver," Tom said to Tracy. "They said that a fragment of the bullet had hit her liver. They removed the fragment and normally the liver would heal, but in this case they can't be sure."

"That's enough about me, how are you Tracy? What are your plans now?" Mary asked.

"That's my problem, I don't have a plan and my boss will be ringing me in a few minutes to hear one." Tracy looked lost.

"Well, if it were me I'd be researching the area and the people looking for anyone known or suspected of being a smuggler. Examine the coast line for say fifty miles either side of Balnakiel, identifying anywhere smugglers could land and get a vehicle to, for moving their goods inland then visit them all to look for recent unexplained activity."

"That sounds like bolting the door after the horse has gone," Tom said trying to deflect any close inspection of the area.

"You're right Mary, why couldn't I think of that? I also need to visit the castle to see if whoever shot you left any clues that could help us. I'll be back after I've spoken to my boss." She left and went outside where she wouldn't be overheard.

"Good morning, Miss Mills. How is DS Howard?"

"Good morning, Sir Bernard, I'm pleased to say things are looking a lot better. She's not totally out of the woods yet, but it's looking promising."

"Very good to hear. What are you planning to do now?" Sir Bernard asked.

"We need to dig deep into the history of this area. The Clan Morgan are strange secretive people, they definitely know far more than they are prepared to tell. I was wondering if Zoe Crump could be spared for a couple of days?" Tracy asked with her fingers crossed.

"Zoe is still on her honeymoon, not operational again until Thursday, but I can make her available then. Do you need her up there or can she do what you need from the office?

"She should be okay working from the office. I also intend looking over any potential landing spots, looking for any that have seen recent activity. Mary is no longer available so I need her replaced, preferably by someone authorised to carry a gun. Is there an agent free to come up and assist me?"

"I don't have anyone I can spare at the moment, but what I will do is get someone sent up from Glasgow police. After all it's one of their own who has been shot they should want to help. I don't understand why the area isn't swarming with uniforms."

"Finally, I want to revisit the castle where Mary was shot looking for anything that could identify the shooter."

"Okay, I'll get onto Glasgow this morning and see what I can get you. In the meantime, see what you can do."

"You bring me only four girls Ivan, when I order twelve. My customers will not be happy. They have many new clubs opening in London and Manchester and need girls."

"I told him you would not be happy father," Yeta said.

Dmitry Lavrov was a senior member of the Russian Mafia. He was temporarily in London to boost his organisations profits from Britain. In six months he had created a network for selling drugs in over two hundred British schools, as he had done in France and Germany in the months previous. Yeta had chosen to stay in England with her son after her husband Mikhail had died. She vowed revenge on the person responsible for Mikhail's death. She would take away Rob Blackstock's partner as he had done to her. He could suffer as she was suffering. She had already had made three attempts to kill Susan Blackstock but all were last minute decisions, badly planned and poorly executed.

"I will bring more girls next trip. This was a new route, we could not risk it with too many girls," Ivan tried to explain. "You have to agree that the four you have are real class."

"Are they trained or fresh from the streets?" Dmitry asked.

"All fresh girls." Ivan answered.

"That at least is something. What about the dope, is that all there?"

"It's all there, I've checked it, it's quality stuff. Now stop messing with him he's not his brother. Mikhail is gone and no one can replace him. Ivan's different. What he say's is true, the places he has found in Scotland are perfect. The Clan Morgan people have been smuggling for five hundred years, they know when not to interfere. Just let him go and do his work," Yeta argued.

"My daughter makes a good point, perhaps she should have been a lawyer. Go and do what we pay you for," Dmitry waved a hand to dismiss Ivan.

Tracy stayed with Mary most of the morning talking about nothing in particular except when Tom left the room to call his office and go out to get her a newspaper.

"I think you're wrong about Tom having an affair, Mary. I've worked with men who were playing away from home and he's not showing any of the signs." Tracy said. "He's been genuinely very worried about you."

"So why is he being so secretive and not getting home until late, twice or more evenings each week"" Mary queried.

"Maybe he's under a lot of pressure at work. It's a very stressful job he's in. What we do is bad enough, just imagine the pressure he must be under with the continuous budget cuts and increasing demand for results."

"Perhaps I am jumping to the wrong conclusion. Quiet, he's coming back!"

Tracy left when Mary's mid day meal arrived. She went back to her hotel room to start her research. She didn't enjoy plodding through endless paperwork and was aware she wasn't very good at that sort of research. So instead, she started to look at the coastline. She fired up her laptop, loaded Google Maps and searched for Thurso. A roadmap image appeared on her screen. She changed the image to a 3D satalite image and zoomed in as far as she could. She was amazed at how clear the image was. She knew, of course, it wasn't a current view but the fact that it was possibly several months out of date didn't have any impact on what she wanted to do. So she slowly moved her way along the coast westward from Thurso.

An hour into her task her phone rang. Caller ID showed her the caller was Sir Bernard, she answered the phone hoping he had good news.

She pressed the green button.

"Good afternoon, Miss Mills."

"Good afternoon, sir

"It's not very good news, I am afraid. Glasgow police can't spare anyone at the moment. They've had a couple of young women murdered in the Glasgow area. The MO for both is similar enough that they think it may be the work of a serial killer, so resources are stretched. They may be able to let us have someone by the end of the week."

"That's better than nothing, I suppose," Tracy remarked.

"However, I do have some slightly better news for you." Sir Bernard continued. "This morning when you asked about Zoe Crump I told you she was on honeymoon and not operational until Thursday. Well, I discovered she's actually back from her honeymoon and having a few days at home. I've been able to contact her and made arrangements for her to fly as far as Wick and pick up a car. She should be with you late Thursday afternoon."

"Thank you, sir."

"Any update on D.S. Howard?" Sir Bernard asked.

"She's still being closely monitored by the doctors, but she's doing well. I'm going back to see her again in a few hours."

"Keep me updated and I'll call again in a day or two."

Yasmin and the other girls had no idea where they had been taken. They had been dragged off the ship in the middle of the night and pushed into the back of a van without windows for them to see anything that might give them a clue as to where they were. The road must have been rough because they were bounced endlessly for about forty five minutes, before being dragged into a dark damp room in an ancient building. They were given a bucket to pee in, there was a pile of blankets to keep them warm and some carpet tiles which they could use against the cold of the stone floor.

Eventually they were given water and some scraps of food. Then a couple of hours later they were back in the van, bouncing around. After about two hours they must have turned onto a better road. It was less bouncy and it felt as if they were travelling much faster now. The journey seemed endless. They stopped to refuel and then again for the girls to pee behind a roadside hedge. When they next stopped, Irina only was dragged out. She didn't return and they drove on further for several hours. From the noise outside Yasmin was convinced they were now in a city. But which city and in what country? Giving her phone to Petra wouldn't help her now. They must be hundreds of miles from where they were when Petra had left and that was a week ago at least. Now there were just four of them.

Tracy worked most of the afternoon until she felt her eyes were just too tired to do any more. In a straight line she'd covered almost forty miles but with the rugged shape of the coatline she estimated it to be close on two hundred miles, so she was happy with what she had achieved and decided she had done enough. She had covered approximately twenty five percent of the coast line she needed to cover and that she would be able to complete the job by the time any help arrived.

She bought a couple of magazines for Mary on her short walk to the hospital. As she walked into the ward she was shocked at what she saw. Mary was laying flat on the bed, she had an oxygen mask over her mouth and nose and a drip in her arm. Tom Howard was in the chair at her bedside looking totally grey.

"What's happened?"

"The doctor says she's had a stroke," Tom said tearfully. "They told me that they don't think she will last the night."

"No, not like this."

"It's all my fault. I've done this. I've killed her. Blackburn you got me into this, I'm coming for you!" Tom said and quickly left the ward.

Tracy stayed until the end. Mary was declared dead at 02:40.

"My knees are still shaking Rob. You could have warned me that canon was going to go off behind me," Sue said.

"I thought you being in the army all those years, you would be used to that noise."

"I was in the Military Police not the artillery. I've never been that close to a big gun when it was fired, certainly when it was unexpectedly fired behind my back."

"I wish I'd had a camera running, the look of terror on your face was amazing."

"Rob Blackstock you are just a horrid bully. I don't know why I love you quite as much as I do."

"Because you love me bringing you to restaurants like this."

After spending a lot of their day in Edinburgh Castle then exploring the city, Rob had booked a table at 'The Kitchen' and they had enjoyed three courses of high quality food and were enjoying a large brandy to finish their evening.

"I must say I can't fault your choice of restaurants. That food was amazing, thank you."

"Well I had to do something to make up for the shock I gave you at the castle."

"You'll need to do a lot more than fill my belly to make up for nearly giving me a heart attack Mr. B."

"I hope you've recovered by morning. We've got to get to Aberdeen tomorrow."

"We're only spending one night there, aren't we?" Sue queried.

"There's nothing much there for us, so on Wednesday we're straight on to Inverness. There's plenty to see there. I'm going to take you to The Malt Room, one of the biggest and best range of whiskies you'll ever see," Rob said enthusiastically.

"I can feel the hangover already. Just so long as we are sober when we meet the solicitor on Friday."

Rob caught the eye of a waiter as he passed their table. "Can we have our bill please and can you call a taxi for us?"

"Certainly, sir."

Chapter 11

"D.I. Howard has gone missing, sir. His last words to me were that it was all his fault but as he left he was talking to himself, I think he said something like You got me into this Blackburn I'm coming for you. I've got know idea what he meant."

****

Yasmin could see they were in a city, she thought it was London because she recognised a few buildings from movies she had seen. Her and the other three girls were taken to a large house on a rural street. They were greeted by an Asian looking middle aged woman, Mrs Chow, who led them to the third floor where she gave each a bedroom, allowed them to shower, gave them new clothes then sat them down at a large table and fed them well. They had the freedom of the whole floor of the house with its eight bedrooms, large lounge and dining room. Access to the stairs was prevented by a locked gate and the windows were also locked. They were still prisoners but now after two weeks they were at least clean, comfortable and well fed.

Late Wednesday afternoon, Sue had jumped onto the jetty in Inverness Marina and tied off the lines to secure the boat. The restaurant this evening was her choice. She had been on the internet browsing, while Rob was preparing their meal the previous night. She had chosen Rocpool, mainly because she could make the booking online.

"Well darling, we are in Inverness, in two days time you'll finally learn what your uncle has left you in his will."

"It won't be much, I'm certain and I'd rather not be thinking about it. Tell me where we're heading next, I'm beginning to like being a tourist?" Sue said.

"Well, we are on schedule and the weather forecast is still good for at least another week. So I thought once we've seen your solicitor, we'd go on to Wick, then on Saturday we'd sail over to Orkney for a few days rest and chill out, or nip across to Shetland,, if we feel like it. Then we turn about and head back to Hull."

"It's sad to think we're halfway through our holiday. I've really enjoyed the last few days, I've never done anything like this before. The pace of life is so much slower, it's nice."

By Thursday afternoon Tracy had completed her search of the coastline. It had taken two and a half days but she was confident that she had been thorough and she had a list of at least a score of possible locations and was going through them one by one, checking for any reason to exclude them, when her phone rang.

"Hi Tracy, it's Zoe Crump."

Tracy didn't respond.

"Tracy, are you there?"

"Sorry Zoe, where are you?"

"I'm in Wick, just collecting a car and wanted to check which hotel you are in."

"The Pentland off Princes Street. I'm in a twin room. I've spoken to reception and they are expecting you."

"Thanks, I should be with you in about forty five minutes."

"I'll look out for you. It will be great to have a friend to talk to. I've had a really crap week. See you later."

Tracy put her phone down, sat upright and said out loud to herself.

"Tracy Elizabeth pull yourself together. People are dying here and you are not doing anything to stop it. Get out there and find Mary's killer. You're a bloody detective, start detecting!"

She shut her laptop down, went for a shower and got dressed ready to greet Zoe down stairs. A quick tidy of the room was needed, then grabbing her phone she left the room, locking the door behind her and went down two floors to reception. Zoe had already arrived and was talking to the receptionist who looked up, saw Tracy and said something to Zoe that made her turn towards Tracy. They greeted one another with a hug.

"I'm so glad to see you," Tracy said. "I've been a bit low but I'm over that now and need to get on with some real work."

"Sir Bernard told me about D.S. Howard. A terrible thing to have happened. After all you tried to do as well. It must have hit you hard?"

"It did for a while, but that's enough about me. I hear congratulations are in order and you and Sarah have made it official. Come up to the room and tell me more," Tracy said as she picked up her colleague's bag and headed for the stairs, leaving Zoe with her laptop bag and a carrier bag containing the remnants of her lunch.

"Christ, Zoe! What have you got in this bag? It weighs a ton"

"Just the usual stuff. Let me take it."

"No I'll manage, we're almost there now"

Tracy placed the bag on the end of the bed then threw herself onto her back on the other bed puffed up her cheeks and blew out.

"Phew, I'm so unfit, I really must find a gym near my flat and start exercising. Wow! That's a wonderful black eye you have! I didn't notice it downstairs, who gave you that?"

"Sarah did, but it was an accident. I got too close to her when she was doing her morning workout and she caught me with an elbow."

"Ouch. How is Sarah, does she mind you coming away so soon after your wedding?"

"Not at all, she left Harlequins and has joined Saracens. It's a little further to travel but she says they play the style of rugby that she wants to play. She's training with them for the first time today. She'll ring me later to let me know how it went."

"I don't really understand the game, but it looks a bit too rough for me."

"Right. What are we doing?"

Tracy explained to Zoe about the research she needed her to do looking into the history of the area and the people, particularly Clan Morgan. She also explained what she had been working on and the list she had made of potential landing sites.

"I can't fault the way you've done this, I think I'd probably have done the same research. So if we start visiting these sites tomorrow, I can do my reaserch as we drive."

"That's what I was hoping. The sooner we get started, the sooner we'll finish. It'll soon be time for dinner. Do you want to freshen up before we go out. Do you like curry? I've found a great little Tandoori place just two minutes from here?"

"Sounds wonderful, I just need a shower. Give me ten or fifteen minutes and I'll be ready."

"Okay I'll ring and book a table for 7:30."

"Good morning, darling." Rob had been up for thirty minutes and brought Sue a coffee. "There's no need for you to rush to get up we don't need to leave here until 10:00, it's not raining and the solicitor's office is only a twenty minute walk away."

"Good morning honey. Is that bacon I can smell?" Sue asked.

"I've just put it on. I thought if we have a good breakfast to start the day. We don't know how long we'll be with the solicitor and if we want to move on up to Wick today we may be have to wait until we're back out at sea before we get lunch. One egg or two?"

"Two please. How long have I got."

"Fifteen to twenty minutes."

"Time for a quick shower then. My hair needs a wash, it feels like straw, the wind, salt and the rain is not doing it any favours."

"Give me a shout when you're out, I'll not start the eggs until I hear you call."

While Sue showered, Rob set the navigation system with the course for Wick, one less thing to do later.

As they ate breakfast, Sue felt a chill pass through her and she shivered.

Rob noticed and asked, "Are you alright darling?"

"Someone just walked over my grave," Sue said, "something bad must be about to happen."

"What do you mean?"

"My Russian grandmother always said when you feel a chill it's because someone is rushing by you on their way to heaven."

"Well if that's the case we'd be cold all the time. Thousands of people die every minute. We'd better get ready to go, it's coming up to 9:40.

Yasmin and the other girls were woken early by Mrs. Chow and all told to go to the lounge. Yasmin felt strange and was glad to sit down when she got to the lounge. There was a man across the room looking out of the window. Mrs. Chow crossed the room and stood next to him as he turned around. Mrs. Chow faced the girls and said, "Ladies this is Mr. Lavrov. You must listen to what he has to say and do what he tells you."

Lavrov took a pace forward. "Good morning girls, welcome to England," he began. "And welcome to my world. Firstly I must tell you that there is a cost for bringing you here. That cost is fifteen thousand Euros and I am not a charity so I must charge you interest on your loan at a rate of one thousand Euros per month. I will help you to pay me back by giving you all work in my clubs. Mrs.. Chow will even give you the training you need at our training school on the floor below. Yasmin spoke out. "What if we choose to find our own work?"

Lavrov immediately replied, "You won't. I think this morning you may all feel a little light headed. That is because for the last four nights your evening meal has contained a sleeping draft. While you slept we injected you with heroin. Not much to start with but enough to get you hooked. Then last night you were each given a full shot which is why this morning you are light headed, by this evening you will be begging me for more. Ladies I own you."

"Ladies there is more good news," Mrs.. Chow said. "Your training starts today. It will last one week and you will learn how to serve, how to dance and how to pleasure. During your training you will live here rent free. Once your training is finished you may live in one of Mr. Lavrov's flats for one thousand Euros per month. Are there any questions?"

The brass plate on the wall read 'Howell Blake McPhee, Solicitors LLP'.

"This is it Rob. It feels odd to be here, to learn about a man I never knew and walk away again with something he left me."

"You don't know anything yet darling, so why don't we go in and find out? Come on, Rob said. He took Sue's hand and pulled her up the two stone steps and through the heavy wooden door. Inside they were greeted by a smartly dressed lady, who Rob judged to be in her late fifties.

"Good morning. Can I help you?"

"We have a 10:30 appointment. Mr. and Mrs. Blackstock."

"Please take a seat and someone will be out to see you."

They had barely sat down when William Blake appeared in the doorway from reception to the rest of the offices.

"Hello again Mr. and Mrs. Blackstock,, we're so happy to see you. Firstly I must apologise for it being so long since we first spoke. But my partners and I all wanted to be present because of the scale of this matter and of your available dates, this was the only opportunity. Can I offer you a coffee?"

"That would be nice, wouldn't it Sue? Thank you Mr. Blake".

Blake turned to the receptionist. "Coffee for everyone in the Oak Room please, Janet."

Whilst Blake had his back to them Rob and Sue gave one another a puzzled look.

"If you'd be so good as to follow me, I'll take you to meet my partners." Blake opened the door into a corridor and they followed him to the door at the end, which he opened and they walked into a large square wood panelled room with a very high ceiling. In the centre of the room was a large oval table with a score of high backed chairs evenly spaced around it. At the far end facing them were a grey haired old man and a slim attractive woman of around forty years old.

"Mr. and Mrs. Blackstock. May I introduce you to Edmund Howell and Miss Gillian McPhee."

"Pleased to meet you," Sue said and walked across the room to shake hands with the two partners.

"Did you fly up this morning?" Gillian McPhee asked.

"No we're on a boat. We've been here since Wednesday, Sue explained.

"A boat, how wonderful. So you are the real outdoor type are you Mrs. Blackstock?" McPhee probed.

"You could say that. I do like to be outdoors"

Small talk continued for a few minutes, then the coffee arrived.

"Let's get down to business, shall we??" Edmund Howell said. "Can we start by explaining Howell,, Blake and McPhee's connection with the late George Rudder. I think I had better begin with how we all came to be here today.

It all began in 1940, the evening of September 21st. Young four year old George Wilson had Chicken Pox and was staying with a neighbour to prevent the Wilson's ten day old daughter, your mother, Mrs. Blackstock, being infected. That night was of one of the first nights of the London bombings and your grand parents' house received a direct hit, killing all inside except the baby. Young George was taken to a local children's home,, where he was cared for by Emma McPhee, Gillian's grandmother. Emma and her husband Reg had a four year old boy of their own, Peter, and the two boys played well together as brothers would. An incendiary took the roof off the children's home one night. All the children were saved and housed amongst the local community, George went to live with the McPhee's, who formally adopted him after the end of the war.

Reg McPhee was Scottish, the son of Robert McPhee, Laird of Sutherland and head of the Clan Morgan, a rather grand but meaningless title. In 1947 the McPhee's emigrated to South Africa. Peter excelled at school and was sent back to England to complete his education and study law. George favoured the more practical things and Robert being a fair man, funded George's education in mining and bought a small local mine for George to manage. In 1965 diamonds were found in George's mine. Robert died in 1967 and in 1970 George brought his step mother back to England to escape the troubles coming from apartheid.

Peter inherited his father's title and land. George bought the land from Peter which allowed Peter to buy into Howell and Blake as an equal partner. His daughter Gillian joined us three years ago but sadly Peter passed away at the beginning of this year.

107

In 2014 George was diagnosed with lung cancer and contacted Peter to help him get his life in order before he died. George had been very keen to trace his family tree. He remembered he'd had a new baby sister and the date he had lost his family. In his research he came across a news paper story about the miracle Baby Wilson, rescued from the rubble three days after the house that had been her home had been destroyed.

"Are you aware of what happened to your mother after she was rescued, Mrs. Blackstock?"

"I am," Sue replied.

George instructed us to locate his sister, sell his mine in South Africa and cash in all his investments to simplify everything..

He died on 30th October 2017. You have proven extremely difficult to locate Mrs. Blackstock,, but you are here now and we can confirm we have no knowledge of any other relative, so we can read you his will. Would you like another coffee before I do so?"

"If I may?" Sue answered.

"And for you Mr. Blackstock?"

"Yes, please."

"I'll ask Janet," Gillian said and momentarily left the room.

On her return Edward opened the will. "This is very simple and very brief. *'This is the will and testimony of George Alexander Wilson. Being of sound mind I bequeath the following: To the daughter of my best friend and adopted brother I give the sum of two hundred and fifty thousand pounds."*

Sue gave Rob a glance and his face showed the same look of surprise that she was feeling about the size of the amount.

Edward continued. *'To my sister,* by default that is now you Mrs. Blackstock, *I leave the remainder of my estate after expences.'*

"So what does all that mean?" Sue asked.

"This is where I come in, Mrs. Blackstock," Blake said.

"Oh do call me Susan," she said.

"Susan, it means you are the new owner of property in Scotland consisting largely of a small parcel of grazing land and several buildings."

"You mean she owns a sheep field, a crofters cottage and a shed," Rob suggested.

"It is a little more than that," Gillian said. "Mrs. Blackstock now owns thirty two square miles of land on the north coast of Sutherland west of Thurso. The buildings consist of Balnakiel Castle, all dwellings in the hamlets of Balnakiel, Durness and Keoldale and the rents from these properties, plus the fishing rights of Loch Boralie and approximately one hundred miles of Atlantic coastline. A land agent has valued the package for estate tax purposes at two point seven million pounds."

"Wow!" Sue couldn't help but express her shock.

Janet entered the room with a fresh pot of coffee and poured a cup for each of them. She had also carried in a small wicker basket, rather like a small Harrods Christmas hamper, which she placed on the table next to Gillian McPhee, who nodded her thanks and Janet left again.

Gillian McPhee continued, "the South African mine was put up for auction in 2016, diamonds had recently been discovered in another small mine just over a mile away, so there were some very keen buyers and the mine was eventually sold for one hundred million SA Rand. That's approximately four point eight million pounds.

His investments on the stock exchange had in the main been very successful. He had bought when prices were low in 2007 during the financial recession and just held on to them as they climbed."

"Thank you, Gillian," Edward said. "As I said earlier we had a lot of investigation to do and I'm afraid our costs have accumulated quite high at eighteen thousand pounds. Other expences, funeral costs etc come to another five thousand ponds. That brings the total of money to be transferred to you after inheritance tax and any other charges, at approximately six point two million pounds plus property."

"Holly shit!" Sue exclaimed. "Oh, I do apologise. I mean that is a great shock."

"I must apologise for my wife, she's ex-army," Rob said and Sue blushed.

"That's quite understandable," Gillian McPhee said. "I can imagine this has come as a real surprise, as you didn't know you had an uncle until a few weeks ago."

"Are you alright, Susan?" Blake asked.

"I just can't take it in," Sue acknowledged.

"Cause for a little celebration perhaps? May I offer you both a glass of champagne?" Gillian McPhee asked as she opened the basket in front of her to reveal a bottle of champagne and a row of glasses.

"I need something," Rob said.

Gillian poured five glasses and handed them around.

"A toast," Edward raised his glass. "To Britain's latest millionaire."

"Congratulations, Susan," Blake added. "I'm afraid there is quite a large amount of paperwork we need to go through, it will possibly take about an hour. Are you expected anywhere this afternoon?"

"Well what's it like being rich?" Rob asked as he and Sue walked back to marina. "The owner of a sixteenth century Scottish Castle and a landlord."

"Just wake me up and this dream will end," Sue said.

"While you were going through the paperwork with Blake I was with Gillian McPhee, learning more about the property. It's in a really remote part of the north coast, it's really wild rugged countryside. She had several pictures of the castle. There are probably copies in that folder they gave you. It's not a castle with turrets, mote and drawbridge, it's more a sort of fortified manor house. It looked habitable but in need of some TLC in places."

"I must read through this folder carefully, to take all this in," Sue admitted.

"When do you get the money??"

"They advised me to speak to my bank and get a new deposit account set up. Once that's done, the money will be transferred directly, should only take a few days, a week at tops," Sue explained. "How far is it to this Balnakiel place?"

"By road, about one hundred and ten miles, but by sea it's approx two hundred miles. Are you saying you'd like to go and see the place now?"

"I think so yes, why not when we are so close. We can do Orkney and Shetland some other time. I just think once I've seen it, I might be able to think about what I'm going to do with it."

"If we get on our way as soon as we're back onboard, we can still get to Wick for tonight, then with an early start tomorrow we can be there by lunchtime. We can spend tomorrow afternoon exploring the castle, getting a feel for the place. We can still get to Orkney on Sunday, spend Monday on the island and still be back in Hull by Friday."

"I'll accept that."

Chapter 12

"Keep an eye on these girls Mrs. Chow. Especially that little blonde Yasmin, she is something special. Don't say anything to Ivan Gorkov but I am very happy with these girls, they will bring in a good price.

****

"I think I can afford to buy you dinner this evening Mr Blackstock, any suggestions?" Sue asked.

"No suggestions at all, I've never been to Wick before. Are you sure you can afford it?" Rob laughed.

"It looks like being a nice fine evening. Are you going to get some clothes on and come with me to find somewhere half decent to eat?" Sue said. "I did see a place by the bridge as we came in, it was called the Bord De L'Eau. Translated that means Waterside."

"Right, we'll start our search there shall we? Give me five minutes and I'll be ready but it's early yet, we've got plenty of time," Rob said.

"Well, it's been a very stressful day, I'm knackered and I'm hoping to have an early night."

Rob was actually ten minutes and by the time they found the restaurant there were no tables available for about twenty minutes. They had looked at the menu on a board outside before entering. They thought it looked good and what they saw on plates looked appetising, so they decided to wait at the small bar and have a pre-dinner drink.

"G and T please, Rob."

"Two gin and tonics with lime please," Rob asked the barman. "This looks a lot better than I expected, for a town this far north."

"The whole town looks better and bigger than I expected," Sue stated.

"I suppose its because of its importance as a port and ferry terminus for the islands. Most of the traffic for Orkney and Shetland must pass through here," Rob surmised. "And probably sum of the traffic out to the oil and gas platforms. Certainly the map shows a sizeable airport."

"Table for two was it, sir," a waiter appearing from behind Sue asked.

"Yes please, Rob answered.

"If you would like to follow me," the waiter said.

Service was a little slow but the food was excellent and they were back on the boat with a brandy before 10:00.

"What time do we need to be away in the morning?" Sue asked.

"I'd like to be leaving by 8:00 if possible to get to the castle by lunch time. That should give us a few hours of good daylight to look the place over. I doubt if it's got electricity."

"If we're up by 7:00 and we hold back breakfast until we're underway that will help," Sue suggested.

"I'll need my coffee before we leave," Rob said.

"We can get that ready while we get dressed," Sue stated.

"That's right girls,, sway your body to the music, please your customer, give the audience what they want, sell yourself to them." Mrs Chow urged on the four Russians. "Tomorrow is your last day of training, we will have an audience for you to perform in front of and they will decide which clubs you will work in based on what they see. They have customers with very high expectations, who will pay a lot of money for you to be with them. Just remember the better you are and the more you give them the more they will pay you. Mr.. Lavrov is a very generous man, he will let you keep forty percent of what they pay you,, so you will quickly pay him for bringing you here, you can then leave quite freely.

This was all alien to the four girls, none of them had even been to a proper night club. They had been to club nights at university and seen performers, even strippers in bars at home, but never anything like they were being trained for. Yasmin wondered whether Oxsana was in one of these clubs and she might see her soon. She'd love to speak to her at least, but she'd given her phone to Petra, so didn't have Oxsana's number. She resigned herself to the fact that in the short term she would be in a place that she hated, forced to have sex with men and women she would despise for paying to do this to her, but realisation was that if she performed as if she wanted to be there, she would earn more money and be able to break free sooner.

Before going down for breakfast Tracy and Zoe planned their day.

"I've got twenty one sites on my list. If we only spent forty five minutes at each site and allowing for travelling we could say an average of an hour per site. There's no way we'll visit them all in two days and there's no flight south on Sunday, even if we could be finished tomorrow," Tracy said.

"Then we might as well split the list evenly and do seven a day, for the next three days. We needn't rush too much and we can do a thorough inspection of each," Zoe added.

Tracy ran her finger down the list. "Balnakiel is 11th on the list. That's half way, and probably our first stop tomorrow afternoon. It's where we were when Mary was shot."

"So we need to do the lot when we're there. Have you got a finger print kit with you, because I haven't?" Zoe asked.

"I haven't, but there may be one in Mary's car. I've still got the keys. I'll check after breakfast.

Yasmin hadn't slept because of the thought of what she was about to have to do today. Last night Mrs. Chow had given each girl a bag of clothes they had to wear today. Yasmin's bag contained a bodice with an under wired half cup bra, a g-string, a pair of holdup stockings and a pair of open toed shoes with four inch heels. They had been told to be dressed and assembled in the lounge by 10:00 to learn how to do one another's make up. Mrs. Chow had told them they would be performing three times, at a 11:00, 4:00 and 10:00, or as Mrs. Chow put it, three chances to earn a place at the top clubs.

At a few minutes to 10:00, Yasmin left her room to walk the short distance to the lounge. She had never worn such high heels before. She struggled walking and wondered how she would manage to get down the stairs or be able to dance. All the girls had been in their nightwear two hours earlier when they had eaten their breakfast in silence, but they looked a lot different now in their performance clothes.

At exactly 10:00 Mrs. Chow walked in followed by two young ladies.

"Jaq and Lottie are with us this morning to show you how to do your makeup. Watch carefully. When they have finished, you will do the same to one another."

One of the two young ladies sat and in next five minutes the girls watched her be transformed from innocent to working girl.

"Thank you Jaq," Mrs. Chow said. "Now girls pair up, you have twenty minutes to make each other look like Lottie."

It took twenty five minutes. "Ladies you take too long, you must be quicker to please Mr. Lavrov," Mrs.. Chow said. "You will gather here again at 3:20 and 9:20 to do the same again. Now we go downstairs for our first performance.

"That's been a successful first day," Tracy said as they turned into the hotel car park at the end of the day.

"I'm glad we chose to start at the furthest point on your list. In the time it took to get there and back, I've just about completed researching Clan Morgan. I'll take you through my findings later," Zoe said.

"I think the best part of today has been the scenery. Totally stunning. Rugged but beautiful and almost totally unspoilt by man," Tracy said as they walked into the hotel and up to their room.

"Certainly beautiful today in the sunshine but I bet it looks different on a dull day. They say that this part of Scotland has two hundred and fifty wet days a year, influenced by the North Atlantic and the Gulf Stream," Zoe argued and placed her laptop on the end of her bed.

"For that reason, I think we can discount the first two locations at Kearvaig. Both the beaches were perfect for getting goods ashore, nice long sandy stretches in sheltered bays but they were so far off the road, must have been five miles down that track. Even today in dry conditions we struggled in a four by four, even a modest sea mist would make impassable," Tracy added.

"Same can be said about the beach at the mouth of the Kyle Of Durness," Zoe said. "I'm heading for the shower."

"Okay, while you're in there, I'll get today's photos downloaded onto my laptop."

Zoe reappeared wrapped in a towel. "The water's not very hot this evening so I didn't wash my hair. If I were you I'd get in there now while there is some warmth in the water at least."

Trace went straight in and when she reappeared Zoe was in leggings and sweater, so she dressed similarly. She didn't actually have much of a choice. She was running out of clean clothes, she had been in Scotland over a week. She had rinsed some knickers and a shirt in the bathroom but there were limits.

"I've been looking at your pics again," Zoe said. "Old shore looked a possibility but I think the land beyond the beach and up to the road is just too steep to carry a load."

"That was the one where the road goes through the village isn't it?" Tracy asked. "Villagers would notice and be curious about strange vehicles passing through, don't you think?"

"Kinlochbervie was just too heavily populated and Sarsgum could be clearly seen by any passing traffic travelling along the main road. But you seemed to think Keoldale was a hot site," Zoe recalled.

"Yes, it's definitely a landing site. The water is not very deep but suitable for a dingy and there is a sound jetty." Tracy explained her reasoning. "Although recent rains have washed much of the detail away there are two sets of vehicle tracks, same as Mary and I saw at the Castle last week. My guess is that they anchored their boat in deep water and brought their stuff to the jetty in a small boat, hence the recent scraping on the jetty planks. Then for some reason they went to Balnakiel Castle."

"That was where Mary got shot, wasn't it?" Zoe asked.

"That's right. We should get there around lunchtime tomorrow. Now let's go and eat and over dinner you can tell me about the Clan Morgan."

"There's not a lot to say really," Zoe reported. "They are believed to be direct decendents of the ancient Pics who gave the Romans so much grief. They were certainly very warlike and were front line for Robert The Bruce at Banochburn where they lost over fifty percent of their number. They again lost large numbers at Culloden and the Clan retreated to the North coast and became crofters. Renowned for their secrecy, they are recognised as prolific law breakers. The majority of the clan were absorbed into the more modern Clan Makenzie when Queen Victoria order the ancient highland tribes to be destroyed. That's about all of it."

"So we're right not to believe or trust them, they look after their own kind, no matter what,," Tracy summarised.

"Tracy and Zoe set off earlier than they had on Friday in order to give them extra time that they would need to thoroughly examine Balnakiel Castle.

Their first location was on the eastern shore at the mouth of the Kyle of Durness, but all the tracks down to the beach were nothing more than goat trails that looked like they hadn't been walked for decades and were unsuitable even for a four by four.

"That's another couple we can cross off," Tracy announced. "It's the castle next."

As they drove down the long drive to the castle Zoe noticed tears running down Tracy's cheeks. She reached out and placed her hand on top of Tracy's on the steering wheel to reassure her. Tracy stopped the vehicle in the same spot that Mary had stopped the week before. She got out and looked down at the tracks in the mud. There were many more than there had been last week. "Look Zoe,, clearly two vehicles," Tracy pointed out.

"Just like the tracks at that place we were at yesterday," Zoe acknowledged.

Tracy moved on to the outbuilding where she had seen the transit. "This is where we need to start gathering finger prints. I was in here when Mary was shot. There was a transit van in here, bits of the engine were out on a piece of sacking on the floor. It looked like someone was doing some repairs."

"I'll get the kit from the car," Zoe said.

"You know it's the police who should be doing this Tracy."

"Glasgow couldn't spare anyone. They're a bit pushed at the moment with Mary gone, her husband missing and a possible serial killer murdering young girls. So we're left with the washing up."

"I've lifted a few good prints and taken a dozen or so pictures. Let's move on," Zoe suggested.

Tracy walked on a couple of paces then stopped. "This is where Mary fell," she said and walked on towards the main building. "Look, one of the panes of glass has been broken, presumably that's how they gained entry. Possibly one climbed in and opened the door for the others."

"That doesn't make sense, look at the door. In particular look at the keyhole. The lock behind that must be huge, probably the original lock and the key would be big and heavy," Zoe observed.

Tracy went to look closer at the glass panel. "This whole section has been rigged so that it can be removed from the other side. I've seen something similar in a Cornish castle. The defenders keep a cannon behind this removable panel, loaded with grape shot to inflict greatest damage. When the castle is attacked the panel is quickly removed and the cannon fired on the attacker to good effect, the panel is then replaced to secure the building again."

"So the glass was broken to get in to remove the panel to gain entry," Zoe asked.

"That's exactly right," Tracy said. "I'm betting that when we push this, we'll find it hasn't been fixed in place because that can only be done from the inside."

Zoe pushed on the panel and it slid away. "Well done you," She said. "Let's go in and search the place."

They both climbed through the space and Tracy closed the panel to show Zoe how it worked. Then they went off to inspect the rest of the building.

Yasmin felt sick when she got back to her room. She had been with a grossly overweight Russian man in his late fifties for almost two hours. Her performance had begun with the four girls pole dancing on stage in front of an audience of twelve or fifteen people of various ages, men, women, white, black African and Asian, all staring at the dancers. Mrs. Chow was directing the show and continually talking to members of the audience. After a few minutes Mrs. Chow took Annika by the hand and led her over to a table where a black man sat on his own. Mrs. Chow said something to Annika who immediately sat on the black man's lap and kissed him. Yasmin and the other two girls continued dancing. Mrs. Chow next took Yasmin's hand and led her to the overweight Russian. Yasmin saw Annika and the black man leave the room. Mrs. Chow said to Yasmin. "You have to please this man, you have to give him what he wants."

Yasmin sat on his lap and put her arm around his neck and drew his face into her breasts. She cringed when he began to lick her breast and was disgusted with herself as she felt her nipples harden. She made herself go into a trance like state for the next two hours while the fat Russian made her do things she would not normally do.

She breathed heavily as she entered her room. She was naked apart from her stained stockings and her shoes. She headed straight for the shower to wash him off her. She felt awful, but she had survived. Then she saw another outfit laid out on her bed and realised she had to do it all again in a couple of hours.

"There should be a jetty somewhere up ahead. We just need to make sure the water is deep enough for us and we avoid the rocks," Rob called out to Sue who was holding on to the bow rail peering into the water, checking for dangers as they moved gently through the water and up the inlet.

"There it is Rob!" Sue pointed out the wooden structure two hundred yards ahead.

As they approached the jetty, Sue caught sight of the roof tops of what must be the castle. Rob carefully brought the boat into the jetty and Sue jumped over the small gap to the jetty and secured the lines. Sue fetched from the day cabin, the oversized key William Blake had given her and together they walked up the path to the building. They saw Tracy's car parked on the drive. "Someone else is here Rob," Sue said.

"Maybe you've got squatters., Rob joked.

Sue tried the door. "It's locked so whoever it is they are not inside." She inserted the key and pushed the door open with a loud screech.

"Zoe there's someone coming in they will know we're here because the car is on the drive. We had best be prepared for trouble." Tracy pulled out her Gloch from her belt holster and Zoe pulled hers from her side holster then together they headed through the rooms back to the front door.

"Sue Blackstock! What the fuck are you doing here?" Tracy called when she saw who had entered.

"I own the place. Why are you here?" Sue challenged.

"You own this place?" Tracy sounded shocked. "Since when?"

"Since yesterday morning."

"Why on earth would you want to buy this place?"

"I didn't. My uncle left it to me in his will, but I don't understand why you're here. Is that Zoe Crump behind you?"

Tracy stepped aside. "Hello Sue," Zoe said.

"We here because it's a crime scene. A police officer was killed here last week."

"What were the police doing here to get shot at in the first place?" Rob asked.

"That's a long story," Tracy responded.

"Come on Tracy tell me. I own this place now, I want to know, I deserve to know," Sue said sternly. "And why are you and Zoe doing scene of crime stuff?"

"Alright," Tracy began. "Well, firstly, MI-6 is working with Interpol, on an international drugs case. All across Germany, France and now Britain, schools are being supplied with drugs. Kids from age six to seventeen are being targeted. Do you remember me telling you all this that night we met in Edinburgh Rob? Did he tell you that we bumped into one another, Sue?"

Sue nodded.

"That's right, you were there to meet a local police officer," Rob said.

"Yes. D.S. Mary Howard."

"I remember now. She's the wife of that inspector who told me to clear off when Justin and I had found that dead girl and I said there was something not right about him."

"Mary ran the drugs unit at Glasgow. She and I were investigating reports that these drugs were entering the country through Scotland. Being landed on remote beaches on the North coast. Mary had received photos taken by someone up here. So we called on the man who had sent the photos to look at more. They showed boxes being unloaded on a beach near here. We left him and saw something suspicious that made us come here and before we had a chance to look around, Mary was shot."

"Is she okay?" Sue interrupted.

"She's dead."

"Oh my God!" Sue said in horror.

"So Zoe was sent up here to help me pick up the pieces and try and find these smugglers.

"You're looking good Zoe, how is Sarah?" Sue enquired.

"She's good. We were married three weeks ago."

"Congratulations. Only been married three weeks and Sarah's let you come up here with Tracey."

"She's not complaining, she's going off with the England squad, training for the autumn internationals in a couple of weeks."

"We had better finish looking around Zoe, we've got a lot more to do this afternoon," Tracy said.

"And we need to start exploring, Rob. I want to take loads of pictures so that we can give thought to what we're going to do with the place," Sue said. "As Tracy and Zoe are working in here, I'm going to go outside and take photos. I promised to send one to Justin as soon as we got here, so I'd better do that."

She framed a photo of her and Rob with the castle in the background. "Would you believe it? I can't send it, there's no signal."

"You'll have to wait until we get back on the boat and link to the satellite via the radio," Rob suggested.

Rob and Sue spent a long time wandering around the outside of the building, looking at the strange construction, the various additions made over the years. They discovered a generator in one of the outbuildings with several cans of diesel.

"So the castle has got electricity, then." Rob said "I was thinking it might be lit with oil lamps or candles. I wonder where the water supply comes from and how the place is heated."

"Trust you to be worried about the practical side of things."

"They are very important if you're going to use the place at all, people will want light, heat and running water whatever they are doing here. It's an expensive business puting in cables and pipes into an old building for the first time, but much less costly just to replace existing wires and pipes."

"This could be made into a really nice place, don't you think Rob?"

"Yes, the building needs a bit of work but could be very attractive. The trouble is its isolation, it's so far from civilisation. We're best part of three hours by road from Inverness or Wick airports and what would people do when they get here?"

"It's good countryside for walking and we've got all the fishing rights," Sue argued.

"But the weather is bad more often than it's good. I think we may struggle to find a solution to this one," Rob concluded.

Rob and Sue turned and walked back to the house when Tracy and Zoe appeared at the front door.

"We've done a good search," Tracy said. "Most of the rooms were tidy and have not been used for a long time. Others show signs of regular use, so we assume they were the ones your uncle lived in. The main hall has definitely had people in recently, there's a pile of food wrappers and there was probably some food scraps before the rats found them. We found these in there as well." Tracy held up an evidence bag containing two bullet cases. "The kitchen has seen use in the last few months but not recently. I think this is a regular spot for smugglers to rest up. How did you two get here, there's no car on the drive?" Tracy asked.

" We came by boat, it's tied up at the jetty," Rob answered.

"Where is the jetty? I didn't know there was one," Tracy asked.

"It's round the back," Rob explained. "There's a gate in the wall on the far side of the kitchen garden and follow the path. It's not far, perhaps one hundred yards, down a slope to the jetty. It's in a good sheltered spot with deep water right up to it."

"We should go and take a look Zoe?" Tracy said. "It sounds like a likely landing point."

"Give us a shout before you leave, we'll be inside," Sue said.

Rob took pictures of each room as they explored the ground floor and Sue wrote extensive notes in a notebook she had brought with her. Most rooms were wood panelled with animal skins hanging on the walls and placed as rugs on the floor. The entrance hall had two rows of deer antlers running the whole length of one of the walls.

Tracy and Zoe shouted they were leaving and Sue and Rob went up to the first floor. There were only a handful of rooms on this floor, the main hall and a row of smaller reception rooms. At one end of the main hall was a massive fireplace big enough for half a dozen people to stand in, the wall opposite had three large windows with very low sills, they looked like they could be opened to allow defenders out onto a flat roof with a low wall running round it. Ideal spot for a handful of defenders with muskets to hold off a small army. On the other two walls were mounted rows of round shields with swords, axes and other weapons mounted behind them. In the centre of the room there was a large oak table with a dozen chairs around it. More chairs of the same style were pushed against the wall. On the table was a pile of food wrappers and in the dust all around the pile were signs that the rats had taken anything edible.

"Look Sue, someone has written something in the dust on here, but I can't make it out."

Sue walked around the table and studied what Rob had been trying to read. "It's Russian it says '*Gospodi, pomogi nam perezhit' eto ispytaniye. Tvoy sluga vsegda Yasmin Kolanski*' which I think translates to 'oh lord help us survive this ordeal. Your servant always Yasmin Kolanski'. Rob its Ana's sister, she wrote this message. She must have been here last week, those people weren't smuggling drugs, they were bringing in girls."

"We must tell Tracy," Rob said

"But we haven't got any phone service."

"Tracy won't have either until she gets to a more populated area, maybe when she gets to Durness. Let's get finished here and back to the boat and make some calls. That will give Tracy time to get somewhere with a phone signal."

"I guess you're right Rob, there's nothing she could do even, if she knew now."

Rob took a picture of the writing and the pile of food wrappers. "There's was only enough food here for three or four girls, five at the most."

"And Yasmin was one of them."

"Who did you say lives here?" Zoe asked.

"James Blackburn, a known small time smuggler who has been setting false trails with some fake pictures, presumably to lead us away from something he had got planned. I want to apply a little pressure on Mr. Blackburn and find out what he is really up to and whether it has anything to do with the gang that murdered Mary," Tracy explained.

Tracy knocked on the door but got no response, so knocked again louder this time. Still no one came to the door.

"He must be in there, I can hear his TV," Tracy said.

"I'll go around the back to see if I can see him," Zoe said.

Tracy knelt on the doorstep and looked through the letter box. She saw no one. So she shouted, "James Blackburn this is MI-6, let us in!"

Zoe came running back to the front. "He's face down on the floor, Tracy he looks dead."

Tracy followed Zoe back round to the rear of the house. She tried the door. It wasn't locked and she pushed it open, drew her Gloch and crossed the threshold. On the kitchen floor Blackburn lay in a pool of his own blood,, obviously dead for at least four or five days. His throat had been slashed open by a broken bottle which lay next to the body. The room was a total mess, signs that Blackburn had put up quite a struggle.

"I have to call this in to Glasgow. They'll have to send someone up here now, the body count is mounting.

"I'll just turn the power on and we'll have a signal for your phone and while you ring Tracy and send Justin that photo, I'll

124

transfer the pictures onto the laptop so that we can look through them after dinner," Rob said.

He stood to one side to allow Sue to step onto the boat first. The tide had come in lifting the boat a couple of feet, so the mooring ropes were a little slack and there was a small gap to step across. Rob went straight to the cockpit and flicked a couple of switches to put the power on. Immediately his phone vibrated in his pocket as messages came in. He went down into the day cabin and found Sue was already talking to Tracy, so he went to the food box to decide what he could cook for their dinner.

"Tracy and Zoe didn't get very far, they found a body in Durness and they've spent the whole afternoon sitting waiting for the police to arrive, but she thanked me for the news about the girls," Sue explained. 'What were all those messages on your phone? It seemed to be buzzing for ages."

"Probably nothing important or urgent, I haven't looked yet." Rob pulled the phone from his pocket and looked at the screen. "That's strange they're all from Luci."

"Read them Rob, it must be important."

"All it says is phone home urgent."

"You'd better call now, something must have happened."

Rob quickly dialed the number. It was answered almost instantly and Rob had a short conversation with someone then ended the call.

"That was Marge," he said. "Everyone is at the hospital, dad had a heart attack this morning."

"Oh no! Is he okay?"

"He was due to have surgery early evening, Marge doesn't know any more than that."

"What are we going to do, we must get back as soon as possible?"

"We need to get back to Wick. We can leave the boat there and fly down to Leeds-Bradford from Wick."

"Do you mean right now?"

"Too risky. It will start getting dark in about three hours, that doesn't give us enough time. But sunrise at the moment is at around 5:00, so if we're up and ready by then, we can be at the airport by noon."

"You had better ring and get some seats booked on the first flight after that,, darling," Sue suggested. "I'll try and find out about Eric."

As it had been Luci who had rung Rob. Sue thought it best to start by trying her first.

"Hello Luci, can you hear me it's Sue?"

"Do you know about grandpa?"

"Yes dear. Your father has just spoken with Marge. Is there any news?"

"It's very serious, Sue. He's in theatre now, it's been three hours."

"We're a long way from anywhere at the moment. Your dad is making some phone calls and we're trying to get back by tomorrow evening. When did it happen?"

"It was about 10:00 this morning. Grandpa was out in the yard walking one of the horses up and down so that Tim could check out a leg problem. He collapsed in the yard and one of the lads came to the house to get grandma. I happened to be in the kitchen with her at the time, so I ran ahead to see what was happening. Grandpa was on his back and Tim was performing CPR. He told me to call an ambulance and to tell them it was a heart attack. It took over half an hour for the ambulance to arrive and all that time Tim kept going. He actually kept grandpa alive until the paramedic took over, if Tim hadn't been there,, I'm sure he would have died."

"How is Rose?"

"She's as you might expect, upset and very worried about grandpa."

"Give her our love and tell her we'll be back as soon as we can. Keep us updated, let us know when he comes out of theatre and we'll see you tomorrow."

"I will do, my love to dad, bye."

"Well?" Rob said questioning.

"It sounds about as bad as it could be, but he's hanging on fighting. How are you doing?"

"Not very well at the moment. I've got a long term berth organised at Wick marina from lunchtime tomorrow but tomorrow is Sunday and there are no scheduled flights to Leeds-Bradford on a Sunday. They gave me the number of a private charter company which I rang. They're checking if anything is available and are going to ring me back in half an hour."

"Well, I suggest we have a drink while we wait. What's for dinner?"

Chapter 13

"Ivan, I did you a favour getting Lavrov off your back. My father is a hard man. The only man I've ever known stand up against him and live is Mikhail. You'd do well to get your head down for a few days. Now you can help me get revenge on the person who caused Mikhail's death. Mr. Robert Blackstock must have his partner taken away as he took mine away from me."

****

At 7:45 a police four by four drove into Durness and pulled in behind Tracy's vehicle. Two uniformed officers slowly got out and sauntered up to Tracy in the drivers seat, she had already had her window down.

"About fucking time you got here, we've been waiting almost seven hours."

The officers face showed he didn't like being talked to like that and he responded aggressively. "Are you the lady who reported finding a body."

"I reported a murder."

"That's for us to decide. Can I have your names please."

"D.S. Tracy Mills and D.C. Zoe Crump.

The officer stepped back from the car and stood up straight. "Sorry miss, I didn't know you were force."

"MI-6,," Tracy corrected him, "and you are?"

"I am P.C.. McBaine and this is P.C.. Taylor ma'am."

"Why as it taken you so long to get here? We expected you here at least two hours ago. Plus I would have expected an officer from the murder squad."

"Sorry ma'am we both had the day off but our Super called us in and sent us all the way up here. We came as quick as we could. We are both seconded to the murder squad, we've been looking into what looks like a serial killer in the Glasgow area, so the team is a bit stretched and our head of section, D.I.. Howard, has gone missing."

"Well P.C. McBaine shall we go and look at the body?? I'm sure you'll see that it's not an accident, nor suicide," Tracy said. "You said D.I. Howard is missing, what exactly do you mean."

"His wife had been shot and was in Thurso hospital and he took compassionate leave to be up there with her. She died a couple of days later and D.I. Howard has not been seen or heard from since."

"I'd be grateful if you would take our statements now P.C. McBaine. We'd like to get something to eat and we've got a two hour drive back to our hotel in Thurso."

"Zoe, get in the car quickly! I didn't mention this to McBaine but when I was at the hospital at the end, when Mary died, as D.I. Howard left I heard him mutter something to himself. I think D.I. Howard came here and did this. I don't think we'll see D.I. Howard alive again."

"Don't you think you should have told McBaine?"

"No, if they do their job correctly they'll soon find out if it is him and why he did it. If we give them all the answers they may not ask the questions. Let's get back to the hotel and have something to eat."

"At least we don't have to drive as far tomorrow, there are still ten locations on your list to check out."

Yasmin lay on her bed for a long time listening to one of the other girls sobbing in her room. It had been 1:00 when she had got back and showered. She felt battered and bruised and very sore but kept saying to herself '*Be good, earn well, get away.*' She looked back on the day remembering the disgusting fat Russian, then next was the smartly dressed woman. She looked only a few years older than Yasmin. She had insisted on tying Yasmin naked to a chair and whipping her with a horse whip. The more Yasmin cried out the more pleasure it seemed to give the woman. The third performance was her biggest worry, Mrs. Chow had given her to a black man. He was mid forties, smelt nice and to start with was very pleasant. However he completely changed when he was aroused, he had been rough with her.

Mrs. Chow had told them all that the club managers would choose which girls they liked and make a bid to Mr. Lavrov. They would be told in the morning and taken to new accommodation at noon, so must be ready. Yasmin closed her eyes trapping her tears and prayed.

"Rob wake up it's 4:35 and beginning to get light. We need to get moving to get to Wick by lunchtime."

"Sorry Sue, I had a terrible night worrying about dad. So I guess I was solid gone when the alarm went off."

"I know you're worried, but his surgery went well and the doctors are confident that he'll recover quickly. You'll be by his side by tea time. Did you ring Ryman?"

"I did, as soon as that charter company confirmed our flight. Ryman will be at Leeds-Bradford when we land,," Rob said.

"Do you think we should tell Ana about Yasmin's message we found written in the dust on the table?"

"I forgot about that with all this other stuff going on and worrying about dad," Rob answered. " I think we should tell her because it means that she was okay a week ago. But I think we should tell her when we see her not over the phone."

"It's a difficult one isn't it? She should be told what we know, but we don't know anything that's going to help find her."

Rob opened the cabin door and looked out, he quickly closed the door again. "It's a bit fresh out there I'll need my coat on in the cockpit this morning. But the tide is full so we don't need to worry about the rocks. We've certainly got enough water under our keel to stay clear of them."

"I'll just pull my coat on and get ready to cast off when you get the engines running. I've boiled the kettle so you'll get your coffee as soon as we're underway," Sue said.

When Yasmin woke she went straight into the shower again, she felt dirty, used and sore. How could she get word to her sister to let her know where she was, then she thought '*I don't know where I am so how could I tell Ana even if I were to speak to her.*' The situation was hopeless. She was also aware that she was becoming dependant on the drugs she was being given, for long periods each day she felt as if she was outside of her body watching what her body was doing.

None of the girls talked about what had happened yesterday, they all had a look of anticipation on their faces as they waited for Mrs. Chow to appear and tell them where their future would begin.

Dmitry Lavrov arrived with three smartly suited men. They were laughing and joking together and stood in a corner of the room away from the girls. Several minutes later Mrs. Chow walked in. She smiled at Lavrov then turned to face the girls. "Ladies the videos of your performances yesterday have been studied this morning and Mr Lavrov has accepted bids from these club owners for each of you. When I call your name you will go with your new owner." Yasmin was shocked to hear that the sexual acts she had been forced to perform had been seen by other people and that had determined her value and she was to be sold like a slave.

"Annika." Mrs. Chow called out the first name. 'The White Lotus'. When her name was called, Mrs. Chow indicated for her to stand and come forward and one of the suited men shook hands with Lavrov, grabbed Annika by the wrist and dragged her away.

Yasmin watched as the same thing happened to the other two girls leaving her as the last. Mrs. Chow smiled at her. "Mr. Lavrov has picked you out as someone special. He has chosen you for his own club 'The Four Aces'. You are most privileged."

As Rob manoeuvered the boat into Wick Marina, his phone rang in his pocket, Sue reached round him and pulled his phone from his pocket. "It's Luci," she said and answered the phone and put it on speaker "Hi Luci, how is grandpa?"

"Grandma rang the hospital a few minutes ago, they said he had a comfortable night and is doing well. Tim is going to drive grandma and me to the hospital. Visiting time is 3:00 to 6:00. Will you and dad be able to get there?"

"Hi Honey," Rob joined in. "We've got a plane booked to takeoff from Wick at 11:30 so we should be landing at 3:30, I've arranged for Ryman to pick us up from Leeds-Bradford airport, so we should be with you around 4:30."

"So Tim won't need to stay or come back for us. Ryman will be able to bring us all back together."

Whilst Rob finished talking to Luci, Sue jumped ashore with the stern line and pulled the back of the boat close into the jetty and tied off the rope. Rob cut one engine, allowing the other to push the bow towards the jetty. He left the engine idling, went forward and threw the bow line to Sue so she could secure it.

They each grabbed their day bags and put all the bits and pieces of perishable food into a bin bag. Rob double checked that the navigation and radio equipment was all locked away and the cockpit made secure, not knowing when they would be back to retrieve the boat. He had paid for the berth through until the end of August and if he needed to extend it he could.

Rob went into the marina office to sign the paperwork and Sue ordered a taxi to get them to the airport. It was still only 10:30,, so they had plenty of time.

Before she had chance to put her phone away it rang, caller ID displayed "TRACY MILLS".

"Hello Tracy, are you and Zoe still scouring the coastline?"

"Good morning Sue, yes we've got a full day today but I've got some news which might be of interest to you. When Rob and I met in Edinburgh the other week, he told me how you Blackstock's have a link with two murders in the Glasgow area."

"That's right, the police thought the first one was Ana's sister and the second one Rob found," Sue confirmed.

"Rob told me he suspected there was a connection between the two murdered girls and Ana's sister and that the sister had mentioned the name Ivan Gorkov. Then you told me yesterday that you found evidence that Ana's sister had been in Balnakiel Castle recently. Piecing all the bits together it seems highly probable that Gorkov is the one that shot Mary."

"Oh my God, you're right!" Sue agreed.

"I thought you might be interested in something I was told last night when I reported in. Ivan Gorkov has been spotted in London. He was seen having lunch with Mikhail's widow, who is known to have run the escort girls that worked for her husband."

"So you're saying that Ivan Gorkov was bringing girls to work in the Russian maffia's clubs and that's where Ana's sister Yasmin could be. Thank you for calling Tracy. I don't know how it helps us, but thank you all the same."

"Rob, Tracy Mills just rang me. She believes that Yasmin is in London,"Sue told Rob when he rejoined her.

"What makes her think that?"

"Here comes our taxi, I'll tell you as we go."

It took just ten minutes to drive to the airport, they passed through security and were met by a young lady wearing a tee-shirt bearing the logo of the charter company. She took them to the company hanger and introduced them to their pilot who talked them through the aircraft safety briefing and at 11:20 they climbed into the two rear seats of the four seater aircraft and moved slowly to the end of the runway, the pilot continually talking to the control tower for instructions. At precisely 11:30 he pushed the throttle forward and they were airborne within seconds.

Once the plane had reached the right altitude, the pilot pulled back on the throttle just a little but it reduced the cabin noise considerably.

"Blackstock, isn't a very common name. You wouldn't know an Eric Blackstock by any chance would you?" the pilot asked.

"That's my father," Rob answered.

"Owns a horse racing yard and some sort of horse training set up for horses used in the movies, both in a village just outside York?" The pilot continued.

"Yes, that's right. Why do you ask?"

"I used to work there. Next time you see him, say Mac says hello. He'll remember me, I'm sure."

"I don't remember you at all. When did you work for him."

"Around twenty years since I left now. I was at those stables 1992 through to July 98. My name is Ian McMillan. I think you and I met a couple of times, I remember you getting totally plastered in the village pub when you came home from university, after your graduation. You were so bad some of the lads had to carry you home. Your mother was so mad, I can still see the look on her face. That was just two weeks before I left."

"Why did you leave?"

"Since a kid I'd always wanted to be a pilot in the RAF but couldn't get in, but I was still accepted for pilot training in the Fleet Air Arm and ended up flying Harriers for fourteen years."

"And now you're flying private charters".

"Well in the navy, and I guess the RAF is the same, every new plane that comes along is more technically advanced than the last and the pilot has less control. I love to fly not be taken around as a passenger by a computer. I was with the FAA Harriers until the last ones went out of service,, then got out at the first opportunity. I bought this plane second hand and with a mate from the FAA, set up Wick Coastal Charter Flights three years ago."

"I bet this is a lot different to fly than a Harrier?" Sue asked.

"You can't really compare a single engine prop to a jet like a Harrier, but the basic principles of flying are the same."

"So is the business doing well?" Sue probed.

"We're making a small profit but it is a struggle and both our aircraft are old and need replacing. We only fly March to October, there no demand during the winter. When we close this October, we'll wind things up."

"What will you do then".

"I'd like to be able to keep flying but for fun at the weekend, rather than to make money. Maybe get an instructor licence. I wouldn't mind getting back into racing again, but I a bit old for a stable lad."

"Are you a family man, Ian?" Sue continued.

"My wife died last Easter, I've got a daughter just graduated with a maths degree but like so many others leaving university at the moment she can't get a job, so she's waitressing. She's another reason I'm ending the business's. I'm all she's got and I'm away so often. Like today I've got to go on to Birmingham later for a booking tomorrow morning, Wednesday I'll be in Shetland and so it goes on."

They continued chatting until they began to descend into Leeds-Bradford. The pilot rolled the plane into a parking bay at one side of the terminal and stopped the engine. He took Rob and Sue to the security check point carrying their bags for them. "Don't forget to say hi to Eric from me." He said and turned and walked away.

"What a nice man," Sue said.

Ryman was waiting for them at the arrivals gate and quickly got on the road for York. They arrived four or five minutes later to find Eric sitting up in bed talking to Rose and Luci.

"You old fraud Eric, you're in here to ogle the nurses, Sue jested.

"You've rumbled me. There is a particular black nurse I wouldn't mind sharing an isolation ward with."

"You silly old fool, you'll give yourself another heart attack. Anyway she'd eat you for breakfast," Rose added

"What a nice way to go," Eric responded.

"Grandpa!" Luci added.

"Really, how are you dad?" Rob stepped up to the bed side.

"Excuse me Eric but we only permit two visitors, it disturbes the other patients otherwise," a nurse said from the end of the bed.

"It's alright I'll go and sit in the waiting room," Sue said.

"I'll go as well. We'll see you before we leave Grandpa," Luci promised.

"So how are you dad?" Rob repeated.

"Tired mainly, a little sore but they are giving me stuff so that I don't have any pain. They're saying if all goes well I could be coming home in a couple of days."

"He looks a lot better than I expected him to look," Sue said to Luci.

"He looked really bad yesterday but Tim was wonderful. He kept him alive until the paramedics arrived and took over."

"We were so worried, being so far away we felt hopeless, unable even to begin the journey home," Sue said.

"Yes, where exactly were you? We all thought you were heading for Orkney."

"Well, you remember I was having a meeting with a solicitor in Inverness about my uncle's will. We saw him on Friday and I've inherited a castle," Sue began.

"A castle! Gosh I bet that was a bit of a shock?"

"That's not all, he's left me all his money as well."

"How much?"

"Several million."

"Gee. Tell me about the castle. Is it on a hill with a moat and drawbridge?"

"No nothing like that. It's more like a fortified house. We counted twelve large bedrooms." Sue explained.

"You counted them. So you've been to see it then."

"Yes, that's where we were when we heard about Grandpa. Its almost at the western end of the North coast, beautiful rugged scenery but very remote, you might say isolated. I've got loads of pictures on my laptop. I'll show you when we get home."

"Dad, do you remember a chap who worked for you twenty or so years ago, called Ian McMillan?" Rob asked his father.

"I remember Mac alright. A great worker. He had a lot going for him. Left me to join the RAF, if I recall."

"He was our pilot down from Wick today."

"It's a small world isn't it? I remember him learning to fly. It was all he ever wanted to do. He spent every penny he earned on his flying lessons. I offered him the head lads position when Charlie retired, but he refused."

"You thought very highly of him then?"

"I did and I was sorry to see him leave."

"That was the last one on the list Tracy, Zoe said.

"How many possible sites have we narrowed it down to?" Tracy asked.

"Five, Keoldale and Balnakiel we know are being used and three that we believe have been used in the past," Zoe summarised.

"We know that Keoldale and Balnakiel were used by the Russian Mafia for bringing in girls from what Sue Blackstock found. Now we believe they have been taken to London. But we don't know if they also brought in any drugs. So while we have missed this shipment, at least we now know that future shipments will most likely come through one of the five locations we've identified and we can keep them under surveillance."

"Does that mean we can go home tomorrow?" Zoe asked.

"If Sir Bernard is happy when I report in later. I'm hoping he'll have a task force ready to replace us."

Chapter 14

"Good afternoon minister, it's Bernard Howe, I know you are busy but I'm sure you would want to know I am about to launch an offensive against the Russian Mafia. I shall be asking two young Russian ladies to share their knowledge and experience of the Russian set up. I also intend speaking with Robert Blackstock. I've had notice from The Palace, that he and his wife will be invited to have tea with Her Majesty at the end of October, for their part in the Venezuelan incident last year.

****

"What are we going to tell Ana?" Rob asked Sue, as Ryman drove them all home.

"What do you mean dad? What do you know that Ana needs to be told about?"Luci queried.

"We know that Ana's sister was taken by Ivan Gorkov and he has been seen in London in the last couple of days," Sue explained

"You have to tell her everything dad,"Luci pleaded. "She'll know exactly what her sister is going through, she may even know where she can be found."

"Hold on a minute Luci, we can't go into the lion's den just like that. The Russian Mafia must be respected," Sue said.

"You've got contacts though, haven't you?" Luci stated.

"Yes, we do know the right people but we can't just go to them with guess work. We need to be certain. We were lucky paying them off for Ana and Eva, as it happened when the Mafia were weakened by their top men getting killed. That was twelve months ago."

"Then tell Ana everything you know, let them add from their own experience, obtain the proof needed to convince whoever you need to convince to take action," Luci argued.

"She's right Rob," Sue said, "Ana must be told everything we know."

"My little girl has become a wise old lady," Rob said.

"Hey dad, less of the old."

"You know what, I think I'm going to take Tim down to the 'Dog and Gun' and buy him a drink or two to thank him on dads behalf," Rob announced.

"He's probably already on his way there anyway. He's spending a lot of time with Jenny. They seem to be getting very serious., Luci claimed.

They dropped Ryman off at his house in the village and Rob drove the final mile and a half back to the stable.

"Do you think we should go and see Ana now, Rob?" Sue asked.

"I think it would look a bit odd if we kept that sort of news away from them too long. I'll drive on round to the Academy and check their schedule and see if their wagons are in the yard. I know they are scheduled to have one wagon for the new Russel Crowe film set in Cornwall, but I think that starts next week. But the other wagon is only local, out days only. That's with that new period drama set in Yorkshire, out somewhere in the Dales. They should have started shooting this week and most of our involvement is in the early scenes," Rob said. "I won't be long."

Sue thought to herself it would be just as quick to walk, it's only half a mile across the fields but over three miles by road. Perhaps he wanted to bring something back from the office, so she said nothing to him.

When Rob drove into the Academy's yard he saw Eva. She was connecting one of the hospitality wagons to the mains power supply to recharge the wagons large refrigeration unit batteries. Her assistant Jules, was chatting with Rob's Academy Manager Billy Martin. They saw Rob arrive and Jules headed off towards the gate. "Bye Billy, Bye Eva, see you in the morning."

"Don't forget we leave at 7:00 tomorrow," Eva shouted back

Jules waved an acknowledgement back at Eva, then as she passed Rob she smiled and said, "Good Evening Mr. Blackstock."

Rob responded with a nod and a smile. "Good evening Eva, I was hoping to see Ava. Is she about?"

"No, she's running around Cornwall looking for Mr. Poldark, Eva said. "Is it news about Yasmin?"

"Yes. They're filming a new series for Netflix on location in Cornwall, set in similar times to Poldark, but I don't think Aidan Turner is starring in it." Rob responded.

"No he isn't, but the leading actor is also very handsome," she laughed.

"I do have some news of Yasmin, but I need to tell it to Ava myself," Eva looked concerned so Rob quickly added. "It's not bad news, she is okay."

"She will be back on Wednesday, I will tell her you wish to see her and you have news of Yasmin."

"How is Jules settling in? She's been with you about three months hasn't she?" he asked.

"She does okay, perhaps she spends a little too much time watching the actors and flirting, but she is only nineteen. She gets her work done and is taking her driving test so she can help with some of the driving of this big beast."

"Was I right in hearing you tell her 7:00 start tomorrow morning, that's very early isn't it?"

"They are doing night time scenes tonight, a burning train and lots of people jumping off as it goes along. We left them loads of coffee and are going back to do breakfast from 8:30."

"Well I'd better let you finish up. Are you going straight home when you've finished?"

"Yes."

"I'll give you a lift then."

"That's very kind, thank you," she said. "I'll only be a minute."

"Hi Rob."

"Good evening, Billy."

"We weren't expecting you back until the end of the week."

"Dad had a heart attack yesterday so we cut short our holiday and flew home to be with him."

"I'm sorry to hear that. Is he okay?"

"It was quite a bad one, but he had surgery last night and the doctors are happy with his progress. He may be home later this week."

"Well that's good news, at least."

Eva came out of the office and locked the door.

"I'll be around tomorrow Billy, we can catch up on work then sometime. Good night Billy."

"Luci tells me you have a boyfriend, Eva." Rob said as they left the Academy.

"Yes he's very nice, he's a doctor at York hospital. We met when I went with Mr. Eric to York races, when you were in America."

"So you've known him several months then." Rob continued.

"Two hundred and forty three days."

"To be that specific he must be someone special."

"He is very special to me."

"So will we be hearing wedding bells soon?"

"I hope so," she laughed

"Good luck to you both," he said and stopped the car at Eva's front door.

"Thank you for your kind wishes," she said, kissed him on the cheek and got out of the car.

As Rob checked his mirror before moving off he saw Tim striding across the car park of the "Dog and Gun", so he reversed past the pub and the car park entrance, then forward into an empty space. As he entered the bar Rob saw Tim stood by a table talking to two of the stable lads who were playing dominos.

"Tim."

He turn to face whoever had called his name. "Rob, you made it back then. How's Eric?"

"He's doing well, thanks to you," Rob said coming forward and shaking Tim's hand.

"I didn't do a lot really, anyone else would have done the same."

"But they didn't, you did and the doctor at the hospital says he would have been dead if not for you. The very least I can do is buy you a drink."

"I was't planning on having a drink until later. You see I've been seeing Jenny and we were planning on a stroll along the riverbank."

"I'll buy you both a drink. I insist."

A smart lady came up to then and slipped her arm through Tim's.

"Hello Jen, can I introduce Robert Blackstock? Rob this is Jenny Buck."

"Pleased to meet you Miss Buck. I was just thanking Tim for saving my dad's life yesterday, I'm buying him a drink, will you join us."

"What's this Tim, you saved someone's life. How?"

"Dad had a heart attack and Tim kept him alive with CPR until the paramedics got there."

"You didn't tell me," Jenny said.

"Honestly, it was no big deal."

"Yes, Mr. Blackstock, he will have a drink with you. Won't you Tim?"

While they waited for their drinks Rob sent Sue a message. *'Found Tim. In D+G home soon.'*

Rob was just half way down his pint when a voice behind him said "I'll have a large Merlot and I'm hungry."

"Sue, what are you doing here?"

"Hopefully having a drink, same as you and I've brought you this to see." She held up an envelope made of top quality paper and some sort of crest embossed at the bottom right corner.

"What is it?"

"I'll show you when we eat. I'll have the Thai curry. Hello Tim, this must be Jenny. Pleased to meet you."

"Jen, this is my boss Susan Blackstock."

"Do call me Sue. I hope Rob hasn't ruined your evening plans."

"No, not at all Sue. In fact I was going to say to Tim let's stay in this evening because I've got something to celebrate. I got a letter this morning. You are looking at the new Performance Director at the Theatre Royal starting 1st September."

"Congratulations, well done," Sue said.

Rob returned with Sue's drink. "Jenny is going to be the Performance Manager at the theatre in town," she said.

"That's great. Shall we grab that table while it's free."

"My round. Same again Rob? We've got something to celebrate now," Tim announced.

They sat at the table with their drinks, Jenny explained what her role at the theatre would entail and how her years as a singer and dancer on cruise ships would help. When the food arrived, Tim and Jenny excused themselves and went and sat at the bar.

"Now what's in that letter? Rob asked.

"It's not a letter, its an invitation, from Buckingham Palace, to attend a private tea with the Queen on 16th October. The Queen has signed it personally. There's a note in with it to say someone from the palace will visit us at a date between 2nd and 9th October, to brief us on etiquette and what to wear etcetera.

"Why us?" Rob sounded a little shocked.

"That's explained in a second letter, this one from Sir Bernard Howe." Sue pulled the second letter from her bag. "It says that Her Majesty wishes to meet us both and thank us for our involvement in the Venezuelan incident. It would not be in the public interest to know of the incident, so Her Majesty herself suggested a private tea at Buck house."

"The kids will be chuffed,," Rob said.

"We can't tell them about Venezuela, you signed the Official Secrets Act. You can't tell anyone why we've been invited."

When Tracy reported in to her supervisor she was told that Sir Bernard was launching an offensive against the Russian Mafia. Additional resources were being made available immediately. With Tracy's own report and that from the Glasgow murder investigation team plus others a clear picture was emerging. It was certain that the Russian Mafia were actively bringing girls in to the country via Scotland. It was highly likely the drugs being found in the schools came in via the same route. Glasgow and Edinburgh have been told to supply six officers each, and MI-5 were sending three agents. The fifteen officers were to be used to provide surveillance during the hours of darkness at the sites Tracy had reported. Tracy and Zoe were to return to London to join an MI-6 task force, specifically targeting the London cell of the Russian Maffia and it's connection into Europe, destroying the network and cutting off the supply of drugs to the schools.

Monday morning, Rob arranged for Ryman to go with him to Wick to collect the boat. On Tuesday Tim drove them to Leeds-Bradford where they caught a scheduled flight to Wick. They spent that night on the boat in Wick harbour and set off at first light, reaching Edinburgh well before dark. The following day they were again up early and completed the journey to Hull late afternoon. Sue drove to Hull to collect them. Sue had spent the week drawing up a shortlist of builders to invite to quote for the extension work. When she drove to collect Rob, she had just heard from Brett Willoby, the appeal against the planning decision had been accepted and planning had been granted. She had also arranged a new account with her bank and Howell, Blake and McPhee had deposited £6,152,020. More than enough to fund the extension.

All week Sue had not interfered with Tim running the stables, once or twice when she looked in she was more than happy with the way things were going. During the week he had only two runners, neither of which were expected to do well, but both were placed.

Everything was coming together in a rush. Tim was managing the current stock, plans had been passed, ample money was available and she even had a shortlist of builders. However, she was nervous, she was on the brink of something that would seriously change their lives and so far it was only her own input. Had she missed something? After thinking it through she decided she needed help, a support team.

Yasmin had spent the week getting to know the staff and the layout of the club. All the dancers were nice to her and when she was with them during the day she was able to put aside what they would be forced to do in the evenings. Each morning they all gathered on the stage to rehearse their routines. On Wednesday she joined their rehearsal in preparation for joining them on stage on Saturday. The girls told her she shouldn't be expecting any extras for the first few nights, maybe even a week. Until the audience got to know her. As far as she was concerned that was the best possible news. She stood in the bar each night and watch the girls perform. They came on stage two at a time, at the end of their routine they left the stage and walked into the audience and the next two came out to perform. She was not in a hurry for Saturday to come around.

"Hi Ana," Billy Martin shouted out across the yard as he came out of the office and saw Ana climbing down from the passenger seat of her catering wagon. "You're back earlier than we expected."

"Filming at that location finished this morning. Only eight lunches so we finished early too," Ana explained. "Is Eva about?"

"Sorry love, you just missed 'er. She left about ten minutes ago. Another hot date with that doctor of hers I expect."

"Thanks Billy, have a good weekend."

Billy walked on towards a cluster of outbuildings where explosives were stored, well away from other buildings and Ana turned to face her assistant who was climbing down from the drivers seat. "Can you connect up the charger for the freezer and secure the wagon for the night please, Paula. I've got to see Mr. Blackstock," Ana requested. "I need you in by 9:00 on Monday, if that changes I'll ring you. Have a good weekend."

"I hope it's good news about your sister, Ana," Paula said. "See you Monday."

Ana quickly checked the office for Rob, not really expecting him to be there at this time on a Friday afternoon. She poked her head around the door and it was obvious that he had finished work for the day and she would find him in the house at the Blackstock Racing stable. So she crossed the two fields that lay between the academy and the stables as fast as she could walk, even breaking into a jog a couple of times. When she got to the house she knocked on the back door.

"Hello Ana, come in," Sue greeted her and smiled to reassure her a little.

"Eva told me you have some news of Yasmin for me."

"Yes we do. Rob is in the lounge. Let's go through and we'll tell you everything we know."

Ana sat on the edge of the sofa and listened to what Rob and Sue had to say about the whereabouts of her sister.

"If she was taken to London she will have been trained to dance in the clubs by now, she could have been taken anywhere after that. Eva and I saw many girls go through club training then shipped on to clubs, Eva and I were very lucky we had worked out our dance routine which Mikhail Gorkov saw had a lot of potential, so we were saved from being sent into the clubs in London and other large cities."

"But Mikhail Gorkov is dead Ana," Sue stated.

"Very little will have changed. The new management will be operating in the same way. To them Mikhail's death was just a hiccup and the wheels must keep turning," Ana explained. "I must go back to London and find my sister, I know many of the girls, they will help me find Yasmin."

144

"You can't go alone Ana," Rob said. "I appreciate you are eager to rescue your sister, but to charge in without thinking of what might happen would be foolish."

"But she is in danger. I must save her," Ana stressed.

"I understand that but we must do our best for her, without increasing the risk." Rob reasoned. "If you find her what are you going to do? You know you can't just walk out with her. The Russians have invested money to get her here, they will think of her as their property. There will be a price to pay. You'll also be puting your own life at risk."

"I don't have a choice. You would do the same if it were your sister," Ana argued.

"What if I came with you," Rob offered.

"Don't be so quick with your offer Rob. It could be just as dangerous for you," Sue claimed. "And what about work? You've just had a holiday, both your crews are working at the moment but you need to be tracking future work. You as well Ana. I'm not saying work is more important than Yasmin but you do need to think of the impact of not being here."

"You're right as usual, darling," Rob acknowledged. "Let's think this through properly. First thing is when can we go."

"Filming in Cornwall is finished, the Blackstock catering is not required next week," Ana said, "so I can go straight away."

"What about Eva's wagon, what does she have? Do you know?" Rob asked.

"She rang to say you had news of Yasmin she told me that filming was not going well and there will probably be an overrun. She was due to finish next Friday."

"Could Paula take Eva's place?" Rob asked. "If she could and Eva is willing she could go to London with you. You could look out for one another and she may well have some thoughts on where to look. After all you were both working together, she might remember something that you don't."

"Paula is capable enough for a simple job like that one. I'm sure Eva will help me," Ana replied.

"What about you Rob, didn't you say you've got three or four meetings lined up for next week?" Sue asked.

"One on Wednesday in London which I must attend. The other three are all stunt design meeting to agree with directors what stunts are required and cost them out, two in Bristol on Monday and one in Birmingham on Thursday. Joe Blunt's team were on the Cornwall shoot which Ana says is done so Joe can cover those, he's done a few in the past, he's well able to cover those. So apart from Wednesday I'm probably free."

"I'd be happier if Ryman goes with you. You could all stay at the flat, there's enough space for you all and I'd know where to find you, Sue said.

"Well, then I suggest we spend tomorrow getting organised and we travel down on Sunday. Ana you'll need to sort things out with Eva and the girls, I'll sort out Joe Blunt and Ryman. I'd like the four of us to meet tomorrow to discuss what we're going to do once we're down there."

"Thank you Rob and you Sue. You're good people," Ana stood ready to leave. "Shall we say 4:00 tomorrow afternoon?"

"4:00 is fine by me. Have a good evening, I'll see you tomorrow."

Sue saw Ana out of the door then rejoined her husband in the lounge.

"Rose says can you help your dad down the stairs, he says two days in bed looking at the same four walls is long enough, so he's coming down to eat dinner with us."

"I'll go up in a minute, I just want to make sure you're okay with this trip to London."

"You can't not help can you? I just wish I could come with you."

"Miss Crump, Miss Mills, that was an excellent piece of work from both of you. I'm pleased to tell you that MI-5 and Scottish Police now have all five of the locations under surveillance."

"That's good news, Sir Bernard, but a lot of the credit must go to D.S. Howard, we simply followed her plan."

"Yes, a sad end to a promising career. I know you had built a good relationship. I'm very sorry."

"Thank you."

"I hope the two of you made the most of the last three days because as of today I'm cancelling leave for all agents until further notice. I'm launching a joint offensive with Interpol against this

Russian mob," Sir Bernard explained. "Agent Mills, I want you to lead the team here in London, Agent Crump you are to assist Agent Mills, four other agents will be assigned to your team next week."

"Thank you again, sir?" Tracy said.

"Agent Mills I believe you are familiar with Miss Oxsana Kolanski and Miss Eva Andelova," Sir Bernard said.

"I know Ana and Eva, yes sir, they work for Robert Blackstock. I've met them several times," Tracy acknowledged.

"Are you aware of their background?"

"I understand they were Moscow students taken by the Maffia,, brought to Britain illegally and forced to work as erotic dancers by the London element of the Maffia. Robert Blackstock paid off the Russians and helped them to get legal papers then gave them jobs and a roof over their heads."

"I understand they worked in the sex trade for several years. During that time they must have become familiar with the Russian operation," Sir Bernard added. "I want the two of you to find out as much as you can about the Russians in London from these girls. Locations, numbers, anything that may be of use to you. This is only a reconnaissance mission, no one must suspect anything. Interpol have asked each country to wait until we are all ready then we will all strike together.

"Yes, sir, we understand, we'll get on it straight away."

"Let me know as soon as you get a plan together. Good hunting ladies."

"I've spoken with Ana on the phone." Rob told Sue. "Apparently Eva didn't go home last night, so Ana spent the evening making notes on places to look for Yasmin in. Eva got in at 10:30 and agreed with what we planned so Ana checked with Paula that she was okay driving out to the Dales and back each day. She's happy, so is Jules. Eva is now adding to Ana's notes.

I've since rung Ryman and he's okay, I actually think he'd like some time away from his parents.

"That's good darling," Sue replied. "While you've been in the office sorting all that out Tracy Mills rang the house phone."

"Oh yeah, what did she want?"

"She staying with her brother, Zoe's with her. They want to talk to us and Ana and Eva so I suggested 5:00 this afternoon, that gives you an hour with the girls to plan your trip to London."

"That's fine. I can't think why she wants to talk to the girls."

Sue had spread her set of drawings out over the kitchen table. "Rob ,be honest with me, do you think I'm crazy doing all of this after just six months in the business.?"

Rob looked down at the plans then at Sue. "I don't think you're mad. Brave to take all this on by yourself, but not crazy."

"Thanks darling."

"But I'm really the wrong person to ask about your layout here, I've only had an interest in horses since I moved up here after Jayne died and then only from a riding and management view point I've never been at the messy end of the business, I don't know what's good and what's bad in the design."

"I was thinking of asking a few people to help me out with things, not to ease the workload, but to reassure me that I'm doing the right thing"

"You mean like an advisory committee?"

"That's exactly what I mean. I was going to ask Tim, he's been at the messy end as you call it all his life, he knows what works and what doesn't. Plus he's got a lot of modern ideas. Also Trisha to watch the pennies and Ana for her tremendous artistic view on things. I want this building to be both practical and appealing. I was also going to ask Eric when he's better. He ran this yard for more than forty years, his experience would be very valuable."

"As usual you've thought things through and solved your problem. I think your advisory committee will work and you should go for it. How are you getting on finding a builder?"

"I've got a shortlist of four. They are all local, I think that's important and they are all large enough to do the job. I've researched each of them and I've got a list of recent work they have done and I'm planning on going out tomorrow to have a look at those, to get a feel for their work. Then on Monday I'll make contact with them invite them in to see the site and discuss the work, let them have copies of the plans and ask them to quote for the job."

"Have you looked at the work Tim's brother is having done?"

"Yes it's looking good. I was there yesterday dropping Luci off. The builders are Moss and Dixons of York, they are on my list, I've got the number of Will Moss who appears to be the key man.

I suppose I'd better clear these plans away, you'll be wanting some lunch.

"Yeta Gorkov and her ten year old son met her brother-in-law outside the Slug and Lettuce by Tower Bridge. Yeta had promised to take her son out for a pub lunch as a reward for his good school report and had invited Ivan along so they could discuss something that needed to be worked on.

They found a table near a window so that the boy could look out onto the street. A waitress came over and took their order and they talked while they waited for their food and drinks to arrive.

"What is it you want to discuss, Yeta?"

"Our revenge on Mr. Robert Blackstock. I want him to have his partner snatched away from him like Mikhail was snatched from me."

"I tried to run her down myself once but that was a hasty decision, chosen in a mood of anger and rage and was never going to work. I had someone try to poison her but they gave the wrong person the poison and almost killed a police officer. I've even had the building she was in blown up but somehow she escaped from the rubble unharmed. The woman has the luck of the devil."

"So you want me to kill her?"

"Yes. But first I want her taken prisoner and held for a few days so that we know we have the right person and Blackstock's heart can bleed in the uncertainty of not knowing if she is alive or dead."

"That sounds suitable. I'm sure we can find a satisfactory end for her."

Ana and Eva were the first to arrive, their little mini shooting gravel across the driveway from its undersized wheels. They went straight to Sue's office which Rob was borrowing for the meeting and were soon joined by Ryman who had walked up from the village and had a hint of real ale on his breath, Rob gave him a questioning look.

"It was my youngest, Kylie's birthday yesterday. She had a party with her mates yesterday afternoon and today we've had lunch in the pub, quite a treat for a twelve year old," Ryman explained.

Rob began. "Are we clear what we are doing this week? We start by finding where Yasmin is, then we plan how we communicate with her, then we work out how we rescue her."

"Ana, you have some thoughts as to where she might be?"

"Eva and I have made a list of places to go to, clubs where she may be working and flats where she may be living. We also have a list of girls who may know her, or know of her, who we would like to talk to. We will also speak to them to discover if anything has changed."

"Okay, are we all happy to leave at about 9:00 on Monday morning, that should give us plenty of time to get to the flat and be ready to go to the first club on Ana's list."

They all nodded.

"Right, 9:00 Monday in the pub car park with your best clubbing clothes. Ryman I'll let you get back to your children, but Ana and Eva I'd like you both to come up to the house with me, a couple of peopl want to speak with you. Don't worry, you've done nothing wrong they just want some information."

Rob and the girls entered the lounge to find Sue chatting with Tracy and Zoe.

"Ana and Eva, I think you've met Tracy Mills and Zoe Crump before?"

"I remember they stayed here one or two nights last year and Miss Tracy is Luci's boyfriend's aunt," Ana recounted.

"Tracy and Zoe are from MI-6, they have some questions they'd like to ask you," Rob said.

Tracy began and Zoe took notes. "I am heading a task force which is spread across Britain, France, Belgium, Holland, Denmark and Germany with a purpose to break and destroy the Russia Mafia's network for sex and drug trafficking. We know that you both were trapped in that network and are hoping you could tell us a little bit on how they operate, the most likely places we will find their leaders and perhaps offer some suggestions as to how we could best learn their plans."

"Hang on a minute, Tracy!" Rob interrupted. "Ana's sister is in the middle of all this crap. I'm taking Ana and Eva down to

London on Monday to try and find her, we may be able to help one another. These two girls know a lot of faces, they would greatly enhance your enquiries. Why don't we work together on this.

"That would put them at great risk and I can't ask them to do that. What if they are recognised? It could blow the whole operation." Tracy argued.

"There are only two people that we spent much time with and they are both dead," Ana said. "It is extremely unlikely that anyone would recognise us, especially without our stage makeup on. To most people all dancers look the same. They are looking at tits and arse not faces, and we're not going to show either of them."

"I'll have to clear it with my boss," Tracy said, "but I think he'll be happy. Now tell me what you are planning."

"Ana and Eva have a list of locations, we'll go to each one observing and looking for Ana's sister and looking for a way to get her out," Rob explained. "I was thinking we would go as two couples partying together. Ryman is coming with us. Ana says that they know a lot of the girls who will help her find Yasmin. I'm sure they would help you as well if it would result in their freedom. They are not there by choice after all."

"That could work well but I need my own people in there with you, so there will be three couples partying and you'll be wired up so that we can give you protection," Tracy insisted. I'll ring to get Sir Bernard's agreement in principle, then meet him Monday to walk him through the detail."

Chapter 15

"Sue, can I tell you something in confidence? You told me that you and Rob were married just a few days after you first met, you just knew it was the right thing to do. I'm thinking of renting a house down in the village and asking Jenny to move in with me. She's got a great new job, so we're both settled and perhaps it's time to begin the rest of our lives together. I'm going to ask her this evening."

****

"I'm not so impressed with this company's work." Sue had taken Rob with her to check out the work of the builders she had shortlisted.

"No," Sue answered. "The first two we saw weren't finished properties, there was still a lot of building work to be done, but the sites were tidy, all unused materials stacked neatly, and no rubbish. They both had oil drums that they burnt their rubbish in as they went, but this building here was finished three weeks ago. The building looks good but the site is a mess, broken bricks, empty cement bags, odd scraps of timber, part of a roll of roofing felt, old paint cans, all just left. I couldn't have a mess like this, we're a working yard, this rubbish would be a danger to the animals." She crossed him off her list.

"Who's next?"

"Moss and Dixon, they are the ones doing Tim's brother's work which I was quite impressed with. They are converting a Victorian warehouse into flats on the outskirts of York."

As they drove Sue said, "Do you remember the pilot who flew us down from Wick?"

"You mean the guy that used to work for dad twenty odd years ago?"

"That's the one. Do you remember him saying he wouldn't mind getting back into racing?"

"Now that you mention, it he did say something like that," Rob agreed.

"I'm thinking of seeing if he would be interested in the assistant manager role I'll need filled to manage the extra workload. What do you think?"

"We don't know much about him but dad thought enough of him twenty years ago to offer him the head lad job. You could do a lot worse."

Sue pulled the car into the side of the road. "This is the right address but apart from a skip and a builder's board, it doesn't look like a building site."

A young woman left the building and went to walk past Sue's car. Sue quickly jumped out and asked. "Excuse me, but I'm looking for a building around here that is being converted to flats."

"Yes, this one. The first three flats are occupied and the builder is working on the other three."

"And you live on the building site."

"Yes, but they are excellent. They even lay a carpet in the hallway to keep the floor clean."

"That must take them longer to do the work."

"I don't think so. They've only been here six weeks and I moved in to the first flat two weeks ago. They are saying another two weeks and they all be finished."

"Did you hear what that lady said, Rob?"

"I did. Fast, clean and top quality," Rob summarised.

"Let's hope he quotes a reasonable figure. Hopefully I can get three of them in at the end of the week. I've got a meeting with Prince Hassan Saleh Al Shammari at The Dorchester at 11:00 on Wednesday morning. I'm thinking it best if I come down on the train Tuesday evening, I should be there by the time you get back from whichever club you're going to be at. You can update me with everything over breakfast on Wednesday. What time is your meeting?"

"Provisionally booked for 11:00 at MGM's London office, it depends when they can get Daniel Craig to come in. Apparently they need some new shots for the opening scenes of 'No Time To Die', the latest Bond movie. They need to be scheduled very soon. It's holding up the production. The meeting is to discuss what's needed, who needs to be involved and estimate how long it will take. It could be a long meeting," Rob explained.

"My meeting is limited to an hour, I just hope I can impress the Prince and he places at least one of his horses with us. I'll catch the 1:30 train back to York."

"Hi Tracy, I've been waiting for you to call. We've been here since 12:45. Not much traffic for a Monday."

"Hi Rob. Zoe and I drove down yesterday afternoon to avoid the traffic and you tell me there was none. Just my luck. I've met with Sir Bernard and talked him through the details of the plan. Like me he wants my guys in there with you, so Zoe and Mark Trent will come to your flat at around 8:00 and fit you with a wire before you get a taxi to 'The White Lotus'. Myself and the rest of my team will be close on hand. Good luck."

"You heard that everyone?" Rob said. "We need to be dressed by 8:00, I guess with being wired and tested, it will be around 9:00 when we get to the club."

"That's a bit early Rob."Ana said. "Most punters go to these clubs after they have eaten, dancers won't be on stage before 10:30. New dancers are generally first up and will do a twenty minute turn. So can I suggest we time our arrival for around 10:20 so that we can get a large table with us all, well away from the stage. If Yasmin is one of the dancers and she recognises us we don't know what she'll do. So long as we stay out of the light from the stage she can't even see anyone's there."

"I'll ring Tracy back straight away. Thanks Ana."

"Mr. Lavrov says he wants eight more girls before the end of October so that they are introduced before the end of year holiday season begins," Yeta Gorkov said to her brother-in-law, as they walked the short distance betweeen The Red Dragon and Stunners.

"It takes time to find good girls who won't be missed until after we have sailed. If I keep taking them from the same place it would draw attention to my activities. This is more than just going to the shop for groceries, it takes patience and planning and as you know, I am the best in my field."

"Well Annika was struggling on stage last night. She looks the part but it's going to take several more nights before she's earning," Yeta said. "So can you deliver eight more girls in ten weeks time?"

"Of course. I will rejoin my ship in ten days when it is in Liverpool. It is in Belfast at the moment having some modifications made. We've lost too many girls keeping them locked up in a container on the deck. Sickness spreads too easily so we are building a cell in the hold large enough to transport ten girls with beds for all, a toilet, a washbasin and most of all, fresh air continuously pumped through."

"That must be costing you a lot of money."

"It's an investment."

"How will you explain the cell if the ship is searched at any time by the authorities?"

"It will be hidden behind a false bulkhead and it's soundproofed."

As Yeta opened the back door to 'Stunners Club' she said, "so we only have ten days to capture the Blackstock woman."

"Zoe come on in. Mark, glad to see you again come in, take a seat, we've got twenty minutes before the taxi is due," Rob ushered the two agents through to the lounge and introduced them. "Mark Trent this is Ana, Eva and Ryman."

Zoe pulled a small box from her bag. I want you each to place one of these buds in your left ear. It's a two way communications device, virtually invisible and completely undetectable."

Zoe passed the box around.

"Tracy, they are all installed, can we test please?" She said to no one in the room, but Tracy and her team outside clearly heard what she said. "Rob can you say your name in a soft voice please?"

"Rob."

"Hi Rob, this is Tracy can you hear me?"

"Good and clear."

"Thanks Rob. Can the next one give me their name"

When the other three had completed their testing, Zoe gave Rob an envelope. "This is from Sir Bernard."

Rob ripped open the envelop to find an American Express card inside. It showed considerable signs of wear and had the name Robert Black on it. "Don't be fooled by the appearance, it is a new card. We felt Blackstock was not a common name so just in case the card gets closely inspected and your name is recognised, we've changed it."

"Are you all members, sir?" the doorman at the 'White Lotus' asked.

"No none of us are,," Rob replied.

"Then your drinks will cost you £12 each sir, we don't have an entry fee."

"What if we don't have a drink?"

"We do have an exit fee for non drinkers of £60, sir. And we know who's not had a drink," the doorman said in a threatening manner then stepped aside to let them pass.

Inside they were met by an olive skinned girl with jet black hair. "Good evening. Are you all together?" she asked.

"We are," Rob answered.

"Table for six. Near the stage?" she queried.

"No, no, one at the back please."

"Yes sir, please follow me."

She led them past the empty stage and out of the circle of light that bathed the stage waiting to welcome the first girls. When they were all seated she said, "my name is Sara, I am your hostess for tonight. I can get you anything you might like, anything." Her eyes sparkled as she said it. "When you want something just lift this marker." She reached across the table and demonstrated how it worked. "What can I get you all to drink?"

The first pair of dancers came on stage just as the drinks arrived and Rob showed his American Express card. "That's £72, sir," she said and pushed Rob's card into the machine she had clipped to her waistband. Rob entered his pin, the machine did it's job and Sara gave Rob back his card.

"£72 for six drinks, you'd have to be rich to get drunk in here," Ryman said.

"And no receipt given, I hope Sir Bernard is okay with that," Rob added.

Ana and Eva studied the two girls on stage and told Rob that the one on the left was very new, this may even be her first night, she looked nervous, not relaxed at all, but it wasn't Yasmin. At the end of their performance the two now naked girls, crossed to the centre of the stage and accepted mild applause from a growing audience, then left from the back of the stage.

"I was expecting a little more than a couple of stripper," Ryman commented.

"That was just the warm up act," Zoe told him. "This place has quite a reputation, it's been raided twice this year."

"I hope it's not the third time tonight," Ryman responded.

"Sir Bernard will have warned the Met that we are active so don't worry about that,," Zoe reassured him.

There was an interval of about ten minutes before the next dancers came out onto the stage. By the noise from the audience these were two well liked girls and Rob didn't need Ana's shake of the head to tell him neither of these was Yasmin.

"We had better have another drink, so at least we appear to be genuine and we also need a bit of conversation and laughter, we're supposed to be friends," Rob said and raised the marker.

Sara immediately appeared at their table. "Same again please Sara," Rob said.

"Can I get you anything else?" Sara said looking from Rob to the stage then back to Rob.

"Not at the moment thanks,," Rob declined.

Both girls were now naked and coming down into the audience letting both men and women touch their bodies. After a few minutes the two dancers came together at the same table near the stage and each held out a hand to a couple in their thirties and led them through a side door.

"How long do we have to stay Ana?" Rob whispered to the young Russian sitting next to him.

"We should be alright to leave after 12:30 without looking suspicious. It's a time when a lot of people leave, I guess it's because they have work the next day. Fridays and Saturdays are different,," Ana reasoned.

They sat through four more dancers before they left, two of the them Eva thought she recognised, but after talking to Ana, agreed that they weren't who she thought they were. They followed three other couples out of the club at 12:30.

"You've reached the phone of Ian McMillan. I can't answer your call at the moment, either leave your message or your name and number and I'll get back to you as soon as I can".

"Ian, this is Sue Blackstock. You flew myself and my husband from Wick to Leeds-Bradford ten days ago. If you were serious about wanting to get back into racing, I have something that might be of interest."

As soon as she ended the call her phone started to ring, caller ID said 'UNKNOWN'.

"Blackstock Racing, Sue speaking, How can I help you."

"Mrs. Blackstock, it's Ian MacMillan, I'm sorry I missed your call but I was outside and by the time I got to the phone it had gone to answerphone."

"But I rang your office," Sue said

"I can only afford a part time secretary and when she's not in the office all calls get diverted to my home number. I'm interested in hearing more and would like to know what you have in mind."

"I'm expanding the stables and I'm looking for someone to run the yard on a day to day basis. I'm adding significantly more capacity by adding new loose boxes and modernising the current ones. I'm also raising our standards by bringing in new high profile owners. I'm talking to Prince Hassan Saleh Al Shammari of the Emirates tomorrow. I'm offering you a chance to interview for the position of Joint Assistant Manager."

"I'm certainly interested. When would you want to interview?"

"The sooner the better really. Are you free anytime next week."

"I've got charters at the beginning of the week but I could be with you on Friday. Is that any good?"

"Friday will do fine, shall we say 10:00?"

"Is the field behind the stable still flat and level grazing?"

"It is."

"Well in that case 10:00 Friday will be fine. I'll fly down and land in that field, if that's okay?"

"Yes of course, I'll give instructions that no animals are to be out there."

"I'll see you next Friday."

"Good evening Rob, Zoe's coming down with a cold so I'm taking her place tonight. I know I'm a bit older than the other two girls, I thought I could team up with you or Ryman. It would look a bit odd a forty year old woman with a twenty five year old partner in one of those clubs. "

"Not totally unheard of but it would certainly draw attention to us," Eva said.

"So we're at the 'Tower Club' tonight, are we? Is the plan the same as last night?" Ryman enquired.

"If we can we'll do exactly the same. It worked well last night so no reason why it shouldn't work every night."

Sue had gone to bed and was well asleep when Rob and the others got home. It had been a far more successful night as Ana and Eva saw two girls that they had known. On the way back to the flat they discussed the best way to get to talk to them and agreed that Ana and Eva, with Ryman for security, should spend the day in the streets around the club.They remembered several places that the girls used to hang out at before rehearsals.

The morning was quite a rush for Sue and Rob, they both had 11:00 meetings across London and needed to be ready to leave at around 10:00, as neither could afford to be late. The others wanted to be back in the area of Stunners night club before noon, but as their timing was not as critical they had kept out of the way until Sue and Rob left.

So as not to draw attention to themselves, Ryman took a separate taxi to the street where they had agreed to start their search. Ana and Eva had walked off about fifty yards down the street by the time Ryman arrived and he started to follow them maintaining the gap. Ana and Eva didn't make it easy for him, they were in and out of the little shops and each time Ryman had to have a reason why he stopped and waited for them to reappear. At the first two shops he just leant against the shop wall and pretended to be using his phone. At the third, he walked past the shop and bought a newspaper from a street vendor and browsed the headlines, until the girls came out and walked past him again.

After several more shops he watched them go into Starbucks, he followed them, ordered his coffee then went and sat at a table near the door. From there he could see most of the shop.

"Oxsana, is it really you?" a squeaky voice said.

Ana looked up from her coffee and a smile came over her face when she saw a friendly smile on a young woman stood at their table. "Rosie. You're still working for a living then?"

"Its alright for you, two ain't it? Luck of the devil I say you have, finding a rich man who likes you so much he buys your ticket from the Russians."

"It wasn't like that Rosie. Go and get a coffee and come and sit with us so we can tell you the real story."

Rosie did as Ana had suggested and sat and listened to Ana and Eva's story.

"I still say you were lucky," Rosie said. "I thought you were back on the game one day last week. I had to run an errand for Tony, my boss. Some papers had to go up the to big boys over at 'The Four Aces'."

"That was Mikhail Gorkov's club," Ana said.

"Now it's Dmitry Lavrov running the show and he's a real hard case. Anyway, I thought you were on the stage, but I was told she was a new girl about to start working. She looked exactly like you, perhaps an inch or two shorter, she could be your sister."

Eva jumped in to prevent Ana giving their true intentions away.

"Is Yeta Gorkov still running the girls at 'The Four Aces' and running the training?"

"No. When Mikhail disappeared a new witch came in, Mrs. Chow. I'm being kind calling her a witch. She watches us like hawks and any slip we make cost us in our pockets. So although it would be nice to stop and chat, she'll know how long I was in 'The Four Aces' to make the delivery. If I take too long getting my coffee she'd know I'd met someone and had been talking. It will end with me being fined."

"We can't let that happen,, but it's been good to see you again." Eva watched Rosie leave then turned to Ana who was staring into space. "Ana, it must be Yasmin. We've found her."

"Perhaps, but how can we get to talk to her? How do we get her out? If this Mrs. Chow is as bad as Rosie says, we don't have a hope," Ana said.

Ryman could see something was wrong but stayed with his coffee until the girls left. He left his table in time to see them climb into a black taxi then hailed one for himself.

"We need to know where she is, Ivan? We know she has a house in Twickenham but she's not been there in months. Robert Blackstock owns a large apartment but she would probably not be alone. If she's home in Yorkshire she certainly won't be alone." Yeta sounded frustrated.

"Why not ring her office and ask to speak to her," Ivan suggested. "You could say you are a reporter doing a profile series on successful women and you'd like to interview her for the series. What woman can reject an ego boost like that?"

"You do have a brain then," Yeta mocked him.

"You could ask to meet her somewhere in York and we grab her in the car park," Ivan added.

"Do you know their office number?" She asked.

"No, but an outfit like that must have a website." Ivan took out his phone and tapped a few buttons. Within a couple of minute he was reading out a number and Yeta was typing it into her phone.

"Blackstock Racing, Terry speaking, how may I help you?"

"Good morning, can I speak to Susan Blackstock, please?"

"Sorry miss, she's in London this morning. Coming back by train this afternoon. She should be back here around 4:00. You can try her then or maybe I can help, Terry Martin Head Lad."

"No I have to speak to Susan. I'll try later. Thank you anyway." She ended the call and turned to Ivan who was doing something on his phone.

"The stables are thirty minutes drive from York railway station. The only train from London any time close to 15:30 is the 13:30 from King's Cross. If we get on that train, we can take her while she's on her own."

"That's a wonderful plan Ivan. We need to get a move on, we've got just ninety minutes to get to King's Cross and get tickets. We'll also need drugs to control her."

"Call a cab, then as we go you call someone for the drugs. Get them to meet us at King's Cross 13:20 at latest, I'll get our tickets online. I suggest we also get someone with a car to meet the train in York and we'll get her back to London as soon as possible."

"I also need to get someone to look after my son for a few days."

Sue's meeting went as well as she could have hoped. The Prince wanted one of his horses placed with Blackstock Racing, but only if it could be housed by 23rd December at the latest. If that proved successful he would place nine more by end of June. If she didn't meet his December deadline, then all ten horses would go elsewhere. He made it totally clear that Sue was his wife choice, trying to get him to treat men and women as equals. "She is the president of the Woman's Rights Campaign in the Emirates," he had told Sue. "A hard lady to ignore."

He smiled and left their meeting. Sue checked her watch. She had been only twenty minutes putting in place a deal that could change her whole life. All she had to do was to get a builder who could deliver on time, to a standard fit for a prince. That was an issue for the next two days,, but for now what she needed was a strong drink and something to eat.

She headed for the 'Bar and Block' just down the road from King's Cross station. She'd been there a couple of times before, so knew she could get a glass of decent red wine and a sandwich. Her hands were shaking as she piled her papers into her briefcase, went out to the street and looked for a taxi. Unusually there were none about. Another look at her watch told her she had over two hours before her train, so she decided to walk. It was about two miles, she'd easily do that in an hour, still leaving plenty of time for a visit to the pub. She could buy her ticket online, first class she thought, then all she had to do at half past one was cross the road and get on her train. Walking calmed her and she soon stopped shaking, she didn't normally get nervous but there again she'd never met a prince before. God what would she be like when she met the Queen?

Sue finished her meal and still had twenty minutes to spare, so she decided to cross the road, stop off and pick up a copy of Racing Post to read on the way home and find what platform she needed. If the train was in she could at least be finding a seat and sitting down, rather than wandering aimlessly.

As she entered the station she passed two men and a woman outside the entrance having quite an argument. The woman was ordering one of the men to do something he didn't want to do, but they were speaking in Russian which although Sue could speak a little she couldn't hear what they were saying clearly enough to follow what they were arguing about.

"Viktor said nothing about me driving to York, only for me to deliver the package." One of the men said. The other looked up at Sue as she walked by, took out his phone and pressed a couple of buttons and said, "that's her. Look." He showed a picture of Sue on the tiny screen.

"Follow her Ivan. Find out where she sits," Yeta said, "and you Boris get back to Victor and tell him that if he doesn't get me a car in York by 6:00 I'll have his balls."

The train was at platform three and as soon as she found a seat,, Sue sent a message to Rob to say her meeting had been a success and asked him how his own meeting had gone. She placed her phone on the table in front of her. There was only one other person in the carriage and as the train pulled off she put her head back and closed her eyes.

She slept for a good hour and a half and when she woke she saw a woman standing in front of her who asked, "are you Susan Blackstock, the race Horse trainer?"

Sue, flattered that someone had recognised her said, "I am."

The next thing she knew, a hand had reached over from behind her and a hand holding a cloth of some sort was pressing against her nose and mouth. She tried to resist but was quickly overcome by whatever was on the cloth.

"Right get the Rohypnol into her before this stuff wears off," Yeta told Ivan.

When they reached York, Sue was totally under the influence of the drug, just about able to walk but unable to resist.

"Get her phone Ivan!" Yeta said.

"No," he replied, "It could be used to find us. I'll tuck it down the side of the seat where no one will see it and then they can track it all they want."

The two Russians helped Sue off the train, out of the station and onto a bench outside the main entrance. Yeta rang Viktor. "Victor, have you sorted a car out for me."

A voice replied "It was on its way before you had a go at young Boris. It's only about 10 minutes away. A silver Audi S4."

It was gone 6:00 when Rob got back to the flat. He had read Sue's message in the taxi and responded with a summary of the outcome of his meeting which had concluded they needed two short clips, no more than two minutes of fast action,, hopefully all filmed in one day, would be sufficient and the 19th August was booked.

As he entered the lounge he saw Eva and Ana sitting solemnly on the sofa browsing magazines and Ryman was in the kitchen preparing a light meal for all of them.

"We've found her Rob, we've found Yasmin! She's at the 'Four Aces'." Eva told him. "We've told Tracy, she'll be here soon to discuss things.

"What's wrong with Ana?" Rob asked Eva.

Eva explained what Rosie had told them about Mrs. Chow and that Ana was sure there was no way she could be rescued.

"I'm sure Tracy will have a solution when she gets here," Rob said.

"Anyone ready to eat?" Ryman called from the kitchen. "I've made tacos for everyone, come and get i!"

"So we're going to the 'Four Aces' tonight, are we?" Rob asked.

"If Tracy is okay with that,". Eva said.

"We'll soon know," Rob said. "I think that's her coming in now."

"Good evening everyone, sorry I'm a little later than I expected. I've had a busy afternoon,," Tracy said as she entered the lounge and sat on the sofa next to Eva.

"After you contacted me this afternoon, Eva I rang Sir Bernard. He was pleased to learn the identity of the new mafia boss here in Britain and that you have confirmed that the 'Four Aces'' is still their headquarters. Although MI-5 have the place watched twenty four seven they had not seen anything to suggest it still was the case. Sir Bernard has authorised a police raid on the 'Four Aces' tonight. He wants the four of you to go there with the same plan as the last two nights. Zoe, Mark and the rest of my team will be part of the force conducting the raid. It is to appear to all that this is just a standard raid looking for drugs and illegal workers. Of course we won't find any, we never do and we do this two or three times a year. However my team will be learning what they can about the building and the people, for when we go on the offensive against the Russians."

"What time will the raid happen?" Rob asked.

"That depends on you four," Tracy answered. "This raid will allow us the opportunity to look closely behind the locked doors of the club. But Sir Bernard is also giving you the chance to get Ana's sister out. This evening you are to take a table nearer to the stage and as close to the main door as you can get. Ana you must have your back to the stage so that Yasmin doesn't recognise you. When Yasmin comes out onto the stage you dial my phone number, Rob. That will be my signal to trigger the raid. Ten minutes later we will enter the club. As the chaos builds you are going to have to act very fast and grab Yasmin off the stage, before the minders take her off the back of the stage. Zoe and Mark will be there to arrest you. You will be bundled into a police van and taken to the station with several others. Rob and Ryman will be released. Ana, Eva and Yasmin will be taken to MI-6."

"It's a simple plan that may well work." Rob said.

"What will happen to Yasmin?" Ana asked. "The Russians will grab her back as soon as MI-6 release her."

"She won't be released. She will die in custody," Ana was rocked by Tracy's reply. "At least that's the story that will be given to the club. In reality she will be smuggled to RAF Northolt and flown across the Atlantic. Sir Bernard asks that you, Rob take her into one of your stunt crews to hide her until it's safe for her to return."

"I can certainly arrange that," Rob said.

Ana was sobbing. "Why is everyone being so nice?"

"Because we are grateful for your help this week, in just three nights you will have helped us learn more about the Russians than we would have found out in three weeks without you," Tracy responded. "Is that Ryman's cooking I smell?"

"Tacos." Ryman announced. "There's some left if you're hungry."

"What's wrong, Rob?" Tracy asked as he put his phone into his pocket."

"Sue isn't answering her phone and she's not at home. They expected her at 4:00 and not heard anything from her. I'm sure she's okay, I'm just puzzled as to where she is and what she's doing."

Chapter 16

"Let the police keep her. It's a shame because she showed great promise and would have made us a lot of money but I've already spent out a lot to get her here. I'm not going to pay out another rouble to get rid of her body. No, we leave her to rot where she lies."

****

"That's him just coming into the car park," Yeta called. "Get the bitch on her feet, get her in the backseat as quickly as you can and don't leave her briefcase behind."

"Do you have any idea where we're going to take her?" Ivan asked.

"Well, definitely not York or London. She could be recognised in either of those," Yeta replied. "We've got houses in Manchester and Glasgow, so we'll go to one of them."

"I know the one in Manchester, it's near the docks, I've used it a few times over the years. It's quite spacious and not overlooked and it's nearer than Glasgow. We could be there in less than two hours."

"Okay, Manchester it is then. Now get her in the back quickly before anyone comes to see what we're doing. Viktor's driver will have to make his own way back to London."

"I wonder what has happened to Sue?" Luci said.

"It's not like her to not be back when she says, or at least let us know her plans have changed," Rose added.

There was a knock on the back door. "I'll get it." Luci called as she left the lounge.

"Terry. Is there a problem down at the yard?"

"No Miss, everything there is fine. Is the Boss in, I'd like a word with her if I may."

"Sorry Terry, she's not home yet."

"Well, when she does get home, can you give her a message?"

"Certainly."

"Can you tell her that she had a call this morning from a lady reporter, foreign sounding, like Miss Ana and Miss Eva. This reporter said she was writing a series on successful women. I told her Miss Susan wouldn't be back until 4:00 and she said she would ring back after that. Well she never did and I thought Miss Susan should know because she's very busy the rest of this week interviewing builders. I thought it best to prepare her for this reporter."

"Thanks Terry. I'll tell her. Good night."

"How long before you need to give her more Rohypnol?" Yeta asked Ivan.

"We should go easy on that stuff. All we need to do is tie her up and gag her. The house is just down there," he said pointing down a street lined on both sides with parked cars. "You're looking for number fifteen."

"Where will we find the key?"

"It's in a lockbox by the door. The code is nine seven four two. I'll help you get her inside and tied up, then I'll nip to the shop and get some supplies. Have you given any thought as to what you're going to do with he?"

"You said you were leaving next Friday."

"That's right, but not until the evening."

"So we keep her on ice until Friday, then finish her. It must be done so that no one can tie anything back to us, but in a way that maximises the pain for Roger Blackstock. We'll start now, take a picture of her tied up, email it to Viktor and tell him to get it printed and in the post to Mr Blackstock. It will drive him mad not knowing who's got her or where she is. The postmark will be London so that won't be of any use to him either.

"Are you four ready?" Tracy asked then stood to leave. "Are you sure you're okay with this Ana? We don't have to do it if you don't want to."

"We have no choice, we must get her out as soon as we can."

"Good girl, don't forget, sit with your back to the stage and don't turn round. It might be best if you and Eva distract the minder and let the men get Yasmin. Okay folks lets go."

"Table for four is it sir?" They were greeted by a young blonde dressed in a short tee-shirt that didn't quite cover her breasts, brief skintight lycra shorts, fishnet tights and basket woven shoes with four inch heels all in emerald green. Rob scanned the club and saw other girls dressed exactly the same but in different colours, he saw royal blue, purple, yellow and orange.

"That table there will do us fine, if it's free." Rob pointed to the closest table to the entrance and next to the side of the stage. He had noticed on the two previous nights at the other clubs, that tables in similar positions were among the last to be taken.

"Certainly sir," she said. "Are you members sir?"

"Not yet," Rob replied. "In that case I must take from you £35 entrance each. Should you choose to join tonight your £35 will be deducted from your membership fee which is £350 per person, per year or £600 per couple per year."

"Four entrances then, please." He handed her his American Express card and she pushed it into her reader then held it for Rob to enter his pin.

"My name is Christina and I'll be your hostess this evening. Can I get you all a drink?"

"The usuals?" Rob asked looking at the other three. They all nodded. "Two Screwdrivers a Mojito and a rum punch please."

The drinks arrived and Rob used his card again. "Sir Bernard will get quite a shock when he gets the bill. Have a drink Ana, it will help your nerves and don't worry it will all be over soon and she'll be away and safe."

The club was filling quite quickly. Rob looked around and saw that the place was now about three quarters full. The tone of the music changed to a rhythmic dance tune, drawing Rob's attention to the stage and he watched the curtains at the rear slowly draw apart, to reveal two heavily made up young women in slender long evening dresses. They slowly walked to the front of the stage stepping to the rhythm of the music. Rob had no trouble at all identifying Yasmin. He was sitting opposite Ana and Yasmin was just behind her. The resemblance to Ana was uncanny, almost identical twins except Yasmin was three years younger and four inches shorter.

Rob had already brought up Tracy's number on his phone, so he carefully pulled the phone from his pocket and pressed the green button with the phone still out of sight on his lap. He glance down and saw the status of the call change. He pressed the red button and returned the phone to his pocket, then picked up his drink, finished it then leant back in his seat looking as though he was ready to enjoy the show.

The two girls were gently swaying to the music and making suggestive movement to the audience, earning them warm applause. The applause increased as they unfastened the halter tie of their dresses and allowed them to fall to the floor, leaving them in their lingerie. Their act now swapped them over, meaning that Yasmin was on the far side of the stage. It would be more difficult to extract her from there, but fortunately after just a few more bars of music they swapped again.

There was a loud noise the other side of the door behind Rob and he heard someone shout something. People looked around at the door with uncertain looks spreading across their faces. Someone shouted, "It's a raid!" Panic was setting in but the team were already in action. Ana and Eva made straight for the minder and in Russian started screaming at him to help them and to hide them. At the same time Rob and Ryman leapt onto the stage. Rob picked up Yasmin's discarded dress and threw it around her shoulders and the two men dragged her off the stage.

Armed police officers had now entered the room and were sweeping across the floor. Then Rob saw Zoe and Mark come through the door with two uniformed officers and immediately grabbed Rob, Ryman and Yasmin as they were the ones closest to the incoming forces. The minder had broken free from Ana and Eva and escaped across the stage. Zoe grabbed both girls by the hair and marched them out.

Outside Tracy was directing the operation. She gave Rob a nod before saying, "Get them into a van and get them down to the station for questioning."

By now there were a large number of customers and staff gathered outside and they witnessed Rob and the other four roughly manhandled into the back of a police van and driven off, followed by several other vans."

"Still no word from Sue?" Eric asked

"Not a word. It's so unlike her. Something must have happened." Rose said. "It's a bit early yet but I'll ring Rob later and see if he's heard anything."

The back door opened and Tim poked his head in.

"Is Sue up yet?"

"She's not here Tim. We don't know where she is," Rose told him. "No one has heard from her. I'm beginning to worry that something might have happened to her."

"I'm sure she's fine. We've got builders coming today and tomorrow to look at the extension. She asked me to help her with the meetings. We were supposed to discuss it yesterday when she got back. Obviously we didn't, so I thought we could do it this morning."

"What do you think we should do about the builders Tim?" Eric asked. "Should we cancel?"

"I don't think we should do that Eric. Sue is desperate to get this work done, she wouldn't want anything to delay it," Tim responded. "You've seen the plans, haven't you Eric and she's talked you through them. Do you think you and I could handle this? Sue has left copies of the plans in the office."

"No Eric," Rose interrupted. "You're still not fit enough to go charging around the yard."

"What if I do all the charging around and Eric sits in the office to answer questions," Tim suggested.

"Just so long as he doesn't get too tired or too stressed."

Rob rang home as soon as he thought someone would be up. He had already tried Sue's phone but got no answer.

"Hi Mum, have you heard from her?"

"No dear, and I'm guessing you haven't either," Rose said.

"I just don't understand it. When she sent me a message she was already on the train sitting in first class. That was at 1:30, twenty hours ago. I'm going to speak to Tracy and get her advice on what we should do."

"Can she help?" Rose asked.

"She's very busy at the moment but I can ask her advice and find out who I should get involved from the Yorkshire police," Rob explained. "There is some good news. We found Ana's sister and got her out. She's going to America until things sort themselves out.

You know I can't talk about things too much but we're all okay and we'll all be coming home on Friday."

Rob could hear someone moving about in the kitchen. He checked the time, 7:37. It had to be Ryman. They had left Ana with Yasmin at the MI-6 offices and Eva was never the first up. If Ryman was in the kitchen then that meant coffee would be available and Rob needed one. He quickly pulled on shorts and a tee shirt then headed for the kitchen.

"Good morning, boss." Ryman always appeared happy and cheerful first thing in the morning.

"You'll be wanting a coffee then, boss."

"Yes please."

"Miss Eva left about forty five minutes ago, sir."

Rob gave Ryman a quizzical look.

"With a bag full of clothes for Miss Ana and her sister. Have you heard anything from Miss Susan yet, sir?"

"No I haven't, neither has anyone at home. I have to say I'm beginning to get more than a little bit worried about her."

Rob could hear his phone ringing in the bedroom and ran to answer it, hoping it would be Sue. But it wasn't.

"Is that Mr. Robert Blackstock?" a voice asked.

"It is."

"Sorry to call you so early sir. I'm Sir Bernard Howe's secretary. Sir Bernard has asked me to invite you to a meeting in his office at 9:00 this morning."

"Thank you. Tell Sir Bernard I'll be there."

"Sir Bernard wants me in his office for 9:00 so I'm going to have a quick shower, get some clothes on and get off. So you'll be on your own."

"That's okay sir, I'll give the kitchen a thorough clean and we're almost out of one or two things, so I'll wander down to the shop later and pick up what we need"

"Well don't plan anything for dinner. I'm going to take you all out for an American treat at Justin's favouite restaurant, to celebrate our rescue mission success."

"Who are you? What do you want? Why have you got me all tied up like this?" Sue was struggling against the cable tie that bound her hands together.

172

"You have too many questions," Yeta responded. "Do you want breakfast?"

Sue nodded.

"Then be quiet and you may get something," Yeta said. "But if you persist in making noises we will have to gag you. You don't want that do you?"

Sue relaxed a little and leant back against the wall. She was sitting on a mattress on the floor where she had tried to sleep last night. The Rohypnol had worn off and left her with a painful headache. "I need a toilet, a shower and some fresh clothes."

"The toilet we can do now, before breakfast. The shower we do later."

Sue struggled to her feet. Her wrists were held tight together with cable ties and her ankles were manacled so that her feet were about nine inches apart enabling her to shuffle along to the bathroom, next to the room she was being held in. There was no window in the bathroom and apart from a bath, wash basin and toilet that didn't have a seat, there was just a toilet roll on the floor. At least she was given some privacy.

She was taken back to her room where her breakfast was on the floor next to the mattress. A bowl of what looked like porridge and two slices of dry toast. She was too hungry to reject it, although it was tasteless, it satisfied her hunger.

"When do I get a shower?"

"No shower, only bath."

"A bath will have to do. When?"

"I have sent Ivan to get you fresh clothes and soap to wash with. When he returns you may bathe but not alone. I must be there with you to make sure you don't do anything silly."

"Thank you all for coming, I appreciate it's early and you all had a busy evening, but we must discuss what's to be done with Miss Kolanski," Sir Bernard began.

"The Russians have cooperated and delivered papers for all the girls we arrested last night. Your sister's papers are here, they are excellent forgeries. I guess we shouldn't be surprised at that, but we will replace them with genuine papers and she will be a British citizen.

"Won't the Russians be expecting her to be released this morning?" Rob queried.

"They will, but we will say she died in custody and the body can't be released until the coroner signs off on the cause of death and there's an inquiry. It could take weeks."

"By which time, we will have taken them down," Tracy commented.

"That's right. In the meantime we have to get her somewhere safe," Sir Bernard continued. "At precisely 12:00 today she will be a passenger in a modified F-35 jet flying out of Northolt to Edwards Air Force Base, two hours drive north of Los Angeles. That's as far as the plan goes."

"So you want Blackstock Stunt to take her from there and hide her for a couple of months," Rob added.

"I'll give you a number for your man to ring at Edwards Base, he can sort out details with Major Eugene Phillips."

"It's still middle of the night in LA. I'll ring my manager out there, Chuck Tanner, at a more reasonable time,"

"Good morning, I'm Reg Blake, Blake and Sons Builders. Here for a 10:00 meeting with Mrs. Blackstock."

"Good morning Mr Blake, Mrs Blackstock is unavailable this morning so your meeting will be with me. Tim Mills Assistant Manager and this is Eric Blackstock former owner and Mrs Blackstock's advisor. Take a seat please Mr Blake."

"Mrs Blackstock said you're wanting two new buildings and the refurbishment of some existing buildings," Blake said.

"Yes Mr. Blake, here is a copy of the plans, the planning permission and an artist's impression of the finished building," Tim said and handed the copy to Blake who immediately opened them up and read the technical specification.

"I'll be totally honest with you, there are one or two items in the material that we've never worked with, I doubt anyone in the country has, so I've got no idea how it will handle." Blake sounded a little uncertain and Tim got the impression that Blake was looking for something to blame if he should miss the proposed completion date.

"Did Mrs. Blackstock explain what she would be expecting from you?" Ian asked. "This is a working stable with certain strict timings that have to be maintained and the work on the extensions must not interrupt that routine.

"She did," he said. "She wants two quotes. One for the two new builds and a separate one for the refurbishment. She'd also like a plan of approach, plus proposed start and guaranteed completion date."

"Exactly. Do you have any questions?" Tim asked.

"I do have a couple. Where will my site access be?"

Eric answered. "We own the field next to the stables, you would just need to pull down a section of the hedge."

"I'll need to have a look at that. How old is the building you want renovated?"

Eric answered again. "There has been a stable block here since the 1850s. The current building was erected in 1911 after a fire destroyed the previous block."

"That means the base is possibly the original and may need replacing. A building that old possibly doesn't have an effective damp proofing layer. That may also need to be replaced. Finally what materials are the internal walls made of?"

"That one I can't answer. I've got no idea," Eric admitted.

"All I can say is the walls are very hard they take a lot of drilling," Ian added

"That may be a serious issue. I'm ready to see the site now, if I may."

Eric walked back to the house and Tim took the builder around the property, showed him where site access could be pushed through. They spent a long time in the old stable block and throughout the tour, Tim continued to get the feeling that Blake was compiling a list of excuses for failure.

When Blake left, Tim went to the house to speak to Eric.

"Well what did you make of Mr. Blake then Eric?"

"If he's the best out there, poor Sue."

"There was something about him that didn't feel right, almost as if he didn't want the job," Tim explained.

"I got the impression the pressure to deliver in a defined timescale is a big worry to him. Perhaps even the job itself is out of his league."

"Are you fit to sit in on the next one at 2:00?"

"See you at 2:00."

"Can you spare me a minute before you dash off please, Tracy?" Rob said the moment Sir Bernard had left.

"Sure Rob. What's the problem, you look worried?"

"I am worried. Sue is missing."

"What do you mean, Sue is missing?"

"She was on the 1:30 from Kings Cross. She sent me a message at 1:40 and no one has seen or heard from her since."

"Well, the police won't be interested until she's been missing 48 hours, but there are some things you can do.

You can use the 'Find My Phone' app on your phone to trace her phone in the hope she's still got it with her. Did she drive herself to York on Tuesday and if she did, is her car still in the car park? Get several copies made of a recent good quality photo of her."

"I can do all that."

"That's good. Then tomorrow lunch time, you ring York police station and ask to speak to D.S. Mike Stevens. Tell him I told you to ask for him. Better say Tracy Longhorn he'll know me by my married name. Tell him everything you know. He's a good detective, I'm sure he'll find her."

"Thanks Tracy. See you again soon."

"It was very nice to have met you Yasmin, I hope you have a good flight."

"I thank you, Mr. Blackstock. My sister tells me you rescue me and you rescue her too and now you help me stay free. I must go now but I will return one day soon."

"Come now Ana, we must let Yasmin get ready to go." The sisters kissed and said their goodbyes. Then Rob and Ana collected Eva and they hailed a taxi to take them back to the flat.

When they were all back together in the flat Rob said, "I think we've had an extremely tiring week and we need to get home. So I suggest we go now rather than tomorrow as we had planned." Everyone agreed with him and they set off half an hour later.

Ivan had gone out after putting Sue's breakfast in her room and didn't return to the house until lunch time. He brought back with him packs of sandwiches, cans of coke and bottles of water for lunch and three microwave meals for dinner. He had also bought a cheap pair of track pants, matching jacket and a pack of medium size tee-shirts as a change of clothes for Sue.

"Has she given you any trouble at all Yeta?"

"She hasn't tried to escape if that's what you mean. She's actually been very quiet. What have you been buying? You were gone a lot longer than I expected."

"I got some stuff for her to wear, some sandwiches for lunch and food for later, so I don't have to go out again today. The less we're seen going in and out the better. I'll take these up to her," he said picking up a pack of sandwiches and a bottle of water.

When he returned he had a frown on his face. "When did you last check in on her?"

"She's been quiet, so I left her."

"She was quiet because she's been working on her bindings. She'd almost bitten through the cable tie round her wrists. I've replaced them now with some heavy duty ones that she won't chew through."

"How is she going to change her clothes with her hands and feet bound?"

"We take them off, but never free hands and feet at the same time and only when we are both about. We don't leave her on her own when either tie is off. You've never done this sort of thing before have you?"

"Held someone prisoner? No, this a first but I'm a quick learner. You're saying she can't take a shower or a bath."

"She can. We free her legs then we refit the manacle again, once she has stripped from the waist down. Only then do we free her wrists so she can strip off to bathe. Do you understand?"

"Yes. And I have to stay in the bathroom while she's in there."

"I've had an idea for what we do with her next Friday. It's Friday tomorrow so I'll be going out before 6:00 in the morning to check a few things out. I'll be back with lunch."

Rob dropped Ryman and the girls in the village, then drove on into York and to the railway station. When he arrived, Sue's car was on its own with a wheel clamp fitted to the front wheel and a note under the wiper. Rob pulled up along side, got out and looked into Sue's car. He could clearly see the parking ticket. Sue had paid for 24 hours parking which ran out at 5:25 yesterday afternoon. The note under the wiper explained the procedure for getting the clamp removed and that there was a penalty of £100 for illegal parking.

Rob returned to his car and just sat for a few minutes thinking things through before driving home. A builder's van pulled away from the drive as Rob approached. That reminded him that Sue had arranged for her selected builders to visit the site today and tomorrow. She wouldn't do anything that would mean she would have missed those meetings, the extension project was too important to her. Something had happened to her that was beyond her control. Then he remembered the three times since they had been married that she had narrowly missed death. She had been almost run down by a speeding car, should have been poisoned but for a mistaken identity and survived when the building she was working in was blown apart. Were these all random events or were they all connected? Is someone trying to kill her? He and Sue had thought this before, but their suspect turned out to be innocent of any wrong doing. But now he wondered, if these were all attempts at murdering his wife and they may well have simply thrown her off the train.

He locked his car and went in through the back door to see Tim drinking tea with Eric and Rose.

"Rob we weren't expecting you until tomorrow. Any news of Sue?" Rose asked.

"Not a word, but let's talk about that later, when I've had chance to collect my thoughts. Was that one of Sue's builders that I just saw leaving here to meet Sue."

"Yes that was Tony Clegg, a site manager from Oliver and Dunhill Builders from Doncaster. Eric and I have been standing in for Sue, we were just talking about this latest one, that he seemed very switched on to what Sue wants and was very positive about everything. Unlike the one this morning who didn't impress us at all."

"Thanks for stepping in Tim, Sue will be pleased you didn't just put them off until some future date. How many more are there to see?"

"Just one at 10:00 in the morning, Moss and Dixons of York," Tim answered.

"Aren't they the firm working over at the Mills place that Sue put at the top of her list?" Rob said. "Any more tea in that pot mum?"

"Help yourself love, there's a clean cup on the drainer."

"Is Justin about?" Rob asked.

"He's probably on his computer," Eric said. "I swear he spends most of his time on that box talking to his mates."

"You do the lad an injustice Eric. Don't let him know that I told you this, but Justin is doing summer school in two subjects, Politics and Economics," Tim said. "He enrolled at Christmas, did two weeks then and another two weeks at Easter. It's a twelve week course with exams in February both at GCSE equivalent. Apparently Peter told him I have got a degree in economics and since he came back for the summer holidays he's been sounding me out. He's decided he wants to join the diplomatic service. The kid is doing eight hours a day on learning and doing test questions. He made me swear not to tell anyone, so for God sake, please don't let on."

"I had noticed his grades were improving," Rob said. "I just put it down to him being a late developer and also one of the youngest in his year. I'll go up and see him. I need his help with my phone."

Rob took the stairs two at a time, Tim's news had given him a spring. He knocked on Justin's door and waited a moment, then opened the door far enough to poke his head through.

"Hi dad, any news of Sue?"

"No son. I need your help, can you spare me half an hour downstairs?"

"Sure, I'll come now." He followed Rob downstairs and into the lounge.

"When I took you back to school after half term and we found that dead girl you used your phone to find her. Can you show me on my phone how to do that?"

"It's very easy you just need to download an app. Here, give it me, I'll do it." He took the phone and tapped a few buttons. "Now we wait a minute for it to load then just follow the instructions. I'll walk you through it if you like, what's the number you want to find?"

"It's Sue's."

"Just type it in and press search."

After a few seconds a map appeared on the screen.

"It's showing you that the phone is at Grantham Station," Justin said.

"Grantham! She was on the fast train, it doesn't stop at Grantham."

"Press the repeat search button at the top of the screen dad."

A new slightly different map appeared, this showing the phone about half a mile north of Grantham station.

"Wait a couple of minutes and do another repeat."

Again a slightly different map appeared this time it showed the phone a 2 miles north of Grantham station.

"She's not in Grantham, she's on the train."

"She may well be but this only tells us that her phone is on the train and the train is coming north," Justin said.

"I've got to get back to York station to welcome her."

"Hang on, I'm coming too."

Rob parked his car next to Sue's car and went to get a parking ticket for an hours parking. They went into the station and looked up at the information board which told them that the London train would be arriving on platform two in eighteen minutes.

Rob looked at his watch at least a dozen times in those eighteen minutes. When the train came to a halt the platform was turned into a scathing mass of people all trying to get out. Rob and Justin stood at the gate until most of the crowd had passed through the gate and then went to go onto the platform.

"Stop. You two stop, where do you two think you're going?" said a short man in a railway uniform. Thinking of a quick reply Justin said. "I've lost my mobile phone. I had it on the train so we're going to have a quick search for it."

"Okay but be quick about it."

"Dad, try that app again."

"A very large scale map appeared showing that the phone was very near."

"We're very close now dad so the app won't help much. Try ringing the number and we'll see if we can hear it."

They walked the length of the train listening and finally heard it when they entered the second first class carriage. Rob was disappointed that it was just the phone and there was no sign of Sue. But maybe it would give them a clue to what had happened and where she was now and they closed in on where the ringing sound seemed to be coming from.

"Here it is dad, stuffed down the side of this seat."

"Be very careful as you get it out. It may have fingerprints on it from whom ever stuffed it down there."

Chapter 17

"Good afternoon Minister, we are waiting for Interpol to coordinate a strike, but it could be a couple of months. We are well ahead, thanks to the efforts of Mr. Blackstock and members of his team once again. Through their involvement and co-operation with an MI-6 squad, we have identified the operations centre of the Russians. We know the layout of their building and we have identified the key players and are watching their every movement. We have clear evidence that they are behind the trafficking of Eastern European girls into the country. We also believe they are behind the drug in schools venture and we can link them now to the two murdered girls in Glasgow"

****

Ivan Gorkov left the house at 6:30 in the morning. Taking the car he drove west on the M62 and at 7:15 he was parked on the side of the road looking out over Crosland Moor Private airfield. He was checking it out through his binoculars and saw there were very few people about. There was a light on in the tower and he could see just one person in there. He stayed watching the comings and goings for over two hours. In that time only one light aircraft took off and in total he saw no more than eight people. This was perfect for his plan.

Next he drove back to Manchester, parked the car in the car park off Chorlton Street and walked the short distance to the Turkish barbershop.

"Ivan, long time since you come to see us."

"Hi Stan. Yeah it's about eighteen months. Is Alex about?"

"Of course, where else would he be? He's in the back room, go through, you know the way."

Ivan pull a curtain aside to reveal a door. He opened it and passed through to the rest of the building. He walked past two closed doors then opened the third.

"Hello Ivan. How is my favourite Rusky?"

"I am well, Alex and how are you?"

"Been better but not bad. What do you need."

"First I need the pin for this credit card," Ivan handed Alex Sue's Visa card.

"Who is S. V. Blackstock?"

"You don't need to know that, just get me the pin. I need a pilot's licence qualifying me to fly a Cessna, pilot's name Sean Victor Blackstock, issued in Munich in 2016 and finally I also need a driving licence for the same name. I'll collect next Tuesday."

"I can deliver all these but by next Tuesday will cost extra."

"How much?"

"For the pin £100, the driving licence £250 and the pilots licence £500. I'll also need a photo of you for the licence. Go and stand against the wall."

Using a digital camera Alex took a series of shots of Ivan.

"You can use the credit card to draw your £850, they can afford it. Just be careful, I don't want anyone to know I'm in Manchester."

"I'm always careful you should know that Ivan."

"Good bye Alex. I'll see you Tuesday."

"Good morning. Will Moss?"

"That's me and you are?"

"Tim Mills, Assistant manager, please come into the office."

"I was just looking around. Some lovely old buildings. They must be a hundred years old. They knew a bit about building in those days. Sorry you said office, didn't you?" The builder followed Tim into the office where Eric was sat waiting.

"Will Moss, this is Eric Blackstock, former owner of the stables. I'm afraid Mrs Blackstock has been unavoidably detained so you'll be meeting with me today and Eric will help out should I not be able to answer any questions."

"I'm sure you're just as able as Mrs. Blackstock. Now as I understand, you're expanding the capacity of the stables and providing living accommodation for staff who are not local. The new build will be in two blocks, one at either end of the existing block. The existing block also to be refurbished. I've been through the planning application documentation submitted to the council and downloaded a copy of the drawings from the council's website. I noticed your architect is Bret Willoby, a good architect, I've worked with him on several projects. He's done another fine job with your plans. The new blocks will look great up against the original."

"Well, Mr. Moss you appear to be fully up to speed with our requirements. Have you got anything you want to ask."

"Not at the moment, I've got enough to build a quote on. Just one or two things I'd like to raise. The new blocks are fine, well defined and straight forward, there will be one or two things that will need to be further clarified as the build progresses. But the upgrade to the old building is very uncertain. It could be very straight forward or very complex, most likely somewhere in the middle. I'll quote minimum and maximum. Site access I assume will be down the edge of the next field. I understand that current access to the stable is via the main driveway and past the house. Have you considered the additional traffic that a larger concern will generate. It may well be worth putting in a formal access road. It would be far cheaper to do that at the same time because all the equipment will be on-site. Permission should be almost guaranteed."

"That's a fair point Mr. Moss, I'll be sure to raise it with Mrs Blackstock when I next speak to her."

"Please call me, Will. I'll also just pass on a couple of observations, if I may. Things you may want to consider."

"Please do Will." Eric added.

"Mrs Blackstock obviously plans to entice new clients but has she considered the first impression this place gives. It's a very attractive house but sadly looks in need of some TLC. The gable end on the north side needs re-rendering and the whole place needs a lick of paint. Also a properly landscaped garden would make the whole place more, how can I put it, up market. It would only cost a few hundred pounds. My team could even do it whilst they're on site which would again lower the cost. My wife is a landscape gardener and I'm sure she could give you some ideas. Anyway they are just a few ideas for you to think about."

"Thank you Will, that certainly is something worth thinking about. Now would you like to look over the site?"

"If I may. I'd also like to take a look at the sub soil, it will help determine the amount of sub ground work needed. I've got a tool in the van I'll just go and fetch it."

He left the office and Tim looked at Eric and they both said, "WOW!"

"What a shame, Sue isn't here. I know he was top of her list, but he said nothing that left me in any doubt that he couldn't deliver," Eric said.

"I'll walk him around and come over to the house when he's gone," Tim said.

Sue had spent the morning sitting quiet, or lay on her bed. She had no idea what day of the week it was or where she was. Yesterday had possibly been the lowest point in her life. She had only wanted to shower or bath and put on some clean clothes, but the whole process was so degrading, she didn't think she would be able to face doing it again. She saw her captors at meal times. They spoke only to give her instructions. None of her questions received answers. She had no idea who these people were or why they were holding her captive.

She had decided she had little or no chance of escape but she was certain Rob would be looking for her and wouldn't give up until he found her.

Throughout her military career she had resorted to exercise when things weren't going well. It always cleared her head and enabled her to focus and resolve her problems. Being trust up like a chicken all day long wouldn't make normal exercises possible, but she had nothing else, to do so even basic exercise, repeated many times would be beneficial. First of all she needed to experiment to see what she could do.

She checked her watch, the woman would be bringing food very soon she would then have four or five hours to try things out then the evening to plan a routine. Tomorrow she would begin.

"Can I speak to D.S. Mike Stevens, please?" Sue had been missing now for forty eight hours so Rob called to report it.

"Hold the line caller, I'm putting you through."

"Serious Crimes, D.S. Stevens, how can I help you."

"Sergeant, my name is Robert Blackstock, Tracy Longhorn said I should give you a call. "

"How is she? We've not seen her since she went down to London last autumn."

"She's doing well. Her divorce was finalised so she's Tracy Mills again now."

"So why did she say ring me?"

"My wife went missing two days ago on her way home from London by train, but she never got there. I'm convinced she has been abducted."

"What makes you think that, she may have been involved in an accident," Stevens suggested.

"Because we know she got on the train, she had no reason to get off before York and her car is still in the car park. If she had an accident then it would had to have happened between the train and her car. That didn't happen, plus I found her phone forced down the side of the seat on the train, deliberately stuffed there I presume, so that it couldn't be used to track her," Rob explained.

"It certainly looks like an abduction. Tracy was right to point you to me. Can you come in to see me first thing tomorrow, and bring with you a recent photo?"

Sue was in a much more positive mood when she woke. Having worked out an exercise programme the previous afternoon and evening, now she was eagerly awaiting her breakfast, so that she could then start her first run through of the programme she had planned and gone through in her mind so many times. She had what she thought would work out to be a fifteen minute programme of gentle exercise which would possibly not be keeping her terribly fit but would give her something to focus on and make her days go quicker.

Earlier when she had first woken, she lay on her bed trying to work out how long she had been held there. She found a discarded hair grip amongst the dust and fluff in a corner of the room and was using it to make tally marks on the wall next to her mattress. She knew that she met with the Prince on Wednesday 31st July, the next day was the day she had a bath, an event she would not forget quickly. Then yesterday she thought of her exercises. So today must be Saturday 3rd August, her 4th day. She scratched four short lines on the wall.

Her breakfast arrived, delivered by the man this time but it was still the same instant porridge and dry toast.

"My compliments to the chef," she told him but got no reaction. After her first run through of her exercise programme she realised she was stretching the same muscles in four consecutive exercises and not at all in the rest of the programme, so she shuffled the order. For the second run through it felt a lot easier. She set out to do her fifteen minute routine then fifteen minute recovery and repeat for two hours morning and afternoon.

"Are you ready to tell me what your plan for next Friday is, yet?" Yeta asked Ivan as he return downstairs.

"Not yet. I have to see a man tomorrow to finalise it. But I'm sure you'll be very happy. It would even have challenged Mikhail to come up with a plan like this one.

"What time are you meeting that policeman, Robert?" Rose asked.

"It's D.S. Mike Stevens mum, at 10:00, I'll be leaving in a few minutes."

"There's a letter for you Rob. The postman just left it with a few bills for Blackstock Racing which I'll take down to the office later." Eric handed Rob the letter. He ripped it open and pulled out a folded photograph. Unfolding it he could see it was a picture of Sue. It was extremely poor quality but it was clear enough to see that it was a picture of his wife lay on a mattress, bound at her wrists and ankles and gaffer tape across her mouth. He dropped the photograph onto the table and sat down heavily, staring at nothing.

Rose picked it up. "Oh my God! the poor girl, and you dear, you must be going mad inside. Why would anyone want to do this. Is there a note?"

"Are they holding her for ransom?" Eric added.

"Just the photo. At least now we know for certain. I must take this to D.S. Stevens." He refolded the photograph and pushed it back into the envelope and gathered up everything he might need and set off for his meeting.

"Mr. Blackstock good to meet you at last. I've heard so much about you from Tracy. She sees you as some sort of hero. Come in and take a seat."

"Good morning sergeant, I've brought you a recent photo."

Stevens took the picture from Rob, turned to a colleague at the next desk. "Mandy can you take this to reprographics and make sure every one on the force gets a copy and get some posters made up, the usual thing 'Have You Seen This Woman' etcetera."

"I've got her phone here as well." Rob placed a polythene bag containing Sue's phone onto the desk. "I thought it may have some fingerprints from whoever hid it."

"We'll get to that later. First I want to go over why you think your wife has been abducted."

"I don't think it, I know it. Here, the proof came in the post this morning." He handed Stevens the envelope containing the photo.

"I agree, there's no doubt. Was there a note?"

"No, only the photo."

"Excuse me a moment, I've just got to call a colleague."

After a short exchange with someone on the other end of the line, the policeman turned back to his visitor. "Someone from our forensic department is coming up to check the phone for fingerprints, he'll take your prints for elimination and then look at the data on the phone to see if it's of any use. Can I get you a coffee or something? It's only vending machine I'm afraid, but it's not too bad."

"Black coffee, no sugar would be welcome thank you."

"Five good prints and half a dozen usable partials, Mike. I'll get them analysed over the next couple of days. I've looked at the data and found that the phone was last used on 31st July at 12:02 to purchase a first class rail ticket for the 13:32 from King's Cross to York. Then at 13:41 to send a text message to person named Rob."

"Thanks Jimmy, can you give those prints priority and let me know if you find a match to any of them. I'll get Mr. Blackstock's prints done before he leaves and I'll send them down to you."

"Well, that's just about all we can do now. I'll get someone to get Mrs. Blackstock's car back to you in the next couple of days. On Monday I'll have a couple of uniformed constables at the station asking around to see if anyone saw anything unusual. Then Wednesday I'll have officers on the 13:32 from Kings Cross asking the same thing. I know it doesn't sound like much but we've got nothing to go on at all. Our best hope is if someone remembers her with someone or if they contact you again with some instructions."

Manchester City traffic was exceptionally heavy on Sunday morning when Ivan set out with a mission to put in place the last piece of his plan. He was heading back to Crosland Moor Airfield and wanted to be there at 10:00, but with this traffic he was going to be late. He didn't have a meeting booked but he wanted to talk with members of the parachute club about their activities. The last thing he wanted was to be stopped by the police so he stayed calm and patient, keeping within the speed limits.

He left the car in the car park and walked across to a static caravan bearing a board with ' CROSLAND MOOR PARACHUTE CLUB' painted on it.

"Are you looking for someone, mate?" a young man in overalls called out and came trotting over.

"Actually I was thinking about the club. Thinking about joining but wanting to know more about what goes on before I commit."

"Hi, I'm Tony Ruffin, Club President. Give me five minutes to see off the day's first load of jumpers and then I'll be free to answer all your questions."

Ivan followed the young man with his eyes and watched him enter the side door into an old hanger. The front doors of the hanger were both open wide and out in front of the hanger was a plane with both its engines idling. Looking into the hanger he could see a cluster of people in orange jump suits, crash hats and parachutes packs on their backs. Ivan watched them climb the steps into the waiting plane. When all were aboard Tony Ruffin pulled the steps back and the plane moved off towards the runway and Ruffin headed back to Ivan. "Well sir, what can I do for you?"

"As I said, I'm looking in the Manchester area for a club, read about yours and thought I'd give you a look."

"How many jumps have you made."

"I made my first jump three years ago and been jumping ever since but nothing in the last six weeks." Ivan was creating a believable story as he went.

"Well then Mr.... I don't think I got your name."

"Blackstock. Sean Blackstock."

"Well Sean, I'm Tony, shall we start over in the hanger?" They walked side by side Tony running through various certifications the club had which allowed it to operate, the safety regulations etc and general information about the club which Ivan paid little attention to.

"Is it right you only jump on Sundays?" he asked.

"Sundays, Bank Holidays. We are licensed and insured for fifty days jumping each year. Sunday is the most popular day so take away the days when weather is not suitable we fit nicely within that limitation."

"If you're only open on Sundays, you must have good security."

"All doors are alarmed, the windows have locks and the whole complex is secure every night. With two night watchmen and four guard dogs running loose between 10:00 and 6:00. Actually there's not much worth nicking. The resale value of the kit is negligible, we don't keep money on site. I suppose the two planes would be worth a bit but there again you need to have somewhere to put them. There are a few bits in the office worth a little but really the biggest threat is from someone breaking in to do damage and the measures we have in place are enough to deter that sort of criminal."

"I see the parachutes are stored in a cage."

"Yes and the cage is locked with six digit coded lock." Tony opened the cage for them to enter with Ivan watching closely as Tony pressed the numbers on the key pad. Six one seven two two four. "I don't know what safety rules you've worked with before at other places, but here we have a tag system. We train jumpers how to pack their own 'chute but when packed they attach a tag to the left shoulder strap then sign and date the the tag. Each 'chute is then checked by two people who also sign and date the tag. No 'chute should leave this cage unless it has three signatures on the tag. As the jumper selects his 'chute he adds his own signature and date. Then finally as the jumper enters the plane the tag is checked then removed. It might seem to be complicated but it works very well."

"So you're saying a parachute that has the first three signatures on the tag is a 'chute ready to be used?" Ivan clarified.

"That's right. Now unless there is anything else you want to see out here, if we go back to the office I've got a leaflet with the general bits and pieces on which you can take away and decide if you want to join us or not."

As they walked the fifty yards or so back to the caravan Ivan checked whether at any time could he see the airfield's main buildings. He was pleased that although the building was in sight, he couldn't see any windows or doors so no one in that building would see someone going from the caravan to the hanger. Only someone in the control tower had a view of that space and there was no reason for any one being in there before 8:15 because flying was only allowed between 8:30 and 6:00. But between the caravan and the car park he could see all of the windows so anybody could see him.

"Thank you very much Tony, I've got a lot to think about. I'll be in touch again soon."

On Monday afternoon D.S. Mike Stevens and two uniformed constables stood at York railway station asking everyone going in or out whether they had been at the station between 3:30 and 4:30 on Wednesday. Those that had been there were shown the picture of Sue and asked if they remembered seeing her or if they saw anyone acting strange. They found one elderly lady who said she saw a man carrying a lady's hand bag with a woman that looked drunk who might have been the lady in the photo, being helped by another, much younger, woman. They had passed her and went and sat on the seat outside the entrance but that's all she had seen. It was the only positive thing to come from the whole day but even that was more than D.S. Stevens had expected to find.

Late afternoon Stevens rang Rob to update him.

"I'm sorry to say that the fingerprints from your wife's phone don't match anything we have on file. But this afternoon we found someone who possibly saw your wife with a man and a woman."

"Is that all?" Rob was disappointed.

"It's more than I expected. We now know there are two people who took your wife, a man and a woman who is much younger than your wife and we know they drugged her because she was walking but not resisting her captors, probably a drug like Rohypnol."

"It doesn't get us anywhere closer to finding her."

"Not yet, but we now know what we are looking for on the CCTV from inside the station and the station car park. I have an officer looking as we speak. With luck we'll get a look at their faces and then we will have something real to work with."

"Are you ready to explain this marvellous plan yet?" Yeta asked.

"I'm almost there. My trip yesterday has left just one last problem to overcome. I need to draw a diagram to get everything

191

finalised. I'll talk you through it as soon as I think it's workable. I've got a meeting tomorrow which will give me the pieces to make it all work," he explained. "How is our guest?"

"She's a strange one that woman. When I took her lunch up to her I found her reciting poetry. She even thanked me for the food."

"I'll get her meal ready and take it to her myself and see if she's the same with me," Ivan said.

Sue was sat on the mattress when Ivan opened the door. Her eyes were closed, her hands were in her lap, palms up. She look like she was in a trance which broke as Ivan crossed the room and placed the plate beside her. As he turned to leave the room she thanked him.

"You were right, she's certainly a strange woman," he said when he returned downstairs.

Sue smiled once Ivan had left. She could just imagine what her captors were talking about. They would be thinking she's going mad or something. If she was to keep this up they would not know what they were dealing with. If she could get them on edge, there was a slim chance of catching them off guard and her getting out. At the very least it gave her something to keep her mind active.

Ivan took a taxi to the Turkish barbershop. He nodded to Stan who had no customers, so was sitting back in the barber's chair reading his paper.

"Go straight through, he's expecting you. Been cursing you every moment of every day since you were last here," Stan said.

"He'd curse if you gave him £1,000,000," Ivan replied and they both laughed. Ivan went behind the curtain and through the door at the back of the shop.

"Good morning, Alex."

"What's good about it. It's just another day isn't it?" Alex pointed at the table. "Your stuff is over there, the pin is written on that piece of paper by the card."

Ivan looked the documents over and held them up to the light to check watermarks.

"These are perfect Alex, you're a true artist. I'll have to trust your Italian on the pilot's licence. I can speak a little but struggle reading it."

"Just remember, I've never heard of you if you get caught."

"Thanks Alex. Until the next time then, good bye," Ivan said as he left.

Back at the house he found some paper and drew a plan of Crosland Moor airfield as best as he could remember. "Okay Yeta, my plan is complete, come over to the table and I'll walk you through it."

"This had better be good," Yeta said and walked to the table.

"Tomorrow, I'm going to use our guest's credit card to hire a plane for Friday from a local airfield. Then early Friday we take her to the airfield and put her in the plane. I then fly her north, you take the car and drive north. I set the plane onto auto pilot, jump out and parachute to the ground, you pick me up and take me to Liverpool. The plane will continue on auto pilot until it runs out of fuel somewhere over the North Sea. Mrs. Blackstock will be lost forever.

Well, what do you think?"

"I like it, I like it a lot," she cheered, "especially the last bit, him not knowing how she dies, will make his grief far harder to bear. Perfect."

Ivan folded his drawing of the airfield and placed it with his forged pilot's licence.

"I didn't know you knew how to fly or use a parachute?" Yeta queried.

"I served my national service in the Air Force," he answered.

"And how will I know where you land?"

"You use an app on your phone to find my phone, you then put my position into the satnav app and let it bring you to me."

Yeta looked blankly back at him.

"Don't worry I'll set it all up for you, show you how to do it and you can practice this afternoon when I go to the shop for more food. Go and get your phone and I'll show you now."

Yeta took her phone from her bag and gave it to him. It took only a few minutes to download the APPs she needed.

"Right, are you ready?" She lent over his shoulder to watch what he was doing.

"First you load up the Find My Phone app and type in my number. Then press find and a little map will appear showing the location of my phone, then you press directions and that's all you have to do. Just follow the satnav instructions and they will lead you straight to me.

"Crosland Moor Aircraft Hire, my name is Jane, can I help you?"

"I'm looking to hire a Cessna 152 for Friday through to Monday. Do you have one or something similar available?"

"I'll just have a look for you. 4 day starting Friday 9th. Yes we do have one available, for that aircraft we charge you £129 per day. So that would be £516. Do you want to proceed?"

"Does that include insurance and a full tank of gas?"

" It does include insurance but you pay for what gas you use. You start with a full tank and we fill it again when you return, you pay for the refill."

"I'll take it."

"Right sir, are you a new customer or have you hired from us sometime in the past."

"I'm a new customer."

"In that case I need to take down a few details. Your name please, surname and initial."

"Blackstock.   S."

"Address?"

"Blackstock Stables, Ashridge York. YO15 7EW"

"What level of licence do you have?"

"PPL."

"Where and when was your licence issued?"

"Milan, 2017"

"You do know sir, that because this is a not a UK issued licence you will have to show it at the desk when you pick up the plane."

"Not a problem."

"Is the phone you are using now the one you want me to record in your paperwork?"

"It is."

"Just one more question Mr Blackstock. What is the purpose for your flight?"

"My aunt has terminal cancer, I'm flying her home to Orkney."

"I'm sorry to hear that, sir. I'll just put domestic medical transfer. Now, how would you like to pay?"

"Visa."

He gave her all the details from Sue's credit card then arranged for takeoff at 8:30 before ending the call.

He turned to Yeta who said, "That sounded as if it went well."

"Everything apart from the phone number," Ivan replied. "I wasn't prepared for that. They now have my number attached to her name. If someone pulls up the phone history they will learn things about me and the organisation we don't want made public."

"Ring them and change it." Yeta suggested.

"Actually it may be best to leave it for now, just in case they have to contact me about something. What I'll do is go onto Blackstock Stables website and find what her contact number is, then get them to change it when I go in to sign the papers on Friday morning."

"We really need some more clothes," Yeta said, "these are filthy. You should have bought more when you bought these. If we get seen like this when we get to the airport they will know something is wrong."

"I didn't have much cash, but now we have the pin for her credit card, take the card this afternoon and get what, you want plus jeans and a polo shirt for me."

"Rob, glad I caught you before you went anywhere."

"Good morning Tim, I must say you've looking particularly happy today. I saw you earlier through the window, you were grinning madly like the cat that's got the cream."

"Was I really?" Tim responded by bringing back the smile. "Jenny has agreed to move in with me."

"Into that tiny flat?" Rob sounded surprised.

"No, we're going to share a house. We're looking at a couple on Saturday afternoon."

"Well done to you both. Are we going to be hearing wedding bells soon?"

"I would like to think that to be a possibility."

"Good man."

"What I wanted to talk to you about Rob are two entries in the stable's diary. They both look like Sue's writing but I don't understand them. One on today's page says 'Mac Tim-field' and one tomorrow just says '10:00 Mac', do you know what they might mean?"

"I do actually. You know that when the expansion is complete, Sue is planning on having a second assistant working alongside you, doing a similar job."

Tim nodded.

"She thinks she's found somebody. He used to work here twenty years ago. Eric wanted him to be head lad but instead he went off and became a navy pilot. Anyway, Sue has invited him in to discuss things. She said she would like you to be involved in the meeting and would like you to train him, like Eric trained you."

"Do you think we should contact him and put him off until Sue gets back?"

"No, I'll handle it. I think I know what Sue is looking for. One, is he right for the job, two will the lads respect him and three will he fit in with you and her as a management team. If you're okay with that, we'll keep the meeting to 10:00. I've got no idea when Sue will be back, I'm waiting to hear the latest from the police this morning."

"I agree that the team bit is crucial. I think Sue and I now have a trust in one another to the extent that I take on board what she wants and she trusts me to deliver it in my own way. If Eric once choose this chap as his head lad then he should be capable and the lads should respect him. I'd be happy to come in on the meeting, do you think Eric should sit in?"

"Thanks Tim, I'll ask him. See you later."

Rob talked things through with Eric and agreed that twenty years was too big a gap for any opinion he had then, to sway a decision to be made now. Rose joined them in the lounge with a tray of coffees.

"Dad and me are going in to town later, do you want anything?"

"I'd like my wife back," he said sorrowfully.

"Sorry dear, I wish I could. It's over a week now and not a trace."

"If D.S. Stevens doesn't ring by the time I've drunk my coffee I'm going to ring him."

No sooner had he said it his phone rang and the display confirmed it was D.S. Stevens. "Good day Sergeant, I hope you've got some good news."

"I wouldn't say good news but I'm pleased to report we have made some progress. Yesterday myself and two P.C.s in uniform repeated your wife's last known journey and we talked to the staff and passengers on train plus's staff on the platforms at both Kings Cross and York. We asked if they had been on the same train last Wednesday and to those who had been we asked if they had see anything. Two people claimed to have seen her. One was the ticket collector who said he had to wake her at Peterborough, so he could check her ticket. The other one was an old lady who said her and your wife were the only two in that carriage but she got off at Doncaster. But my team have searched the videos from York station at the time your wife arrived looking at clusters of two women and a man. They did find some good footage of the three leaving the train. Your wife was certainly under the influence of drugs, she was struggling to walk. They were on camera as they walked along the platform and again in the car park. They were there for a good ten minutes before the arrival of a Silver Audi S4."

"We're you able to recognise who these people are?" Rob asked.

"The woman's face was not shown to the camera either on the platform or in the car park. However we found several good images of the man, although we did not get a hit through facial recognition. But we've distributed copies to all UK forces and interpol. I'll send you a copy. We have been able to trace the car to a Mr Osbourne of Hammersmith who reported it stolen last Wednesday."

"So you are still in the dark really," Rob said.

"To a degree yes, but now we have a face, a description of the woman and a car which is far more than we started with."

Chapter 18

"Miss Mills, Bernard Howe here, I thought you might be interested in the news I've received from Scotland about the murder of James Blackburn up in Durness. Apparently the murderer was D.I. Howard. He confessed in a note found when his body was discovered. He had hanged himself in the garage of the family home. He confessed to being a long term partner of Blackburn in a smuggling enterprise bringing in alcohol and tobacco, but Blackburn had got greedy and was taking money from the Russians for helping smuggle drugs and more recently, girls. Howard's note said this was the reason his wife had been killed and after the deaths of the two other girls as well, the price was too high and he wanted out but Blackburn wouldn't let him"

****

Sue's usual breakfast came early. It was only 6:00. Before eating it she added another tally mark to her calendar. A quick count up told her it was Friday 9th August, her tenth day in captivity, Rob must be close to finding her by now. She ate her porridge and toast and stood to begin her exercise plan. She was finding it a lot easier than earlier in the week, so she was happy that it must be doing her some good. But her limbs felt heavy this morning and she felt sleepy all of a sudden. She heard voices but couldn't understand what they were saying. Someone was pulling her up on to her feet and helping her walk. They were talking to her all the time, then there was a second voice and another person helping as she went down some stairs.

Yeta and Ivan bundled Sue into the back seat of the car and an empty large hold-all went into the boot. Ivan and Yeta were in their new clothes and they had pulled a tracksuit top onto Sue to cover her stained tee-shirt, Her shoes looked odd with a track suit but they would have to do.

They reached the airfield just after 7:00 and Ivan parked down a track that ran down the outside of the perimeter fence.

"Sit tight, I'll be twenty minutes, certainly no more than thirty, Ivan said as he left the car, taking something from the boot on his way. He walk a little further along the perimeter fence until he reached the point closest to the parachute club buildings. Making sure he kept the club caravan between him and the main airport buildings he took out the wire cutters he had taken from the boot, cut a hole in the fence and crawled through. He swiftly moved to the back of the hanger and on round to the window on the far side. Using the handle of the wire cutters, he smashed a small pane of glass next to the lock. It then took him several minutes to pick the lock and open the window. He climbed into the hanger and made for the secure cage. He pressed the buttons on the keypad allowing the cage door to swing open. He grabbed the first parachute he found with three signatures on the tag and left the way he had come in. When he got back to the car he put the parachute into the hold-all in the boot.

"Sorry I was a bit longer than I said, I had trouble picking a lock to get in. We're now running a couple of minutes behind schedule so we need to get to the main building."

"Mr Blackstock is it?" A smart woman in a blazer stood behind the counter greeted him.

"That's right, here to pick up a Cessna."

"I have your information here on the computer. Can you read through it and confirm it is correct."

"That's not the correct telephone number but everything else is correct."

He gave her the new number and she keyed it in, overwriting the previous number.

"Can I see your licence please sir? I need to scan it into our records."

He handed over the document. Alex had done an excellent job he'd even made it look like it had been folded and unfolded hundreds of times and also looked a little grubby.

"Right sir, all I need now is to see some ID and for you to sign."

He pulled out the driving licence Alex had produced which she checked and updated the notes on the computer to say 'ID confirmed by driving licence'. Finally he signed on an image reader and was handed a key.

"Your aircraft is waiting for you outside hanger number three, the registration is GOLF ROMEO MIKE NOVEMBER NOVEMBER. Have a good flight, sir."

Ivan got back into the car and drove down to hanger number three. He unlocked the plane and with Yeta's help, manhandled Sue up onto the wing then into the right hand seat. Yeta grabbed the bag from the boot and tossed it in behind the seat. Ivan climbed into the left seat as Yeta left with the car. Ivan went through all the preflight checks then looked at his watch, 8:28, almost time to go.

"GOLF ROMEO MIKE NOVEMBER NOVEMBER calling Crosland tower."

"Crosland tower receiving you."

"GOLF ROMEO MIKE NOVEMBER NOVEMBER requesting permission to take off."

"Affirmative GOLF ROMEO MIKE NOVEMBER NOVEMBER. Please proceed to runway for immediate take off. Once airborne climb to four thousand feet and set your course to twenty eight degrees. Leeds- Bradford tower will pick you up after three miles. Your weather is good with light winds all the way to Orkney, have a good flight. Over."

"Thank you Crosland tower. Over."

Ivan quickly got the plane into the air, turned left slightly onto the correct heading. It took ages to climb to four thousand feet. Sue was beginning to come out from the effects of the drug, she heard a voice on the radio.

"Leeds tower calling GOLF ROMEO MIKE NOVEMBER NOVEMBER. Over."

"GOLF ROMEO MIKE NOVEMBER NOVEMBER hearing you loud and clear. Over."

"GOLF ROMEO MIKE NOVEMBER NOVEMBER increase your height to four thousand two hundred feet immediately."

Ivan did as instructed.

"GOLF ROMEO MIKE NOVEMBER NOVEMBER you are currently passing south east of Leeds-Bradford, please prepare for a slight course change. On my mark change course to zero five degrees. Three,two,one,mark."

"Thank you GOLF ROMEO MIKE NOVEMBER NOVEMBER, please maintain course, height and speed until further notice. Over."

Ivan pushed a few buttons and turned a dial on the autopilot, then flicked a switch in front of him, a red light lit up on the autopilot.

Sue was becoming more aware of what was happening around her, but not enough to know Ivan was puting on a parachute. She was also getting feelings back in her arms and legs and could move her head a little. She slowly turned toward Ivan in time to see him open the door, climb out onto the wing and jump.

To start with Sue couldn't understand what was happening. As the drug wore off, her senses began to return but so did the sickness and the blinding head ache that she remembered from a week ago. It took all of fifteen minutes before she realised she was on her own. The reality of the situation and the emotion of fear broke the final hold that the drug had on her. Fear was now her driving force. She was almost certainly going to die. If she did nothing the plane eventually would run out of fuel and fall out of the sky, if she tried to land she would probably kill herself. But that was a 'probably' not a 'certainly', it did at least give some hope.

She looked out of the windows. To the left was rough hilly almost mountainous terrain, to the right as far as she could see there were pockets of buildings and a larger built up area in the middle. A city and its suburbs she thought to herself. Ahead the ground looked like gentle rolling country side. It could be farmland or maybe moorland, she was too far away to make it out clearly. So her best option would be to land on the ground in front of her. But she had never been in the cockpit of a plane before. The closest she had come was when she was doing physics at school, studying flight. The class had a trip to an aircraft training facility and they all had tried a flight simulator, but that was twenty five years ago. How much could she remember from that day. She certainly remembered kissing Billy Johnson on the back seat of the coach, he was the first to use his tongue. But what were all these controls and instruments? The thing in front of her she remembered was called the yoke, turn it clockwise and the flap things at the end of the back edge of the wings moved, one up and one down making the plane bank to the right, turning the yoke anticlockwise made the plane bank left. Pulling the yoke forward pulled the nose up and the plane should climb, pushing it forward would push the nose forward would make it dive. The dial that was blue on the top half and brown on the bottom with a black line across the middle she knew was the one she needed to watch to know she is flying level. The one next to it looked like a clock, she knew was the altimeter, it was telling her she was at four thousand two hundred feet. The next was easy because it said Airspeed across it, she looked closer and saw it was segmented in different colours. White, green, yellow and red. Instinct told her that green was the segment that was safe flying speed, the needle was currently near the top of the green segment at eighty five knots. Next to that a dial that looked like the rev counter in her car, she guessed that's what it was above the throttle lever. Then there was a lever labled flaps and finally a dial, a row of buttons, a switch and a light glowing red.

"That must be the autopilot," she said to herself. "It's no use waiting Susan, you might as well get on with it."

She grabbed the yoke and flicked the switch on the autopilot. Instantly the yoke felt different. With just the slightest movement the plane either turned or went up or down, whenever she tried to compensate she over did it, so it took her ages to get level again. She spent the next ten minutes playing with the yoke and watching the effect her movements had on the instruments.

A voice above her head interrupted her thinking. Someone was talking on the radio. She could do without that distraction, so she looked up and pressed a small red button and the voice stopped.

"If I'm going to land this thing I need to be a lot lower and a lot slower."

She pushed the yoke forward and watched the altitude drop, but at the same time her airspeed increased, so she levelled out again and the airspeed settled.

"Well that wasn't right girl, let's try slowing the engine." She pulled the throttle towards her a little watching the rev counter drop. Her airspeed dropped and her altitude started to drop very slowly. Then she pushed the yoke forward again. This time she got the result she wanted, less height without increasing the speed.

"What about the flaps. Won't the drag from them slow me down. I'll try."

She pulled the lever a little and saw the effect instantly, she slowed but the nose came up and she had to push the yoke forward. Her airspeed was now at the bottom end of the green segment, so she raised the flaps again. The altimeter was now telling her she was at eight hundred feet and she had a clearer view of the land. It was definitely moorland and looked quite level.

"It's now or never girl. Full flaps." The plane dropped very quickly. "Steady on Susan, not too quick!" She lifted the flaps back to half way and her rate of decent slowed. She pulled the throttle a little more and the airspeed needle moved into the white segment.

She looked out of the window and was surprised how close to the ground she was. "Here goes." She pulled the throttle lever and the flaps lever both all the way. The nose lifted and the plane dropped the last few feet and the rear wheels hit the ground with such force that she bounced. It was not the cleanest of landings but she'd done it. The nose dropped and the nose wheel touched the ground. As it did so the plane veered sharply to the left, the right wing began to dip and in a second it hit the ground ploughing a trench until it could not go further, but the momentum flipped the plane over, ripping off the right wing, breaking the fuselage in two before it came to rest.

Sue didn't move at first until she saw the engine was sending out sparks and she could smell fuel. She was sitting in a bomb.

Three thousand seven hundred feet above Sue, another light aircraft was flying south. A young woman's eye was caught by sun light reflecting off something ahead and below then. At first she thought it was a car but then she could clearly see it was a plane almost at ground level. She watched it land in a wide open stretch of the North Yorkshire Moors. Just seconds later she saw it flip over and shatter.

"Dad, I've just seen a plane crash down there on the moor!" she said to the pilot.

"Are you sure, honey?"

"I'm sure dad. We have to go down and look."

"Hold on," he said and banked right into a sharp descent then levelled out at three hundred feet.

The wreckage, approximately a mile ahead of them suddenly exploded sending a large fireball high into the sky in front of them. The pilot took evasive action by pulling the yoke hard towards him and right at the same time, then pushing the throttle fully open. When he was a safe distance away from any danger of a shock wave he levelled out and began to circle the site. The explosion must have consumed all of the aviation fuel because although the wreckage was burning, flames were no bigger than you'd see from a garden bonfire.

"Leeds Tower this GOLF DELTA BRAVO TANGO UNIFORM. Over."

"Leeds Tower receiving, go ahead GOLF DELTA BRAVO TANGO UNIFORM. Over."

"We have just witnessed a plane crash at this location. Over."

"We have you on screen at one thousand three hundred feet GOLF DELTA BRAVO TANGO UNIFORM. Can you land a check for survivors? Over."

"Negative Leeds Tower. Will descend and circle. Over."

He took the plane down to three hundred feet again and circled the wreck. The explosion had blown the fuselage apart and parts of the cockpit lay twenty metres away from engine block.

"There's no way anyone survived that, dad."

"Most unlikely."

"Leeds Tower, no visible survivors. Over."

"Thank you GOLF DELTA BRAVO TANGO UNIFORM. Will pass to rescue services. Have a good onward flight.Over."

"No sign of Sue's Mr. Macmillan yet, Rob. It's not giving a good impression for an interview."

A plane flew low over the yard, as Tim and Rob were talking. They watched the plane go off into the distance, circle round and come back towards them even lower.

"What is this idiot doing?" Tim said.

"He's landing in our field," Rob said and he ran out of the yard to the gate into the field from where he saw Ian MacMillon and a young woman climbing out of the plane. Ian walked towards Rob his hand held out to shake Rob's.

"Mr. Blackstock, good to see you again. Can I introduce my daughter, Stella?"

"Pleased to meet you Stella." Rob said.

"I'm sorry we're a bit late but we witnessed a plane crash on the North Yorkshire Moors. A bad one the plane exploded. We circled looking for survivors, but didn't see any, so left it to the rescue boys to sort out."

"Nasty," Rob said. "Can I offer you both a coffee? Please, come into the office."

Luci had seen the plane land from her bedroom and had rushed out to see what was happening.

"Luci can you get some coffee organised and bring it to the office please darling?" Rob requested.

"I hope you don't mind me bringing Stella with me. I've spoken about my years here many times and she wanted to see the place for herself."

"If you'd like a guided tour of the yard while we meet with your dad, I'm sure Luci could show you around?"

"That would be very kind."

"Let's have our coffee first."

"Isn't Mrs. Blackstock interviewing me?" Ian asked

"Sue isn't available this morning, so I will be standing in for her and this is Tim Mills, Assistant manager here."

"I thought I was here for an interview for that job." Ian said.

"You are Ian." Tim interrupted. "Sue is about to expand to more than double the capacity of this yard from 1st January. Because of that she needs to build a larger management team."

"Ah coffee, thanks Luci," Rob smiled "Ian this is my daughter Luci. Luci after we've had coffee do you think you could show Stella around the yard. She might like to see the horses exercising.

"Ian, did my wife know you would be flying in this morning?"

"Sure, she promised to make sure there were no animals in the field."

Tim and Ian talked over the details of the role with Rob adding bits here and there.

"From what you've told me this morning, this is going to be an exciting place to work in the next few months, but I don't have recent relevant experience."

"That's not an issue," Rob explained. "Sue's plan is to appoint someone by early November and for them to work alongside Tim learning about the job by doing it supervised."

"Well, I am certainly interested in the job but moving down here would be a huge step for Stella and me. Stella would need to find work and we would need to find somewhere to live locally."

"I may be able to offer a solution to both of those. I'm currently making use of the flat above the old stable, but next month I'm moving into a house in the village with my girlfriend. I'm sure Sue would rent you the flat. It's small but has two bedrooms and would do you until you see somewhere more permanent. My girlfriend is the daughter of the pub landlord and has been helping out behind the bar, but she's about to start a new job in York. The landlord is looking for someone to work lunches and evenings."

"Your daughter has a maths degree if I remember correctly Ian," Rob asked

"That's right, a two:one."

"Well I'm thinking on my feet here, Sue has just engaged a new accountant who is going to get someone in part time to do Sue's bookkeeping. I'm about to enter a similar contract. Somewhere in all that there seems to be a full time job for a junior accountant."

"You are both making this very attractive and I'm very interested," Ian responded.

"Of course we'll report and discuss today's meeting with my wife when she gets back and she'll be in touch with you in the very near future," Rob said. "Now would you like to look around the yard?"

"Yes please, see what changed since I was here twenty years ago."

"I don't remember any of the lads having children back then. In fact it was even rare for any of them to be married," Rob claimed.

"No, Stella is my step-daughter. I met Pauline, Stella's mum, soon after I left here. The two came as a package deal. Pauline was a single mum struggling to bring up a baby on her own and Stella had just turned one and was learning to walk. Three years later she was bridesmaid at our wedding. We've always been close, but even more so this year, what with Pauline dying at Easter just days before Stella's finals and then only being able to get seasonal work. It's been hard."

The office door opened and Luci entered. Luci said, "Sorry to burst in on you but the rain has arrived. The sky is bright all round so it won't last long but it's throwing it down at the moment."

"Stella, Mr. Blackstock thinks there may be an accountancy job vacancy near here."

"It's nothing certain, but I know our accountant is looking to take on a maths student, initially as a bookkeeper, but to train and help train up to FCCA level. I could find out more if you are interested."

"Yes please, Mr. Blackstock. That sounds exactly what I'm looking for, I love working with numbers."

"I don't suppose I could see the plans for the extension?" Ian asked.

"I don't see why not," Rob replied. "Tim have you got a copy handy?"

Tim went to the filing cabinet, pulled open the second draw and found the folder containing the plans, took out a copy and spread it across the desk.

"Wow. Now that is very impressive and ambitious, I can see why it will need a larger management team."

"The rain has stopped, shall we go and have a look around?" Tim suggested.

"Yes please," Ian eagerly replied, "and if Eric is about I love to see him again before we go"

"Luci, why don't you and Stella go up to the house and wait for us in the lounge. If you see granddad, tell him Mr. MacMillan would like to see him."

"This is exactly how I remember it, I can almost see the faces of the lads. It really is a beautiful old building, but you're right, the insides do need modifying. It's ridiculous that in this day and age you've only got one small light in each stall and water has to be carried in from the yard. With modernisation this place would run with possibly twenty percent less staff. You've got lads out there with horses just walking them because its their rest day. Install a couple of treadmills and one lad could do the work of five in the same time. A mechanical sweeper for the yard would do the job quicker and needs only one person to operate it."

"Where have you got all these ideas from Ian?" Rob asked.

"Well, in my business I spend a lot of nights in hotels, the sort of magazine they leave around are things like 'Horse and Hound' or 'Country Life' and they are full of adverts for these sort of things. I see you are still mucking out into wheelbarrows. But a trailer on a quad bike would be so much more efficient."

"I guess we should be looking at this sort of thing." Tim said. "There's no point modifying the buildings if we don't modify our methods. It could reduce the number of new staff we need to find."

"Another thing I noticed Tim, in the plans for the new block you've laid out accommodation to a similar style to the flat that you are currently using. That surprises me. Both you and Mrs. Blackstock have military experience. Surely units for eight or ten in a barracks style would be more economical. Two dorms like that could share a common room, a kitchen and bathroom. In the space you've designed to house six twin bedded rooms you could actually sleep twenty."

"I must say you've given us a lot to think about Ian and I'm sure Sue will take your suggestions on board. Let's go and find Eric."

They found him in the lounge talking to Stella.

"Hello Eric," Ian held his hand out to shake Eric's.

"Mac, you haven't changed a bit."

"A few pounds heavier and a little less hair."

"And still flying I see," Eric commented. "I've been talking to your daughter. She's been telling me about the problems of finding work in Wick."

"I don't know of anywhere quite as bad, Eric. There just isn't a great turn over of people. A high proportion of families have lived there for generations. There are very few new businesses coming to town. The oil and gas businesses gave the place hope but even that is reducing these days. My business is having our worst year ever."

"So that's why you're looking for a new job."

"Partly that and partly the new planes are getting more automated, flying isn't the fun it once was. The sky's are too crowded, you are told how high to fly, when to turn, how fast to go. Anyway Eric its good to see you again and I hope to see you again very soon."

"Same here, have a good flight home."

"Rob, is there a café or somewhere in the village where Stella and I can get some lunch."

"The 'Dog and Gun' is your best bet, good food and plenty of choice."

"The plane won't be in your way for the next couple of hours will it?"

"No, go and have some lunch before you fly home."

Rob went to his own office at the academy. Business was quiet at the moment, just one team out working on a period drama, staring Sean Connery, at the Warner Brother studio in Watford. Eva was with the catering truck and Ana was busy in the office working on a food order to replenish her stocks.

Billy Martin was at his desk working out a new stunt. The director wanted a car chase to end with a car rolling end over end. He had worked out how to achieve the stunt and was now deciding how many cameras he needed and where they should be placed.

For once Rob had very little to do and he'd caught up on his paperwork in just a couple of hours. He checked his emails and started to delete those he didn't need to keep. He came across the email D.S. Stevens sent with the photo of the man who took Sue. He opened the email to look at the picture once more. Maybe he had been watching Sue around the yard and someone saw him. If he printed it off he could pass it around to find out. Ana was at the printer as Rob photo came out.

"Rob, did you just print this?"

"Have you seen him somewhere?"

"You don't know who this is, do you?" Ana asked him.

"It's one of the pair who took Sue."

"Then she's in great danger."

"You know who it is don't you?"

"It's Mikhail Gorkov's brother. It's Ivan Gorkov."

Chapter 19

"I'm very happy that Susan Blackstock is finally dead. I can just imagine the agony Robert Blackstock is now going through. Almost two weeks and no word from her and no clue as to where she could be. I've decided to send him a note, make him fear his own safety and perhaps give him a scare or two but there is no need to hurry. I can wait until my son goes back at school in September."

****

Rose heard someone knock on the front door. "Who can that be? It only 7:00." She opened the door and gasped at what she saw. It was a total surprise and it worried her. "Sorry to bother you this early on a Saturday morning. Is Mr. Robert Blackstock in? I need to speak with him on an urgent matter," the policeman at the front door said.

"You'd better come in out of the rain1 constable, I'll go and get him."

"I'm Rob Blackstock, my mother said you wanted an word urgently. Is it news of my wife?"

"In a way it is sir. On Wednesday your wife hired a light aircraft for four days, Friday 9th to Monday 12th. The plane was collected at 8:20 yesterday morning and signed for by your wife. Take off was at 8:30 with a destination of Orkney. At approximately 9:30 the plane crashed and a subsequent explosion totally destroyed the aircraft. Emergency teams arrived on the scene at 10:05. A lady believed to be Mrs. Blackstock was retrieved from the wreckage, no other bodies were found."

"Are you saying she is dead?

No sir. I understand that the lady did suffer burns, a broken fibula, several broken ribs, some cuts and bruising plus a nasty bang on the head, which the doctors are most concerned about because she was unconscious when the rescue team found her and she still hasn't woken. D.S. Steven has asked me to take you to the hospital to confirm this is Mrs. Blackstock."

"Certainly constable I'll just grab my jacket and I'll be out."

He rushed back to the lounge. "They think they've found Sue, mum. She's been in a serious accident but she's alive."

"What sort of an accident dear?"

"A plane crash."

"Oh God!" Rose put her hands to her face.

"The constable it taking me to the hospital, I'll call when I know more."

Rob was met at the hospital door by D.S. Stevens.

"How is she Sergeant?"

"She's just gone into surgery to remove a blood clot that is causing pressure on her brain. I've got a photo of her here which I'd like you to look at to confirm that it is your wife." Stevens held out his phone so that Rob could see the screen clearly.

"Yes, that's my wife, Sue."

"Thank you. There's a room upstairs we can wait in. The medics will bring us news when there is any development. I've got a few questions you might be able to help me with."

They travelled up to the third floor in the lift and sat in a small empty waiting room.

"Before we start sergeant, can I just say that one of my staff has positively identified the man that took Sue as Ivan Gorkov, a known member of the Russian Maffia."

"From the description given by the people the plane was rented from, he was the one who signed for the plane and used your wife's credit card to pay the bill. His body wasn't found in the wreckage so we're assuming he bailed out before the crash."

"Do you know why it crashed?"

"Not yet. The black box will tell us but that will take weeks so we're hoping your wife can shed some light on what happened when she wakes."

A doctor appeared at the door. "Mr. Blackstock?"

"Yes, I'm Robert Blackstock, how is my wife? Is she going to be okay."

"The procedure went well and I'm optimistic about the future. I was able to remove the clot that was causing her problems and I'm expecting to see a significant improvement when the anaesthetic wears off. She may even wake."

"What about the other injuries?"

"She has a broken fibula. It's a clean break, it won't need surgery and we'll get it plastered up as soon as the bruising goes

211

down. Her left side from shoulder to ankle and her left arm suffered some burns as the track suit's cheap fabric melted rather than flamed, so the skin was scorched rather than flame grilled. That fabric probably saved her life, the burns are minor and will heal quickly. The fire did not damage her lungs which is good news. All in all she was extremely lucky. From what the paramedics have told me the largest piece left of the front of the plane was the seat your wife was strapped to."

"Thank you doctor. Can I see her?"

"She's in post op at the moment but a nurse will come and get you as soon as she's settled in a recovery room."

D.S. Stevens had been on the phone while Rob was talking with the doctor. When he ended the call he turned to Rob and said. "We've put out a warrant for the arrest of Ivan Gorkov, for the kidnap and attempted murder of your wife and in connection with the murder of D.S. Howard and two unnamed Russian ladies found in the Glasgow area. I wish I could say he'll be put away for a very long time, but I very much doubt he'll see any time behind bars, these Russians have all got friends in high places. Evidence will go missing, reports will be altered and statements changed."

"By bent coppers?" `Rob questioned the sergeant.

"Not just the police force, the whole legal set up is riddled with people prepared to turn a blind eye for a favour in return."

Rob rang home to update them, then the two men sat talking about many different subjects for almost an hour until a nurse arrived.

"Mr. Blackstock, your wife is awake and asking for you."

Rob stood up to follow the nurse but turned to the sergeant before he followed and looked quizzically at him.

"Go and see your wife Rob. I'll wait here until she's ready to talk to me about what happened."

Rob smiled then followed the nurse.

His emotions took over when he saw her lying in the bed all wired up and a drip high up, feeding something into her arm.

"Hey, I thought you were a tough guy," she said in an unsteady voice.

"Obviously not as tough as you," he replied. "By all accounts you are lucky to be in one piece. What happened?"

"I don't remember much. I think I'd been to sleep. I seem to remember something about sitting in the back of a car, but that feels like it was in a dream. Then I remember being in the front of a plane as it took off but that's all fuzzy like in a dream as well. But when I woke up I found I really was in the front of a plane and I was alone. I remember thinking that my only chance of survival was to try and land the plane, which I did. It was then that things went wrong so I ended up in here."

"There's a police officer down the hallway waiting for your memories of what happened and to learn about what's been happening the last ten days. But he's happy to wait until you feel up to speaking with him."

"Not yet. I need a bit of time to think it over first."

"There were two witnesses to your crash. Well, actually only one saw the crash but two witnessed the explosion."

"Have you spoken to them, what did they say they saw?"

"It was Ian MacMillan, flying down for his meeting with you. He had his daughter with him. It was her that saw you crash. Ian said they turned back to check the wreckage when your plane exploded sending up a massive fire ball that almost wiped them out as well. It was Ian who reported the crash and triggered the rescue. But he was quite certain there couldn't be any survivors. Of course we didn't know then that you had been on that plane."

"How long have I been gone? What day is it? What happened about all the meetings I had planned?"

"Calm down and relax."

"How can I relax? Those meeting were about the future of my business, they were important. Now they are not going to happen for some time and if I don't get accommodation built for Prince Hassan by Christmas, he'll take his horses elsewhere."

"Don't panic! Tim stepped up and has done an amazing job. He and Eric did the interviews with the builders last week and he and I interviewed Ian yesterday."

"How did the interviews with the builders go?"

"You'll need to talk to Tim about that but from what Eric has told me, the first one was a washout, the second was a possibility and the third one was outstanding and has even made some suggestions to improve things. They've all been asked to get their quote in by the end of business Monday."

"And Ian, how did that go?"

"Amazing. He's got so many brilliant ideas about improving the running of the place. Ideas about modernisation and efficiency. Honestly Tim and I were shell shocked by the amount of good practical thinking he came out with, such good ideas and we think you need to offer him the job as soon as you can."

"Did he say what he felt about the job?"

"He made it very clear to both of us that he is keen to get it. I'm going to speak with Trisha on Monday morning because Ian's daughter, Stella, graduated with a two one in maths and wants to train in accountancy. She would be a good match for what Trisha is looking for, to do your bookkeeping. We also spoke about accommodation for them both. Tim and Jenny are moving in together into a house in the village, so we said to Ian that the flat could be available until he finds something more suitable."

"I appear to be surplus to requirements," Sue stated.

"Not so darling, they have all been told that you'll be deciding who gets what?"

"Excuse me Susan," a nurse stood at the door said. "Sorry to interrupt but there is a young lady out here who would like to see you".

"Send her in please nurse."

"Only for a few minutes then I need to do your obs and change your dressings. So your visitors will have to leave until after the doctor has been."

"Luci, how wonderful!"

"I had to come to see you, gran drove me in," Luci said with tears rolling down her face.

Sue reached out to hold her hand. "As you see I'm in one piece. I can't give you a hug because I'm a bit sore. Don't worry I'll be out of here soon and we'll have a girly day out together, go shopping and have a good lunch. How's Peter?"

"Really stressed out. I'm keeping out of his way at the moment. He's very worried about his results, they are due out on Thursday."

"I'm sure he'll get what he needs to get into Edinburgh," Sue tried to reassure her stepdaughter.

"That's what I keep telling him, but he is so on edge."

The nurse came back and asked them to leave.

"I'll go home now with mum, have a shower and get into some fresh clothes and come back after lunch. That policeman will want to talk to you once the doctors been, don't let him tire you out," Rob kissed her forehead. "I love you".

It was still only 10:30 when they got back to the house.

"I'll get some coffee on, are you ready for one?" Rose asked.

"Not for me mum, I'm going to have a nice long hot shower," Rob said.

As Rob opened the front door of the house another vehicle pulled into the drive.

"It's a builder." Rob told Luci and Rose. "I wonder what he wants?"

"Mr. Blackstock, I assume? I'm Will Moss of Moss and Dixons. I was invited to quote for the building work Mrs. Blackstock wants done. Is she about?"

"I'm afraid not Mr. Moss." Rob said.

"That's a pity, I've brought my quote for the work and wanted to explain it to her. It's a complex project and I've tried to keep the quote as simple as possible, I really need to talk through the quote with Mrs. Blackstock to be sure she is clear about every part of it.."

"I'm afraid my wife won't be back for some days, she's in hospital following an accident."

"I'm sorry to here that. I hope she makes a full recovery."

"I will be seeing her every day, so you can explain it all to me and I'll pass it on to her. Let's go into the office and you can talk me through it."

Will Moss followed Rob down to the yard then up the steps into the office. They sat facing one another across Sue's desk and Rob moved the overflowing intray to one side. Will Moss then had somewhere to put the bundle of papers he was carrying.

"I've also enclosed a build projection," Moss said.

"What is a build projection?"

"It's a sort of timeline, let me give you an example: I work out how long each stage is going to take and plan out the whole job so that materials and a crew are ready. So here foundations might take two days to dig so I plan concrete pouring for foundations for day three, four days for that to go off, so brickwork can start on day

215

eight and I know that I have to have materials on site and men ready for that day. If the men are on another job until day ten, then I know I've got two days leeway in the first seven days and so on through the whole project. That gives me an estimated completion date or as I prefer to call it a target date. I also plan for bad weather by adding three days to the date for each month."

Rob looked at the builder totally confused.

The builder explained, "What I'm trying to say is, if my plan tells me that a project is to finish on day sixty, then I add three days for every twenty and set the target date as day sixty nine. So for this contract with Mrs. Blackstock, I've split it into four phases, because I'm guessing she will need to keep her business running while the work is being done. Here is my breakdown and costs." He pulled some papers from an envelope and handed them to Rob.

BLACKSTOCK STABLE MODERnISATION AND EXTENSION

Assumed start date 02 September 2019.

Phase one –North end stables £420,000 Target Date 31/10/2019

Phase two –Strip and refit existing block (cost dependant on unknown structure of building and possible strengthening required)

Minimum £32,000 Target Date 26/11/2019

Maximum £48,000 Target Date 02/12/2019

Phase three – South end stables £490,000 Target Date 17/01/2020

Phase four –Re-lay yard floor £12,000 Target Date 31/01/2020

OPTIONAL EXTRA

Laying new vehicle access and parking for six vehicles £12,000

Prices include:- Electricity, hot and cold water supply to all stables and accommodation units. Warm air central heating to all accommodation units, Integrated fitted kitchen, sealed unit windows and doors, all bathroom furniture(white) in six x two bed accomodation units. Removal of all waste.

It does not include:- floor coverings in accommodation units or fixtures and fitting in stable units……

Rob gave up after reading the summary page.

"The rest is a full breakdown of material costs and sources including fridges, cookers,washing machines and heating boilers," Moss told Rob.

"Can you explain why the second stable unit will cost £70,000 more than the first unit?"

"Most of that cost is because of the soil in that area, the samples I took last week show very poor soil structure at that end of the site and we will need to have far deeper foundations. It will also sit over your existing site drainage, so drains will need rerouting." Moss explained.

"And the two quotes for refitting the existing building is because you don't know what you'll find when you strip it out?"

"That is correct."

"Well thank you for all this, I'll sit down later and go through it in detail. We have got other quotes coming in, they need to be in by close of business Monday so we'll let you know which we select early after that. But you say you can start 2nd September."

"That's right. The first job is to push through an access road then dig out for foundations for the first block. For that I need my digger and its on another job all next week."

"As I said, I'll talk my wife through all this and get back to you with her decision early next week. Thank you."

Rob walked Will Moss back to his car then went back into the house for his shower.

From his bedroom window Rob had a good view of the front garden. The dominant feature was the driveway. Starting at the far end some eighty yards away the gatehouse where Madge lived, the gravel drive with lawns either side came straight towards the house, twenty yards short of the house the drive widened to the full width of the plot. Rob visualised looking at the house from the gatehouse. To the left of the house the driveway continued past the house and on down to the yard. This was the only vehicle entrance to the yard, even the horse boxes had to go that way. To the right of the house the driveway continued to a double garage that was rarely used for cars. Will Moss was right it all looked a mess. There was no edging to the drive and in many places the grass was creeping across the gravel. The gravel itself had large areas where weeds had taken over and the grass desperately needed a cut. The hedge that marked the boundary of the property had gone wild and look like a farm field hedge.

Madge's husband Reg used to keep it all looking tidier, but it all got too much for him as he got older. He had died suddenly last November and Rob had paid a stable lad to cut the lawns a couple of times. It certainly gave a poor impression to visitors.

After a light lunch, Rob drove back to the hospital. When he got to her room the nurse he had seen earlier told him that Sue was doing very well and she had been move onto the wards and she gave him directions. When he eventually found her, someone was in a high backed chair by the bed with their back to him. Whoever it was they were making Sue smile. He stood at the end of the ward for a moment, Sue spotted him and beckoned him towards her and he saw that the mystery visitor was Tracy Mills.

"Tracy how on earth did you find out Sue was in here?" Rob asked.

"You forget we're almost family, Rob," she answered, "your Luci told Peter and he told me."

"You just happened to be in Yorkshire."

"I'm actually on the trail of Ivan Gorkov. I'd been told he was involved in Sue's abduction. Then when Tim rang me this morning to tell me about him and Jenny Buck, he mention that Sue was in here. So I got straight in my car and drove up to ask Sue if she had heard anything in the last ten days that might help. I arrived about half an hour ago, told the nurse I was Sue's sister so they let me in."

"I've told her they talked Russian all the time and they didn't speak much around me, but I did her two words repeated several times. Sudno which is Russian for ship and Liverpool." Sue said.

Tracy added, "I'm guessing he got on a ship in Liverpool docks yesterday and by now he's half way to Russia."

"I hope you are not getting too tired, Sue."

"I'm fine, you should know by now I'm immortal," she smiled. "Tracy was telling me about those clubs, no wonder you were keen to go with Ana."

"I didn't look, honestly."

"Well, I think I'd better be off and leave you two love birds alone. Hope you're better soon."

Rob settled into the chair.

"What news have you got for me?"

Rob told her about Will Moss turning up with his quote.

"Tim says he only expects one more quote. Oliver and Dunhill seemed keen to get the job, but he thinks it's too big for the others."

"You said earlier that Ian MacMillan had some ideas. Can you talk me through them so I can give them some thought while I lie here."

"Not just Ian but Will Moss also made some valid points."

"Well out with it."

"Will Moss pointed out that the first thing your new customers will see is the house and front garden, which if you hadn't noticed are in a right mess. First impressions count with new customers. He reckons the house needs a coat of paint and some rendering and we need get the front garden properly landscaped, also put fresh gravel on the drive and have the drive edged. I was looking this morning and think we also need to get some security. We could start by getting some remote controlled gates installed and some motion detecting lights."

"What else did he have to say?"

"He asked if we had considered how much additional traffic will be generated and passing by the house. He suggested making a new entrance specifically for the yard. He said permission would be quite straight forward and it would be cheaper to have it done while his equipment was on site."

"Any more bright ideas?"

"Ian, or Mac as he likes to be called, questioned why you had gone for two bedroom apartments. He pointed out that two dorm type rooms with shared facilities in each block would be cheaper to build, easier to maintain and give you more capacity."

"He's right about that, we'd get twenty in the same space as we'd planned twelve. Can you speak with Brett Willoby and get the plans changed and find out if this impacts the planning permission?"

Rob continued, "Mac has suggested several ways to improve the yard, simple things mostly, like when we're mucking out use a trailer behind a quad bike rather than the traditional wheel barrows."

"Such a simple thing, why didn't I think of that Rob?"

"You said a couple of weeks ago you were worried that you were doing this all alone and you were thinking of creating an advisory committee."

"And I've done nothing about it," Sue stated. "All of these suggested changes are very good and need looking at. I need to get out of here as quickly as possible."

"Don't be in too much of a rush. It's Saturday afternoon in the middle of August and the weather this weekend is hot and dry, nothing needs to be done until Monday. If you are so eager to get back in the saddle I'll bring you the Moss and Dixon quote. It's quite a document, you'll need time to digest it all."

"Rob, can you tell the nurse I need a bed pan please?"

Rob left the small ward looking for a nurse. When he came back he was followed by a nurse pushing a wheelchair.

"Doctor says we're to get you up this afternoon Susan, so we'll ask hubby to wait in the common room while I wheel you off to the ladies."

When Sue was back in bed the nurse told Rob he could go back in.

"You look worried Rob. What's up?" Sue asked.

"Not worried, I was deep in thought," he replied, "I was thinking you could put your advisory committee together from here, they are only a phone call away. You could even run a meeting from here using video conferencing."

"That's something worth thinking about, but I haven't given any real thought as to who I want on the team."

"Well you don't want too many, they have to be people who will add value and accept that you have the final say. Tim is an obvious must, after all he'll be the one who's got to work the place."

"Ian as well, if he takes the job."

"I'm sure he will. I also think Trisha would add value by challenging cost versus benefit. Can you think of anyone else?"

"I was thinking that Ana would be useful, she's got a good eye and when it comes to soft furnishings in the accommodation units she'd be an asset."

"Is that it?"

"Yes, I think the four of them will do."

"I'll see if D.S. Stevens still needs to keep your phone as evidence."

"He left it with me this morning. I think he put it in my drawer here."

Rob looked, found it and passed it to Sue.

"The battery is flat," she announced.

"I'll bring a charger when I come in this evening."

"I didn't expect you back again today."

"I can't leave you here without anyone to talk to, when everyone else has visitors."

"I'd be alright, Tracy brought me a few magazines."

"It might be best for you to rest. I'll go and ask if they've got a phone charger at the nurse's station."

He was gone for ages.

"Sorry I was so long but I had to go to the hospital shop for one. I just hope it's long enough to reach the wall."

He fitted the lead to the plug and plugged it into the wall behind her head and lay the phone on her bed side unit.

"You should be able to reach that. When it's got some charge check that you've got all the numbers you need and give me a call if you need any."

"Thinking about what you said earlier Rob, about an access road to avoid all the traffic going past the house. It would be good to see a bird's eye view of the whole site. We've only got a block plan for new blocks and I think it would be good to have a view of all the land belonging to the stables. We could then see what something like a new access would give us."

"Sounds like the sort of thing Justin would have an app on his phone to do, I'll get him on it as soon as I get home. Anything else you need?"

"Not that I can think of. I can always call you if I think of something."

A bell rang to sound the end of visiting and all the visitors on the ward were standing and saying their goodbyes.

"Ring me in the morning, let me know how you're doing. Visitor time tomorrow is two 'til four. I'll be as early as I can," Rob said and lent forward to kiss his wife goodbye.

Chapter 20

"We have DNA results from the two murdered girls, sir. Traces of the same DNA was found on each of the girls, which confirms they were connected in some way. We were unable to match the DNA to anyone but we did get a partial hit which indicates that the person is a sibling of Mikhail Gorkov."

****

"Where were you last night, young lady? You'd gone even before I got back from the hospital?" Rob said when Luci came down to breakfast. "It was gone 1:00 this morning when I heard you come in."

"Dad, think about it. It was the second Saturday in the month. 6th form party night. I went early because I was one of this month's organisers, That's the reason I was late home as well. Peter's dad drove us."

"Sorry Luci, but when you didn't answer your phone, all I could think of was what happened to Sue."

"You know we have a no phones rule at these parties so that no photos get taken. Everyone has to hand their phone in at the door and collect it at the end, I didn't switch it on again until about ten minutes ago."

Justin appeared and went straight to the fridge for a carton of milk and poured himself a glass full.

"I had a look for an app that would do what you want, I found a couple but they required measurements to be entered and photographs to be loaded."

"If it can't quickly be done then I'll do something freehand."

"I didn't say I hadn't done it. I've used google maps, I got a satellite view which I took a screen shot of and loaded it to a photo editor then drew around all the buildings etcertera to create a tracing which I'm printing out now."

"You clever lad, I told Sue you could do it. Can you show me?"

Justin ran to his room and was back quickly with two sheets of paper which he laid on the table in front of Rob.

"I enlarged it to print over two sheets."

"This is fantastic son, well done."

"You're all up early for a Sunday," Rose said as she walked into the kitchen. "Has anybody put the coffee on?"

"I'll do it gran, you sit down."

"Thanks Luci, grandad will be down shortly."

Before Rose had chance to sit, someone knocked on the backdoor behind her, so she turned and opened it.

"Madge what ever's wrong, you look terrible. Come in and sit down."

"Oh Rose," was all the housekeeper could say before she burst into tears.

Rose put an arm around Madge's shoulder and guided her to a chair at the table.

"What ever is wrong dear?"

Holding back the tears Madge explained.

"My daughter Beth has breast cancer."

"How terrible. So soon after having the baby as well," Rose said.

Madge continued. "She is starting treatment almost immediately, first session is next Monday. I will be needed to look after the baby. I've been up all night thinking about this and decided I'm going on Friday, that gives me three or four days to get things sorted."

"Of course you must go, don't worry about us. We can look after ourselves if we need to, take as long as you need."

"No Rose, I mean leave for good. I won't be coming back."

"Don't make any hasty decisions Madge, take a few weeks to think about it then decide," Rob suggested.

"No Robert, I've given this a lot of thought. I'm not getting any younger, I'll be sixty six in a few weeks and qualify for my state pension, so I'll have money. If I'm to be perfectly truthful I hated being in that house on my own since Reg died last November. The house is too big for one person and everywhere I look I still see Reg. As much as I love you all, this has been my family for thirty five years, it's time to look after my own family, while I'm still fit and able.

"Where will you live?" Luci asked, tears building in her eyes.

"The top floor of Beth's house is like a flat with a lounge, bedroom,bathroom and kitchen. It's even got its own front door."

"What about your furniture?" Rob asked.

I've only got one or two bits I want to take. It should all fit in my car. I was thinking if I left it all you could rent out the house as furnished accommodation."

"Although I'll hate you for leaving, I understand completely why you have to go. It's family, of course you must go, they have to be your number one priority. I'm lucky I've got my family all around me," Rose added.

"Thank you Rose, that means a lot. I have to go now and talk to Beth, I'll be back later."

Sue was sitting in the chair reading a magazine when Rob got to the hospital.

"This is a bit of a surprise, seeing you out of bed like this. Two days ago we thought you were dead."

"I keep telling you I'm immortal," Sue replied. "I've had a busy day. I've been walking on crutches and had a shower. That was an experience with my leg in a plastic bag stuck to my skin above the plaster, but I insisted. I felt so dirty, I knew I must stink, I hadn't had a shower for over a week. The house I had been held in wasn't very clean and then there was the crash. I just needed to feel clean again and a bed bath just wasn't enough. I must say the nurses were very good, two of them helped me. They put a stool in the shower so I didn't risk falling, helped me in and out, then help me dry and dress and got me back to here. One got so wet she had to change her uniform."

"How is your leg?" Rob asked.

"The doctor says it is a good clean break with no displacement and should heal quickly."

"And the burns?"

"Apparently all very minor. Fresh dressings were put on after my shower only to stop the material of the gown rubbing them. But they say that in a couple of weeks they will be completely healed and probably no scars.

I've also had another MRI and there are no more head problems."

"You've been incredibly lucky."

"From what Tracy was saying yesterday, Gorkov and an unknown woman were the only two responsible and I must have been held somewhere near Manchester," Sue said.

"That's about all the police have to go on. But let's not talk about that, look what Justin has done." Rob handed Sue a copy of the bird's eye view he had created.

"That's great, exactly what I wanted. Thank him for me please, darling."

"He's done this as well." Rob handed Sue another piece of paper.

"It's a satellite view of both Blackstock Stables and Blackstock Stunt Academy. See, he's marked out the borders of the two properties," Rob pointed out the red lines marking the properties. "Do you see how close they actually come at that one point there is just about one hundred yards between them. I've lived there all my life and didn't realise they were that close."

"Is that because the two points are parts of the properties that are down in the hollow, always wet and boggy and totally overgrown?"

"That's right. As kids we used to go down there to shoot rats. Whenever we walk from the stables to the academy, we always go over the brow of the hill in a line between buildings across Russell's property which more often than not he's got livestock on."

"What are you trying to say, Rob?"

"That bottom part of Russel's field is totally useless to him. He's always had it fenced off. So I was thinking of offering him a good price for it, just a strip of about twenty yards and then driving a path through to connect the two properties. Nothing too fancy but enough to be able to ride a quad bike through. It would mean we could get from one to the other in just a few minutes rather than twenty minutes walking across the field or the three mile drive on the road."

"Sounds to me you've already decided," Sue concluded.

"Well, when I'm home, I do that journey three or four times each day so it would save me about an hour a day."

"So go and see Russel and see what he says," Sue suggested. "Now what have you brought me?"

"These are the first two quotes, Oliver and Dunhill's quote was hand delivered this morning to Tim. I don't expect much from the third company. Dad wasn't impressed with them at all. Price wise there's not much between these two but Moss and Dixon appear to be more modern in their thinking."

Rob handed Sue the two quotes and spent a long time telling Sue what Will Moss had explained to him about his planning process.

"You said the quote was delivered to Tim. How is he?" Sue asked.

"Work wise things are going very well. I think it was three winners last week. But he was very down this morning. He and Jenny were looking at houses to rent in the village yesterday, they looked a four and didn't like any of them. Two didn't have a garage which he must have because apparently he's spent years restoring a 1960s MG. It's in an old shed at his brother's place at the moment, but that's coming down as part of the changes up there, so he needs a secure garage to keep it in. They are looking now at other options further away."

"That's not so good. It's a shame the flat at the stables isn't a bit bigger," Sue said.

"Oh I must tell you this. Madge is leaving us."

"Oh no, why?"

"She's going to live with her daughter who has been diagnosed with breast cancer. Madge says she needs to look after the baby while Beth has treatment."

"I can understand that. It's still a shock though. She's been with your family so long, you're all going to miss her. How's Rose with the news?" Sue asked.

"Upset, but already planning to get the place deep cleaned and decorated then advertised as a fully furnished rental."

"Would it suit Tim and Jenny? It's a big three bedroom place and it has a garage. I want him to take on some of the vet workload once we have a second manager, it would be wonderful if he was virtually on site."

"Brilliant idea, I'll sound everyone out over the next few days," Rob promised.

He stayed until the end of visiting time. Sue told him he was looking tired and he shouldn't come back for evening visiting and he conceded that a relaxing evening would be beneficial.

Rob was late for the start of visiting on Monday afternoon.

Sue greeted him with, "I was thinking you weren't coming."

"No spaces in the car park, I've had to park about a mile away," he explained.

"I've had a very busy day. I now have a review committee and our first meeting is on Wednesday afternoon."

"Do you need me to bring in a laptop for your conference?" Rob asked.

"No need," She said smiling, "they say providing I can get myself to the toilet and wash myself tomorrow morning, I'll be discharged."

"That's great news."

"I'll need you to bring me some clothes this evening. You'll have to bring a skirt because of this plastered leg. Get Luci to sort something out for me."

"Good idea."

"Like I said, I've had a busy day. I've spoken to Tim and Trisha and they are happy to be part of the committee. I haven't been able to get hold of Ana yet but I rang Ian MacMillan, he wasn't there but I had a lovely long chat with Stella. She sounded a very nice young lady, she told me about seeing a plane crash when they came down on Friday and was shocked when I told her it had been me. She didn't see how anyone could have survived. Neither can I. She sent me some pictures she took of the wreckage. Look!" Sue showed Rob the pictures on her phone. "Ian rang me back about an hour later and I offered him the same contract as Tim is on. He accepted with one condition, he wants to bring his plane and use the field until he finds somewhere permanent to keep it. He starts 14th October. He also agreed to join my committee and will take part in Wednesday's meeting via video link.

This afternoon I rang Will Moss. Moss and Dixon's start on 2nd September. Will is also going to get together with Brett Willoby to cost up an access road and a parking area with sufficient space for four horse boxes and six cars. He says he'll change the entire look of the entrance so you'll turn off the road into a wide entrance with options to turn into the gatehouse, the house or the yard. Plus he'll revise the accomodation based on two dormitories for four bunk beds and storage for eight people above each new block. He is also happy to be a member of my committee.

Finally this afternoon I've been speaking with Eric about landscaping the garden and getting the work done on the house. I said I'd pay if he and Rose would contact Will Moss's wife. I also asked Eric to try and find two new horse boxes."

"You have had a busy time."

"Yes and I'm knackered, so I'm going to have a rest now."

"I'll leave you quiet then and come back at 6:00 with a bag of clothes."

He kissed her and left.

"What have you been up to Luci, you look like you lost a penny and found a pound," Sue asked Luci when she came down to the kitchen for a mid morning coffee.

"Peter just rang me from school he's just got his A Level results. He got four A's so he's got his place at Edinburgh vet college.

"That's wonderful, give him my congratulations! That will be you next year, then you'll be off to Oxford."

"It is wonderful and I'm thrilled for him but it gives me a huge, huge problem."

"Tell me, I might be able to help."

"Peter's dad is taking the family out to dinner tonight as a celebration of Peter's results and I've been invited. But it's Madge's last night and gran is expecting the whole family in the 'Dog and Gun' to see her off and I really want to be there. If I don't go and dad doesn't get back in time, it's not going to be much of a party."

"Your dad said he will try his best to be back in time."

"I still don't think it right, him going off to London for two days, the same day that you came out of hospital, after almost being murdered."

"It was something he had to do himself," Sue defended her husband.

"What do I do?, I want to see Madge off but I also want to celebrate with Peter."

"If it were me and Peter was my boyfriend I wouldn't want to share the celebration, I'd want it to be the two of us. I'd want to hug him, kiss him, show him some emotion and I don't think I could do that in front of his family."

"Certainly not, it's embarrassing enough eating a meal with them."

"Why not decline the offer, tell his dad something like you think it should be a family thing because it might be the last chance before he goes off to uni in four weeks time. Then see Peter face to face and tell him exactly how you feel and you want the two of you to celebrate together. How about cooking him a meal sometime before he goes to university, followed by a movie?"

"I don't think my cooking is quite up to that." Luci admitted.

"I'm sure granny will help and I'll take everyone else down the pub so you get the place to yourself for a few hours."

"Thank you so much Sue, I knew you'd know what to do, you're the best step-mum ever!" Luci gave Sue a kiss on the cheek and ran back upstairs.

Friday was an emotional day for everyone. Rob and Justin helped Madge load the few bits she wanted to take with her into her car, fortunately the chair she wanted came apart otherwise they wouldn't have got it through the car door. Eventually everything was loaded and the whole family came out to see her off. After hugs, kisses, a few tears and promises to keep in touch she left.

Tim was at the door at 8:00 on Saturday morning. Madge had shown them round the house earlier in the week and he and Jenny loved it and wanted to move it immediately. They had agreed to clean and decorate the place in lieu of a month's rent, he'd come for the keys so that they could move in.

Rose had helped Luci plan her special meal the following Friday. It was basic but should taste fantastic and most importantly there was no last minute work to be done. She had chosen Peter's favourite starter, prawn cocktail, the main course was beef in red wine which was cooking in the slow cooker all day, with new potatoes, peas and carrots and to finish, she made individual cheesecakes.

Rob wasn't too happy about leaving them in the house alone but Sue talked him round, she also convinced him to get them a bottle of Prosecco. Rose volunteered to drive, she didn't drink but knew the others would want a drink. They left at 6:45 and Luci went upstairs to change. Eva had done her makeup and Sue had helped her choose what to wear, telling her to look sexy for him but not to be silly. Luci knew what that meant.

Back downstairs she poured two glasses of fizz and turned the veg on to cook while she waited for Peter. She had told him 7:15.

Peter was just leaving as Rose pulled the car up to the house.

"Are you walking home, Peter?" Rose called jthrough the open car window."

"I am Mrs. Blackstock," he replied.

"Then hop in and I'll drive you home."

The other four went into the house and through to the lounge. Luci was in the kitchen loading the dishwasher and putting leftovers into the fridge.

"Do you want a malt dad?" Rob asked.

"Yes please, Rob."

"I'll have a whisky too please, Rob," Sue said.

"And me," Justin asked.

"You can have a beer and be thankful," Rob told his son and headed into the kitchen to get the drinks.

"Hi darling, how did your dinner go?"

"Perfect, thanks dad." She gave him a hug and kissed his cheek.

As Sue sat down on the sofa she saw something sticking out from under the cushion. Recognising immediately she discreetly screwed it up and put it in her pocket.

Later Sue knocked on Luci's door and waited to be called in. She closed the door behind her, went across the room and sat on the edge of Luci's bed.

"These are yours I assume," she said holding out a pair of knickers. "It's a good job I found them and not anyone else. Are you going to tell me what happened?"

"Nothing really we just played around a little. We didn't have sex. Where did you find them? I looked everywhere, I thought Peter had kept them."

"Be careful young lady. You are playing a dangerous game. Next time you may not be able to say nothing happened. You're not eighteen for another few months. If he's as infatuated with you as you are with him, he'll wait."

The last week of August flew by. Because of the plaster on her leg and persistent rain, Sue had to leave almost all the day to day work to Tim and didn't even leave the house. On the plus side it gave her time to make small changes to the plans. She confirmed the new access road and got Ana involved in the new look accomodation units. Brett Willoby drew up revised plans and Will Moss took responsibility for getting the necessary planning authorisation.

Yesterday was the last Sunday of the school holidays. Rose had prepared a full roast beef Sunday lunch and insisted that all the family attended. That meal also marked the end of the old Blackstock Racing Stables. Today work would begin on the New Blackstock Racing Stables. Sue had looked out at 7:00 and Will Moss was already there. He was stood in the field talking on his phone and making gestures with his other hand. She saw a digger arrive and start to rip out the hedge where the new wider entrance was to be.

Two men with surveying equipment marked out what was to become the new access road. Will Moss, with two other men, plus the digger had moved to approximately where the new North stable block was to be built. Moss was walking round waving his arms and pointing at things. There was no doubt who was in charge and he was giving his men their instructions for exactly what he wanted from them.

By the end of the first week, two neat rows of curb stones, set in concrete marked the access road and car park, the top soil between the two rows had been scraped off and piled high in a mound in the field. The sites of the two new stable blocks had been cleared, this also entailled breaking away sizeable strips off the edge of the concrete yard. The North block foundation had been dug and the concrete poured.

Rob had been down to London again but he had to come back for the weekend to take Justin back to school on Sunday. He was able to get away at 2:00 and was home at 5:30. He went straight to look the building work over while it was still daylight and was amazed at the progress made. He then went in the house with a large bunch of roses and a small gift bag.

He walked into the lounge saying, "Hi everyone, I'm home." He held out the roses to Sue. "Happy anniversary, darling." He bent down kissed her passionately and placed the roses and gift bag on her lap. She slowly opened the bag and took out a small jewellery box. Inside was a pendant in the shape of a rampant horse carved from pure jet black opal.

"It's beautiful darling. What I've got you is nothing like this." She handed him a long white envelope. He ripped it open carefully and pulled out a certificate of ownership of a barrel of whisky.

"I've bought you a full barrel of single malt from Tayside. It's only three years old at the moment. When it reaches ten year old they will bottle it as 250 bottles of Blackstock single malt."

"Wow, that's something to look forward to! I think I'll have a malt now. Anyone going to join me?"

Yeta Gorkov had sent Rob a letter on Tuesday which had arrived Wednesday when he was in London. It had been put on the mantle piece behind a photograph of him and Sue taken at their wedding. Yeta had taken her son to school on Thursday. He was a first year boy at St Anne's Boarding School For Boys. All first years were starting on Thursday giving them two days before the rest of the boys return. On Friday she drove to Yorkshire, she stopped on the roadside at a spot where she could look down at Blackstock Stables through binoculars. Rob Blackstock's car wasn't there, but she knew Blackstock had a son away at school in Edinburgh, he would be taking him up there this weekend. So where ever he was now, he'd have to come back here in the next couple of days. If she could get a tracker on his car she would know where to find him when she needed to. She didn't want to kill him yet, that would come later when he had grieved for a good period. She had rung ahead and booked a room in a small village inn about six miles from the Blackstock Stables, so went there now to register and have something to eat. She could return later to check if he was home, it wouldn't be dark until almost 8:00 so she had plenty of time to eat before driving back. There should still be enough light to see if the car was there.

The sun was just setting in a ball of fire behind the hills when Yeta returned to the spot where she had earlier looked down on the stables. Looking down across the front of the house she could just make out the car she wanted to see. If she moved her car down into the village she could park in the pub car park without it attracting any attention. She could then walk to the stables, it was only just over a mile, at least two thirds of the way was well lit so she could be there and back by 10:00 easily and be away in her car while there were still several cars in the car park.

There were lights on in the gate house but the curtains were drawn and music was playing quite loud, so she just walked by on the other side of the driveway making as little noise as possible. As soon as she was through the gateway she got off the gravel and onto the grass where she could walk almost silently. The rear of the house was all lit up but all the windows at the front were in darkness and she was confident there was no one around to see what she was doing.

Rob's car was parked right up against the grass, so she was able to go right up to it and place the tracker in the wheel arch. Then she simply retraced her steps back to her car.

The tracker didn't move all day Saturday but when she checked the monitor app on her phone at breakfast, the car was already fifty miles north on the A1. They must have left about an hour ago. The round trip should take around eight hours, so she had approximately six hours to get into position. She had already selected the place where she was going to ambush him. Rob was almost certainly going to leave the A1 at the junction with the A59, half way up the slip road, the road passed a small wooded area. Yeta planned to lie in the undergrowth with her sniper rifle, watch the tracker on her phone until Rob was nearing the junction. She would then shoot out the near side front tyre as he passed here. He would be slowing for the junction so he should maintain control of the car and get it off the road to change the wheel.

Everything went as she had planned it and Rob had to spend twenty minutes changing a wheel, thinking how unlucky he had been to pick up a puntured. It wasn't until he took the tyre for repair that he found out he had been shot at.

While Rob was out next day some post arrived for him and Rose put it on the mantle piece behind the photo. She remembered to tell him they were there when he got home and he sat and went through them.

"What's wrong? You've gone white!" Sue asked.

He said nothing just handed her the letter.

'Now you know what it's like when your partner is murdered and you are left to grieve. But your suffering will end soon. I killed your wife and you are next but not yet.'

Every day there was something new being done on the extensions, drainage pipes were laid, the floor base was put down and walls began to rise. By the end of September the shell of the first block was finished including windows and external doors. The bricklayers were now working on the second block getting it up to damp course and the access road was ready for tarmac. Sue had been back to the hospital to have the plaster removed. Ryman had assumed his post as Rob's bodyguard and everyone was being extra cautious, especially with new faces on site almost daily.

Sue had given little thought to her Scotish property until she received a letter from Howell, Blake and McPhee, telling her that they had just transferred £18,800, into her account, payment of tenants rent for second quarter. The solicitors office was acting as agents, an arrangement she had made when she went through the mountain of paperwork. Luci had been pestering to see the castle ever since she had first heard about it. Thinking back, Sue recognised she had not had much of a look round the place herself because they had to rush back when Eric had his heart attack.

Rob came in through the back door of the house just at the moment that Sue ended a call on the house phone.

"You've just missed your son on the phone," she said.

"He hasn't lost his phone again has he?" Rob enquired.

"No, nothing like that, in fact I think you'll be quite impressed. He rang to say he wouldn't be home at half term, he's arranged with his tutors for extra classes in a couple of subjects that he's struggled a bit with," Sue explained.

"He's finally got the message that he is there to study and none too soon," Rob commented.

"Rob, I've been thinking about my castle and we didn't really have time to explore, consequently we still don't know the place very well. So how can we decide on what we're going to do with it? We do need to spend some time up there and if we don't go soon the weather will make it difficult. I'd like to spend a couple of days producing a set of floor plans. Luci is also keen to see the place, so I thought we could go up for half term week if you are free. What do you think?"

"Good idea. If we take the Range Rover we could take the trailer and some trail bikes and spend some time checking out the area. See what local facilities there are for food and other essentials. I've got a couple of things in the diary for that week but they could be rescheduled. But what about you, isn't the first block supposed to be finished that week?"

"That was the original plan, but Will needs his bricklayers on another project at the time they should be working on the original block, so I've agreed to a few changes. We are focusing on the loose boxes in both units first, so that we can move the horses out of the old block and have a bit of spare capacity for three or four early new arrivals. We'll still have the first dorms ready for when we need to increase staff."

"Okay then," Rob said, "we'll travel up on the Sunday, there will be less traffic and we can probably do the journey in about eight hours, we don't want to be arriving in the dark. We can come back on Saturday, it's not so critical to get home in daylight."

"We'll need everything we would take if we were going camping except we don't need a tent. We'll need provisions for the week but without a fridge we'll need to find whatever local shops there are," Sue said.

"We've got three weeks to get all that sorted out. We should get Luci onto it, with Peter away she's got time on her hands. With all her camping experience she should have no trouble."

Chapter 21

"Father, it's Yeta, I've had a message from Ivan Gorkov, he's bringing you ten girls. He says that twelve is too many, it needs more than one vehicle to transport them and that would attract too much attention. His ship will dock in Felixstowe to offload part of its cargo on evening of 28th October. I am to meet him there. He will meet his men with the van the next morning, then together we will drive to Scotland. The ship is due to be at the jetty at midnight 31st."

****

"Rob, we've had a letter from the palace. We are to make ourselves available to meet Sir Rodney Leverage who wants to come and talk to us about our invitation to tea with the Queen. He's coming here on 7th October at 11:00. We both have to be here when he comes. He's going to tell us how to dress, where exactly to go and how to behave when we are with the queen."

"I appreciate it's an honour but I'd rather it wasn't happening," Rob complained.

"Don't be silly, She's not interested in you she wants to know whether I'll have space for some of her horses," Sue laughed.

"It was 23rd when we are supposed to be a the Palace isn't it?" Rob asked.

"Yes dear, why."

"I was just thinking, I've got some business I need to arrange in London. So if I were to arrange meetings for 21st and 22nd, it would give you time in the city to find the new outfit you will obviously need for tea with Her Majesty. Of course you have nothing suitable in your wardrobe."

"You're learning quickly," Sue smiled. "We'll know more about what to wear on Monday when this Sir Rodney has been."

"I shall have to move my meeting on 23rd back a day."

"I was a bit cautious flying down on the 13th but we did say I would start on 14th and to me that meant first thing, not half way through the day."

"Good afternoon Ian, nice to meet you again," Sue offered her hand. "This must be Stella. I understand Trisha is interviewing you on Tuesday."

"That's right Mrs. Blackstock. It would be the perfect position for me and I'm very interested in the accountancy training. I know a lot of accounts procedures from my degree course and would very much like to learn more."

"My name is Susan, or Sue as most people call me."

"And I'm Mac," Ian added.

"Well Mac, you don't appear to have much luggage. Do you need help unloading and carrying stuff up to the flat?"

"No thanks, we've only a couple of bags of clothes each and four or five boxes of personal items. We learnt the practicalities of keeping possessions to a minimum when I was in the FAA and we were continually moving around."

"Well if you are sure," Sue said. "We'd like you to join us for dinner this evening, Tim and his girlfriend Jenny will be there, plus Eric and Rose.

"Love too, wouldn't we Stella?"

"Come over when you are ready, have a drink before dinner. Rose is doing roast pork for 6:30. See you later."

"Sir Bernard, how are you?"

"I'm fine thank you, Sir Rodney."

"Excellent," Sir Rodney Leverage, member of the Palace security team reported. "Her Majesty was most impressed with Mr. and Mrs. Blackstock, she felt they were very modest about the part they played in the Venezuelan incident. She was extremely interested in Mrs. Blackstock's racing stables and the work she's having done to modernise. They spent a long time discussing the training method Mrs. Blackstock employs and how Sir Henry Herbert trains the Queen's own horses."

"They are the sort of people this country needs more of," Sir Bernard suggested.

"The Queen would like to reward them more publicly. She is suggesting an MBE for services to national security."

"We need to be very careful not to let what actually happened to be known to the general public. There are possibly only ten people who know the full story and I intend to keep it that way," Sir Bernard said.

"That was not what I expected. She's just like a posh version of my grandmother," Sue said when they were back in the car driving back to the flat. "I didn't expect to be in there for over an hour. She is so knowledgeable about breeding and training racehorses, you'd think it was her day job."

"It's remarkable that at ninty three she still manages to go riding regularly," Rob added.

"At least we've got something we can tell everyone that we talked about. She didn't even mention Venezuela once," Sue said. "Rose is bound to want to know every detail."

"And Luci will," Rob added.

"She'll be too busy getting things ready for Scotland," Sue suggested. "I'm going to be far too busy when we get home Friday afternoon to help her. I've got to meet with Will Moss for a progress report, speak with Tim about Mac's progress and Eric wants to go over the landscaping design."

"I should be free on Saturday to help her, to get the Range Rover packed and get three trail bikes onto a trailer hitched behind it," Rob said.

"You'll also have to take her to the supermarket for provisions. Luci's got a list but I suggest there will be less people in the store Friday evening than Saturday."

"Maybe we should think about driving home when my meeting finishes. It won't be until 5'ish so it will be late when we get home but would give us all day Friday, as well as Saturday," Rob Suggested.

At breakfast on Friday everyone wanted to know everything about the their tea at the palace.

'We're they the only two?'
'What was she wearing?'
'Did she pour the tea?'
'Was there anything to eat?'
'We're any other family members there?'.......

Once the interrogation was over Rob, went shopping with Luci's list. He had to pass her college so dropped her off first. Meanwhile Sue sat in the lounge with Eric and looked over the proposed landscaping. Hedges on both sides to be ripped out and replaced by fences, the drive to be edged by curb stones and re-gravelled, spring and summer flowering shrubs planted in large half moon shaped beds, cut into the grass on either side of the drive. Remote control gates mounted on brick pillars would be installed, these would trigger switching on driveway lighting when opened. Finally either side of the front door would be a raised flower bed giving colour for most of the year.

"I like it Eric. What do you think?" Sue asked.

"It's simple and low maintenance, I'm more than happy."

"Then we'll go with it shall we? Send me the bill."

As she walked out and towards the building work, Sue saw Tim and Mac walking towards the exercise gallops. They were obviously getting on well , she would check with Tim later to see how Mac was getting on. She found Will Moss with Ana upstairs in the new north block. It was just an open space from one end of the building to the other at the moment, no internal walls had been built yet, just marks on the floor where the walls would be. They were looking over the latest redesign of the accomodation, which had one dorm with six bunk beds at one end, next to that were four shower rooms and four washrooms each with toilet and wash basin, the final one third of the length would be the day room with soft furnishings, dining area and kitchen.

"What's all this? Secret meetings?" Sue asked jokingly.

"No, no, Ana has made a very good point. She's pointed out that we haven't allowed for separate areas for boys and girls, we were up here discussing options to bring to you, but as you're here now we can show you. The solution is actually very simple."

"Show me on the plan," Sue said.

"This end wall of the dorm has a door in the centre of the wall." He place a finger on the plan to show where he meant. "We replace that with two doors six inches apart and we run a stud wall the length of the room effectively creating two dorms."

"Excellent. But isn't it a bit late. Sue said looking around at all the plumbing and electrical wiring that had already been installed.

"No. All we have to change is to move what was to be a central light in the larger dorm. It only has to move a few feet so that its central in the smaller dorm, then add in another loop for a light in the other dorm."

"Good answer. Well done you two. Anything else you need to discuss Will? If you remember you won't be able to contact me next week.'

"No, Sue we're good. If anything, we are slightly ahead of schedule. I've checked with the council and we are okay to go ahead to put a drainage ditch in next to the access road and run it into the stream at the bottom. So that will done early next week and the tarmac should go down on Thursday."

"Brilliant. I must get on to the sign company and get a board made up for the entrance, maybe I can do that this afternoon."

Luci had the back seat to herself apart from three air beds and three sleeping bags piled on the seat behind the driver, who was Sue. Although her left leg was not back to full strength, this was an automatic, so her ability to drive was not in question. In the five minutes it took them to reach the A1 she had got used to pulling the trailer and its load of three trail bikes and jerry can of fuel. Rob, in the front passenger seat, was keying something into the satnav trying to avoid possible hold ups. It was telling him that the journey would take eight hours thirty three minutes. That would be without stopping which he knew they would have to do. It was now 6:50 and they were being treated to a most spectacular red sunrise. With the trailer on tow Rob, resigned himself to the journey of four hundred and sixty five miles taking close on ten hours. He had check sunset time in Balnakiel and it was 4:40. If the journey took any longer than ten hours they would be arriving in the dark. At least the traffic was light at the moment and Sue was two or three minutes ahead of the satnav prediction which had dropped from 3:23 to 3:20. Maybe if they managed just two quick stops and ate their lunch on the move, they could perhaps only add forty five to sixty minutes to that time. But he said to himself all they can do is hope for no holdups and for the weather to stay dry.

Rob took over the driving from Queenferry Services just before the Forth bridge. From here their journey began to slow down as roads changed from motorway to just single carriageway. Towing a trailer made it difficult to pass any slow vehicles and Rob slowly lost the time that Sue had gained. For the last few miles before Inverness, the A9 again became dual carriageway but with a speed limit, at least he was able to get past most of the lorries. He just hoped there were no speed cameras.

Their journey just got slower and slower as the roads got narrower and narrower. Eventually they were on the track to the castle.

"There it is Luci, our very own castle," Sue said.

"It's not as grand as I expected," Luci said disapointedly. "It looks more like a big Manor House."

"Well it has been the site of at least two fights," Sue said. "In 1745 cannon fired from the roof tops saw off an attack by Clan Macleod. Some argument over a bride's dowry. Then in 1942 soldiers billeted in the castle, fired on a German U-Boat surfaced in Balnakiel Bay, forcing it to submerge."

"We're a little earlier than I expected," Rob said. "We've got about thirty minutes of daylight left. I'll drive right up to the front door, then if you two begin unloading, I'll attempt to get the generator running,"

Rob moved quickly to the outbuilding where the generator was. It was dark inside so he needed the light on his phone to read the instruction plaque which for some reason he read aloud.

"1. Ensure there is fuel in the reservoir and the valve is in the open position.

2. Pump the primer until pressure builds

3. Pull regulator to full open position

4. Press starter repeatedly until engine runs

5. As engine warms, turn regulator to achieve optimum running speed

That seems simple enough. Where's the fuel can?"

He wedged his phone on a ledge so that the light shone on the generator. The fuel can, when he found it, was almost full and next to it was a funnel which he place in the generator's fuel tank, then poured in a good amount. He found a small brass pump which he pumped four or five times and felt it being resisted. The regulator was next to the starter button and in just a few minutes the generator was ticking away sweetly. The overhead light in the out building was burning brightly, as did the outside light above the front door.

Sue met him at the door. "Can we turn on all the lights we need?" she asked.

"I don't really know. I assume there is some sort of safety device that prevents nasty things happening if we overload the system, but I don't know what or where to find it. So just be a little cautious and we'll experiment tomorrow in daylight," Rob warned her.

"Everything is in from the car but it's not locked," Sue told him.

"Okay, I'll push the bikes into one of the outbuildings in case the weather turns, we can find somewhere for the Range Rover in the morning."

He pushed the bikes and the trailer into an outbuilding that smelt of animals, locked the car and went indoors. Locking the door behind him he went up the stairs to the main hall where he could see lights on.

Luci was kneeling in front of the fireplace, gently fanning a small pile of smouldering chopped sticks, trying to encourage some flame. Sue was about the room closing shutters at all the windows.

"The shutters at the end window are broken but the rest work. The temperature in here dropped rapidly when the sun went down, so we're shutting these and getting a fire going to make it nice and cosy," Sue explained.

"Where have you put the bedding?" Rob Asked.

"In the first two side rooms," Sue answered. "They are obviously bedrooms because we found a washstand in three of them but strangely no furniture. In the end room we found a pile of sheep fleeces that have been cleaned and dressed, so we won't be cold at night."

Luci spoke up. "I know what happened to the bedroom furniture. It's been burnt. There are still a few bits of polished wood at the back here under these logs."

"I wonder why, because there's a pile of split logs outside big enough to last all winter." Rob said.

"I can't think my Uncle George would cut up his own furniture to burn, if it was him. He died years ago so why is it not covered in dust and why is there no dust on the table?" Sue queried. "When we were here before we read Yasmin's message written in the dust on the table. Somebody has been living here for some time.

I'm guessing they were here up to about a week ago, I say that because when I first came up the stairs today I got a face full of cobwebs, it would take a spider about a week to construct something of that size, any longer and it would have been dusty and I would have seen it."

"I can see why people keep telling me what a great investigator you are," Rob said. "That's a cracking piece of detection. It also explains why the generator started so easily, it's been running recently. Have either of you found a bathroom?"

"There is a toilet in a tiny room under the stairs. It's a chemical one like you get in a caravan. Could do with a good clean, it stinks," Luci screwed her face up in disgust.

"What I don't understand is why didn't the surveillance teams see anything?" Sue said.

"Because they were removed six weeks ago," Rob said. "I rang James Bull at MI-5 last week to tell him we were coming up here, so he could make his team aware. He told me that financial cuts have forced the removal of the surveillance teams, and replace them with motion triggered cameras and alarms."

"Well obviously the alarm doesn't work," Sue claimed.

"Tomorrow we'll be able to have a good look around in daylight," Rob said.

"You don't think it was Ivan Gorkov, do you Rob?"

"It may well have been."

"Egg, sausage and beans okay for you two?" Luci interrupted.

"I hope you haven't planned scout camp food for every meal," Rob moaned.

"I have, but I think you are going to be very surprised with what you get," Luci defended herself. "I planned this for tonight because I had no idea what we would find here or even when we would get here and this is quick and easy."

"Egg, sausage and beans will be fine," he said.

"With a glass of Prosecco to make it more classy," Sue said.

"Now you're talking my language," Rob smiled.

"That smells like coffee," Rob said.

Sue was up and dressed. "It probably was once but it's been brewed for ages. It's 9:15, you been asleep for about twelve hours."

"Gee, I must have been more tired than I thought," Rob said, "I'd better get up, there's a lot to be done."

"There's water in the jug by the washstand. It's probably cold by now," Sue told him.

Rob shivered as he washed in cold water, dressed and went out to the main hall where Luci and Sue were chatting. They stopped as soon as he appeared.

"What are you two secretly hatching?" Rob asked.

"Just girly stuff dear, nothing for you to be bothered about."

Out of sight from Rob, Sue squeezed Luci's hand and whispered, "we'll talk later."

"There's coffee in the pot if you want one, dad. It's been made a long while but it should still be drinkable. I put a bag of rubbish out earlier and found another bag outside that some animals have ripped open and I could see all manner of fast food wrappers. I've also had a good look downstairs. I discovered a massive kitchen with a large table with twelve chairs around it."

"Servants dining room I expect," Sue said.

"In the kitchen I found a small microwave and one of those dual cooker rings and grill units plus a fridge. They all look quite ancient. The fridge had a half bottle of vodka, a can of Scotish Ale and some mouldy cheese in it."

"I think that proves someone has been living here for a few weeks," Sue claimed.

"It looks like being a pleasant day today, so we should go exploring the area, find out where we can get food supplies from etcetera, start to get to know our surroundings."

"Where do you think the best chance of finding a shop is Rob?" Sue asked.

"Probably Durness, a mile east or so. Some of the Croft's have roadside stalls selling their surplus. There are always eggs and vegetables somewhere," Rob said.

"Actually dad, there are quite a few shops in Balnakiel," Luci claimed, "I looked it up on the internet. There's a craft village with loads of little outlets. All the normal things you'd expect to find like potters, wood turner, painters, and art gallery. But there is a chocolatier called 'Cocoa Mountain' that is also a coffee shop. There's a small restaurant and even a boat builder".

"That might be worth visiting. It could be a nice place for a meal one evening," Sue suggested.

"There are quite a few places in Durness, including a Spar shop and a pub, there is also a health centre which is worth knowing," Luci added.

"I'll go and get the car into one of the out buildings and get the bikes ready. Maybe we'll check out Durness this morning, have lunch at that pub, have a good look around to see what else there is, then pick up anything we need from the Spar. We could possibly look in at the craft centre this afternoon if we have time or we can do that another day. Are you ready to go?"

The trail bikes proved to be perfect for the tracks and narrow roads in the area and it took just a few minutes to get to Durness. There was far more there than Sue or Rob had expected to see. They walked on the beach but it was a bit too cold to stay long. They looked into most shops, just interested in what they had to offer. Rob bought a bottle of local ale from a craft shop to take home for his dad. They had lunch in the pub. The food was good basic pub grub but reasonably priced. Luci went into the Spar and bought pate and Fremch bread for their tea

By the time they got back to Balnakiel they decided it was too late for the craft village, better to do it when they had time to do it properly.

Tuesday started with similar weather and they walked down to the village. Because it was half term the shops were all open, they spent a long time browsing all of them. They stood and watched several people working on their crafts. At the chocolatier they enjoyed a free sample which tempted them to buy a large box. After an early lunch of panini and coffee at the small restaurant they called in at the village museum, they read about the 1942 U-boat sighting. With photographs showing just how close it had come to the shore. Other pictures were of the six soldiers who had fired on the U-boat and their officer. Luci noticed that the background in these pictures was not the castle, but an extremely rocky terrain and reading the text with these exhibits there was some sort of military building somewhere north of the castle. As they walked back to the castle they agreed that they should check out and explore the area north of the castle.

They collected their bikes and set off following the track past the castle over increasingly rocky terrain, almost entirely bare rock jutting almost a mile out into the North Atlantic. The only vegetation was odd patches of moss. This was possibly the most inhospitable place in mainland Scotland, yet there it was, the remains of a military outpost, complete with a twenty yard diameter concrete circle with the remains of a painted H on it.

"I didn't know helicopters were used in the Second World War," Luci said.

"Oh yes. They had many uses right through the war by us, the Americans and the Germans who were even landing them on ships," Sue explained.

"What gets me is if in the war the authorities felt they needed to watch this area for enemies landing here, why are they surprised when they discover smugglers are using it," Rob queried.

On Wednesday and Thursday it poured with rain all day, so they used the time to produce accurate plans of each of the seven floors, the cellar and the attic, plus the roof. They made notes about everything as well as taking photographs. The rain eased on Thursday afternoon and eventually stopped in the evening.

Rob suggested that they could explore south if it was dry tomorrow. Also that they should pack as much as they could so they'd have less to do on Sunday. That way they could get away earlier. It was going to be a long trip home.

Chapter 22

"Sir Bernard, it's Tracy Mills. I've heard from Robert Blackstock, he had some news you'll be interested to hear. He, his wife and his daughter are spending the week at Balnakiel Castle in Scotland. Last night he had a visitor, Ivan Gorkov. There were others with him. They were in a white van and a sports car, like I saw when D.S. Howard was shot."

****

"Get the van open lads, they are just bringing the first girls ashore now," Ivan called out.

"Dmitry was not happy when I told him you only had ten girls when he had ordered twelve," Yeta told Ivan.

"Lavrov can go fuck himself, he doesn't take the risk, I do. Ten is all we can get in a van. Using more than one van would only draw attention to us. These villages don't get much traffic and to see two vans in the middle of the night just never happens."

They heard a splash, then another, followed by shouting coming from the jetty. Ivan and Yeta were only twenty yards from the jetty but there was no moon or stars so the scene was in total darkness, all but the light from a single torch.

"What's happening down there?" Ivan called out.

"All the rain has left the jetty very slippery," came a reply from someone on the jetty. "Two of the girls have slipped and fallen in the water."

"Get some fucking lights on them and get them out before they fucking freeze to death," Ivan ordered.

"They are going to need dry clothes Ivan. It's a freezing cold night. If they stay in those wet clothes they will be dead before you get them to London," Yeta claimed.

"I know woman, you don't need to tell me," Ivan responded aggressively. "Let me think."

All ten girls were now in the van. The two who were wet were wrapped in old blankets from the ship, but were shivering madly.

"I'll get some of the old boys clothes from the castle for them to change into. They'll be far too big and dirty but will keep them warm." Ivan thought out loud. "Wait here I won't be long."

A noise disturbed Rob's sleep. There it was again. *'Bloody rats.'* He thought. *'I hope Luci put all the food back in the fridge'.* Again he heard it, louder this time. *"That wasn't a rat. That's someone trying to get in.'* He climbed out of bed and went to Sue and gently shook her to wake her. He gently laid a hand across her mouth to stop her calling out and he whispered. "There is someone trying to break in. Go next door and wake Luci quickly and take her up to the attic. Both of you stay there until I come and get you."

"What are you going to do?" Sue whispered.

"Beat the shit out of who ever it is." He slipped the belt from his jeans and wrapped it round his hand leaving a long tail, ending with the heavy buckle. He carefully opened the bedroom door and held it open to let Sue follow him out. He watched as she opened the door to Luci's room then moments later he watched them climb the narrow stairs up to the next floor and onwards towards the attic.

He was bare footed so made no noise as he crossed the boarded wooden floor towards the hand rail at the top of the broad main wooden staircase. The glowing embers in the almost dead fire gave him just about enough light for him to avoid bumping in to any furniture. He looked over the hand rail down at the stairs. All the rooms on the ground floor and the first floor had high ceilings so there were a lot of steps in the staircase and two turns. He could see a faint light coming slowly up the stairs to the first turn. They were immediately below him so he could only see the glow from the light, which he guessed was from a phone, as is didn't penetrate the darkness very far.

Rob knew that as soon as whoever was coming up the stairs got his head level with the floor they would see him, so he quickly moved into the alcove next to the fireplace. He listened to the footsteps slowly coming up the stairs, each step creaking as the intruder's weight shifted. Then the sound changed a little to a slightly hollow sound as he, or she, crossed the floor moving towards the fireplace. Knowing he was about to be discovered Rob made his move, he stepped out of the alcove. The intruder was a man, similar in height and build to Rob and he held a gun in his hand.

Rob had surprise on his side and before the intruder had a chance to raise the gun, he swung the belt at the gun hand. The heavy belt buckle struck hard against metal, knocking the gun from the intruder's hand. It slid across the floor to the top of the stairs and they heard it clatter down many steps. The intruder reacted quickly and threw a punch at Rob, catching him on the side of the head. Rob launched himself at the other man. His shoulder caught his opponent in the midriff and drove him backwards hard against the wall.

The intruder clenched his hands together and brought them down heavily on Rob's neck and driving him to his knees. Before he could move away the intruder drove his knee up under Rob's chin sending him flying backwards across the floor on his back. The intruder followed him and went to drive his boot into Rob's ribs but Rob caught the foot and twisted it, causing the other man to fall. Rob was quickly on top of his opponent again and hammered his fist down into the other's face repeatedly, drawing blood from his nose. The man managed to throw Rob off and got in several blows of his own. Hearing all the noise, Sue had come down from the attic, seeing the intruder pounding Rob with his fists she rushed over and grabbed him by the hair and pulled. In his attempt to get rid of her, he swung round with his elbow catching Sue on the side of the head and sending her backwards across the floor leaving her senseless. Rob and the other man were now on their feet again exchanging blows. One blow from the intruder forced Rob to his knees again and the man lifted a chair and smashed it across Rob's back. He collapsed flat and didn't move. Sue had regained her senses, the intruder was stood next to the fire and she could now see who he was.

"Ivan Gorkov," she said.

"Mrs. Blackstock, I thought I'd got rid of you but it seems not. I'll have to have another go." He turned and picked up a leg from the broken chair. Sue turned and grabbed at one of the ancient shields hanging on the wall. It came away easily and the weapons behind it clattered to the floor. In a split second she raised the shield and was ready to protect herself from Gorkov coming at her with repeated blows with the heavy chair leg. Sue pushed back and Gorkov stumbled and fell. His hand landed on the fallen weapons and as he got back to his feet, he had a battle axe in his hand. He rushed at Sue and hammered the axe down hard on the shield. He was now in a wild frenzy of blows, hitting the shield eventually forcing Sue to her knees.

"This is the end Mrs. Blackstock. I don't know how you escaped from the plane but you will die now." With that he raised the axe high above his head and grinned. As he was about to bring the axe down his expression changed to a look of surprise. The tip of a sword burst from his chest. He collapsed to his knees, then fell onto his side motionless.

"Sue are you okay?" Luci asked.

"I am thanks to you. I thought he'd done for me there. How's your dad."

"I'm okay," Rob called out. "Who is he? Is he dead?"

"It's Ivan Gorkov and yes he's dead, thanks to Luci."

"Is he alone do you think?" Luci queried.

"I don't think anyone else is in the house, but I will take a look outside." Rob said. "I'll pick up Gorkov's gun. It should be on the stairs somewhere. You two go back to the attic, I don't want to be worrying about your safety when I'm outside."

He first went to the bedroom to pull on his jeans, sweater and a pair of shoes, he then picked up the gun on his way downstairs and went out through the front door. There was nothing in the driveway so he started to walk down the path to the jetty. It took a while for his eyes to adjust to the dark. He didn't want to use a torch just in case there was someone else about and he gave himself away to them. He slowly made his way down the path to the jetty. There were no vehicles there either but there were lights showing off shore and they were slowly moving out to sea.

Now that he was convinced no one else was about he felt it was safe to use the light on his phone to examine the jetty. He found dozens of footprints on the jetty where one or more people had walked across the rain soaked sand and then walked along the jetty leaving sandy footprints. It was clear to Rob that Ivan Gorkov and several others had been here to smuggle someone or something ashore. But he didn't understand why Gorkov had gone into the castle. Maybe he'd find a clue in Gorkov's pockets. So he headed back to the castle. As he came back round to the front of the castle he heard and saw a sports car race off down the drive. In its headlights he saw a white van driving away.

Sue and Luci were in the main hall when Rob got back.

"There was a lot of noise down here and then it all went very quiet, so we came down to investigate," Sue explained.

"What have you done with Gorkov?" Rob asked.

"I thought you'd moved him," Sue replied.

"Are you sure he was dead?" Rob asked

"If you mean did I check his pulse, no I didn't. I assumed a two inch blade pushed through his heart would kill him. No, someone must have come in and taken the body. But why should anyone risk doing that? Shouldn't we notify the police, Rob?"

"I don't think there is much point as we haven't got a body."

"What about letting Tracy know."

"She'll be interested for sure. I'll go down the village first thing, find somewhere with a good signal and ring her. Now let's all try and get some more sleep."

None of them slept deeply and as the sun lifted itself from the horizon at 7:30 Luci was already down in the kitchen making porridge. The smell of fresh brewed coffee lured Sue and Rob downstairs in their pyjamas.

"She does make a good cup of coffee, this daughter of yours," Sue said.

"Her cooking's not bad either. She's fed us well this week on this very crude equipment, I'm quite impressed," Rob added.

"Grandma is a good teacher." Luci claimed.

"That she might be, but you've got talent and you obviously enjoy doing it," Sue said.

"Well, I need to be able to feed my family one day."

"Not for a few years yet, I hope." Rob spoke up.

"Well I want four children and I want to have them before I'm thirty, so that I'm still young enough to play with them, like mum played with us."

"Yes she did didn't she? I think she was happiest when she was playing with her children or watching them play. Even the night she died she'd been with Michael at football training."

There was a silence now that Sue felt she needed to break.

"You're only seventeen Luci, you've got years to think about having children."

"I shall be eighteen in exactly seventy five days, my life is already drifting by."

"Does Peter know about you wanting four children?" Sue asked.

"He thinks the same as I do," Luci replied.

"Well he's not going to be earning for the next four years while he's at college. Then he's got to find a job and pay off his debts. It will be a long time before he can afford to have children." Rob explained.

"We know all that dad. I'll be graduating at the same time. If I get the grades that Durham University want it's a three year course."

"I had better get dressed and go and ring Tracy Mills," Rob announced.

It was a gorgeous autumn morning, the sun was bringing out all the colours in the rocks, the grasses and the heathers. There was just the odd gust of wind coming off the North Atlantic as a reminder that winter was just around the corner. It was about half a mile to the village and it was only 8:45, so he decided to walk. He was in the heart of the craft village before he got a decent signal.

"Good morning Tracy, it's Rob Blackstock, I've got some news you might be interested in, have you got a few minutes?"

You'll have to be quick Rob, I've got a very busy day. The Interpol job is on for this evening, Manchester, Birmingham, Glasgow and London all at 8:00." Tracy explained."

"Wow, good luck with that," Rob said. "Sue and I have spent the week at the castle exploring and measuring the rooms and the area. Last night, just after midnight we had a visitor, Ivan Gorkov. We fought and he's dead. There were others with him, at least two. They were driving a white van and a sports car like you saw the day Mary was shot."

"You say Gorkov is dead?"

"Run through with a claymore, but the strange thing is his body has disappeared."

"What do you mean, it's disappeared?"

" I went out to check if there was anyone else about and when I got back the body was gone and the sports car and van were leaving in a hurry."

"Very strange," she said. "When are you home again?"

"Tomorrow. We should be back around 6:00."

"Right I'll give you a call sometime tomorrow evening to tell you how this Interpol thing goes. If all goes to plan, it should be safe for Yasmin to come back."

Rob walked back through the craft village heading back to the castle. Several shop units were already open and some of the craft workers were hard at it. Rob was pleased to see that the boat builder was one of the ones working.

"Excuse me, mate," Rob called out.

"Yes, can I help you?"

"I was wondering if there is anywhere around here where I could by a quality padlock?" Rob asked.

"The closest hardware store is in Thurso, two hours drive away. But I do keep a few bits here and I may have what you're looking for. Have a look in that cabinet, second drawer." He pointed towards an old office filing cabinet against the wall.

Rob pulled the draw open and turned over the contents until he found what he was looking for. "What do you want for this one mate?"

"Is a fiver okay with you?"

"It's a bit low if anything," Rob suggested.

"That stuff came from a saleyard, all the stuff in that drawer and the one above it for £10. If the keys are with it, a fiver will be fine."

"Thanks a lot mate, see you again sometime."

When Rob got back to the castle he explained his plan to leave the trail bikes and the trailer.

"We'll need the bikes today but when we've finished with them I'll wheel them into the servant's dining room. I found a length of chain in one of the outbuildings and I bought a heavy duty padlock when I was in the village. I'll chain the bikes together. The trailer can stay in one of the outbuildings but I'll remove the hitch. Without the trailer we'll travel a lot quicker tomorrow and we'll need bikes whenever we're up here."

"That's a good idea," Sue said. "That will mean next time we come up here we can come in the car, far more comfortable than the Range Rover for such a long journey."

Yeta had reached Edinburgh before sunrise. It was a bit early to ring Dmitry Lavrov but these were exceptional circumstances.

"Father, Ivan is dead. Killed by the same man who killed Mikhail. Stabbed him in the back."

"What about the girls?"

"I have ten. We're at Edinburgh so should get the girls to you early evening."

"Good I'll get Mrs Chow. to get rooms ready for them and prepare a reception."

"Father, did you hear me I said Ivan is dead. His body is in the boot of my car. A couple of the girls needed clothes so Anton, Ivan and me went to the castle to search for something for them. We found someone was sleeping there. Ivan went upstairs and was set upon. As Anton and I watched from the stairs Ivan fought one against three. They eventually stabbed Ivan to death. That's when I recognised it was the Blackstock bitch and her husband. Anton and I hid until the coast was clear then carried the body out and into the boot of my car."

"Why have you got his body in your car? What if you are found with him. You need to dispose of him as soon as you can and make sure you get rid of every trace."

"Actually there's a reason I've got his body. He failed doing a job for me when he was alive, I'm going to give him a second chance now he's dead."

"I won't even pretend to understand what you mean, just be careful,"   Dmitry said. "Just make sure those girls get here this evening."

"They will be, but I won't. There is something I have to do tonight. Ivan's man Anton is here to help me."

Yeta spoke to the van driver. "Vasily go straight to the Four Aces with the girls and make sure they are there before 8:00. My father is expecting you, he will pay you and give you a job."

Then she got back into her car and set off with Anton travelling south west and picking up the M6 to Manchester. By lunchtime she was back in the house where they had held the Blackstock bitch two months earlier. She was there to collect a few items she needed for her plan. Wearing a glove she collected the manacle, several discarded cable ties, a towel, a shirt and pulled the belt from the trousers Sue had been wearing when they had taken her from the train. She stuffed everything into a plastic bag. These items were certain to have Sue's DNA all over them, perfect for what she was planning.

She waited until 11:00 before driving on towards Yorkshire and the Blackstock Stables, arriving a little after 1:00. The entire estate was in darkness apart from a solitary dim light in the stable yard way beyond the house. The sky wasn't clear but was giving enough light for Yeta to turn off her headlights and let the car roll past the gatehouse and the splendid newly laid tarmac entrance to the house and stables, then down the lane a little further and into the field gateway. The lane only went another couple of hundred yards to an electricity substation, so no one would be coming down there at this time of night. She was sure that she couldn't be seen from either the main house or the gatehouse.

"Google maps shows that there is a patch of woodland and wild undergrowth by a stream at the bottom of this field. That's where we'll leave Ivan's body," Yeta explained to Anton.

They lifted the body from the car's boot and lay him on the ground for Yeta to add what she hoped would be the evidence that would get a conviction. She fitted the manacles to his ankles, put some of the bag ties in his pocket. She tore the shirt and used strips of it to bind his wrists.

"Open the gate, Anton and we'll carry him down to the trees!" she ordered.

When they reached the little stream at the bottom of the field they discovered there were not as many trees as she had thought. Instead it was a mass of tangled briars twisting through hawthorn bushes and stunted holly trees. Yeta got Anton to pull away what he could of the undergrowth and make a small clearing big enough to lay Ivan's body in. They covered the body with some dead branches and freshly fallen leaves. Then they pushed briars back over where the body lay. As Anton stood back to check that the body wouldn't be seen unless some of the debris was moved, Yeta slipped the belt around his neck and pulled hard. As his life slipped away, he fell forward and slid down the bank and into the stream dragging briars and brambles down on top of him. Yeta pulled more down, plus some broken tree branches and the remains of an old horse blanket.

Satisfied that it couldn't be seen unless you were stood in the water she went back to the car, turned it around in the gateway and left.

The Blackstock's got on the road a little after 8:30. Luci had cooked some sausages and made a batch of sandwiches so they could eat breakfast and lunch as they went, then they would only need to stop for the toilet. While Sue and Luci had folded the bedding and loaded it on the seat behind the driver, Rob had shut down the generator, noting how little fuel it had used in the week. Without the trailer they made easy progress and were able to pass the slower vehicles.

"How are you Luci?" Sue asked as they drove through Inverness. "You've not said much about what happened Thursday night."

"I've not seen a dead person before and I killed him."

"You shouldn't think like that, he was about to chop me in half, you saved my life. You didn't kill him, you saved me."

"I guess if you look at it that way, it's not so bad," Luci conceded.

"It's the only way that you can look at it."

They stopped for the toilets at Edinburgh and Sue took over the driving. They were home at 4:20.

"Seven hours fifty minutes. I don't think we could do the journey any quicker than that, there were no holdups at all. The new entrance looks good. I'm going to walk back down and have a look to see what they've done," Rob said and Sue went with him but Luci went into the house to see her grandparents.

The forty or so feet of the side boundary hedge had been ripped out and a area of tarmac, approximately twenty feet square edged with curb stones, created a single entry to the three properties. On the left was a six foot spur to the short gravel driveway of the gatehouse. Straight ahead there was a ten foot spur running off at a slight angle towards the house. This would obviously join the gravel driveway to the house when the new edging goes in. Either side at the end of the spur were slabs of concrete that were the bases for gate posts for the new gates. The final ten feet of the square was the start of the new access road leading down to the yard with curb stones the whole length and drainage pipes every few yards. There were also bases for gate posts either side.

"All that we need is a big sign saying who we are," Sue said.

"Or have it worked into the gate somehow. The gate will always be shut and on a remote control won't it, so it can be read from the lane? I just think having a big sign with just the words Blackstock Stables on it would look a bit daft," Rob argued.

"I hadn't thought of that but you're right of course. You clever old thing," she said and gave her husband a squeeze as they walked back down the drive in the twilight.

"Luci has been telling us all about your intruder on Thursday night," Eric told Sue when she and Rob had joined them in the lounge. "Isn't he the same one who tried to kill you in that plane?"

"The very same, but he's no longer a threat to either of us. So we can stop looking over our shoulders," Sue answered.

"The new entrance is looking good dad," Rob said.

"It does doesn't it? They laid the tarmac on Thursday. The landscapers start on Monday, then we'll look even better with the hedge ripped out and a five foot fence replacing it plus the drive cleaned up and properly edged. They estimate it being a three week job," Eric said.

"And your builders have got on really well Sue," Rose said. "The roof timbers went up on the second block yesterday and the roof tiles have arrived, so I expect the roof will be finished this week. I saw Tim on Thursday and he was saying you'll be able to move horses out of the old block and into the first of the new ones by the end of the week."

"That's wonderful news to come home to. That means they are about a week ahead of schedule."

Rose had cooked curry for their dinner and they were still at the table when Rob's phone rang.

"It's Tracy, she should have news about the raids on the Russians last night. Hi Tracy how did it all go?"

"It was all a bit of a mess actually. We had two officers shot, one's critical the other just a bullet in the thigh. But we did achieve what we set out to do. That was to shut down the Russian operations

258

in our major cities. London was our main focus, as we knew it to be the centre of operations in this country. We particularly wanted to take their head of operations Dmitry Lavrov. But he was just taking delivery of his latest batch of girls when we went in."

"That could be what they were bringing in on Thursday night," Rob interrupted.

"Very possible," Tracy continued. "Well Lavrov decided to make a run for it out of the back door. He almost got away as well but he was hit by a red London bus and was dead before he reached hospital. The ten girls brought in were rescued and will be returned to Russia. The madam, Mrs. Chow, was the one who shot our two officers before she was taken by return fire from our own armed officers. Lavrov's daughter wasn't found but she is reported to drive a red sports coupe. So it could have been her you saw Thursday night. We did round up several other big players including Vladimir Zhukov, known to be a key person in the drugs distribution to schools."

"What about the other raids? How did they do?" Rob enquired.

"Birmingham, Manchester and Glasgow were all taken down. Internationally Germany, Italy and Spain all had similar stories to us but we hear France was a total blood bath, fifteen dead officers and several Russians got away. But overall the operation was a big success. We could never hope to totally destroy the Russian Wolves but we have given them a good kicking, it will take them a long time to rebuild. Most importantly we've cut off the drugs to schools. It will mean a hard few weeks for lots of kids as they detox and a struggle to keep other dealers from moving in."

Chapter 23

"Mr Truman, I am Prince Hassan Saleh Al Shammari. An associate of mine recommended you, as someone who can find the dirt on someone if there is any, no matter how deep it's buried. I need to know everything about Mrs. Susan Blackstock, Racehorse Trainer in Yorkshire.

****

Yeta was back in London by breakfast time, she had crossed the river on Kew Bridge then parked her car at Richmond Royal Hospital using a fake staff parking permit. From there she walked the last half mile to the Richmond flat rented in her maiden name.

She slept until lunch time then tried ringing her father but got diverted to voicemail. It was still early for him if he'd been up late in the club, so she decided to try again in a couple of hours and went into the kitchen to make her lunch. She turned the radio on to catch the mid day news bulleten. The first item was about the leader of the opposition, Jeremy Corbyn's reaction to PM Boris Johnson calling a general election on 12th December. It was the second item that grabbed her attention.

'Police in more than sixty major cities across Britain and Western Europe are this morning celebrating the total destruction of a major international drugs ring, in simultaneous raids, coordinated by Interpol. A spokesman for the Home Office said in Britain one hundred and fifteen arrests have been made, mainly of Russian Nationals, at locations in London, Birmingham, Manchester and Glasgow. This was an interpol led operation to stop the supply of hard drugs to more than eight hundred schools across Europe.'

Yeta turned the radio off immediately. "Shit!" she said out loud. Her brain was working double time to sort out her next move. She would have to get away, out of the country, back to Russia. But she was sure airports and ferry terminals would be on the lookout for Russian Nationals. She also had her son to consider, she couldn't leave without him.

As she thought her problem through, she remembered something Ivan had said. He was going to deliver the girls to her father Friday evening. Then he had to get to Liverpool to meet his ship which would be sailing mid afternoon on Sunday. If she were to drive up to St. Annes this afternoon, she could take her son out of school and drive to Liverpool docks and be on that ship when it sailed. The hard part would be getting her son Gregor. If the police were looking for her they would certainly be watching the school. Then she saw the answer on the table in front of her, a poster from Gregor's school advertising the school fireworks evening, all family and friends welcome to join their boys, gates open 6:30, food and mulled wine available. St Annes was a four hour drive so she could easily get there in time, park away from the school and walk in with the crowd. First thing to do was send Gregor a text.

'I'll be at fireworks meet me 6:45 by hot dog stand.'

But first she had too try and get hold of Gregor Rakmanov at the White Lotus to see if he knew what had happened. After trying several numbers she eventually got hold of him. He told her that he believed someone on the inside had given the police information that enabled a targeted attack to be made. They knew exactly where to go and who they were after. He said that one of his girls had been seen with the two dancers that now worked for the Blackstock's. The girl had been beaten and confessed to telling them details about 'The Four Aces' club. She arranged to pick up the girl, Rosie, half an hour later. Next she packed clothes into a small suit case and then she was off.

Yeta had torn a strip of material from Sue's tee shirt and when she stopped at the motorway services on the way, she parked in a remote part of the car park and when Rosie and her were walking back to the car after a toilet stop, Yeta slipped in behind Rosie, using the strip of cloth strangled the girl and piled her into the car boot.

"Sir Bernard, this is Agent Jones at Gregor Gorkov's school. There are crowds of people arriving, they've got some sort of do going on. There must be 400 or 500 people here, it's impossible to see whether the target is here. Can you get back-up here quickly, so that we can go in and mingle."

"I'm sorry Jones, Tracy Mills and Zoe Crump are in Manchester observing the cleanup after last night's raid. They are the closest to you, I'll get them to your location a soon as I can. In the meantime go in and see if there is a red convertible sports car in the car park and report back to me.

261

Sir Bernard called Tracy immediately, and got them heading towards the school.

With so many people at the event it was easy for Yeta to move with the crowd and make her way to where Gregor would be waiting. She found him easily and together they went back to her car.

They were on the M55 just five miles from the school but moving slowly through road works, the road was restricted to one lane in each direction, with so many portable lights it was almost daylight.

"That's her Zoe," Tracy said excitedly. "The red sports car on the other side, coming towards us. A woman driver and a child in the passenger seat."

"It might be her," Zoe watched the car as it passed them going in the opposite direction.

"It was her, that's the car I saw in Scotland. Put the two tones on and hold on tightly, we're coming off at this junction." With siren blasting and light flashing, Tracy pushed her way through the cones that were keeping traffic away from the works and had workmen jumping out of the way as she raced the one hundred yards to the junction, round the roundabout and onto the slip road down to the other carriageway. But the red sports car was out of sight. She turned off the siren and lights because there was no way of getting past the cars in front until the end of the roadworks. This lane had concrete barriers rather than cones.

"Zoe, ring Sir Bernard, tell him what's going on."

"The number's engaged."

"Keep trying, we're nearly at the end of the roadworks."

"I think we should stay back, Tracy. At least until we've spoken to Sir Bernard."

"We've got to find her first. I'll just get past these cars, we'll then have a clearer road and may be able to pick her out."

"Isn't that her just indicating to take the slip road for the M6 South?" Zoe pointed.

Tracy liften her foot off the accelerator and drifted across to the slow lane and they followed the sports car at about fifty yards back, letting that extend to one hundred yards, once they were on the motorway again.

"That's not the same car, Tracy. It's a nineteen reg. The one we were following was a seventeen reg."

"How did that happen? Bugger!" Tracy said.

It was a two hour drive to Blackstock stables, but Yeta did not intend leaving the body in the same place as she had left Ivan and Anton. She had researched the area and found that the patch of overgrown woodland went through to a minor road that ran past Blackstock Stunt Academy. She pulled off the road into a gateway that appeared to be regularly used by fly tippers. She dragged Rosie's body from the boot and into the undergrowth. Fly tippers had trampled a path into the undergrowth and created a clearing ten yards in. Yeta dragged the body in and threw an old mattress over her then threw a pile of black plastic bags and an old TV on top so that the body was completely hidden. Satisfied with what she had done, she turned the car around and headed for Liverpool.

It was a full twenty minutes before Zoe could get hold of Sir Bernard, by which time they were on the M62 heading for Liverpool.

"She'll be heading for the docks sooner or later, hopeful of a Russian ship to take her home," Sir Bernard surmised. "Hang around that area and watch for her, do not apprehend her, just get the name of whichever ship she boards. The Russians want her back, let her pay for her own extradition. Selling her sports car and the white van will at least ease my overtime bill for these last two days."

Rose cooked roast pork for Sunday lunch. Plates had been cleared away and Rose was slicing up an apple pie to have with custard.

"Anyone got any thoughts on what we're going to do for Christmas this year? Marge and Gran have always cooked Christmas dinner together, but we won't have Marge this year." Luci asked.

"Why don't you take Marge's place Luci?" Rose said.

"That's a good idea Rose, she's a grand cook." Sue added.

"I couldn't do that gran, I'm not good enough," Luci panicked.

"But you would be helping me not doing it alone. It's really a very simple meal, its just a roast with a few extras and on a grander scale," Rose said.

"Well, I suppose it would be an experience. Can Peter come?"

"Won't he want to be with his own family? Rose asked.

"Not if I tell him I'm cooking, so he's got to come," Luci said convincingly.

"You can see who wears the trousers in that relationship," Rob smiled.

"Not at all. I'll be quite happy to spend Boxing Day with his parents and I can't go there on Christmas Day, because I'm cooking dinner for you lot."

"I expect I'll be at some racecourse or other on Boxing Day," Sue said. Boxing Day is a Thursday, so we'll probably be somewhere Friday and Saturday as well and then there are a couple of big meets around New Year."

"Talking of New Year I've booked a table at the 'Dog and Gun' for New Year's Eve," Eric Announced. "My treat. I booked for twelve provisionally, I thought we should invite Mac and Stella and Tim and Jenny, plus Ana and Eva of course."

"That's very kind of you, Eric. It was an excellent evening out last year," Sue said, "apart from almost getting run over."

"It's a ticket only event this year. £15 per ticket, that gets you one drink and a plate at the buffet," Eric added.

"Sid has asked Jenny and Stella to work behind the bar and he's booked Ana, Eva and me for the evening to do a couple of sets. So that's four that won't need tickets, Granddad. I'm already working on a few ideas with the girls," Luci said. "He has also offered me a weekend bar job, as soon as I'm eighteen. Friday evenings and Saturday lunch and evening. He offered a lot more but I said no because of school work. He's desperate for someone full time."

"I don't like the idea of you walking home alone at midnight Luci." Rob said.

"I won't be dad, Stella has bought a car and she does Wednesday to Sunday evenings and has offered me a lift until I sort out my own transport. That's why I've applied for my provisional licence. Granddad has offered to give me a few lessons to get me started and I've spoken to Toby Read in the village, he works for '17+' and he said he can start lessons with me from 1st December."

"You've got it all worked out haven't you," Rob conceded.

"She certainly is her father's daughter," Sue proclaimed.

"I suppose you'll be wanting a car for your birthday," Rob suggested

"That would be good, dad. I'll have a car instead of a party," Luci laughed.

"What's going to happen to Yasmin Rob, now that the Russians have been removed," Sue asked.

"I'm waiting to hear from Sir Bernard. Apparently there is still one high ranking Russian at large," Rob explained. "It's the woman with the red sports car. She's the daughter of Dmitry Lavrov and the widow of Mikhail Gorkov."

"So she's Ivan Gorkov's sister in law," Sue concluded. "Then she was probably the woman who held me captive."

"Most likely," Rob answered.

"And that's also the reason Gorkov's body was taken from the castle, some sort of family loyalty," Sue reasoned.

"Maybe. This is all the latest information that MI-6 have. Tracy rang me this morning to update me, but really she was asking if I made a note of the red sports cars registration, which I didn't. I didn't even see what make it was. MI-6 assume she will flee the country and go back to Russia. But Tracy told me that this woman has an eleven year old son, he is a first year at St Anne's Boarding School For Boys, so MI-6 are watching there closely to see when she turns up and they'll take her then. Once they have her, Sir Bernard will ring me and we'll make arrangements to bring Yasmin back."

"So it could be soon?"

"Yes, but I don't think we should tell Ana yet, let's wait until we have something definite.

"Good morning Rose, has Rob gone to work already?" Sue asked then poured a coffee.

"No dear, he took his coffee into the lounge. I think he's talking to Bernard Howe on the phone."

"Morning darling." Rob came into the kitchen and put his empty mug down next to the sink. "I've just been talking to Sir Bernard."

"So Rose was just saying".

"Yeta Gorkov is onboard a Russian ship in Liverpool docks. It leaves this afternoon. The Russian authorities will catch her when she reaches Russia. He is still concerned that Ivan Gorkov's body hasn't turned up. But he says he sees no reason why Yasmin can't come back to be with her sister. Ana should be in the office this morning, so I'll let her know. I'll also ring Chuck in The States and get him to book her on a flight to Bradford-Leeds airport. She'll be here before the weekend."

Sue checked the office diary, she had a busy week ahead. First up was a review meeting with Tim and Mac in a couple of minutes, but her big task for today was to arrange meetings with a few potential new owners. She also wanted to invite her favourite jockey, Willie Jobe, to come and see the new look stables. From what she had seen walking around yesterday, the place no longer looked like a builder's yard. There had been an extensive clean up and there were two skips full of rubbish waiting to be taken away. The first new block was almost finished, all the loose boxes were ready for straw to be laid down and horses moved in. Upstairs all building work was complete, the kitchen, washrooms and showers had been fitted out, leaving just the walls and ceiling to be painted and furniture to be installed. In the second block the loose boxes just needed their floors laying, the upstairs was still just an empty space with a few pipes and electric cables here and there. Outside, sand had been laid over the areas where the concrete had been broken away to get the foundation for the new blocks. The car park at the end of the access road looked massive sitting empty, it would look a lot different with four horse boxes parked there. She had walked from the car park through the gap between buildings which the horse boxes would come through to load and unload. It looked too small a gap but she thought no one would make that sort of a mistake. She still had to step it out to convince herself it was okay. There was a similar gap the other side of the yard, through which horses going for exercise would pass. Also stable vehicles would come in through there from the barn where they were kept. It was all beginning to look very impressive. It had been hard work for the last ten weeks, trying to keep the business going while men were walking and working all around. She was glad she'd recruited Mac, even while he was learning the job, he was taking some of the pressure off her and Tim.

Tim and Mac arrived together, laughing about something, as they always seemed to be doing.

"Good morning guys, what have you been up to then while I was in Scotland?"

"Ian has done a grand job teaching me the job," Mac began.

"He's a good pupil. On Thursday I let him run three horses at Doncaster. I was there to observe but he had it all under control."

"I had my first winner."

"Yes it was Ross Jenkins's horse, so Mac's definitely the blue eyed boy with the Welsh ma,." Tim smiled.

"There is one thing I struggle to get my head around and that's race classes. Are they different for flat racing than they are for the rest?

"Slightly, I can try and explain it," Sue said.

"I'm not sure I fully understand it either." Tim said.

Sue began. "It's all about handicaps. After a horse has raced three times it is given a handicap by the twelve member British Handicapping Association. This gets reviewed weekly and changes are made depending on performances. The handicap determines what class of races a horse may race in and what weight he has to carry. It's all designed to give all the horses in a race an equal chance of winning, ensuring also that the best horses race together, for the biggest prizes. So a race might be for a horse with handicaps between seventy six and ninety, the horses with the higher handicap would have to carry extra weight to take away the advantage."

"I never did understand why some horses had to carry weight and others didn't. I assumed it was because they kept on winning," Mac said.

"Well it is, sort of," Sue continued. "A trainer can rig a horses handicap by running the horse in a race not suited to the horse, perhaps longer than it likes or weather it dislikes, so that it finishes well down the pack and consequently gets its handicap reduced. Then the next race it runs in, it will actually be a better horse than it's handicap shows and therefore has a better chance of winning."

"Surely that is cheating," Mac said.

"It's legal and all trainers do it. Class determines the quality of the race. Class 1 is the highest class and will be championship races. Here at Blackstock we only have two or three class One horses, so although we get a good number of winners we have very little chance of scooping one of the classics.

The purpose of all these changes are to attract more better class horses, so that we can be involved in more of the big races, competing for the bigger prizes. As a management team we need to learn to play the handicap game. But for now our priority is to fill the stables with quality horses. I've got seven new owners lined up. Three are owners dissatisfied with current trainers and four are new owners with very deep pockets in the market for class One horses."

"Quite a challenge," Tim said.

"Now you know why I need you both. It's not all about getting a horse fit enough to win a race but about entering them in the right race and targeting the right ones to win," Sue concluded. "I understand you're ready to move horses into the new building Tim."

"That's right, I discussed it with Will last week and agreed that we'd move all the horses out of the old block into the first new block, so that he can get a team in at the end of the week to gut it. At the beginning of next week we start work updating the old block's plumbing, electric, drainage etcetera. That's going to take two weeks to complete. The loose boxes will be built in the two weeks after that. Completion date 7th December."

"That's great news! It means we'll have maximum capacity well before Christmas. If there's nothing else, I think we had all get back to work," Sue said.

Sue went off to find Will Moss for a full update.

"Hi Sue, how was Scotland?"

"Mostly good, but a lot colder than down here," Sue replied. "Tim says you're going to be finished in early December."

"As far as the construction work we will be done but there are two jobs that are giving me a problem."

"What problems are they?"

"The biggest problem is laying a new yard. The concrete will need four days minimum to get hard enough for horses to walk on, so I'm currently thinking about doing it in two phases. Phase one involves laying a four foot band of concrete around the perimeter and using steel bridges to get the horses from loose box to the centre and from the centre to the path to the exercise area. Then phase two the next week, get the horses to walk on the perimeter band while we fill in the middle."

"That sound workable."

"The issue is that with a week needed to break up and remove the old concrete it becomes a three week job, which I can't start for two weeks because the crew will be working on the new storm water drain. So it will take us right up to Christmas."

"Why not do the yard before the drain?" Sue asked.

"That brings me to the other problem. With two new roofs, the access road and the bigger yard you will be capturing approximately eight times the amount of storm water. The current nine inch pipe won't cope, so we need to put in a new twenty one inch pipe across the field down to the stream. If we don't do it first and it rains the whole area could quickly get water logged and ruin the concrete in the yard before it has chance to go off."

"I've got a very important client bringing his horse here a couple of weeks before Christmas, so I need the yard finished before that. We'll just have to take a gamble on the weather and do what ever we can if we do get a storm."

"Okay, so long as you understand the risk," Will said.

Rob drove Ana to Leeds-Bradford airport on Friday morning to meet the flight from Los Angeles. On the journey back to the stables Ana sat in the back with her sister and they chatted away in Russian for the whole journey. As a thank you, Ana invited Rob and Sue to go to her house for a traditional Russian meal the following evening.

"But Ana can't cook," Sue reminded him.

"That's right but apparently Yasmin is a very good cook and it was her suggestion."

"In that case I look forward to it. I used to really enjoy my grandmother's cooking."

The next week the builders started breaking up the concrete slab of the old yard. Using a hammer drill attachment on the digger was extremely noisy. Because of that and the disturbance it would cause the horses, Sue had agreed that it would only be used for two hours each morning. It took three busy half days to break up the concrete and take it away. In the afternoons Will Moss got his men puting in the drive edging stones.

Once the concrete had been broken up and cleared away a pipe was laid to carry storm water from the second new block to a manhole behind the first new block, another pipe was set for a drain in the yard.

Everything was beginning to take shape. Two of the new owners delivered their horses, both were Class One with promising futures. The first advert for stable hands had produced three new workers, one from the village but the other two would need to take up residence in the dorm of the first block. Two of the current lads, who had to travel several miles each day also claimed places in the dorm, as did Sally Ball, a stable girl who lived locally but who Tim believed was suffering physical abuse at home. She was often seen carrying bruises. Sue and Ana had chosen the furniture and soft furnishings for the first dorm. Moss and Dixon's painters had decorated throughout. A flooring company had laid vinyl in the bedrooms and bathrooms, a short piled carpet in the lounge with Vinyl again in the kitchen area. By the end of the second week of November the first block was ready to be occupied and Sally Ball plus the two lads who lived miles away, moved in over the weekend.

The house too was beginning to look good. The drive was finished, the fences were up, the beds for the flowering shrubs had been prepared and the lawns mowed and tidied up. The house itself was getting a makeover too. The damaged rendering had been repaired, necessary repointing had been done and painting work had started. Another week and the house and garden would be finished apart from the new gates which would not be ready until the end of the month.

"This is a major milestone Rob," Sue claimed. "New owners, new staff and the first new building. I think we should have a small celebration, just the two of us, a bottle of Merlot and two steaks down at the 'Dog and Gun'".

"That would be nice,"Rob agreed. "It's been a long time since we had an evening out together. How about Saturday? I'll ring Sid and book us a quiet table."

"Thanks Rob." Sue kissed him then put her arms around him and pulled him in tight to her. "We need, sorry, I need, to think about what we are going to do to celebrate when its all finished."

"You mean a grand opening."

"Sort of."

The yard was busy on Saturday morning. Tim and Mac were getting ready to take five horses to Redcar, all with very good chances of a place at least.

"Good morning, Mrs. Blackstock." A voice behind her made her jump.

"Willy Jobe, good to see you." Sue turned and greeted the jockey she rated very highly.

"I was passing on my way to Redcar, I've got four rides there this afternoon, one of yours in the third race I believe."

"We're a bit out of the way to be just passing, Willy. I wasn't aware you were riding one of my horses. I'm afraid I've been rather tied up with the expansion work and the racing has been left largely down to my assistants."

"I must congratulate you on your assistants, they actually listen to me when I tell them stuff, unlike most trainers who treat their jockeys as the hired help. Those two engage with the jockey, make them one of the team."

"Thank you for sharing that with me, Willy. Now would you like me to show you around?"

"Very much."

They talked as they toured. Sue told him about Prince Hassan Saleh Al Shammari and how his feminist wife was pushing him to place his horses with her. She also listed the other new owners she was communicating with. He seemed impressed.

"What do you think, Willy?"

"If this all works, it could push you up amongst the leading trainers which is a remarkable achievement for just a few months."

"Can I look to you to take more rides from me next year?"

"I'm certainly interested."

Rob had booked the table for 7:30. Rose offered to drive them down and pick them up later. They were greeted by Stella MacMillan when they entered the pub.

"Hi Stella, Luci said you were working here. How's the accountancy training going?"

"It's going well, thank you Mr. Blackstock. I'm learning bookkeeping at the moment, Trisha says that by the New Year I'll be ready to do yours and Mrs. Blackstock's bookkeeping, spending a day a week with each of you, two days in the office with her and one day at college. What can I get you both?"

"Actually, we've got a table for two booked and I'd like a bottle of Sid's Australian Merlot and two glasses please."

"Table six over in the corner Rob," Sid called from the other end of the bar.

"I'll bring your wine over to you." Stella offered.

The pub door swung open and Ana walked in followed by Yasmin. Then Eva and a tall thin man in his late twenties entered. Eva was holding the man's hand.

"A bottle of Champagne please, Sid." Ana ordered.

"Special occasion is it Ana?" Sid asked.

"Very special," Eva responded holding up her left hand and showing off an engagement ring.

"Congratulations to you both. May I wish you both a long and happy life together," Sid said. "The Champagne is on the house if you promise to get the karaoke going later, Ana."

"Okay Sid," Ana replied and the four of them sat at a table near Sue and Rob.

"Congratulations Eva," Rob called across.

"Thank you Rob. You've not met Paul have you?"

"I don't think we have met."

"Paul, this is my boss and dear friend Robert Blackstock and his wife Susan. Rob and Sue this is my fiancé Dr. Paul Polinski"

"Polinski is that Russian?" Sue asked.

"My grandfather was Polish. He came over in the war and never went home. Pleased to meet you both, I've heard so much about you," Paul replied.

Ana and Yasmin were flicking through the karaoke play list and whispering. Then Ana stood and walked to the stage picked up the microphone and switched it on.

"Good evening everybody. Our landlord has asked me get this evening's entertainments going. But I'm not going to."

There were several boos and jeers from the customers and a scowling look from the landlord.

"Instead I'm going to give you a very special treat. I'd like to introduce my little baby sister who is a much better singer than I am. Ladies and gentlemen. Yasmin."

Ana stepped off the stage and dialled in a number on the machine as Yasmin took to the stage. The music started and was instantly recognisable as *Cilla Black's 'You're My World'*. As she finished the song the entire audience stood and applauded. Ana got back on the stage and took the microphone from her sister.

"There you are, didn't I say she was something special?" Ana handed the microphone back as the applause swelled again.

"Thank you, thank you so much. I first must apologise for my poor English. Ana and me both learn from listening to English pop songs. Cilla was our father's favourite. That song was one he sang to us often. Ana is going to join me now in a song that we'd like to sing to say thank you to someone we both owe our lives to, Mr. Robert Blackstock."

Rob felt himself start to go red as Sue pushed her chair back and the applause rang out again. As it died down Yasmin said, "We first heard this song sung by Barbra Streisand and Donna Summer about fifteen years ago. Hope you like the way the Kolanski sisters perform *'No More Tears'*."

The customers were again on their feet applauding as they finished the song. They both took a bow and returned to their table. Sid took the microphone.

"Thank you girls. Now is anyone brave enough to follow that."

Will Moss was on site early Monday to supervise the preparation for the cement arriving Tuesday. It had to be very precise, so that the whole yard would drain. The whole area had to slope by six inches diagonally across the twenty five yard square, so that all water would run to the lowest corner where the drain was set.

Eric and Rose stood and watched as lorry after lorry load of concrete arrived and was laid. More than half of it had to be barrowed across the square. It was hard work and almost dark when they finished.

The following Monday the team prepared for filling the middle section. It would require four times the amount of concrete, but it could all be pumped directly to where it was wanted. The first load arrived with the sun only a glowing light just below the horizon. They kept on coming all day until sunset. It was almost dark when the final square yards were levelled. The following morning showed them that it all was as near perfect as it could be and they all congratulated one another.

The new gates were ready and would arrive on Thursday, so the team turned to building the brick pillars for the gates to the specifications supplied by the gate manufacturer. There were two gates for the house drive and one gate for the new access road. They were to sit on a pair of hinges each mounted into the brick pillars. The opening mechanism was a simple motorise wheel mounted on the end of each gate. Sue was at home on Friday when the gates were hung. They were very heavy and it took four men to lift them and drop them onto the hinge pins. It only took minutes for the electrician to connect them up. Once he was happy, he gave Sue the two remotes.

"They are dual controlled Mrs. Blackstock, you can either press the remote or you can enter the four digit security code, I'll show you how to set that. Sensors will detect when the vehicle has passed and the gates will automatically close again. Sensors will also detect vehicles leaving and open the gates. They can be operated manually by inserting a key into the hole on the side of the motor." He handed Sue three keys, each labelled.

"What about the drive lights?" Sue asked. "What makes them come on?"

"They've got motion sensors, set to operate when they detect anything larger that a medium size dog coming within fifty feet of them and stay on for five minutes. Just like you've got in the yard," he explained. "Now all I need you to do is show me where you want the monitors placed."

Luci had been out four times having driving lessons with Eric before her first lesson with Toby Read on Sunday morning. He quickly assessed that Luci was quite confident, so he was happy to allow her to drive to the outskirts of York, then return to the village.

The family were all in the kitchen with a pre lunch drink when Luci arrived home.

"How did it go Luci?" Eric asked.

"Excellent, really great. I drove to York and back. Toby thinks I'll only need half a dozen lessons. He wants me to apply for my written test straight away and I should get a slot before Christmas. If I pass he says I should book my practical test immediately. They're coming through with about three weeks notice at the moment. Extra lessons could be fitted in during the school holidays if needed. I could be driving by my birthday."

Chapter 23t

"Sir Bernard I've just had a report from the Russian police. Yeta Korkov and her son were not on that ship when it docked at St. Petersburg. They believe she transferred to another vessel somewhere in the Baltic and is now hiding somewhere in Estonia"

****

The building site had all been cleared away and the yard was fully functional again. An open ditch now ran the length of the access road to carry away storm water from the road. Over the last week everyone who had come to the stables had said how impressive the gates were. The pair for the house each had a two foot high rampant horse facing the centre, held in place by bars in a starburst pattern. The gate to the access road was four foot high, divided into three vertical sections, the middle section was the stables logo of a rampant horse, over a scroll bearing the words *'BLACKSTOCK RACING'*. The two outside panels were identical and contained a central ring six inches in diameter, held in place by rods in a starburst pattern."

Work was still going on. It was the final job in the contract, puting in the storm water drain. Will Moss had surveyed the route from the oversized manhole behind the first new block down to the stream. Every 5 yards was a stake in the ground with markings on them saying how deep the trench needed to be at that point. The pipe had to be a minimum of two feet below the surface, fortunately the slope of the field was enough to mean the pipe would end at the level of the stream bed.

The digger straddled the line of the trench and slowly dug a two foot wide trench to the marked depth, sand was spread in the bottom of the trench and the four foot long section of concrete pipe was chained to the digger and lifted in to the trench. The length of pipe then had to be manually manoeuvred so that its collar overlapped the end of the previous length. The chain could then be pulled out and the pipe bedded on the sand. The digger then dragged the soil back in to the trench. Progress was very slow, only three lengths could be laid per hour and they had ninety to lay. If there were no problem they could be finished by Friday.

Sue was in the office Tuesday afternoon, working on a presentation to give to two potential owners. Mac had suggested that if they had a professionally produced web site with a linked video tour of the stables, Sue wouldn't need to do this sort of preparation. Sue had told him to find someone who could produce it and come back with some options. In the meantime she had to continue preparing these presentations. The phone rang.

"Blackstock racing, Sue Blackstock speaking."

"Good afternoon Mrs. Blackstock. My name is Abdullah bin Zayed Al Maktoum. I am personal secretary to Prince Hassan Saleh Al Shammari. His Highness has asked me to supervise the delivery of a racehorse into your care on Thursday this week."

"Thank you for calling sir, you can assure His Highness the Prince that everything is ready for his horse and that over the next few weeks we will assess the potential of the animal and present him with a proposal for which races we enter it in."

"We will arrive at 2:00, please be ready to receive us. Thank you," he said commandingly and ended the call before Sue had chance to respond.

Looking at her diary she had to reschedule two meetings to clear her diary for Thursday. Her future success was at this moment resting on the relationship with Prince Hassan. It was crucial she was there to ensure everything went smoothly on Thursday.

From half past one Thursday afternoon Sue stood in the car park looking up the access road for a horse box to arrive. At exactly 2:00 it arrived preceded by a black Rolls Royce. Sue pressed the remote control she had in her pocket and the gates opened for the two vehicles. She stood by the car park and directed the two vehicles into the yard. A large Arab man, looking like a night club bouncer, emerged from the front passenger seat of the car and opened the door for the passenger behind him, who approached Sue.

"Mrs. Blackstock?" he enquired.

Sue nodded.

"I am Abdullah bin Zayed Al Maktoum."

"Pleased to meet you, sir."

The driver of the car had climbed out and had opened the other rear door. And a pair of expensive looking shoes were followed out by a slender body, also looking expensive.

"May I present Manal bin Rashid Al Shammari, first wife of Prince Hassan."

Sue was surprised to see a slender figure in her thirties alight from the car dressed in a tailored white trouser suit under a pastel blue fur trimmed coat. Her long jet black hair hanging loose making her look more like a film star than a traditional Arab princess.

"Pleased to meet you your Highness."

"No Susan, please call me Manal. I may call you Susan may I, as I think we could be friends?. I have read so much about you. I feel I already know you."

"As you see, Your Highness."

The princess just looked at her.

"As you see Manal, we've recently had a lot of building work done. Would you like me to show you around."

"Yes, I'd like that but first can we conclude our business. I'd like you to meet *Red Stone Girl*." The big Arab unhooked the tailgate of the horse box and led the filly out. Typical Arab lines and looking every inch a winner.

"What a beautiful horse," Sue said.

"She is, isn't she? I was there when she was born, she is my horse really but in my country women are not allowed to own such things."

"What a gorgeous colour, almost red."

"In some light she is red, her stable name is Ruby." She turned to the secretary and took a folder from him.

"Here is all the paperwork you need." The Princess handed Sue the folder. "You will see that both her parents were big winners, so we do expect great things from Ruby."

"Would you like to lead Ruby into her new home?!" Sue asked.

Manal took the halter from the big Arab and followed Sue to one of the four isolation boxes in the second new block. Only one other box was occupied.

"This will be her home for the first three weeks. She'll be closely monitored in here, with a daily check from our resident vet. It's something we are introducing for all our new residents as a precaution against them bringing anything nasty into the yard."

"A very wise precaution. Now you said about showing me round."

She stayed for an hour talking to Sue about living in The Emirates, and the countries problems in moving away from the ways of former generations and adopting a more Western life style. She explained how her husband supported her feminist campaign in private, but in public he had to be very careful. He had agreed with her that all decisions about Ruby would be hers, but in public he must be recognised as the owner.

As she left, she said she would be back in the New Year to see how Ruby had settled in and possibly select her first races.

All week Sue had an uneasy feeling that she put down to this being the very last week of the extensive work she had taken on, deep down she was still uncertain that she had done the right thing. By Friday she was feeling really rough. Rob had come home late the previous evening, after three nights away. He'd had a bad journey because of fog, so was too tired when he got in for her to unload onto him and he was still asleep this morning. At least Rose had come up with a solution for how they could celebrate the completion of the work, as she termed it *'a winter barbecue party'* with hot spiced mulled wine and Hot Toddy made from whisky, honey, lemon, cinnamon and cloves. The food would be baked potatoes topped with either chilli, beans or cheese. The whole thing would be a family party with members of the family preparing and serving the food and drink. It was all to happen on Saturday 21st December. Invites had gone out to everyone involved in the work from the architect to labourers who worked for Moss and Dixon's. Also to everyone working at the yard. All were told to bring a plus one. Potentially there could be one hundred and twenty people turn up, but being that close to Christmas and children not included, it was likely that the number would be closer to eighty.

Two more horses were due to arrive this morning. A mare owned by premiership footballer Jimmy Boil and a second mare, the first horse to be owned by someone new to racing, Boris Navalny, one of three Russian millionaires who owned the club Jimmy Boil played for. That would fill the last two isolation boxes until after Christmas.

Jimmy and Boris both arrived together sharing the same hired horsebox. They didn't arrive until 11:00 and only stayed long enough to see their horses stabled, hand over the paperwork and pay for three months in advance. As Sue watched them leave, she heard a great commotion coming from down by the stream. Obviously the team had laid the last pipe and were celebrating so she set off across the field. Before she had reached half way the party had gone quiet and she could see Will Moss hurrying up the field his face as white as a sheet.

"What's up Will, what's gone wrong?"

"The lads have found a body miss, a man's body."

"Where, show me."

"No miss," he grabbed her arm to stop her. "He's been down there some time and the rats or a badger, maybe a fox has been at him. You don't want to see it."

"We must call the police," Sue said.

"That's what I'm going to do now, but there is no service down there by the stream."

While Will rang to report the finding to the police, Sue stood and watched the other four men slowly trudge up the field, heads low.

"The police will be here shortly, they have asked that we move nothing and no one leaves," Will reported.

"I'll go and open the gate for them," Sue said and went for the key then walked to the gate, inserted the key to disengage the motor, then hauled the heavy gate open.

Two female constables in a patrol car were the first police on the scene and Will walked to meet them. They both looked to be in their mid thirties.

"Are you the one who reported finding a body?"

"Yes, I'm Will Moss. Myself and my men here were working down there by the stream, when we found the body hidden in the undergrowth."

"And you madam, who are you?"

"I am Susan Blackstock, this is my land."

"Down there by the stream you said, sir?"

Will nodded.

"Sarah go take a look and confirm there is a body down there," one constable instructed the other.

"I wouldn't go down there if I were you love," Will said.

She ignored him and set of across the field. They watched her down to the stream, saw her bend to look at something, then quickly come away double over and throw up.

"Sarah, are you okay?" The constable called over her radio and the constable down by the body waved to signal that she was and she walked back.

"It's certainly a body, but it looks like animals have been at it."

"The investigation team will be here in about thirty minutes."

"I think we could all do with a cup of tea and get out of this cold," Sue suggested. "Come into the house and sit while we wait."

It was an hour before leading investigator D.I. Rory O'Brian arrived and the investigation team could start work. A further four hours passed before the body was taken away and the workmen were allowed to lock the digger but not move it and go home. The police had taped off the area as a crime scene and told Sue that she would be notified when work could continue. Will Moss had said that if there was heavy rain, the pipe was far enough down the hill that the water would go to the stream anyway.

The police were back again at first light Saturday. O'Brian had called Will Moss in to use the digger to help clear the undergrowth. Just before lunch a second body was found. Again it took hours to process the body and the ground where it lay. Daylight was failing when it was finally taken away and the search was abandoned for the day. With so many vehicles going in and out of the field during the last two days the edge of the field was a mass of muddy tracks and the heavy mortuary van had to be towed up the slope and out onto the lane by the digger.

O'Brian's Sunday breakfast was disturbed by a phone call from the station.

"Good morning sir, sorry to disturb you at home on a Sunday morning but I have some news about the bodies at Blackstock stables."

"Well out with it, Constable Sherman!"

"Yes sir. A woman came into the station about an hour ago, said her name was Unis Ponta. A migrant farm worker from

Romania. She lives in a camper van but we took her mobile number. She said that the news paper headlines this morning were about the murders and she said she had information that might be useful. She said that on Friday night she was walking her dog around 2:00 Saturday morning on the road overlooking Blackstock stables and she saw someone dragging something into the undergrowth at the bottom of the field. She said it could have been a body and it looked like it was a woman dragging it. She said she saw the same again on Saturday and again on Sunday. She also said, that at the time she thought it odd that someone would be working at that time of night. But when she saw today's Sunday papers, she thinks it must have been the murderer she had seen."

"If she's right, then there's another body to be found. We'll have to continue looking tomorrow. Thank you constable."

He rang Will Moss and asked him to be ready with the digger first light Monday. He also rang the three constables who had been at the site on Saturday and the duty coroner from Saturday, telling him what was happening and that he was needed as he expected to find a third body on Monday.

Will continued ripping out the undergrowth all day Monday but they found nothing. By the end of the day they still had thirty to forty yards of dense undergrowth ahead of them, plus a considerable amount of fly tipped rubbish. This end of the belt of undergrowth ran close to a minor road which ran past Blackstock Stunt Academy.

A third body was found just ten yards from the road. It was hidden under a discarded mattress piled high with black plastic bags, full of rubbish. Looking back across the area that had been cleared, the full extent could now be seen. It was an area approximately thirty yards by one hundred yards, most of it was boggy, made so by water flooding from the stream which ran through the centre of the patch. Will had dragged the rubbish, the brambles and briars, holly and elder, plus a couple of small trees that looked like they might be apple trees and he had piled it into a heap, intending that it be burnt as soon as the police had finished.

There was little going on in the racing world during the last week before Christmas so Sue had time to sit down with Rose to plan the party on Saturday. Each day Rose baked twenty potatoes and froze them. Ana's food supplier sourced some large cans of beef chilli and cans of beans. The brewery allowed Sue to have two cases of mulled wine and a case of whisky at cost price and they borrowed two five gallon hot water geysers from Sid at the 'Dog and Gun', for the wine and the toddy. Rob and Eric were given responsibility for the drinks. Luci, Rose and Sue would manage the food, using the microwaves from the two dorms, the one from the flat and the one from their own kitchen to heat the food. They were forced to use plastic glasses, plastic cutlery and paper plates because they could not risk broken glass injuring the horses.

On the morning of the party Rob fetched two large gazebos and four trestle tables from the academy catering truck and constructed a makeshift kitchen in a corner of the yard. Eric went to the loft and fetched a game that Rob remembered from his childhood. It was a very simple game consisting of six one foot tall wooden horses on wooden trolleys, each with four wheels and twenty yards of string attached to the trolley. The game is a straight race between horses, the speed of the horse dependant on someone winding the string onto a spool. The horses were very top heavy and had a tendency to fall over if jerked too hard. Rob had good memories of the game. It would be perfect for this event. Luci brought out her CD player to provide background music.

Sue was happy that this would be the family party she wanted, no frills, entertainment for everyone to enjoy and they did, most of them staying well into the evening. Justin was the only one missing having stayed at school to play in the last rugby match of the term. Rob would be leaving early in the morning to fetch him home for Christmas.

The clearing up didn't take long. Rob put the gazebos and the tables into one of the empty loose boxes, the remaining drink went in there as well to cool down and the food was taken into the kitchen where Rose and Luci bagged it and put it in the freezer. Rob and Eric picked up what little litter was lying around and by 9:00 they were all in the lounge relaxing and discussing the party. A bell rang in the kitchen. Someone had pressed the intercom call at the gate to the house.

"Who can that be at this time?" Rob queried as he got up to answer the call.

A couple of minutes later he returned. "It's the police," he said.

"I wonder what they want?" Rose queried.

"Possibly something about the body that was found. Maybe they've come to tell me it's okay to get the builders back to finish that pipe," Sue suggested.

"I'd better let them in," Rob said and went off to open the front door.

When he returned he said, "they want to speak to you Sue." He was followed into the room by three men. Two in uniform and the other, a middle aged man with a beard, in plain clothes.

The plain clothes officer stepped forward and began to speak.

"Susan Blackstock?" he questioned looking straight at Sue.

"That's me," she replied and recognising the tone of his voice she stood.

He continued, "the bodies retrieved from this property between 13th and 16th December 2019 have been examined and results thoroughly investigated. We now know who the victims are, how the victims died and without any doubts who was responsible for their deaths." He paused.

"Susan Blackstock I arrest you for the murders of Anton Levetov, Ivan Gorkov and Rosie Katavlich, sometime between 1st and 4th November 2019. You do not have to say anything. But, it may harm your defence if you do not mention when questioned, something which you later rely on in court. Anything you do say may be given in evidence."

Printed in Great Britain
by Amazon

66693912R00163